PRAISE FOR JAMES TUCKER

THE
HOLD OUTS

ALSO BY JAMES TUCKER

Next of Kin

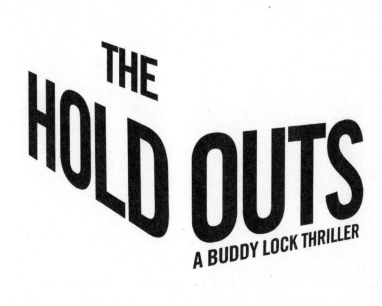

THE
HOLD OUTS

A BUDDY LOCK THRILLER

JAMES TUCKER

THOMAS & MERCER

Text copyright © 2018 by James Tucker

Published by Thomas & Mercer, Seattle

www.apub.com

Amazon, the Amazon logo, and Thomas & Mercer are trademarks of Amazon.com, Inc., or its affiliates.

ISBN-13: 9781503903982
ISBN-10: 1503903982

Cover design by Ray Lundgren

Printed in the United States of America

for Megan

DAY 1

1

They saw the bodies when they opened the trawl net. Thousands of fish fell onto the deck, their silver scales flashing under the slate-colored skies. And together with the fish, the barely clothed figures of a man and a woman, a black medallion hanging loosely from his neck, her long graying hair threaded with fish still shaking with life.

Mack Berringer's crew of two men looked at him, their puffs of breath visible in the late-January cold. Midmorning, the wind broke across the Atlantic's rough swells and needled their faces, making their eyes water. They'd left the docks on the north side of the Shinnecock Inlet in Hampton Bays at half past three that morning. They were tired and cold, and they wanted to get back to land. To deliver the fish. To get warm. But now they had a delay and a problem.

Mack glowered at his men but didn't speak. He moved toward the bodies, using his boots to nudge the flounder and the black sea bass out of his path. The body of the woman was closest to him, and he squatted beside her.

He could see that something wasn't right. It wasn't that she was Asian and maybe sixty years old, similar to the man lying a few feet from her. And it wasn't her plain silver wedding band or her engagement ring with a diamond of more than a carat. He leaned over, nearer her face and hair. She stared, eyeless, out at him. Fish had eaten off her eyelids and the soft jelly of her eyeballs, and most of her lips were also missing. Leaning closer, he noticed the tip of her tongue was gone, chewed roughly and relentlessly by sea life. Her pale-blue blouse had compressed to a wreath around her neck, and fish had gnawed off her nipples and exposed tissue that was faintly pink with blood. Her body was bruised the length of her left side. Otherwise, she remained whole.

Mack Berringer pulled his blue knit cap more tightly over his ears. *This doesn't add up,* he thought.

They were thirty-two miles from shore. The fish lived here and moved farther out every year due to the warming ocean. He knew that if these bodies had fallen into the Atlantic near land, by the time the currents had carried them dozens of miles from shore, they'd have been nearly devoured by sea life. After twenty-nine years working these waters, he knew that freshly dead human corpses were a delicacy—rare and, for many fish, delicious. Even if the sea life had ignored the bodies—an impossibility—it would have taken days for the currents to take them to the area he'd been midwater trawling. As he stood, he estimated that they'd been in the ocean no more than four hours.

Turning to his crew, he said, "Either of you see or hear another boat?"

The men shook their heads.

Clearing a path through the fish with his boots, he went around the body of the woman to that of the man, put his hands on his thighs, and bent over for a better view.

This one was balding and also missing eyelids, eyeballs, lips. Bruises on the feet and legs. The dead man's gray shirt was torn open, revealing a nearly hairless chest and the necklace with the black medallion.

The fisherman studied the necklace. The string was black leather, thick with water. From it dangled a round black stone containing a symbol and image he didn't recognize. He patted the man's pants pockets, rolling him sideways to check the side pockets, but he found nothing.

No wallet, keys, money, or identification. No jewelry other than the leather string with the medallion. Once again he looked up at his crew.

One of them, the older man who was about thirty, slowly shook his head. "Give them back to the sea, Mack. This is nothing but trouble."

The younger deckhand nodded and added, "But take the lady's ring."

He considered this idea. It had merit. He could wash his hands of the matter. These two people were already dead, and bringing them ashore wouldn't solve anything. But then he realized they might have families: children, brothers and sisters, parents. The relatives would want to know, wouldn't they? And one of the crew might talk, and then he'd be caught up in it anyway and blamed for not doing the right thing.

He reached down and pulled the necklace and its pendant off the dead man. Then he returned to the woman, squatted beside her, and used his gloved hands to work the rings off the rigid fingers. He took off his gloves and put the pendant and rings in the inside pocket of his Carhartt work pants.

When he stood, the younger deckhand said, "What's our share of the diamond?"

Mack Berringer laughed. "It's going to the police."

"Aw, come on!"

He didn't respond, just said, "Wrap them in a tarp. I'll take us in."

A moment later he stood in the wheelhouse with the barely functional heater and thought about the police. He'd heard that another fisherman had found a body the year before. Far from shore, but not this far. He'd read about it in the *Southampton Press* and heard from other fishermen that, months later, the Long Island police still hadn't figured out who it was. Unknown and unclaimed, the body had been buried in an unmarked grave. Mack Berringer thought that if he reported his discovery to the same police, the same thing would happen. But what if he contacted someone in the city?

5

He didn't know anyone there. Hadn't been to Manhattan in nine years and would never go back. As he surveyed the eastern rim of the overcast sky with no hint of land at its end, the wisp of a name ignited in his memory. He did, he realized, know of someone.

That cop—the police detective who'd handled the Death Clock Murders and then another big case a few weeks ago, the one involving the rich German family. He'd seen the guy on CNN. And in the *Gazette*'s articles. What was his name? Buddy something. Buddy Luke? No. *Buddy Lock*. Detective Lock. That was it. He thought Lock had seemed like a straight shooter. Maybe he should give Detective Lock a call. Wouldn't hurt. Better than involving the Long Island police, who'd give the NYPD a call anyway. Pulling out his mobile phone, he confirmed what he already knew.

No reception.

He put the phone in his pocket, grabbed the steering wheel and throttle, and swung the boat around in the direction of Shinnecock Inlet.

2

■

Ben was afraid the judge would take him away from Buddy and Mei.

He watched Buddy, especially Buddy's face. He liked the face. It was handsome but not refined. Dark, watchful eyes and short black hair. Tall, over six feet, with a powerful chest. But also the kindest man he'd ever met, much kinder than his own father. He really liked when Buddy smiled, although today Buddy only frowned. He saw the muscles on the sides of Buddy's jaw tense.

Ben was sitting in Judge Sylvia Miles's chambers in New York County Family Court at nine in the morning. At a hearing three weeks earlier, his aunt and uncle had argued that they should have custody of him. Today Judge Miles wanted to speak with him, but he didn't want to speak with her. He wished she'd let him be, let him continue living with Buddy and Mei. He shifted uncomfortably in the big chair, the muscles of his right thigh hurting where a knife had been thrust weeks earlier. Mei put Aquaphor on the stitches every night to keep them from getting dried out and hurting worse. For a few days he'd been in a wheelchair, but now he walked with only a slight limp.

Mei Adams was in the chair to his right, holding his hand. To his left stood Buddy, in front of the windows showing a sky with clouds the color of pepper. Along the wall to Ben's right, past Mei, stood a neatly dressed man in a suit and a red bow tie. This man was younger than

Buddy, with thinning blond hair, and he wrote on a yellow legal pad whenever the judge spoke.

Judge Miles rested her elbows on her large wooden desk and leaned forward, peering down at him over her reading glasses. She said, "You've lost your parents at ten years old, and there's a dispute about custody. About where you'll live. With whom you'll live."

Ben didn't know how to respond, so he kept his mouth closed. He didn't like Judge Miles, didn't like her pinched face, her mousy gray hair, or her shapeless brown sweater. He felt himself go hot and knew his forehead had turned sweaty. Letting go of Mei's hand, he touched his forehead but found the skin dry. Then he set his hands in his lap and tried to look Judge Miles in the eye.

She said, "I'm required to make my decision based on your best interest. So I wanted to visit with you this morning. Do you understand?"

Ben clasped his hands so tightly his fingers hurt. He wished the judge couldn't see or hear him. He wanted to be home with Mei and Buddy, and never have to see Judge Miles again. He looked up when he heard Buddy's voice.

"I'd ask you to keep the situation here in mind," Buddy said. He'd moved closer, so he was two feet from Judge Miles's desk. He towered over her, his voice strong. He said, "Ray Sawyer is Ben's guardian and has chosen to give custody of Ben to Mei Adams and to me." Buddy pronounced Mei's name clearly, like the fifth month of the year, to be sure the judge got it right. He continued, "We've willingly accepted that responsibility. We love Ben very much and he's become the most important part of our lives. He's family now. He has his own bedroom, and we can provide everything he needs. As Ray Sawyer noted during the recent custody hearing, Ben's parents were clear about custody. They did not want him to live with any of his aunts and uncles."

Judge Miles knit her brow and held up a hand. She said, "Quiet, please."

Buddy stopped talking.

Judge Miles looked at Buddy and then at Mei. She said, "I'd like to speak privately with Ben. Would the two of you leave us for a few minutes?"

Buddy's face reddened, but he nodded.

And when he nodded, Ben began to feel the fingers of panic wrap around his heart. He looked up at Buddy, who came over to him and knelt beside his chair.

Buddy said, "You'll do great. Just tell the truth. Tell her what you want, all right?"

As always when he was with Buddy, Ben's confidence rose. He said, "Can't you stay?"

Buddy hugged him and said, "You'll be in here alone, but I'll be here, too. Because I'll be thinking about you the whole time." Separating from Ben, Buddy said, "Then it will be over and you can go to school or we'll go home. Or out for pizza. Whatever you want."

Ben wanted to leave now. He wanted to be like every other kid. He clasped his hands so they didn't shake. "Is it okay if I go to school?"

Buddy touched his shoulder. "Sure it is."

Mei had stood and now leaned over and kissed Ben's cheek. She said, "Judge Miles will talk with you for a few minutes. We'll be right outside her office, not far from you at all." Mei smiled. "You'll do well, Ben. I'm sure of it."

He felt as if he'd lost his stomach, as if he'd just started down a roller coaster's steepest drop and the ground was rushing toward him, making his body weightless. He couldn't help but cry a little as he watched Buddy and Mei walk out into the hallway, and the man with the thinning blond hair and the bow tie and the legal pad shut the door behind them. Slowly, Ben turned from the door and faced the large desk and the pale woman behind it.

Judge Miles removed her reading glasses and set them on her desk. She said, "Ben Brook, you've had a rough few weeks. Would you tell me why you don't want to live with your surviving family?"

Ben felt his stomach churn. He thought he might throw up. He swallowed and tried to sit up straight. After he noticed his hands shaking, he clasped them together. He hoped Judge Miles and the young man with the red bow tie hadn't noticed.

For a moment he was silent. He didn't know how to answer the question. He didn't want to anger his aunt and uncle, but he wouldn't lie. He thought of Buddy and Mei and the love they'd shown him, the trust he had in them.

He opened his mouth and began to speak.

3

Buddy's mobile phone rang.

He stopped his pacing outside Judge Miles's chambers. He shook his head, angry at the interruption, and pounded his right fist into his open left palm. Again and again. He ignored Mei's annoyed expression, ignored the ringing phone.

Nobody, not even Judge Miles, should find Ben's aunt and uncle preferable to us, he thought. *Nobody.*

He recalled last Saturday afternoon, when he and Mei and Ben had braved the January chill and gone to the Wollman skating rink in Central Park. Buddy had tripped, fallen, and lain on the ice, assessing his arms and legs to be sure nothing was broken. Realizing he was unhurt, he'd looked around.

Ben, a devilish grin on his face, had skated over and jumped on top of him. Ben had giggled and then laughed loudly, happily.

Mei had approached and jumped on the pile. She'd leaned down and kissed them both.

Buddy had groaned in mock agony but had held them tightly, not wanting to let go, in that moment filled with more unbounded joy than any other in his life. Beneath their warm bodies and laughter, with the hard ice under him, he'd thought it was they rather than he who were holding him up. *This is what I want,* he'd said to himself. *Nothing more. Now I've got it all.*

Afterward, when they'd returned the rental skates, they'd gone to Starbucks for hot chocolate, with extra marshmallows for Ben. For those hours, they'd forgotten the tragedy that had brought them together, the brutal deaths of Ben's parents and too many others. Since that terrible time a month earlier, they'd become a family. Buddy was surprised that he'd begun to think of Ben as his son. Maybe that was what happened when a ten-year-old boy needed you, and you discovered you needed him even more. You formed a bond out of need that rapidly evolved into love. *Yeah,* he'd thought over and over again. *Love.* How else to describe the feeling he had when Ben suffered nightmares and melancholy while thinking of his late parents and little sister? *Love.* But also anger at anyone or anything that threatened Ben or Ben's place in Buddy's world. The way Judge Miles was doing right now.

She doesn't understand, he thought. *She's just focused on the money.*

As one of the surviving family members who owned Brook Instruments, the orphaned Ben had inherited several billion dollars. *That money,* Buddy thought, *is a curse and the only reason Judge Miles would award custody of Ben to his aunt and uncle, two cold-as-fish liars who have no love for the boy.* They were the ones who wanted Ben's money. Buddy didn't give a damn about it. He and Mei had told Judge Miles they'd keep the money in trust and would use it only for Ben's school tuition and college, and that Mei had family money. Yet Buddy wasn't certain the judge believed them.

His cell phone rang again. He glanced over at Mei and saw her shake her head. So he pulled the phone from the left breast pocket of his suit coat and prepared to mute it. But when he checked the screen and saw the number, he experienced the usual thrill at the main number of the New York City Police Department. His blood quickened as he thought that maybe, just maybe, he'd been brought back on active duty and been given a case. He hit the talk button. "Lock here."

"Hey, Buddy. It's Jackson. Got a call from a crank. Some fisherman on Long Island reported an old man and woman caught up in his nets. He was . . . let me find it here . . . thirty-two miles offshore when he found them. Says he'll talk only to you."

Buddy thought about the bodies found out in the Atlantic. Where exactly had the fisherman found them? And in what condition? And why were they in the ocean when nobody went boating, not this time of year, during an unexpectedly frigid January? He thought they might be suicides. But that didn't make sense to him. People rarely drowned themselves. It was too unpleasant and took too long. No, something else had happened in the waters off Long Island.

As Jackson continued talking, now about how Buddy's recent television interviews made everyone else look bad, Buddy paced back and forth from the door to Judge Miles's chambers to the dirty beige wall at the far end of the hallway. He thought about Long Island—far beyond his jurisdiction. Forcing himself to breathe deeply, he reached the end of the hallway, turned, and headed back.

"Buddy?" It was Mei, not Jackson. She'd stood and was watching him, her beautiful face showing concern. "Is everything all right?"

He held the phone against his chest. "Yeah. I've got a case. Catch up with you and Ben tonight?"

Her forehead wrinkled briefly. She'd wanted his help in taking Ben to school and handling the emotional turmoil from the boy's interview with Judge Miles. But she understood him. She said, "You'll be home for dinner?"

He nodded briefly, kissed her cheek, and walked toward the other end of the hallway. He looked up at the pale fluorescent lights and thought of ways to be reinstated in short order. This was a major obstacle. He might be able to swing it if Chief Malone were in his corner. Or Mayor Blenheim, for that matter. But as of this moment, he couldn't do anything. He remained on administrative leave due to his being part of an officer-involved shooting three weeks earlier—the shooting that had brought the murders of Ben's family members to a close. Today, he had no badge or service weapon. He couldn't investigate. Couldn't work at all.

But he *would* work. That was how he was made. That's why he rarely took vacation. Because he was a detective first grade with the NYPD, and that meant a hell of a lot to him. For more than twenty years, his job had been his anchor. He'd built his life around being a detective, and in return, he'd received pride, honor, purpose, and a way to fight off the demons of his past. An essential trade, because without the NYPD, he didn't know what he was supposed to do with his life—not during the day when Ben was at school and Mei at Porter Gallery.

He turned at the end of the hallway and began walking toward the elevator. He thought of the bodies found thirty-two miles from shore.

An accident? he wondered. *Or something else?*

Into the phone he said, "The fisherman out on Long Island. What's his number?"

4

Late morning, Buddy stood on the dock next to Mack Berringer's forty-foot trawler, the *Salty Lady*. He was trying to follow Mack's explanation of the currents off the coast of New York City and Long Island. Ignoring the bitter wind coming off the water, Mack pointed in a southerly direction. "So they come up from the Jersey Shore, and then they're like a slingshot out along Fire Island and the Hamptons. At that point"—Mack started rotating his swollen and weathered hands—"they gather force off the coast and swing out to the real depths where I fish."

Buddy nodded, but he didn't know exactly what Mack was telling him. He glanced around. The air around the docks smelled acrid with brine and the strong, almost overpowering smell of fish, raw and pungent with decay.

The continuous sounds of rigging clanging lightly against metal. The cawing of gulls that wheeled overhead or stood on the tops of the dock posts yards away, waiting for the men to leave so they could search for scraps on the deck of Mack's boat. Buddy saw these pretty vultures and how they relied on others to do their killing for them. A beneficial arrangement, as long as the killers did what they were supposed to do. He turned to the blue-painted trawler to his right, touching its cold fiberglass hull and finding it slick with seawater. He rubbed his hands together to dry them; Mack Berringer seemed not to notice.

"So," Mack concluded, "that's why they didn't enter the water from shore—not from *any* shore, right?"

Buddy hesitated, cocked his head. He said, "Because any current would have taken them out into the deep, eventually, but to get from any point on shore to where you found them, they'd have been in the water for days."

Mack nodded. "Yes, sir. And now we'll take a look at them, and you can tell me if you think they've been in water for days or for hours."

Buddy followed Mack up the ladder on the side of the trawler. He said, "I'm not a medical examiner."

"Me neither," Mack called back to him. "But I'm not stupid."

On the deck, Buddy kept his feet wide apart. He didn't want to fall onto the deck that was greasy with the remnants of fish. He watched as Mack knelt down, took hold of an olive-green tarpaulin, and pulled back the waterproof fabric, revealing two corpses. At once the trawler, the gulls, and Mack faded away. He was alone, not so much thinking as observing, absorbing.

He noticed both bodies were bruised, but only one side of the woman, and the man's limbs. Pulling out the latex exam gloves he kept with him at all times, he squatted down and looked at the woman's hands, touching them, feeling the stiffness of rigor mortis. The fourth finger on the woman's left hand showed signs of two rings.

Mack Berringer said, "Detective Lock. Here they are."

At the edge of his vision, he saw the flash of metal under the gray skies. He turned over his hand, and Mack set an engagement ring and a wedding band in his palm. He studied the engagement ring. A sizable square-cut diamond that flashed white and blue under the clouds. On the inside of the ring were markings. Bringing it closer to his eyes, he read an inscription in cursive: *for L.*

He looked up at the fisherman. He was beginning to trust Mack Berringer. Mack stared back at him, his face inscrutable. Buddy again studied the ring before pulling out his cell phone and taking several photographs of it.

When he'd finished, he asked, "You found the bodies thirty miles from shore?"

Mack said, "Thirty-two."

Buddy had observed their condition, had made the same mental calculations that Mack Berringer had. Given their state of decay and their susceptibility to the teeth of fish and sharks, he knew they couldn't have been in the water more than a few hours. Maybe even less. He didn't know the ocean and its tides and currents as Mack did, but he knew he'd heard a wrong note.

Buddy said, "Any other jewelry?"

Mack Berringer reached into the bib pocket of his work pants and handed Buddy a black medallion on a leather string.

Buddy tilted his head. Turned the medallion around in his hand. It was heavier than he'd expected. One side was smooth black stone. On the other side, the image of a white flower on the black background, and in the middle of the flower petals, a slightly yellowish bulb. He didn't remember the names of flower parts. Maybe the yellowish part was called the *pistil*. But maybe not. He guessed the black was onyx or synthetic. The white and yellow parts seemed to be ivory and gold inlay. Below the image of the flower was a symbol carved into the black stone. The symbol looked like Chinese lettering, but to his untrained eye, it could be Korean or Japanese or another language that used symbols. He held the medallion close to his eyes. He thought it might be old, but maybe it was only made to look that way. He didn't recognize the flower. Given the ethnicity of the dead man and woman, he guessed it was Chinese or, at any rate, Asian, but he didn't know. He said, "Know what it is?"

Mack Berringer shook his head. "Some kind of flower, maybe."

A second time, Buddy pulled out his phone and took a few photographs of the medallion. Once he'd put it in the right side pocket of his parka, together with the wedding band and the diamond ring, he zipped up the pocket and patted down the woman, followed by the man.

He found nothing.

Mack Berringer said, "No ID. I checked when we picked them up."

Buddy nodded slowly, then stood and looked over the transom to the frigid water of the inlet. This time of year—late January—you'd last a few minutes if you were lucky. He thought these people might have been dead before they got wet. He breathed in the wind as it screamed toward the land and froze his ears.

Mack Berringer called from behind him, "Need me for anything else?"

It took a few moments for Buddy to hear the older man. When he did, he shook his head but didn't turn from the ocean. He said, "I'll have people come for them."

He sensed rather than heard Mack Berringer leave the boat. The starboard side dipped and rose as the fisherman stepped off. A more intense quiet enveloped Buddy even in the midst of the howling wind.

Buddy was thinking about the dead couple and how they'd been found more than thirty miles off Long Island in a snowless winter gale. His experience and training had taught him to see patterns and to expect and even to know with certainty what the next note would be. Long before he'd flubbed his senior recital at Juilliard and given up the piano, he'd been a child prodigy. Since he was three years old, his mind had been trained to observe at a freakish level of detail. For a long time, he'd succeeded.

Before turning fourteen, he'd performed in London, Paris, Milan, Saint Petersburg, Berlin, and Vienna. His mind absorbed structure and pattern in a way few others did. And because he saw patterns that others couldn't, he saw exactly where patterns failed. He saw the wrong note among a hundred or a thousand right ones. Even more, he was interested in discovering why the note was wrong. He obsessed about the wrong note and making it right. It was this obsession that led to his relentlessness. He couldn't help himself. He always felt like he *must* figure it out. He couldn't stop his work until he understood what was wrong and had tried to fix it. Tried, using all tools available to a first-grade detective.

The badge. The full force and power of the NYPD. Search warrants. If necessary, his fists and his gun: tools of aggression and violence just this side of legal.

And sometimes beyond.

5

But he had no jurisdiction over this case.

He turned from the water and the sharp wind, and again observed the dead bodies of the older Asian man and woman, the docks and the other fishing boats behind them, and behind these, the shore and the low-slung commercial buildings, gray and weathered from years of a harsh climate in all seasons.

He thought the case properly belonged with the police on Long Island. He'd have to pull some strings if he wanted to work it. And he did want to work it.

He pulled out his mobile phone, his exposed hand burning from the cold, the wind, the fine icy spray coming over the gunwale. After dialing, he held the phone to his right ear and listened over the whistling wind.

He waited for the ringing. He thought about what he'd say in order to grab the case. He thought he could *do* something with it. His mind had begun circling it. He felt a sort of compulsion to figure it out—the what, the who, the why. Once, late at night, he'd admitted to Mei that he couldn't control the need.

Her head had been on his chest, her silky black hair smooth against his skin. She'd reached up with her warm hand and touched the line of his jaw, soothing him. "Yes," she'd whispered, "I know."

"You aren't angry?" he'd asked.

"No."

"Then you'd be the first woman I've dated who isn't."

"*Shhh,*" she'd said, placing an index finger over his lips. "As long as you need me more than your job, I can't find any fault."

In response he'd rubbed her back, bent his head, and kissed her hair. She'd lifted her head and looked at him faintly in the darkness.

"Do you?"

"Do I what?"

"Do you need me more than you need your job?"

He'd smiled, although she couldn't see him. Laughed and said, "Yes. Yes, I need you more than anything."

She'd slid off him, kissed his chest, reached down, slowly, below his navel, and touched him. Softly at first. Then she used her fingernail with just enough pressure to cause pain and surprising pleasure. She'd said, "Show me how much you need me."

He'd waited a moment, to be sure she meant it. His reaction to the pressure of her hand told him he could do it again if she were sincere, even if they'd made love twice over the past hour. He'd said, "Again?"

"Do you want me to beg?"

"No. I just didn't think you wanted more."

"Well, I want more. *Now.*"

Then he'd taken control. He'd moved. His large body against her slender one.

Standing on the deck of the fishing boat, listening to the phone line ringing, he knew that he wouldn't do anything to put what he had with Mei in danger. What he had with Ben. He wanted a normal case that he could work eight-to-five and not bring home with him. This one seemed to fit the bill. It was old-fashioned detective work that had no connection to Mei and Ben. In no event would he take a case that might bring death or worse to the two people he loved. Not after the case regarding Ben's family that he'd resolved less than a month ago.

If I take this case, he thought, *they'll be safe.*

21

6

At the security checkpoint, the guards recognized Buddy. Nobody smiled, but they watched him carefully.

It was past three in the afternoon when he walked into One Police Plaza, the large red brick building that was home to the NYPD. He was the only detective, other than Mike Malone, chief of detectives, who'd been a regular on television after solving two high-profile serial murder cases over the past couple of years. After the very public events of three weeks earlier, the guards knew he was on mandatory administrative leave.

Standing before the scanning machine, he removed a Glock 26 from his IWB—inside-the-waistband—holster and set it in a plastic container to be examined by one of the guards. This "baby Glock," his personal weapon for which he had a specially issued permit from Police Commissioner Quinn, didn't raise anyone's alarms. Without being asked, he took out his permit and held it up for the guard on the other side of the conveyor belt. The guard glanced at it, nodded, and Buddy walked through the metal detector. On the other side, the guard passed the Glock to him, and he put it back in the IWB holster.

He visited One Police only when necessary. He didn't like oversight and avoided management whenever possible, although he trusted Chief

Malone. Investigating was his thing, not politicking. But today his pulse jumped. This was the heart of the NYPD, and he belonged here. Today, he wanted something.

After depositing with the property clerk in room 208 the wedding band and the engagement ring that Mack Berringer had pulled off the dead woman, he took the elevator upstairs. In the front pocket of his trousers, he kept the medallion he'd taken from the John Doe. Despite regulations requiring him to leave all evidence with the clerk, he thought mere photographs of it wouldn't be enough.

In Malone's office, the chief of detectives' domed forehead shone in the overhead fluorescent lights. His red-rimmed eyes showed fatigue but also amusement. He said, "Why are you here? Did you miss me?"

Buddy didn't answer or sit down. In Chief Malone's large office with the tired furniture, the framed photographs of Malone with the governor and with Mayor Blenheim and with two presidents of the United States of America, he hesitated, but only to impress upon the chief the right amount of gravity. Finally, he told Malone of the bodies found early that morning off the coast of Long Island: two sixtysomething Asians, no ID, far out from shore but physically intact. While he was still speaking, Malone picked up his desk phone, punched in an extension, and said, "My office." Then he hung up the phone and watched Buddy.

Buddy finished describing what he'd found. "Chief, would you give me a month?"

Malone scowled. "We have enough cases in the city. Why bring in a Long Island case that's got nothing to do with us?"

Buddy said, "It's connected."

Malone laughed heartily, clearly enjoying himself. "Connected to what?"

"To the city."

Malone widened his eyes. "How did you figure that out? So quickly? And with no evidence?"

Buddy said, "That's how it would make sense."

"Make *sense*? Buddy, you're full of shit."

Buddy said, "It's all wrong, Chief. The bodies. Where they were found and how. The pattern's off."

"What pattern?"

Buddy was about to explain, but restrained himself. He'd sound crazy because he was relying on intuition and experience from music and twenty years with the NYPD. He couldn't give a logical explanation. And in Chief Malone's office, logic and evidence held sway. Malone could be emotional and filled with bluster, but at heart he was conservative. He didn't like his detectives to rely on intuition. Logic, information, evidence—these were the things Malone respected. So Buddy repeated, "Give me thirty days, Chief. It'll get me back in the groove. I don't want to deal with robbery-homicide today. Not after what happened three weeks ago. Okay?"

Chief Malone glared at him. Until they heard a knock at the door.

Both men looked over and saw Rachel Grove standing in the doorway.

As part of the NYPD's Force Investigation Division, Rachel examined all firearms discharges, partnering with District Attorney Mahoney. Her father was of Swedish descent and her mother was Puerto Rican. She had curly brown hair, dark eyes, smooth skin, and a nicely curved figure. Before he'd met Mei, Buddy had asked her out for a beer. She'd smiled and said she was with someone. Buddy didn't inquire further and didn't ask again. Rachel always wore black or gray pants, never skirts, and her single extravagance was a yearly trip to Carnival in Rio de Janeiro. She'd been a detective—one of them—for several years.

Rachel said, "Hey, Buddy. How're Mei and Ben?"

Buddy smiled briefly. "They're good. You?"

"Good."

As usual, Malone didn't bother with greetings. He said, "Can you clear Buddy tonight?"

She looked at her wristwatch and shook her head. Turning to Buddy, she said, "Administrative review usually takes longer. You sure you want to jump back into it?"

"Yeah," he said. "I'm ready."

She looked over at Malone. When the chief pointed at her, she said, "Given the highly unusual circumstances of Buddy's last case, there's nothing controversial and so we'll get it done. I have some related paperwork tonight, but we'll clear him in the morning."

Buddy nodded. "Thanks, Rachel."

Chief Malone stood behind his desk and crossed his arms. "Yeah, thanks, Rachel. Now Buddy can go find out what happened to an Asian couple found off Long Island while murderers go free here in the city. I'll have to invoke jurisdiction under the governor's roving task force, pissing off the Long Island police and everyone in our department. Thanks *so much*."

Buddy and Rachel didn't laugh or even smile at the chief's joke, if it was a joke.

Malone's mouth curled up on one side. He said, "One month, Buddy. Not a day more. And I'm doing this out of the kindness of my heart since I'm a fucking sentimental asshole. You had a shitty time last month, so I owe it to you. And your working a case, even a stupid one, will get Mayor Blenheim off my back. Always the mayor's asking me when's Buddy coming back. *Jesus.* It's like you shit diamonds since you've been on CNN a couple of times and got someone at the *Gazette* to write love letters to you. Yeah, in an election year, everyone loves the NYPD. By December, they'll have forgotten us." Malone barked out a laugh. "So thirty days, Buddy. Enjoy your vacation."

"Appreciate it, Chief," Buddy said.

Buddy thought Malone would further criticize him, but the large man motioned for him and Rachel to stay. Once again, Malone picked up his desk phone and dialed. "Mingo?" he said. "My office. Now."

7

Malone cocked his head and held open his palms. He said, "You really think these are homicides?"

Buddy nodded. "They might be."

"Might?"

Buddy crossed his arms. "No promises."

A moment later a young Hispanic man in his early thirties entered Malone's office. Buddy recognized him as Mario Mingo. He was handsome but carried a few extra pounds—more extra pounds than Buddy, who stood about six foot three, with Mingo several inches shorter. Mingo had medium-length jet-black hair brushed neatly into a side part. His eyes were dark and his smile easy.

"You called, Chief?" Mingo said. He had a reedy, excitable voice.

Still looking at Buddy, Malone said, "Here's your new partner. Mingo, you're headed to the Nineteenth Precinct."

Buddy turned to the younger man and offered his hand. His new partner had a firm handshake, he noticed, trying to warm to the young detective. Mingo's reputation was that of a solid detective who was enthusiastic and clean, but Buddy thought he might be too slick, might not have the patience to get into a case's details. And it's in the details, Buddy knew, that a detective finds the pattern that solves the case. But he hoped that maybe Mingo could improve, could be an asset. No, he had to do more than hope. He had to believe in the younger man. He had to trust Mingo with his life.

Malone held up a meaty forefinger as his eyes bored into Buddy's.

"The bodies from Long Island will be brought to OCME," he said, referring to the Manhattan Office of the Chief Medical Examiner. "Take a look. But so help me God, you're on a short leash."

8

As Buddy left Malone's office, he pulled out his phone and dialed Mei.

"Buddy? Where are you?"

He stopped, could barely hear over the noise of the corridor where he was standing. Other detectives, clerks, secretaries, and cops passed him as he stood against the wall watching them pass but not really seeing them.

He said, "I'm at work."

"You'll be leaving soon?"

"Probably, yeah. This thing turned out to be more than I expected. Two bodies were found in the Atlantic. Everyone else thinks I should let it go. They were suicides or victims of an accident, people are saying. But I think it's a double homicide from here in the city."

He looked up, suddenly sensing people nearby who'd overheard him. He saw the backs of a man and woman he didn't recognize walking away from him. He glanced left, and an office door closed abruptly. Lowering his voice, he said, "I'm sorry for leaving you and Ben at the courthouse."

"Don't apologize to me. But talk with Ben tonight. He's still upset after talking with Judge Miles, and he's worried he said the wrong thing and the judge will take him away from us."

A hard, angry feeling welled up within him. *Take him away? It's not going to happen,* he told himself. *No fucking way Ben's going to live with people with hearts of ice. No fucking way.*

But now he was at One Police, he'd gotten the case, and in a nice way, Mei was letting him know that he'd failed. He knew she was right. *Goddammit.*

He heard Mei's confused voice. "You're on leave, Buddy. How can you work a case?"

"They're reinstating me tomorrow," he told her, digging into his left trouser pocket. He felt for the medallion from the dead man he'd seen on the fishing boat and lifted it up to the light.

Mei was silent. He knew she wasn't happy, knew she believed he needed a break longer than three weeks. After what he'd been through. What he and she and Ben had been through.

He said, "Hang on a second."

He pressed the home screen button on his phone, touched the photos icon, and found the image of the medallion. After he texted it to Mei, he raised the phone to his ear and said, "I just sent you a photo. Would you let me know if you recognize it?"

She said nothing.

He waited, thinking she was furious. He half expected her to hang up.

Yet a moment later she said, "I don't read *hanzi*, the characters used for writing, but I'm certain this is Chinese. You might go to Chinatown and show it in the jewelry stores. But please do it *tomorrow*. I'm going to leave the gallery now and pick up Ben. Don't be late tonight."

When they'd ended the call, he turned to his left. Two men he didn't know were walking away from him, one with light hair and the other with dark. A third strode past, glanced into Buddy's wary eyes, then looked away. Buddy waited a moment, and the man passed. Buddy turned to the right. An attractive black woman walked toward him, and behind her he could see the retreating figure of a woman with gray hair.

He recognized no one, but all of the retreating figures would have heard parts of his conversation with Mei.

But which parts? he thought. *And why would they care?*

He realized he'd been holding his breath, listening. He heard nothing but the typical office sounds. Yet he felt something, as when a bass in an orchestra played so softly it was almost undetectable, but the note played was in a minor key and spread unease throughout the concert hall.

They don't care, he told himself about those who might have over-heard his conversation with Mei. *This is nothing but a boring missing persons case. Right?*

9
■

Buddy glanced at the darkening sky and kept going. He walked away from One Police, buttoning his navy-blue overcoat, putting on his wool hat, scarf, and gloves. Instead of heading west toward Centre Street, where he could more easily catch the 6 train to the Upper East Side, he began walking north toward the Spring Street station.

He did his best thinking on the streets. The sidewalks acted as a tonic to him, a drug that cranked up his brain while helping him focus. But tonight he wouldn't go far. He had to be home for dinner. And it was too cold: twenty-one degrees Fahrenheit, with a fierce wind snaking between the buildings.

A second time, he looked up at the sky. For a week the days had been nothing but gray. The color matched his mood. He shook his head at the memory of the visit with Judge Miles that morning. He didn't understand how the judge could go against the decision of Ben's guardian, Ray Sawyer. But then he'd never understood how lawyers could twist the law to do what they wanted. When he got home, he'd talk to Ben about what Judge Miles had said, if she'd said anything. Buddy thought she had a great poker face. He didn't know where he stood with her, and he didn't like that feeling.

Lowering his head against the cold, he continued on to the Spring Street station. That would take him home, and his family—what he hoped would be his family—would be complete.

Though maybe not for long.

Passing a liquor store on Cleveland Place, he looked through the windows at the brightly lit shelves of bottles made of clear, green, or blue glass. In the windows' reflection of the street, he saw a man in a lightweight tan jacket, a dark knit hat, and a scarf, but no gloves. The man had one hand at his side, the other in the pocket of his jacket. The man walked several yards behind Buddy, and his image disappeared wherever the windows were covered by banners advertising beer, wine, and liquor.

Buddy anticipated tonight. Sitting in their living room and having a drink, a Jack Daniel's for her, a Michelob for him, while Ben did his homework at the small desk in his bedroom. And later, after Ben was asleep, going to bed with Mei. He liked to leave a faint light on in the master bathroom so he could see her, admire her.

The burn of wanting filled him, and he quickened his pace.

He saw two people walking in his direction: a twentysomething in a Carhartt jacket, jeans, and boots, and an older, hunched woman dressed in a long coat that extended nearly to her ankles. Both of them bundled up on a frigid evening. To his left was a small, triangular park with pavement, trees now without their leaves, and benches, all mostly surrounded by a wrought-iron fence. In warmer weather, people would be sitting there, smoking, drinking surreptitiously, waiting for buses, flirting, skateboarding. But in tonight's cold, it was empty.

At the intersection of Lafayette and Spring, Buddy turned the corner in front of the Duane Reade store with its high stone façade and neoclassical columns. Ten yards ahead on his right were the steps down to the Spring Street station. Instead of proceeding down the steps, he passed the entrance and slowed his pace, stopped, and stood with his back against the building.

Something about Tan Jacket bothered him. *Why wear a lightweight jacket in this cold and also have a hat and a scarf?* he thought. *Doesn't the man own a heavy jacket? And why had Tan Jacket's left hand been at his side, exposed to the cold, while his right hand was tucked into the right side pocket of his thin jacket?*

Buddy had glimpsed the pocket for only an instant, but now he tried to recall its shape. He breathed in and focused. The pocket had been filled, but with more than just a hand. A pack of cigarettes and a lighter? An item bought at a nearby bodega?

No. The contour wasn't right.

Most people, even most cops, wouldn't have noticed. But he'd been trained since childhood to notice patterns in which even the smallest detail was out of place. This detail, he'd become certain, was wrong.

Buddy looked left, at the corner. Tan Jacket stood there, looking straight ahead. Buddy moved his hands in front of him, pulled off his right glove, and reached into his overcoat for his Glock. This gesture was second nature, but today the gun wasn't there.

Shit!

Now he remembered. Malone would give it to him tomorrow at his reinstatement. But he had the baby Glock in his waistband holster.

Again he checked the street corner. Tan Jacket had turned and was staring at him.

10

He pushed off the building wall and began walking along Spring Street. He didn't slow down. Holding his hands in front of him, he removed his left glove, put both gloves in his overcoat pockets, and dropped his hands to his sides in as natural a way as he could. He knew that Tan Jacket could shoot him in the back. He also knew that in the cold the stream of pedestrians was sparser than usual, so there might be nobody between him and the pursuer he estimated was fifteen feet behind him.

He pivoted left and jogged through traffic, across Spring Street and north on the west side of Mulberry Street, putting more distance between himself and Tan Jacket.

This was a commercial and residential block, the left side of the street marked with a few parked cars and short staircases descending into lower level offices or living spaces. A few trees barren of leaves. Adequate light only between streetlamps. He saw places to hide but no good ones. It didn't matter, because a bad hiding place was better than getting shot in the back. He quickened his pace, noticing especially steep concrete steps—about five or six of them—down to a below-grade real estate agent's office. In one motion, he grabbed the metal railing, swung himself around, and dropped down the steps.

Hearing nothing, he bobbed his head upward and glanced down the sidewalk.

His face was nearly blown off by a single muffled gunshot.

Fuck.

Tan Jacket was using a suppressor. And he was close.

Buddy thought quickly. *One guy, or more?*

He wasn't sure.

Taking the Glock out of the IWB holster, he felt the familiar weight of the gun. He was good to go.

He backed up a pace so that he was pressed against the exterior wall of the office. Again he raised his head just enough to look over the steps. A flash of fire, the sound of a bullet, concrete shards flying up around him.

Crouching again, he assessed what he'd seen. Tan Jacket, about twenty yards from him, standing behind another descending concrete staircase. Tan Jacket didn't have a clear shot as long as Buddy remained low.

A standoff, Buddy thought. *You move, you die. Unless . . .*

He looked up Mulberry and saw nobody coming south toward him. He glanced right, around the steps, and saw a group of four people—one man and three women—walking north from behind Tan Jacket's position. They didn't seem alarmed by Tan Jacket, who, from their angle, must be standing harmlessly by the concrete steps. With each stride toward Buddy, they formed a screen from Tan Jacket.

But only for the width of the sidewalk. There were no parked cars near him. He needed something to protect him once he reached the street.

He looked left and saw a BMW X5 SUV, its bluish-white xenon headlights sweeping along the asphalt as it drove south—the wrong way on the one-way street. As the SUV approached slowly, Buddy noticed its Illinois license plate.

Tourists, he thought.

To his right, the pedestrians approached. Ten feet away, they still hadn't noticed him.

To his left, the BMW drew closer.

Buddy's pulse spiked, but he controlled his adrenaline by counting silently. *One. Two. Three. Four.*

He bent low and ran in front of the four pedestrians. Crossing the sidewalk, he slid behind the SUV.

But it was moving, even accelerating. If he didn't stay connected to it, he'd be exposed and dead.

Standing, he leaped onto the back of the SUV, grasping the spoiler above its rear window, his feet not finding purchase on any bumper. So he hung there, his head lying sideways on the window, his feet dragging on the asphalt. As the SUV moved, he glimpsed Tan Jacket crouching in the stairway, staring north to where Buddy had been.

Thirty feet farther, and he dropped from the BMW and ran to the west side of the street. Now he was behind Tan Jacket, and Tan Jacket was exposed.

Buddy crouched in another stairway. He listened for footsteps rushing toward him, but there were none. Mulberry was strangely silent.

He took out his mobile phone and texted his half brother, Ward: In the shit. Pick me up in Little Italy on Mulberry, 50 feet north of Spring.

Not waiting for a response—Ward could be in London, for all Buddy knew—he put away his phone. Still breathing rapidly, he waited until he got his adrenaline under control. Then he brought his head around the stairwell.

At first he couldn't see anything but a seemingly empty stairwell down to a basement apartment. He felt a chill on his neck and wheeled around.

Yet there was no one behind him.

He exhaled. *Okay. Stick with the plan.*

He edged north along the buildings on the west side of Mulberry. Inch by inch, until Tan Jacket came into view.

Buddy narrowed his eyes in the dim light.

Tan Jacket was squatting in a stairwell at the entrance to the office of T. J. Evers, CPA. Around the steps ran a railing made of pewter-colored metal. He still wore his black hat, yet Buddy couldn't see the gun with the suppressor screwed onto the end of the barrel. But he knew it was there.

Tan Jacket watched where Buddy had been and seemed patient, even relaxed. He must have believed he had Buddy cornered. He must be waiting for Buddy to make a mistake.

As Buddy considered calling for backup, he heard the ring of a cell phone. He quickly checked his phone, but saw the screen remained dark. Nobody was calling him, and Ward hadn't responded to his text. He put away his phone.

But Tan Jacket now held his cell phone to his left ear. He spoke in a low voice.

This guy isn't working alone, Buddy thought. Tan Jacket was coordinating, telling another guy he had Buddy cornered—a second thug who would be on the scene in seconds.

Over the concrete sidewalk, some of Tan Jacket's words carried. Buddy didn't recognize them. They were in a foreign language. Not French or German or Spanish. A different alphabet, the words with a different intonation. He couldn't be sure, but he thought he was hearing Russian.

11

Buddy determined he had three choices.

He could sneak away. But it wasn't his nature to sneak away from anything. Moreover, Tan Jacket would find another time and place to take him out.

Or he could announce himself as police, order Tan Jacket not to move, and call for backup. He could give Tan Jacket the opportunity to do the right thing. But if Tan Jacket spun around and tried to shoot him, Buddy would have to kill the man, leading to yet another suspension because of an officer-involved shooting. Which would mean he couldn't get his badge and service weapon tomorrow, and he wouldn't be able to investigate the dead couple found off Long Island.

No, he needed to avoid shooting, avoid a fatality.

The third option? He couldn't remember it.

As he stood against the building wall fifteen yards behind Tan Jacket, he waited until he saw another couple coming up Mulberry. He put the Glock back in his holster. When the couple pulled even with him, he stepped behind them, bending over to bring his height in line with theirs.

The couple neared Tan Jacket, who was crouching low in the cold and keeping the gun between his chest and the concrete steps, his left hand holding the phone to his ear.

The couple passed Tan Jacket. Buddy didn't.

From the higher elevation of the sidewalk, Buddy stepped behind Tan Jacket at the same time that Tan Jacket ended his call and put the phone in his back trouser pocket. Sensing Buddy behind him, Tan Jacket muttered a guttural word that sounded like, but wasn't, the word *terrible*. He turned around and began to straighten.

Buddy pressed forward. He raised his leg and, with all his strength, drove the bottom of his shoe into the man's head. The heavy skull jerked sideways, crashing into concrete. Tan Jacket fell and lay crumpled at the bottom of the steps.

Buddy stood over him, ready for more, but Tan Jacket didn't move. He was out, a bloom of dark blood spreading over the concrete.

Buddy didn't hesitate. He picked up the man's gun, took the cell phone from the back trouser pocket, and stuck them in the pockets of his overcoat. Then he reached down and went through Tan Jacket's pockets.

He found no wallet.

No ID.

No money, other than a single ten-dollar bill.

Not a real New Yorker, he thought. *Maybe not American.*

Rolling Tan Jacket over, he took out his own phone and snapped three photos of Tan Jacket's face. Narrow, angular, bloody. He stood there for a moment, thinking. He wanted more, needed more. Then he heard a siren, getting closer, louder, quickly. Hearing the gunshots, even dampened by the suppressor, someone might have dialed 911.

One minute, he thought. *No more than two.*

He pulled his own wallet from the right breast pocket of his suit coat. Holding the wallet in both hands, he removed his Visa card. He breathed on it and rubbed both sides of the card on his overcoat. Then he knelt down, grabbed Tan Jacket's left hand, and pressed the tip of the loose index finger on the front surface of the Visa card. He adjusted the card and made a second print. At that point he removed his tie and wrapped it around the credit card and put the bundle in the left side pocket of his suit coat. At last, he climbed the steps and looked up and down the sidewalk. He saw no immediate threat. Nobody had emerged from the offices of T. J. Evers, CPA. He saw no undue interest in what he was doing, although the siren was drawing close.

So he headed north on the sidewalk. He was hot now, filled with nerves. From almost dying. From kicking Tan Jacket's head into immovable concrete. His mind alert, he resisted the instinct to run.

He formulated a plan.

In case Tan Jacket had a crew, Buddy would take cover and call the Fifth Precinct two blocks away on Elizabeth Street. They could scoop up Tan Jacket and question the hell out of him.

At the intersection with Prince Street, he dropped Tan Jacket's gun in a garbage can and ducked into the vestibule of a bar. He stood by the door and texted Ward his new location. Then he studied Tan Jacket's phone. He saw it was a burner, but he checked the call log anyway. He found no record of outgoing calls, but one incoming call was listed. Must have been the one Buddy saw him take. The number on the screen seemed familiar, yet Buddy couldn't place it.

He tapped on the number and held the phone up to his ear. He heard a ring, two rings, three. Then a click as a female voice answered.

"Good evening," she said. "New York City Police Department."

12

Mei gathered her things and threw away her empty coffee cup. She checked her watch.

Twenty minutes.

The 4 train from Fifty-Ninth and Lex. Transfer to the 7 at Grand Central. Exit the subway at Hudson Yards.

I'll be at Vista School just as Ben finishes science club.

This was new for her, planning for someone else, cutting down her hours in order to care for a child. She found it difficult to leave work so early. Guilt and stress plagued her. She feared that she couldn't make anyone happy. But she wouldn't give up Ben, not for anything.

"Mei, could you come into my office?"

She swiveled her chair around and looked up at Ms. Anta Safar, the assistant director of Porter Gallery.

Anta Safar stood just behind Mei's chair and to the right. She was dressed as usual in tight black pants, black boots, and a black blouse. Only the color of the scarf around her neck changed. And today it was red, almost a perfect match for her lipstick. Safar was in her late fifties, about twenty years older than Mei, but she remained pretty, if not as slender as she'd once been. Her bottle-blond hair wasn't really blond but several colors in the yellow range, mixed together.

Her hair, Mei thought, *needs work.* Yet she smiled at Anta Safar. Usually Anta Safar returned her smile—usually Anta Safar was like her favorite aunt—but not today.

Mei asked, "How can I help?"

"Let's talk in my office," Anta Safar said, tilting her head toward the private offices behind the exhibition space.

Mei stood, grabbed her phone, and began to follow. She glanced down at her friend Jessica, who sat to her left and whose desk also faced the large gallery with its polished concrete floors and multimillion-dollar paintings hung on white walls.

Jessica, a tall skinny blonde originally from Bozeman, Montana, widened her eyes and shrugged.

Mei and Anta Safar entered the private office. Safar closed the door behind them and walked around her pristine white desk with absolutely nothing on it except a white iMac computer. Safar indicated the chair. Mei sat down, but Safar didn't.

Anta Safar looked down at Mei with concern in her eyes. She said, "I'm terribly sorry, Mei, but we've decided to go in another direction."

Mei sat quietly, waiting to hear more. Perhaps her work on the upcoming show of Titian's paintings hadn't considered an important part of the artist's biography. When Safar offered nothing further, Mei said, "In which direction are we going?"

Safar lifted her chin. "What I mean is that Porter Gallery has decided to go in a new direction staffing-wise. We're letting you go. It wasn't . . . it wasn't my decision. I'm so sorry."

Mei felt herself grow hot all over. She felt as if an invisible being were sticking sharp pins into her arms and legs, into her feet and hands. She had difficulty breathing and her mind clouded. Lowering her eyes for a moment, she looked at her hands in her lap. She saw the pretty silk of the eggplant-colored dress she wore, together with, on the ring finger of her left hand, the diamond solitaire Buddy had put there only recently. Everything had seemed to be going so well! They'd saved Ben, who'd come to live with them. They'd begun the process of adopting him. Her wedding to Buddy—the man she loved more than any other—would be in two weeks, in the City Clerk's office. And now Ms. Safar had told her . . . had told her . . .

She raised her eyes, knowing they'd soon be filled with tears. "What happened?"

Ms. Safar's blue eyes widened. Her face softened. "I can't . . . I can't explain, Mei. I can say only that the gallery has decided to go in another direction."

Mei leaned forward. "But did I do something wrong?"

Safar shook her head. "No, Mei. You did nothing wrong. Nothing at all. Not as far as I'm concerned. This will be the end. For us. But I'm sure not for your career."

Mei sat back, stunned.

It's my short hours, she thought. *My caring for Ben. But Anta isn't saying that's why. She's hiding the reason.*

Anta Safar walked around the desk and held out her hand. At first Mei thought Safar intended to shake her hand.

Safar said, "I'll need your iPhone, please."

Mei held her phone but didn't hand it over. She said, "It's my only mobile phone. Could I drop it off in a couple of days after I buy a new one and port the number over?"

Safar shook her head. Flexed her outstretched hand. "I'm sorry, but I must have it now."

Reluctantly, Mei handed Anta Safar the phone.

Safar opened her office door, stood to the side, and said, "Goodbye, Mei. And good luck."

13

Something in Mei changed with that ultimatum, that unfairness, that taking of the phone. Her fortitude, momentarily diminished as a result of being laid off, reasserted itself. She pushed herself up from the chair, left the office without looking at Anta Safar, and walked along the short corridor to her desk by the south wall of the gallery.

Jessica looked up at Mei.

Mei didn't meet her friend's eyes. Instead, she set her oversized Bottega Veneta tote bag on her chair, picked up her few personal belongings, including a photograph of her with Buddy on Waikiki Beach—their Hawaii trip, the only one they'd ever taken together—and began loading the bag. Exhibition catalogues for which she'd written the introductory essay. Thick and heavy-as-iron monographs on various artists. Her minimal collection of tea, lipstick, two mugs, toothpaste, and a single pink toothbrush with a cover.

Jessica swiveled to face her. "What's going on? What are you doing?"

Mei looped the tote straps over a shoulder and faced Jessica. "Stand up and give me a hug," she said. "I've been fired."

Jessica's mouth fell open. "*What?*"

Mei reached out her hands. "Safar says I have to go now."

"But—"

"Come on!"

Jessica stood, towering over Mei. She leaned down and gave more than the fake hug so common among New York women. She held Mei tightly—for a good ten seconds—and said, "Let me know where you land, okay? I'm sure you could work at any gallery. Any of them. I'm sure of it."

Mei said, "I hope you're right."

Jessica grasped her upper arms and stared at her. "I'm right. Of course I'm right. This layoff, whatever"—she tilted her head in the direction of Anta Safar's office—"isn't because of you. There's some management issue or money problem. I'm probably next. Oh, God. I'm next, I think."

Mei smiled. Jessica had a good heart, but everything intersected with Jessica's life, even things that had nothing to do with her. Mei's friend, really her work acquaintance, was self-absorbed but affable and not unkind. Mei said, "Goodbye."

Jessica shook her head. "Not goodbye. We'll meet for drinks. And if you need time to recover, you can use Oliver's country house. I'm sure he wouldn't mind. Let's talk, okay? *Soon.*"

Mei smiled and said "Soon," although she knew they probably wouldn't. With that, she turned and walked across the polished concrete floor toward the doors onto Fifty-Eighth Street. She didn't look at the paintings hanging on the walls. She didn't look at the few visitors who'd entered the gallery while she was in Anta Safar's office. They were no longer her concern, though she wished they were. She'd liked working here and didn't understand what mistake she'd made or why Porter Gallery wanted to go in a "different direction."

It hurt, being let go. What a euphemism. *Fired* was a better word because it described exactly how she felt. Perhaps she'd contact Jessica in February to learn if Anta Safar had explained. But she knew her firing wasn't right. She knew she'd done nothing wrong, other than meeting the needs of a ten-year-old boy. And now that she'd lost her job, would Judge Miles hold that against her?

Her thoughts swirled with uncertainty. She felt perspiration on her brow.

Pulling open the gallery doors, she stepped onto the sidewalk and into the city after dusk, with its multitude of lights and cacophony of sharp noises. As she traveled a few paces and was about to step off the curb and hail a cab—her tote bag was too heavy for the subway—the cold air surprised her. Shocked her. The wind whipping the cold between the buildings woke her as if from a horrible dream, and she realized she'd forgotten her coat.

God no, she thought. She'd have to return to the gallery and grab it. She couldn't leave it, not on a day as cold as this one. And it was a nice coat, worth far more to her than the embarrassment of going back to her desk. As she turned away from the street, she saw a large man dressed in black pants, a black parka, and a black baseball hat, walking straight toward her.

Immediately she sensed danger. She didn't know why. Maybe it was being fired. Maybe it was the shock of the cold. Maybe it was the way she'd nearly been killed weeks earlier, during Buddy's last case. She felt unsafe, even on a street and in a neighborhood as expensive as this one, even with other pedestrians on the block, though not close to her. There was something about the man dressed in black, and his wearing sunglasses under dark skies, the man who strode so quickly and purposefully toward her. She couldn't see his face, not really. A patch of skin on either side of his nose, but no more.

She backed up toward the gallery doors, never taking her eyes off him. She watched as he reached into the right front pocket of his parka and began to pull something out of it.

In the streetlights she could see the pale glimmer.

A cell phone? she thought. *Or a knife?*

She stepped backward, her left heel catching in a metal grate in the sidewalk. She nearly tumbled over, the extra weight in her tote pulling her off-balance.

The man in black neared her. Fifteen yards. Ten. He held his hand by his pocket, and the metal object in it remained mostly hidden. He walked quickly but seemed unhurried, as if he had plenty of time to take care of her, as if she couldn't escape.

And she couldn't. She seemed frozen, trying to catch her balance, trying to shift the tote, failing to steady herself. Afraid of turning her back to the man to rush for the gallery doors, she faced him and knew this would be either an example of her paranoia, if he was just holding a cell phone, or the end, if he was holding a knife.

"Mei!"

It was Jessica, her statuesque figure pushing through the gallery doors. Jessica held up Mei's knee-length Moncler winter parka, nearly blocking the sidewalk as she did so.

Mei caught her balance. She held up a hand to warn her friend about the man in black.

Jessica must have thought she was reaching for the parka. So Jessica held it toward Mei. "Jesus Christ, Mei!" she called. "You can't be out here without your jacket. You're not a Montana girl, after all!"

Mei tried to look around her friend, but the big puffy down jacket was blocking her view. She feared for her friend, feared for both of them. But then she saw the man in black.

He'd turned from the sidewalk. His right hand was plunged into his jacket pocket, hiding the metallic object. He was angling left and stepping between two parked cars. Then he jogged through traffic across Fifty-Eighth Street.

Mei turned back to Jessica. She forced herself to smile and take the coat and air-kiss Jessica's cheeks.

When her friend went back inside the gallery, Mei was left standing on the sidewalk, alone and afraid. She looked right and left along the sidewalk but saw nothing unusual. The man in black had gone, at least for now. Yet she believed she wasn't safe. Something had happened that led to her being fired and then to her feeling threatened on East Fifty-Eighth Street. She sensed the two events were somehow connected but couldn't understand how.

All at once she had a premonition of many knives cloaked in darkness, of these knives moving across the island of Manhattan like a plague that was coming for her and Ben and probably for Buddy, too. *Ben,* she thought. *Is he all right? Or did they already come for him?*

14

Buddy waited for the silver Range Rover to approach and pull along the curb. He peered through the front passenger window. His brother's driver, Brick, was at the wheel. Brick had sun-bleached hair and was rail thin. He looked like he'd grown up surfing in Malibu, and he had. His fellow surfers had given him the nickname because his stomach was as hard as the building material. Buddy had never heard his real name. Brick pointed to the right rear door. Buddy took a final look around and, seeing no immediate danger, opened the door and climbed into the car.

Buddy studied his brother, who was sitting in the back seat. At forty-one, Ward was a couple of years younger than Buddy but seemed to be five or more. Buddy saw the perfect navy-blue suit under an unbuttoned camel hair overcoat. The perfect suntanned complexion even in midwinter. The perfectly cut and styled sandy-colored hair worn slightly long and pomaded back and to the side. The dark-blue eyes. Buddy also noticed something new. A wristwatch so large it must be some kind of machine.

Ward asked, "You all right?"

Buddy considered how he felt. His pulse thumped twenty beats more per minute than usual. He wasn't nervous; he was angry. "Yeah," he said. "A hundred percent."

Ward leaned closer. "What the fuck happened?"

"Someone put a hit out on me."

"Why?"

"No idea," Buddy replied, though he did. He was thinking of the dead couple lying on the deck of Mack Berringer's boat.

Ward asked, "But aren't you on administrative leave?"

"I'll be reinstated tomorrow."

"So why kill you tonight?"

Buddy turned to him. He didn't want the questions. He needed to think, and then act. A plan was forming in his head—one involving Mei and Ben. He changed the subject by pointing at Ward's wrist. "What does it do, other than tell time?"

Ward Mills held up his wrist, showing him a large black watch with a profusion of dials and numbers and arrows. "You can activate a beacon that communicates with a satellite system so you can ask for emergency help anywhere in the world. It's a GPS, meaning the service knows your exact location. And it's also a phone, so I can communicate with Brick. Or with the police if things go south. It's a satellite-based SOS."

Buddy thought for a moment. He said, "By the time someone could help you, you'd be dead."

Ward smiled. "You never know how fast help can get to you."

Buddy thought about how quickly Brick and Ward had shown up tonight and asked the question his brother had never answered. "Do you have a place in the city?"

Ward held up a hand. "Enough."

Buddy didn't press further. His brother had a big country house up in Greenwich, Connecticut, but he was always in the city and never had luggage with him. Buddy thought his brother was odd, especially for keeping secret where he stayed in Manhattan. In the past few weeks, he'd come to appreciate Ward, even to need him. For most of his life, he'd hated his half brother, the secret love child resulting from his father's relationship with Ward's mother. Buddy's father had left Buddy and his mother in near poverty while marrying Ward's mother, heir to a manufacturing fortune. Ward had inherited hundreds of millions of dollars or more. Buddy had been a scholarship student at Juilliard, where Ward had been BMOC, the most precocious performer, tutored by their father, the legendary teacher of several of the most famous pianists on earth. Buddy had learned from his father, too. Not only piano, but how to destroy a family. By leaving it. By caring for only one of your two sons. By going for the money.

Ward's wife, Anna, had been murdered over two years ago in Rome. These days, somewhat recovered, he traveled the world by private jet and dated movie stars. Buddy worked all hours studying the worst of humanity for modest pay. Yet Ward had helped him and Mei and Ben, and all of them had grown close.

Ward touched his shoulder, leaned closer to him, shifted the conversation. "Hey, man. Tell me what happened."

Buddy didn't answer, not right away. In his mind he replayed the events of the last hour and kept going through the entire day.

Ward gave him time, didn't press. Covered up the large watch with the sleeve of his camel hair overcoat.

Buddy thought about Judge Miles. Were Ben's aunt and uncle trying to take out Buddy in order to gain control of Ben and his money? No, he'd learned they wouldn't go that far. He also considered his meeting with Mack Berringer at the Shinnecock Dock, and the bodies of the man and woman lying on the deck of Mack's trawler. Discovery of the bodies wouldn't have been enough. But then he'd told Chief Malone about what Mack Berringer had found and that he was going to investigate. By accident he'd told others, unknown to him, who'd passed him as he stood in the hallway outside Malone's office and spoke with Mei by cell phone. He might have a target on his back for any one of these reasons. He thought he wasn't paranoid. He thought he was hearing that bass in the orchestra playing a single B-flat, louder now, that set his teeth on edge. Shaking his head slowly, he said, "I don't know. But I touched the third rail."

Ward cocked his head. "What third rail?"

Anyone who'd grown up in the city knew that in the subway, the first two rails carried the train cars; the third rail, the electricity that powered them. When Buddy was a child, his mother had given him repeated bleak warnings: *If you touch the third rail, you'll die. You can't survive. Nobody can.* Now he opened his hands and said, "No fucking idea, but someone wants me dead—and fast."

Fast.

He realized that speed mattered. If he'd been marked for death because he'd decided to pursue the bodies found off Long Island, the speed with which that had happened meant something about the bodies and those who'd tried to kill him. Speed also meant he'd have to move even faster and learn who was hunting him. *It's a race,* he thought, *in which the loser dies.* Other men would have been more shaken if someone had tried to kill them. Not Buddy. He was jumping ahead, trying to figure out *why.*

Removing his gloves, he checked the NYPD directory loaded into his phone, and dialed.

Two rings, and he heard the clear, youthful voice: "Mingo."

"Mario, I got into a scrape with a hit man in a tan jacket on Mulberry just north of Spring. He's lying at the bottom of the entrance stairs to the office of T. J. Evers, CPA. Have someone from the Fifth Precinct pick him up and find out who he is."

Mingo asked, "A *hit man*? You're . . . you're okay?"

"Yeah."

Mingo waited a moment, then said, "Buddy, are you telling me someone tried to *kill* you?"

"That's right."

"What for?"

"No clue."

Mingo's voice showed skepticism. "You sure about this?"

"It was pretty damned obvious," Buddy said. "Details later. For now, have the patrol scoop him up. He might need time in a hospital."

Mingo took this in silently.

Buddy thought his partner had ended the call. He said, "Mario?"

"I'm here. But . . . you think the guy is where you left him?"

"He's there," Buddy confirmed. "No way he's going for a jog."

Mingo paused. Then he said, "I'm on it."

Buddy said, "I already printed him, using my Visa card. I'm going to leave it on your desk in the morning. Send it to the lab, would you?"

Buddy ended the call. *Speed,* he thought again. Tan Jacket and someone in the NYPD—they'd come for him in a fucking blitzkrieg. And what had he done just before they'd tried to take him out? He'd told Mei about the case and even texted her an image of evidence.

Sweat formed on his forehead as he dialed her mobile number. There was no answer.

He hung up and called their home phone.

The line rang again and again before going to voicemail.

He ended the call but held the phone tightly in his lap. Gazing out at rush hour traffic in the quiet comfort of the Range Rover, he saw they were heading uptown on the FDR Drive but slowly, stop-and-go the entire way. To his right lay the black water of the East River and beyond it, the residential towers and the few remaining warehouses around Bushwick Inlet.

He checked his watch. The drive home was taking too long. He thought Mei and Ben might be exposed.

15

After Mei picked up Ben from school, a taxi brought them to the Carlyle Residences. When the car had pulled along the curb on East Seventy-Sixth Street, she put a hand on his arm, indicating he shouldn't open the car door.

He turned to her, his eyes questioning.

"Wait," she told him, staring at the door to their building. "Just a moment."

She didn't want to make the journey of a few steps to the door unattended. Not when the man in black might be pursuing them. So she waited for Schmidt, the doorman whose head remained bandaged from a recent assault on the building and on her and Ben, to pull open the car door.

From under the black canopy that extended from the building door to the curb, Schmidt recognized them, smiled, and opened the door. "Welcome home, Ms. Adams and Benjamin!" he said heartily.

"Thank God," she told him, allowing him to walk beside them and then open the building door. His presence, and their arrival at home, eased her fears.

As they entered the small lobby with the gray-and-white marble floors, the white walls with generous molding, and the comfortable black leather furniture, she made straight for the elevator. When they were inside, she held her access card in front of the electronic reader and pressed the button for the twenty-fifth floor. Moments later, as the elevator eased its upward motion and came to rest, Mei again held her key card up to the reader on the interior of the cab. The reader chimed, the elevator door rolled back, and they walked into the foyer. She set down her heavy tote bag along one wall by an antique Chinese medicine cabinet in black lacquer.

Ben shrugged off his navy-blue peacoat and set his backpack on the floor next to her tote bag. He stepped out of his New Balance running shoes and stood there in stockinged feet, khakis, and a button-down shirt under a wine-colored crewneck sweater.

Without his coat and backpack, he seemed more like a little boy than ever. Her heart swelled with affection for him. "Come here," she said. "I need a hug." When he lowered his eyes, suddenly shy, she walked over and embraced him. "I love you," she told him.

He stood on tiptoe and kissed her cheek.

I can't give him up, she thought. *Not ever.*

16

Later, after getting home and making sure everyone was unhurt, Buddy used the landline in the kitchen to order pizza for delivery, took a Michelob out of the refrigerator, and looked across the granite countertop to Ward and Mei.

Too much, he thought. *Too much has happened in too short a time.* Something was way off, he realized. Someone had declared war on his family, and he didn't know why.

Looking first at his fiancée and then at his brother, he said, "They have power—power that can reach all of us. That can order the killing of a cop, which requires coordination and expertise."

Mei's eyes widened. "Which cop?"

He put his hands on the counter. "They tried to get me downtown after I left One Police."

"Get you?"

"A guy shot at me."

"My God, Buddy."

"I'm all right."

"What about the guy?"

Buddy looked away. "He's not so good."

"My God," she said again. "Maybe it's true."

He turned back to her. "What do you mean?"

"I was fired today. And then—"

"*Fired?*" he asked. "Why?"

She glanced toward the hallway that led to Ben's room, put a finger to her lips, and said, "When I left the gallery, a man in dark glasses was approaching me. He might have had a knife. But Jessica came outside and he went away."

Buddy listened, but he wasn't sure why anyone would threaten Mei. He suspected she'd become nervous after the events of the last month. But what if he were wrong and his experience with Tan Jacket were related to the man outside Mei's gallery—the man who might have had a knife?

It hit him then like a brick smashing into his chest.

He reached across the counter and touched Mei's arm. "You're not safe here."

Her eyes flashed defiantly. "Neither are you."

Buddy knew she was right. Yet despite concerns about his personal safety, his mind churned through question after question.

Is Chief Malone or one of the others in the chief's office dirty?

Did someone hear me in the corridor outside Malone's office?

How did the bodies found off Long Island get there?

He had no answers, but he knew that here, in the city, he couldn't protect Mei and Ben.

He said, "I'm being reinstated tomorrow. I'll be armed with my usual service weapon. You won't have that."

She said, "I still have the small revolver Ward gave me last month."

"That's not enough. You know it isn't. And what about Ben?"

Mei looked at Ward and then at Buddy. She was about to say something when Buddy interrupted her.

"Maybe you should take Ben and get as far away from me as possible. Until I've cleared this up."

"Yes?" she asked, voice rising. "What then? I can't be in danger, not anymore. Your last case was all I could handle. And it isn't fair to

Ben. You need to solve this problem, Buddy, so we can be safe and stay together. We can't go on like this."

Buddy recognized the warning for what it was. He knew she wasn't worried only about the events of today. She was thinking of the future. That is, she wanted one that was safe and secure. For her and for Ben. He understood. He knew he had to change the situation and provide her with what she deserved. And yet her threat made him uneasy. As his chest tightened, he glanced down at Mei's hand to be sure she was wearing the engagement ring he'd given her. Seeing that she was, he exhaled.

Buddy said, "I hear you. Things will change, okay?"

Mei only stared at him with her lustrous brown eyes. She said, "There's risk in taking Ben out of the city—that's against Judge Miles's order."

He set down his beer, put both palms on the countertop, and leaned toward her. "There's more risk in staying. I don't know what's happening, Mei. I don't know if the attack was related to the man and woman found off Long Island or if it was related to something else. Give me time to find out." He realized he'd made the same plea to Chief Malone, and at the thought of Malone's possible betrayal, his mood darkened. He said, "While I find out who attacked us, I can't keep you safe. I admit it. So you should leave the city, go somewhere nice with Ben."

Her cheeks flushed. "You're forcing me to leave town?"

"I'm *asking* you. For your safety, and Ben's." Buddy saw her mouth tighten and expected the worst.

Ward must have seen it, too, because he gently touched her forearm before saying, "I know a place you can stay. You can rest up and decide the next step in your career."

Mei remembered the terrible event weeks ago and shook her head. "Ben and I won't go back to your house. Not after what happened there."

He said, "No, no, no. I'd like you to stay with a friend of mine I've known since grade school. You'll be safe. Buddy can work the case and figure out what's happening. When he's resolved it, you and Ben can come home."

Mei was quiet for a moment. Then she said, "We'll stay at a house owned by the boyfriend of one of my friends."

Ward asked, "Where is it? And who is the friend?"

She shook her head. "It's safer if I tell no one."

17

Mei left the kitchen, walked down the hallway to the master bedroom, and closed the door. Sitting on the edge of the bed, she picked up the phone on her night table and dialed.

"Mei! I'm so glad you called!" Jessica's voice was all Montana—Midwestern with a hint of relaxed California. "How are you doing?"

Mei's spirits rose when she heard her friend's concern. "I'm okay, but I'd like to see if the offer of Oliver's country house stands. Just for a few days."

"Of *course* it does."

"Jess, I could pay you something."

"Oh, please. That's crazy! Why don't I give you the address?"

Mei closed her eyes, grateful her friend was closer to her and more generous than she'd believed. She picked up the pen and pad of paper next to the phone and said, "That would be wonderful."

Jessica gave her the address of a house near Rockridge, a small town west of Bloomingburg and about ninety minutes northwest of Manhattan. Jessica said, "There's no key, just a code to unlock the door and disable the alarm. The code is 1-8-3-2. Got it?"

Mei repeated and wrote out the numbers: "1-8-3-2."

"Right," Jessica confirmed. "Now don't expect too much. It's rustic and in the middle of nowhere. But it's pretty and has a good kitchen and wireless."

Mei said, "Is there a password for the wireless?"

"Yes," Jessica told her, "it's j-e-s-s-i-c-a."

"I can't thank you enough."

After replacing the phone on its cradle, she stood and opened her closet doors. On tiptoe, she reached to the shelf above the rack of clothes and took down a heavy nylon case. After setting it on the bed, she unzipped the case and looked at the small revolver Ward had given her. She opened the cylinder and looked through the chambers. As she expected, all were empty. She replaced the gun in the case, zipped the case, and from the closet took down a box of .38-caliber bullets. Then she set the gun case and the box of ammunition in the bottom of her large Bottega Veneta handbag.

About to walk into the bathroom to collect toiletries and add them to her bag, she heard the chime of the doorbell. Her chest tightened with fear.

Who? she thought.

She stared at the gun in her handbag before leaving the bedroom and proceeding along the hallway. She stopped walking, ceased breathing, and listened.

18

Hearing the doorbell, Buddy hurried to the foyer. He took the small Glock from his IWB holster. Standing against the side of the elevator, he switched off the emergency lock and allowed it to open.

Nobody stepped into the foyer.

"Hello?" came the voice.

It was Schmidt, their doorman.

Buddy stuck the Glock into the holster and stepped out where Schmidt could see him.

The doorman stood in the elevator. He was of medium height, stout, with dark hair partly covered by bandages, and blue eyes. In his dark uniform, he looked impressive, even formidable. In both hands he held a large pizza box.

"Hey, Schmidt," Buddy said. "Thanks for bringing it up."

Schmidt handed him the pizza box. "You're welcome, Mr. Lock. Have a good evening."

As Schmidt backed into the elevator, Buddy lifted the box and read the computer-printed label on the front of the box. It stated his name, the order of a large pepperoni pizza, the time he placed the order, and, in handwriting, the time of delivery to Schmidt downstairs. The order was correct. He again thanked Schmidt, set the elevator lock when the door had closed, and returned with the box to the kitchen. Mei was waiting with Ward, neither of them talking.

After setting it on the counter, he walked along the hallway to the bedrooms. He came to the doorway on the right leading to Ben's room. As he expected, Ben was sitting at the desk that had been Mei's. His headphones plugged into a MacBook Air, he was typing rapidly. Buddy walked two paces into the room. He saw that instead of the expected text or email, Ben had begun typing a response to his assignment's question about Mesopotamia and the Fertile Crescent. He hated to tear Ben away from his homework and from his new home, but he had no choice. He said, "Ben?"

The boy continued typing.

More loudly: "Ben?"

The typing ceased. Ben turned slightly and pulled off his head-phones. He said, "Hi."

"How are you?"

"Okay."

"How'd it go with the judge?"

"I don't know."

"What did she ask you?"

"Where I wanted to live."

"Yeah, we knew she'd ask that, didn't we?"

Ben said, "I told her."

"Good."

"I told her I hate my aunt and uncle, that they're horrible, and I hate them."

Buddy touched his shoulder. "You told the truth. That's all you could do."

Ben's light-brown eyes, glimmering with worry, looked up at him. "So can I stay here with you and Mei?"

"I hope so."

Ben sat quietly for a moment.

Buddy said, "Would you come out to the kitchen? We're talking about you and Mei going to stay out of the city for a little while."

Ben didn't move. He said, "Out of the city?"

Buddy hesitated. "Mei can tell you."

"But why do we need to leave?"

Buddy jerked his head in the direction of the kitchen. "Come on. Let's talk it over with Mei. The pizza's here."

In the kitchen, Buddy and Ben sat on one side of the counter while Ward and Mei stood on the other. Mei had taken out four white plates and put two slices on each one.

Mei looked at Ben and said, "You and I are going on a little vacation, just for a while."

Ben put his arms across his chest. "Why?"

"Buddy's working a case. We can stay in the country until he's finished."

"But *why*?"

Mei said, "The case involves some very bad people, and we want to stay away from them. Okay?"

Ben looked at Buddy and asked, "Is it because of my aunt and uncle? Or because of something I told Judge Miles?"

"No," they replied in unison.

"No," Buddy repeated. "This is about something else—a case I'm working that relates to a couple of people out on Long Island. Nothing to do with your family, okay?"

Ben seemed uncertain.

Buddy said, "This is just my job. Sometimes I have to deal with bad people, and I don't want them to know about you or find you. Let me put the bad guys in prison, and then you can come back, all right?"

"Okay," Ben said softly, relaxing his arms.

Buddy nodded at him. Ben had been in danger before, and Buddy knew he wanted his life to be calm and normal, even boring. He said, "Good. It's settled."

"Plus," Ben continued, "I can attend school on the web."

Buddy was confused. "The web?"

Ben's eyes shone with excitement. "I can connect to my classes, Buddy. They're all on camera because so many kids are gone with their parents."

With Ward's help, Ben had recently gained admittance to Vista School, at Tenth Avenue and West Twenty-Eighth Street in Chelsea. Tuition for Ben was $45,000 per year, and the parents of his classmates were movie stars, hedge fund managers, and other wealthy people who had second or third or fourth homes and used all of them. Buddy knew the school accepted its students' absences and realized that Vista must have begun doing live broadcasts of classes—or even taped classes—for students out of town.

Mei said, "Yes, you can attend remotely. So pack your laptop and everything else you'll need."

Ben turned to her. "When are we leaving?"

Mei glanced at Buddy.

Buddy said, "Fifteen minutes."

As Ben began walking, favoring his left leg, toward the hallway and his bedroom, Ward said, "Hang on, Ben."

Ben stopped and turned as Ward went over to his camel hair overcoat draped over a barstool. He fished in the pocket and withdrew a small square box of the most perfect white.

Ben's eyes brightened. "For me?"

Ward offered him the box. "For you."

Buddy said, "What is it?"

Ben turned to him. "It's an Apple Watch. A new one, with cellular."

"You already have a phone," Buddy said.

Ward nodded. "This watch has cellular. Even if he forgets his phone, he has the watch. He can text and make calls. Just in case."

Buddy thought the gift was unnecessary since he'd never seen Ben without his phone. Yet he appreciated Ward's generosity. He said, "Thanks, Ward."

Ben smiled. "Yeah, Mr. Mills. Thank you!"

Buddy noticed there wasn't any plastic wrap over the box. *A hand-me-down from Ward?* he wondered. That seemed unlike his brother. But maybe Ward had discarded it in favor of the enormous satellite watch-phone-GPS, whatever it was, he wore. Buddy also noticed Ben's expression of wonder as he took the top off the box and saw the black watch and the royal-blue band. Buddy was amazed by how quickly Ben attached the watchband and strapped the device to his wrist.

Ward patted his shoulder. "Need my help pairing it with your phone and laptop?"

Ben laughed. "I can figure it out."

Buddy thought he'd need a few days to figure it out, or longer, or never. He said, "Good. But you still need to leave in fifteen minutes. Wear your jacket and pack your boots."

As Ben and Mei left the kitchen to get ready, he looked at Ward and then drank his beer.

Ward put both hands on the counter and leaned across toward Buddy. He said, "There's something I've been hiding from you for two years."

19

Buddy knew his puzzlement showed on his face. "Hiding from me?"

Ward nodded. "I wanted to thank you for visiting me at McLean."

Buddy remained impassive. He was uncomfortable at the mention of the psychiatric hospital outside Boston where Ward had lived for six months following his wife's murder. He remembered the large gothic building and Ward's room: fake wood floors, tan walls, plain bed made of dark wood. Like a hotel room, but one with a lock on the outside of the door.

Buddy had sat in his half brother's private room every Saturday afternoon for six months. For two months, he'd talked, and Ward had stared at him or at the ceiling or out the window but had never replied. *I'm talking to myself,* Buddy had thought. *And I'm not much of a talker.* He'd left recent copies of the *Gazette* and issues of the *New Yorker* and *Rolling Stone* for his brother, who hadn't seemed to notice.

The third month, Ward had listened, focusing his dark-blue eyes on Buddy's face.

The fourth month, in response to questions from Buddy, Ward had nodded or shaken his head.

The fifth month, Ward had begun to speak.

The sixth month, Ward had met Buddy in the dining room and conversed with Buddy like a sedated but otherwise healthy man.

A week later, Ward had been released, and returned to live in his mansion in Greenwich, looked after by Ms. Gallatin, his sixtysomething housekeeper and cook.

"At McLean," Ward continued, "I lived for your visits. For a long time, I couldn't even acknowledge them. I couldn't do much more than breathe and shit. You couldn't have known they were important to me, but it's true. After Anna's murder, dying was all I could think about. Each day, I told myself that I'd live until Saturday morning. And if you visited, I wouldn't take a sheet from the bed and hang myself from the bathroom door. But you came to see me every Saturday for six months until I was released. If you hadn't come—or even if you'd missed a Saturday because you were sick or working or with a girlfriend, I wouldn't be here. So when you call me, the way you did tonight, and ask for my help, I'm here. It's that simple."

Now it was Buddy who couldn't speak. He felt his entire body grow hot. His throat swelled up. He stared at his brother. His heart pounded in his chest like a bass drum.

After a moment, he nodded.

Ward reached his hand across the counter.

Buddy took it.

Competitors and rivals, but brothers, too.

20

Mei and Ben moved swiftly through the lobby of the Carlyle Hotel. Following them, Buddy and Ward carried their bags. In case of surveillance, Mei had asked the valet to bring her car to the Carlyle Hotel entrance on Madison Avenue rather than to the Carlyle Residences entrance on East Seventy-Sixth Street. They didn't have to go outside since the residence building was connected by a short hallway to the hotel if you had a key card. As she walked, Mei's stomached tightened with fear.

What if somebody sees us leave? she thought. *What if we're followed all the way to the country house?*

She had the revolver in her handbag, but she knew that wouldn't be enough to save them. Their escape needed to be anonymous to succeed. Nobody could find out.

Buddy and Ward handed the bags to the hotel doorman, who took them out to Mei's SUV. Mei and Ben stood in the vestibule, looking at Buddy and Ward, not knowing what to say. Ward took out his money clip and handed her several hundred-dollar bills and a few twenties.

She pulled back her hands. "No," she began.

"You must," he insisted, taking her hand and pressing the bills into it. "You can't use credit cards or an ATM, because your charges could be tracked."

Reluctantly, she closed her hand around the money and turned to the door. She wore her black Moncler down parka over jeans and boots. Ben wore his navy-blue peacoat, khakis, and New Balance running shoes. Both wore gloves and hats.

Buddy said, "We won't communicate unless there's an emergency. Keep your phone—Ben's phone—off unless you're using it. If you need to check emails and voicemails, keep the phone on for a few minutes at the most, okay?"

"Yes," she said.

"You won't give me the address where you're staying?"

"I shouldn't."

He said, "You don't want me to visit. I get it."

Of course she wanted him to visit. To hear his voice, to watch him laugh with Ben, to lie against him in bed. Yet she resisted. Now she needed and was demanding safety—in the present and in the future—for herself and for Ben. She met Buddy's eyes and raised her chin. "Not until it's safe here for us. You have to solve this, Buddy. You have to change things."

His eyes showed warmth, but his expression hardened. He said, "I know. I'll deal with it."

Sensing she'd blamed him unfairly for things he perhaps couldn't control, she put a hand on his chest, stood on tiptoe, and kissed his lips.

He responded, holding her tightly. In that moment, she felt secure and safe, but she knew he couldn't be with her constantly. When they finally separated, she felt less safe, but she also sensed anew the fear driving her away from the city. Her skin crawled with anticipation and the desire to flee.

She drove away from the hotel with Ben sitting quietly in the front passenger seat. As they crossed the George Washington Bridge and headed north, she saw fine snowflakes in the Audi's headlights. Tightening her hands on the steering wheel, she realized her grip was already too tight. She let go with one hand and opened her palm. Her hand shook. She looked over at Ben and saw that he'd noticed her agitation.

After a while he said, "Mei?"

"Yes?"

"Will we be okay?"

"Yes. We'll be okay. We're just going to have a little vacation. That's all. And then we'll go back home and you'll be in school, just like usual. Does that sound all right?"

Ben didn't respond. He pulled up the left sleeve of his jacket, revealing his new wristwatch. He pressed on the screen, and it lit up with colorful icons and white letters. The device occupied him for a half hour. Then he let down his wrist and stared at the snow swooping up over the windshield as they pressed north.

21

Buddy stood in the living room, looking down at the lights of the traffic crossing through Central Park. He wished he could see Mei's car. Yet he knew that by now she was out in the dark countryside. Ward had eaten a final slice of pizza with Buddy and gone, too, either to his house in Greenwich or to his obscure perch on the island.

Now Buddy paced by the windows, anxious to be reinstated tomorrow. Reinstatement, he knew, would give *him* some power. And he needed to work, to learn why he and Mei had been targeted. He needed to show Mei that life with him could be safe.

Turning from the window, he walked through the living room and along the back hallway to the master bedroom. In the closet, he opened the safe and pulled out his shoulder holster. He replaced the IWB holster he'd worn that day, as well as the Glock 26, and closed the safe door.

As he kicked off his shoes, he thought about Tan Jacket. And about the call Tan Jacket had received from the main line of the NYPD.

He knew that outgoing calls from One Police Plaza came through the same line. So the call might have come from any of the hundreds of people who worked at One Police—or from someone visiting One Police who'd used one of its phones.

At this idea, Buddy's sense of the case's difficulty increased.

His phone buzzed. He took it from his front trouser pocket and answered. "Yeah?"

"It's Mingo."

Buddy's pulse jumped. "What'd you find?"

"I went down to Mulberry Street, just like you said."

Buddy's hand tightened around the phone. "You found the guy?"

Mario's voice grew louder. "I'd already checked with the Fifth Precinct patrol, the detective bureau, and local hospitals. Nada. So I drove down to the spot. I found a pool of fresh blood but no guy. Maybe he got well enough to walk away."

Fuck, Buddy thought. But his frustration was replaced by foreboding. A nearly dead man, scraped up from the sidewalk and taken away not by an ambulance but by someone else. *More than one,* he thought. *Tan Jacket hadn't been working alone.*

He said, "No, Mario. The only place Tan Jacket could go was the hospital—and not on his own two feet."

"Maybe a Good Samaritan helped him," Mario offered.

Buddy said, "Maybe. But more likely it was a bad Samaritan."

"A *bad* Samaritan?"

"Yeah. Someone from . . ." Buddy almost said *Someone from the NYPD,* but he didn't. He couldn't say it. He had no real evidence to make that leap. He had only the One Police main line on his attacker's burner phone. Moreover, Mingo worked for the department—could he be trusted? Buddy said, "Someone from the guy's crew."

"You're probably right," Mario agreed. "See you in the morning."

"10-4. Hey, Mario?"

"Yeah?"

"Thanks for checking on it yourself."

"Sure thing."

Buddy went into the bathroom and washed his face, then climbed into bed. It was too quiet in the bedroom without Mei, without her form under the covers. The sound of her breathing. Her face on the white pillow. He missed it all.

After an hour, he slept. His dream was first a recollection of a week ago, a better time when he and Mei had taken Ben to the Intrepid Sea, Air & Space Museum down in Hell's Kitchen on Pier 86. Where Ben had gotten to see fighter jets and an aircraft carrier and had toured a submarine. Ben must have seen movies with military men, because he'd begun saluting—with his left hand—nearly everyone they came across. When anyone returned the salute, he grinned and laughed. "Your right hand," Buddy had reminded him. "Your *right* hand."

Yet mischievous Ben had continued using his left.

Afterward, they'd returned home, where Mei had made French toast (Ben's favorite) for dinner. They'd watched *Raiders of the Lost Ark*, a movie Ben hadn't yet seen but loved. As in real life, they'd been eating and talking, Buddy sitting next to Ben at the bar in the kitchen, and Mei standing across from them at the counter. But from that point onward, the dream changed everything.

Buddy turned, and Ben wasn't on the stool next to his. He walked through their home, yet Ben had gone.

Buddy went outside and searched for him. But in the enormous city, he didn't know where to begin. When he remembered how much Ben had enjoyed the Sea, Air & Space Museum, he began walking rapidly toward it, but the journey through an impossibly dark night seemed to take forever.

When at last he reached the building on Pier 86, he pulled open the large doors, and stepped inside.

Blackness everywhere. He could barely see. When his eyes adjusted, he made out the massive, terrible outlines of the planes, the missiles, the tools of war.

Weaving through the displays, he called Ben's name, but there was no response. Buddy could hear nothing but his own footsteps. Yet he kept going and eventually reached the submarine. Climbing the steps to the conning tower, he reached the top and looked at the ladder that led down into complete darkness.

Then he heard them. Faint cries from inside the coffinlike shape. Buddy stepped onto the ladder and climbed down into the dark, dank space that pressed against him on all sides.

Now the cries were louder. He went toward them, step-by-step, careful not to run into the bulwark. From his previous visit, he knew he was passing through the torpedo room and the officer's wardroom to the sonar room. Careful not to bang his head, he needed a long time to reach the source of the cries.

But in an instant, the cries ceased. When Buddy saw why, panic gripped him.

A large man, his back to Buddy, stood over Ben. The man's large, muscular hands squeezed Ben's neck and then shoved him backward.

Ben tumbled onto the metal decking, screaming in pain and fear.

The man closed a glass door, rimmed with steel and rubber, between himself and Ben. As Ben banged his small hands against the glass, the man turned a lever that locked the door and created a seal. A moment later, the man pressed a button hidden in the darkness.

Buddy could see it then. The water, rising in the room where Ben was imprisoned. Rapidly, the water level rose. To Ben's ankles. To his knees.

His hips.

His chest.

His chin.

His nose.

Finally, to the top of his head.

Buddy saw the boy he loved thrashing in the water, trying to climb up the sleek metal wall to the remaining air pocket. But Ben couldn't. He could only stare at Buddy, his mouth moving, creating words Buddy would never hear.

In a last gesture, he raised his right hand, and saluted Buddy.

Buddy tried to lurch forward toward the man, to grab the lever and turn it the other way, to open the door so the water would run out of Ben's cylindrical grave and he could take Ben in his arms and carry him to safety. But he couldn't run or even walk.

He couldn't lift his feet.

He could only stand there as Ben's eyelids closed and the boy floated, lifeless as a fallen leaf.

22

Mei shook Ben awake. "We're here," she told him.

She watched his eyes open in the soft light of the Audi's interior. He looked at her, then forward.

In the headlights, they saw a small house with gray siding and a red brick chimney. There was no garage, and the house's front door faced the asphalt driveway that showed in oil-colored patches where wind had cleared the snow. The house had a narrow blind-covered window on the left side of the door.

Mei shut off the engine, and they climbed out.

She shivered. The cold here was stronger than in the city, the wind more cutting. Turning to look behind her, she saw only the dimmest contours of the long steep hill they'd taken and the serpentine driveway that terminated right here. Above them to the west, the same hill rose even more steeply. In the darkness it seemed they were halfway up a mountain. There were no houses around them, only what appeared to be open land studded with evergreens. It was quiet and serene up here, she decided, but without neighbors who could help if you got into trouble.

While the car's running lights illuminated the house, they took their bags from the Audi's cargo area and carried them to the door. As they did, two exterior lights on motion sensors flashed on, brightening the area at the front of the house. She punched in the access code—1832—that Jessica had given her.

The lock clicked and drew back.

She turned the handle and pushed open the door.

They stepped into the dark house, whose interior was warmer than outside but not warm.

Mei felt along the wall behind her, searching for a light switch. Finding it, she pressed the rocker switch, and recessed lights bathed the space in a warm glow.

The house's interior was clean and sparsely furnished. Cheap paintings of landscapes hung on white walls, and the floors were white oak. A sofa and two chairs, covered in navy-blue leather, faced a large flat-screen television on the wall to the left. At first it seemed to Mei that the house was one large room that included the entry, kitchen, dining table, and living area. Then she noticed a doorway to the right.

She and Ben passed through it and into a hallway that led them to two bedrooms, one large, the other small. In addition to a king-sized bed, the larger room had a sofa in gray leather.

Ben went over to the sofa and looked at it. Then he turned to her, his eyes uncertain, and said, "Can I sleep here?"

She smiled at him. "You don't want the other bedroom?"

He shook his head. "I can't sleep by myself. I don't like it here."

She said, "I realize it isn't home."

"That's not why," he told her. "When I was in the country on New Year's Eve, my family . . ." His voice faded. But he swallowed and continued. "Then we were at Ward's house, and we were attacked. The same thing's going to happen here."

"No," she replied quickly, going over to him and putting her hand on his shoulder. "No, it's safe here. Nobody except Jessica knows we're here. It's just you and me. And besides, we're here because of Buddy's job, not because anyone wants to hurt us."

I'm stretching the truth, she thought. *But I'm probably wrong about the man outside Porter Gallery who must have had a pen or a phone rather than a knife.*

Ben seemed to sense her uncertainty. "I want to go home," he pressed. "I want to be in my own bedroom. I want to go. Can we go?"

As he spoke, her smile faded and she felt great concern for him, for his fear of being out here in the unfamiliar wilderness, so far from the familiar, and from Buddy. Instead of telling him no, she dropped her bag, sat down on the sofa, and held out her arms to him. He moved closer to her, and she embraced him, held him against her.

"Everything will be okay," she told him. Yet she thought about his day: the meeting with Judge Miles, the strange conversation in the kitchen, the rapid packing and leaving their home, the furtive drive late at night to this house at the edge of Wurtsboro Ridge State Forest. *This is hard,* she thought. *Hard for anyone, let alone a ten-year-old.*

Ben began to cry. Not loudly. She felt his warm tears on her neck.

When he grew calm, she went into the smaller bedroom and returned with the sheets, blanket, and comforter from that room and made a bed for him on the sofa.

He looked at the sofa and then at her. He said, "Is there anything to eat?"

She felt immediate concern. "I don't know. Let's find out."

She opened the refrigerator and saw only a bottle of wine. The freezer had a bottle of vodka and a carton of vanilla ice cream.

Ben had walked over and now stood beside her. "May I have the ice cream?"

She scooped some into a bowl for him and searched the cupboards for other food. Finding a box of Triscuits, she opened it, began to eat, and felt better about being so far from the city's dangers. Then she heard noises outside the house.

Ben heard them, too. He put his spoon down in the bowl and stared at her, his eyes fearful.

She stopped breathing.

23

The footsteps moved around the exterior of the house, from the north side of the house to the area to the south—and the front door. Outside, the two lights on motion sensors came on.

Mei stared at the door. She noticed she hadn't set the lock.

She rushed over to the door, turned the latch to set the dead bolt, and turned off the small foyer's overhead light.

The sound of the lock, the faint abrasive sound of metal on metal, seemed loud in the silence.

At the same time, the noise outside ceased.

They waited in the darkness. One minute passed. Two.

The motion lights on the exterior of the house went out.

Ben said, "Is he gone?"

She didn't move. She swallowed. Then she crept silently to the window to the right of the door. Her body cold with terror, she reached up and pulled at the edge of the blind. Peering through the opening she'd created, she scanned the ground beyond the window to the extent that she could see anything in the faint moonlight reflecting off the snow. She saw movement, about ten feet from the door.

There it was. In the dimness, she could see it. Not well, but well enough.

Stepping back from the window, she let the blind fall into place. She turned on the light, faced Ben, and tried to smile. "It's a coyote, or a wild dog. I'm not sure which. But he wants nothing to do with us."

Ben opened his mouth and breathed, gulped for air.

She hugged him, felt his chest shudder, took his hand, and led him back to the kitchen.

He finished the ice cream. She ate another Triscuit. Then she turned out the light, and they went back to the larger bedroom.

They didn't brush their teeth. She opened his bag and took out his pajamas. He put them on and slipped under the comforter she'd spread over the sofa.

He looked up at her with his big brown eyes. "Would you sit with me?"

"Sure." She sat down and smiled at him.

"Mei?" he asked.

"Yes?"

"Are we going to stay together?"

She wouldn't lie. He'd suffered too many lies already. "Buddy and I are doing everything we can so that you can stay with us forever. Judge Miles will decide. Soon, I hope."

His eyes shone with anxiety. He asked, "What if she says I have to go live with my aunt and uncle?"

"Then Buddy and I will keep fighting to keep you. We could go before another judge."

Ben was quiet for a moment. He touched her hand and said, "Mei?"

"Yes?"

"Do you want me to stay with you?"

She leaned down and hugged him, kissed his cheek. "Of course," she said. "Of course I do. You know I want you to stay with us."

"But I'm worried."

She pulled away and brushed his hair away from his eyes. "Worried something will change?"

He nodded.

"I had the same fears," she told him. "My biological parents left me at an orphanage in Shanghai, a large city in China. My American parents adopted me when I was five months old. For a long time, I worried they'd leave me. I'd already been left once. Why not twice? Don't bad things repeat themselves? And maybe I was the one to blame. Maybe I wasn't lovable. That's what I worried about until I was more than twenty years old. I certainly thought these things when I was your age. But you know what, Ben?"

"What?"

"I made it. I grew up. I lived on my own for a while. Then I chose to be with Buddy. And with you. It was my choice," she repeated. "And as you get older, you'll have more control over your life. You'll be able to choose who you want to be with. I just hope that when you're older, you'll still want me to be in your life."

Ben had tears in his eyes. He said, "I always want you to be with me."

She leaned over, kissed both his cheeks, and caressed his shoulder.

No longer fearful, he soon fell asleep.

Mei shut off the lights, took off her clothes, and put on one of Buddy's T-shirts. She sat in bed with the covers over her legs, listening for the sounds of the wilderness outside. Yet she heard nothing except wind interspersed with an eerie silence.

When at last she slept, she dreamed that she and Buddy were falling into warm water. Except that when she looked down, she saw they were hurtling toward not water but a vast expanse of ice. Now she was going to die. She knew it for certain. She reached for him as he reached for her. His faced showed worry. He knew they were doomed. Their hands got close, but she couldn't grab hold of him, couldn't touch him. And then she looked again at the ice and winced and put her arms around her head.

No!

She woke.

Sat up in the strange bed.

Leaning her back against the wall, she grew calm as she listened to the breathing from Ben's hidden form on the sofa. As she stared into the room's darkness, all the assumptions she'd made about her life swirled around her in confusion.

If Ben and I have to leave the city every time Buddy takes a case, she thought, *we won't live in the city at all. We won't be the family that Buddy and I want. If we survive this case, what about the next one?*

Without realizing, she'd begun to turn her engagement ring around and around her finger. She stopped herself, adjusting the ring so the diamond was up, and slid back down into the bed.

Surviving, she told herself, *is more important than marriage. But I don't want anyone other than Buddy. I'd be so unhappy, so lonely. And if we had a kind of joint custody, where I'd have to see Buddy, I'd want him in my life. I'd want him to stay the night, to stay forever.*

She sighed, seeing no way out of this dilemma.

DAY 2

24

Buddy waited in Chief Malone's office, the gray light from outside coming through the windows. Malone sat behind his scuffed metal desk, his large face pale and lined. His eyes bulged a little more than usual as he slid the Glock 19 and badge across the desk to Buddy. Taking up the gun, Buddy checked the magazine, saw that it was empty, and placed it in his shoulder holster. He took the badge, put it in his badge wallet, and put the wallet in the left breast pocket of his suit coat. Then he turned to go.

"Hold on, Buddy."

Buddy remained still.

Malone stood. He was about Buddy's height but outweighed Buddy by more than seventy-five pounds. He crossed his hands over his ample stomach and said, "That's it?"

"What do you mean, Chief?"

Malone narrowed his eyes and laughed. "Buddy, I leaned on Rachel Grove to get you an expedited review. I pissed off the Southampton Town Police Department by yanking the bodies your fisherman found away from them. I'm letting you work a John and Jane Doe suicide or accidental death case when you're a homicide detective and we need man power. I do you all kinds of favors, and you don't give me the time of day. What's your problem?"

Buddy felt his face warm. "Yeah, Chief. I'm sorry. Thank you for all you've done. I just want to work the case. I guess I'm already focused on it."

"Focus on me right now, okay?"

"Yes, sir."

"Turn, Buddy, turn to the door."

This was an odd command, yet Buddy did as Malone had asked. He turned and saw, in the doorway of Malone's office, Rachel Grove of the Force Investigation Division. And behind Grove stood Police Commissioner Garrett Quinn. As they filed into the office, Buddy saw Mingo. The younger man walked up to Buddy and gave him a bear hug. Buddy tried to push him away, but the younger man wouldn't have it. Kept hugging him for three seconds too long, until there was laughter in the room. Buddy took a ziplock baggie from his pocket and handed it to Mingo. Inside the bag was his Visa card. He nodded meaningfully at Mingo, who seemed puzzled. But then Mingo's expression cleared as he remembered that Buddy had printed Tan Jacket. Mingo tucked the bag and the card into the side pocket of his suit.

Malone's secretary, Alicia Bravo, also walked in. And then there was a slight commotion in the corridor outside Malone's office, and Buddy saw Mayor Susan Blenheim, tall and elegant in a navy-blue dress with long sleeves and a string of pearls around her neck, enter Malone's office.

They fanned out on either side of him, and they seemed to appraise him silently.

He looked around, confused. He hoped he was being reinstated, not fired. So what was the brass doing here? What did they want with him? And the mayor—didn't she have more important things to do?

From behind him, Malone said, "Buddy, you're a pain in the ass, but you're a fucking great detective. Your work has saved a lot of people at the same time it's put you through hell. What you did three weeks ago impressed the hell out of all of us. We owe you our greatest thanks."

Here Malone turned to face Commissioner Quinn, a sixty-year-old veteran of the force with white hair, a ruddy complexion, and ramrod-straight bearing. Quinn nodded at Malone, but he didn't smile when he looked at Buddy.

With a solemn voice, Commissioner Quinn pulled a small black box from the side pocket of his jacket. He said, "Detective Cyrus Edward Lock, I, Garrett Quinn, on behalf of the New York City Police Department, hereby award you the Combat Cross. This honor is for your heroism and engagement in armed combat with an adversary at great personal risk to yourself." Commissioner Quinn opened the box and lifted out its contents.

Buddy didn't think much of awards, but when the commissioner pinned the green bar to the lapel of his suit coat, he was surprised by the strong emotions he experienced. His entire body warmed with pride. He couldn't control these feelings. His heart thumped in his chest, and he felt as if he might shed a tear. Because his respect, appreciation, and love for the department went that deep. He loved his job, loved what he and his brothers and sisters in the detective bureau did. He understood their mission—to protect and serve—and it was the purpose of his life. His voice cracked as he said, "Thank you, Commissioner. I'm honored."

He knew Commissioner Quinn needed the ceremony to be private, given how he'd earned the award. But that was all right with him. He'd had enough publicity for a lifetime, both as a pianist and as a detective. He wanted to keep his head down and do his work. Anything more was a distraction. Anything more could be a danger to Mei and Ben. But that didn't mean this private recognition meant nothing to him. It did, because it tied him even more tightly to the mission. He might be a bit of a loner, but he wanted the commissioner and the chief to know he did his best.

The commissioner's blue eyes narrowed, the crow's feet around his eyes deepened, and he clapped Buddy on the shoulder. "Keep up the good work, Detective. The city needs you."

Buddy nodded. "I try, sir. Thank you."

When Commissioner Quinn had left the office, Chief Malone congratulated Buddy. Mario shook Buddy's hand so vigorously that Buddy wasn't sure if his new partner was mocking him. Malone remained standing. Mayor Blenheim walked over to Buddy.

He stood up a little straighter.

25

The mayor offered her hand. It was warmer and stronger than he'd expected.

Mayor Blenheim was in her late fifties, Buddy guessed. Until now, he'd never seen her up close. She was prettier than she appeared to be on television. More serene and yet commanding. Her light-brown hair alloyed with strands of gray hung straight, framing her clear, fair-skinned, attractive face. She had dark-brown eyes and a prominent nose. She smiled at him. "It's an honor to meet you, Detective Lock."

Her voice was calm and deep—fitting, he decided, for someone who had a large presence in the city. A little over three years ago, he'd voted for her, and she'd won reelection to her second term.

He said, "The honor is mine, Mayor Blenheim. And you can call me Buddy. Everyone does."

"All right." She smiled. "Buddy, then. I heard about your award, and I wanted to thank you personally for what you've done for the city over the past few months. The Death Clock Murders and then the—"

"I'm not ready to talk about it," Buddy interrupted, holding up a hand. "Especially not here."

The mayor nodded, her eyes never leaving his. "I understand. Really, I do. My father worked for Madigan-Hyland as an engineer. When I was eleven, he was supervising a cabling repair near the top of the Tappan Zee Bridge, and he fell. My mother and I were left alone, with nothing but union death benefits. Those were enough to keep us from having to move into a shelter, but not much more than that. I thought everything would improve, and for a time, it did. Until my late husband went missing in action. It was extremely difficult," she explained, "picking up the pieces. I couldn't talk about what happened to my father until about five years ago. So I know how things can hang on for a long time."

This story surprised Buddy. He thought Mayor Blenheim had a royal-sounding name, excellent manners, and educated speech. She didn't seem to be working class, but she was. Or had been. He said, "Thanks, Mayor. It's been a tough few months."

"For you, it has been," she agreed. "I'm glad you've been reinstated. I feel much better with you on point. If you ever need anything—if there's a roadblock to your doing your job as effectively as possible—feel free to contact me personally."

Buddy nodded, sensing this was a politeness rather than a real offer. "Thanks," he said.

He glanced at Malone, whose eyebrows rose dramatically. He looked at the mayor. She stood motionless, hands clasped together in front of her. There seemed to be nothing more to say.

As Buddy turned to go, he heard Malone's voice bellowing behind him.

"Coffee!" Malone said. "On me. Now!"

Before Buddy could react, Mario had put an arm around his shoulder, and Buddy was swept up in their group as it moved toward the elevators. As he smiled and accepted their congratulations, he thought about it.

Betrayal.

Joking, giving Mario a high five, he tried to recall which of those standing in the elevator with him now had also been present in Malone's office when he'd described the bodies found off Long Island.

He smiled, but his eyes recorded those around him. Chief Malone, red-faced and blustery. Rachel Grove, lively but watchful. Mario Mingo, young and enthusiastic. Mayor Blenheim, dignified but friendly. Alicia Bravo, Malone's secretary, quiet with the boisterous detectives and the mayor.

But even in the midst of the high spirits, he knew that everyone in that office might have been innocent, and innocently told someone else who was dirty. And that person might have ordered Tan Jacket to kill him. But he didn't believe in innocence—not after twenty years as a detective. He believed that at least one person in the building, if not in Malone's office, if not in this very elevator, intended to kill him, and to kill Mei and Ben.

Who?

He realized he was a blind man walking through a field littered with land mines.

26

Who betrayed me? Buddy thought.

He wanted to leave his fellow officers, but he had to be here. He couldn't be rude, even though he wanted to begin work on the missing couple found off Long Island. He also couldn't help thinking that someone having coffee with him wanted him dead.

Who? he thought again, forcing himself to smile, to keep his voice upbeat. Yet his stomach burned with anger.

Having official business to attend to, Mayor Blenheim had parted from them on the steps of One Police Plaza. But everyone else from the elevator had walked over to Chambers Street and the Blue Spoon for coffee. It was good coffee, Buddy admitted, though not his customary Dunkin' Donuts. But it wasn't his money, and he needed some caffeine. After they'd placed their orders, some sat at an empty table and a few of them stood. Buddy sat on one of the stools by the window. He felt a tug at his elbow and turned to see Rachel Grove perched next to him.

"Congratulations," she said loudly, and then leaned closer to his ear. "Can I talk with you?"

He could smell the mint in her shampoo. "Yeah. What about?"

She shook her head. "Not here."

He stared at her until Mario joined them and said, "How the hell am I going to compete with the Combat Cross? I mean, *Jesus*. It's like working with Sherlock fucking Holmes."

Malone turned and scowled. "Stop it, Mingo. He's had enough praise for one day."

"For one year," Rachel Grove piped up.

"You guys don't know a good thing when you have it," said Alicia Bravo, her face coloring as she chided the others. "That's the problem with cops."

"You'd know." Buddy laughed, alluding to her boyfriend, currently in patrol out of the Twenty-Eighth Precinct in Harlem.

It went on like this for longer than Buddy wanted. But eventually the coffee was gone, and they left the Blue Spoon and headed southeast on Chambers. Minutes later, as they neared the front doors of One Police Plaza, Buddy held back, as did Rachel. When the others were out of earshot, she put a hand on his shoulder until he stopped.

She pushed her brown hair behind her ears, alluring even in the bitter cold. Her voice was low when she spoke. "You know I can't discuss IAB cases," she began, referring to the Internal Affairs Bureau.

Buddy wasn't sure where this was headed, but he was going to tread carefully. He said, "They're confidential. Everyone knows that."

Rachel nodded. "Right. But I'm going to bend the rules here because you're our best detective, and I know you're clean."

Buddy didn't react.

She said, "I can't give you details, but we're looking at Malone and Mingo."

Buddy felt himself tense. "What do you mean, 'looking at'?"

"I can't say more."

"Bullshit, Rachel. You opened the door. You have to give me something."

"I can't."

Buddy pointed at her chest. "You've *got* to. You can't drop a bomb and walk away. That's not how it's done."

Rachel looked around him, and behind her, to be sure they were alone. She said, "Mingo has a bank account." Then she stared at him knowingly.

He smiled. "BFD. I have a bank account. So do you."

Rachel raised an eyebrow. "A numbered Swiss bank account. You have one of those?"

Buddy thought about Mingo. He'd figured the kid was green, but not green in the sense of having money. Had he misjudged his new partner? He wondered why Mingo had set up an account at a Swiss bank. *Payment for selling me out?* he wondered.

Rachel didn't stop there. She said, "We're also watching Malone."

"What?" Buddy whispered loudly. "Why?"

"I can't tell you."

"Come on, Rachel. Give me more."

"Not on the chief of detectives, Buddy. We're monitoring him. IAB doesn't have anything solid yet, but he's hiding something. If I told you more, my job would be at risk."

From the way her mouth had set and her expression had hardened, he knew she'd disclose nothing else. But he made a final request. "Rachel, could you tell me who at One Police called a certain number?"

She considered it but shook her head. "I couldn't get a warrant, not without more."

He held up a hand. "The call was from the NYPD trunk line. From a department phone. You don't need a warrant for that."

Slowly, she nodded. "All right. What's the number?"

He took out the burner phone he'd lifted from Tan Jacket, switched it on, and checked the number. She took out her phone and typed in the number.

"Give me till tomorrow," she told him.

"Thanks, Rachel."

She touched his shoulder once more. And then she removed her hand, turned from him, and hurried into One Police Plaza.

Buddy stood there, alone, an empty coffee cup in his hand. He stared up at the large brick edifice of One Police, doubting whether he should ever enter it again. He couldn't trust anyone—not his boss or his partner. He was exposed, and he knew it. Making a rapid decision, he pulled out his phone and dialed his brother.

"Ward Mills." The voice calm.

In the background was another voice, soft, female.

Buddy paused and then said, "I need you to check on two people for me. Mike Malone, chief of detectives, and Mario Mingo, my partner."

The female whisper on the other end of the line ceased. Ward said, "What's your reasoning?"

"Inside info. See if Mingo has a Swiss bank account."

"Why would he have a Swiss account?"

"That's the question."

Buddy ended the call. He had many questions, all with answers that might prove fatal.

27

Ward set the phone on the nightstand. Staring at the ceiling of the spacious bedroom, he thought about Swiss banks and money and payment for services rendered. He thought about access and how to get it. He thought about wire transfers from the United States and realized the money could have come from anyone. No, he needed the receiving end of the money, not the origination. Mario Mingo would have used a bank that people—people like Ward—commonly used.

He turned and looked at the woman lying beside him. She was blond, slender, and she had a husky voice he liked, especially when she urged him to be more strenuous in bed.

She smiled at him, touched his stomach, and began to move her hand lower.

He pushed himself up on one elbow and admired her. She wasn't wearing anything, and neither was he. They'd pushed the covers down to the foot of the bed and then, as they'd grappled with each other, onto the plush carpeting.

She had the figure of an eighteen-year-old girl, but she was in her early thirties, ten years younger than he. Hazel eyes, full lips, wonderful breasts. She spoke well, in her husky voice, the product of attending university in England. He liked her hair that she colored blond, and the darker hair between her legs. But duty had called, quite literally.

Gently, he took her hand and set it on the sheets.

She raised an eyebrow.

He said, "I have to check my computer."

"Really?" Her breathy voice made him yearn for her. "You're tired?"

He laughed. "No, I'm not tired. I have to do something for my brother."

She sat up, swiveled around, and put her feet on the floor. "I have to meet some girl who says her mother abandoned her as a baby. Probably nothing to it."

He knew she wasn't pretending to have work. She was a leading reporter at the *Gazette*. And he couldn't tell her anything about the case Buddy was working. He watched her firm backside as she stood and walked into the master bathroom, closed the door, and switched on the shower.

He sprang out of bed, pulled on a pair of Burberry boxer briefs, and went over to the leather chair and ottoman on the other side of the room. Opening his laptop, he waited for the wireless connection, then typed in the web address of Zurich Cantonal Bank. He put in his identification number and password. A moment later, the screen showed his account activity and balance.

It was over a quarter of a billion dollars. This was his escape hatch. His fuck-you money. His ability to disappear and survive, if it ever came to that.

He heard her turn off the shower. Heard the whir of the hair dryer. He exited his account, went over to the nightstand, and picked up his phone. He pressed a number he had on speed dial, walked into the sitting room, and gazed out at the snow and skeletal trees of Central Park.

It was near the end of the day in Zurich, and he wasn't sure Helmut Borer would answer, but the Swiss rarely left their offices early.

"Helmut Borer" came the voice. Stiff, formal, severe.

"Good evening, Helmut. Ward Mills here."

"Hello, Mr. Mills. How may I be of service today?"

"Helmut, I need to locate a numbered account owned by an American gentleman named Mario Mingo." Ward spelled Mario's name aloud before asking, "Does Zurich Cantonal have an account owned by Mr. Mingo?"

Helmut made a noise of displeasure. "I am sorry, Mr. Mills. I cannot divulge the names of any of our account holders."

Ward waited for more, but the Swiss was quiet. Ward said, "Helmut, have you forgotten how much business I give you?"

"No, Mr. Mills. No, of course not."

"You wouldn't want me to move my account to Credit Suisse, would you?"

"I . . . I think understand, Mr. Mills."

Ward said, "You have my word that the information you give me won't be made public and won't cause harm to anyone. But I must have your help."

For a long time, Helmut was silent. At last he said, "I'm looking in our system, and I can report that Mr. Mingo has no account with Zurich Cantonal Bank."

Ward said, "Would you check with your fellow bank managers—Reichmuth, Banque Bonhôte, and the others—to see if they have a numbered account owned by Mario Mingo?"

"No, Mr. Mills. You know that is not legal. To get that information, you would need a court order."

Ward thought of Buddy and the mortal danger he'd be in if Mario were taking kickbacks for betraying his partner. He lowered his voice almost to a whisper, something he knew the powerful often did. "Helmut, ask your fellow bank managers for the information. If I don't have an answer by tomorrow, New York time, I'll move a hundred million out of your bank and over to Credit Suisse."

Without waiting for Helmut's response, Ward ended the call. He stood up from the leather sofa and returned to the bedroom.

"Hello?" he called. "Sophie?"

The scent of her Chanel No. 5 remained, but she was gone, having slipped out during his phone call. He picked up the sheet, blanket, and duvet, and made the bed. His chest ached with a new pain, one he hadn't felt in many years, not since he'd fallen in love with his late wife.

28

Buddy got out of the Dodge Charger he'd taken from the motor pool and scanned the street. He looked to his right, left, straight in front, and behind him. Then he headed toward the chief medical examiner's offices at 520 First Avenue. In the cold morning, the wind had disappeared, and the city lay noisy and hard under a blanket of gray clouds that didn't seem to move. Despite the cold, he began to sweat, and he touched his gloved hand to the left side of his jacket. He felt the Glock 19, which he'd loaded before leaving One Police.

Betrayal, he thought, *is only the beginning.*

He walked through OCME's metal doors and showed identification at the security desk. Riding an elevator down to the examination rooms, he could feel his mind sharpening. He hoped the bodies would show him something, some clue to the killer's identity.

An assistant showed him to the room in which Dr. Silva, the chief medical examiner, stood between two bodies on stainless-steel tables. Silva had short dark hair and olive skin, and was perhaps five foot four. In contrast to his white lab coat and shirt, he sported a tie of purple paisley below his kindly expression. Buddy guessed the ME was fifty-five, twelve years older than he. Buddy wondered if he'd be so well preserved at that age, or if he'd even be alive.

Silva walked around the table and smiled. He said, "Detective Lock, you're finding bodies all over America for me to work on, aren't you?"

"Sorry, Doc. I had to do it. Thanks for handling my cases personally."

"Hey, no worries. These won't take long."

Buddy said, "You've opened them up?"

"Not yet. We took delivery last night. Interesting situation."

"How so?"

In response, Silva turned and extended a hand toward the bodies.

The overhead lights made the color of their skin darker and yellow, as if they'd been dipped in iodine. Extensive bruising on both bodies, one side of the woman and the legs and arms of the man. Some visitors to the morgue might forget these bodies were, until recently, people who'd talked and laughed and slept alone and together. Buddy wasn't one of those people.

Silva said, "Fingerprints don't match anyone in NCIC or IAFIS. So they're Jane Doe and John Doe, unless you've learned more."

Buddy shook his head.

"No tattoos or jewelry."

Buddy said, "Not anymore, as to jewelry. Jane Doe was wearing a silver-colored engagement ring with a single diamond, plus a silver-colored wedding band. I gave them to the property clerk. John Doe had nothing." He didn't tell Silva about John Doe's medallion with the Asian symbol that was in the left front pocket of his trousers.

Silva nodded and continued. "Nothing remarkable about the dental work. Probably American."

Buddy asked, "The victims are Chinese?"

Lines formed on Silva's forehead as he looked down at the woman on the table in front of him. "Probably Chinese American, but they could have been Chinese nationals living here."

Buddy avoided looking directly at the faces. A glance was enough to confirm they were the same bodies he'd seen on Mack Berringer's trawler in Southampton. The missing eyelids, eyeballs, and lips made them appear like terrible ghosts, unnerving even to him. But avoiding their faces left him studying their naked torsos and limbs. In these he saw nothing unusual, except for the bruising. He asked, "How long were they in the water?"

Silva shrugged. "Impossible to know. An hour? Two? I'd say not more than three. More than three, and there wouldn't be much left."

Buddy winced at the image of fish and sharks eating human flesh.

Either this image didn't occur to Silva, or it didn't bother him. Silva said, "So we have Jane Doe and John Doe. Might be related. Might not be. In a few weeks we'll have results from the tox scan. Which might show something or might not." Silva paused for a long moment, studying the bodies.

Buddy said, "What about the bruising?"

Silva said, "I haven't started the postmortems."

"Got it," Buddy said. "But what do you think? What can you guess?"

Silva's face reddened. "I don't *guess*."

Buddy waited. He'd worked with Silva for more than a decade. Wouldn't his friend give him something?

"But," Silva continued at last, "most or all of the bruises appear to be from impact."

Buddy leaned forward. "Beaten to death?"

Silva's face remained impassive. He said, "Jane Doe and John Doe suffered impact to the entire body. They might have been beaten with something dull and hard. Nothing sharp. See, there are no cuts."

Buddy scanned the woman's body in front of him, saw that the skin was unmarked by cuts or gouges. He said, "So we have two people beaten using an unusual weapon."

Silva widened his eyes. "Yes, possibly. Or possibly an ordinary weapon, such as a telephone book wrapped in cloth. Or not."

"Not?" echoed Buddy, watching Silva carefully.

Silva said, "Jane Doe and John Doe have injuries consistent with another fate." Here Silva paused, looked meaningfully at Buddy, as if Buddy should pick up on the hint.

Yet Buddy had no idea. "What fate?"

Silva said, "They jumped off a bridge. Or they were pushed."

29

A half hour later, Buddy parked on Mott Street, between Canal and Bayard Streets, in the heart of Chinatown.

He switched off the ignition and the radio and sat quietly. He checked his left front trouser pocket and felt the medallion.

For a good two minutes, he scanned the street, the cars, the pedestrians on the sidewalks. He studied the scene in front of the Dodge Charger through its windshield and in the side and rearview mirrors. The Fifth Precinct was a block away, on Elizabeth Street, but he'd avoid that building and anyone who worked there.

Observing nothing worrisome, he unlocked the car, climbed out, and stepped onto the sidewalk on the west side of Mott, which was a one-way going south. He'd been in Chinatown many times before. Only yesterday, he'd walked north on Lafayette, which bordered the western edge of the neighborhood, past Cleveland Place, and to the Spring Street subway station. But today, by parking on Mott Street, he'd gone from the edge to the heart of the historic district.

Immediately he noticed the narrow street lined by a pleasant mixture of buildings of different materials and heights. Most were four to six stories high, in red, white, or tan brick. Fire escapes, many painted green, red, or black, cluttered the sides of the buildings in a way that showed the neighborhood's vintage. Below the fire escapes, signs and awnings in bright colors: royal blue, yellow, bright green, maroon. Lettering on the signs and awnings in different colors. Red rice-paper lanterns and other merchandise hanging from corrugated metal hangers. Even in winter, inventory was set on the inside edge of the sidewalks: shirts, sweaters, sunglasses, stickers, tea, ice cream, dresses, bags, leather goods, and books and magazines written in Chinese. The doors of some of these shops were open despite the cold, with the proprietor sitting or standing by an electric heater. Food markets specialized in fish and vegetables—ginger, cabbage, bok choy, white radishes—not found in most supermarkets Buddy had visited. A feast for his eyes and his memory. He and Mei had walked through Chinatown many times, and she knew the better restaurants. *Mei,* he thought.

Picturing her safe in a house far out of the city, he felt twinges of regret and desire. Great motivation for finding and stopping his—their—pursuers.

As if I need it.

He walked south along the sidewalk on the western side of Mott, looking for a particular kind of store. Thirty yards farther, he saw necklaces, bracelets, and watches displayed behind a plate-glass window.

Pushing open the door to the jewelry store, he heard a buzzer and encountered two Chinese men behind the counter, one about seventy, the other, who resembled the older man, in his forties.

Father and son, Buddy thought. *The family business.*

They greeted him but didn't smile.

He took out his badge wallet, opened it, and held it up. "I'm Detective Lock, with the NYPD. I'm hoping you can help me."

The men didn't comment, only waited patiently.

Buddy unbuttoned his overcoat, reached for the medallion with the symbol, and set it on the glass counter in front of the men. He said, "Can you tell me what the symbol is? What it means?"

The younger man bent over, squinting at it.

The older man took a gold-colored jeweler's loupe, placed it in his eye socket, and did the same. He muttered something Buddy didn't understand.

At the same time, both men shook their heads.

The younger man said, "I'm sorry, Detective. The writing at the bottom of the stone can be translated as 'sacrifice.' But we're unsure of the symbol. It may be a flower, but it seems to be old and worn. Some of the clarity has been lost."

Buddy felt disappointment, but this was only the first shop he'd tried. He said, "Is it close to anything else you know?"

The younger man looked to the older man, who said, "No, it's not close to anything—anything familiar to me."

"What's it made out of? The black stone?"

The older man's voice was low. He said, "Onyx."

Buddy thanked them, picked up the medallion, and left the store. He continued along the block until he came to a store that sold Asian antiques and décor. He went inside.

And came out minutes later. No luck.

He worked his way down the street, stopping in every shop regardless of whether it sold jewelry or not. When he reached Bayard, he turned around and canvassed the shops on the east side of Mott. He spoke with the owners or workers in more than a dozen shops, but nobody could tell him about the medallion's symbol.

At the corner of Mott and Hester, he noticed a restaurant. Or at least that's what he thought it was. The signs were in Chinese characters.

He looked to the right of the door and saw a clear Plexiglas box. Inside the box was a menu. Peering closely, he read the English translation of the dishes offered. Then he checked his watch. It was 10:34 a.m. Too early for lunch, but he tried the door anyway. It was unlocked, so he went inside.

The lights were on, but he saw there were no customers. He heard sounds of metal and skillets from the kitchen hidden behind a wall. On the wall hung pictures of traditional Chinese nature scenes: finely drawn temples on the sides of mountains, thick groves of bamboo and other trees, and below, a black bridge over a curving stream. He stood unmoving and looked around. The tables had been set with place mats, napkins, utensils, and teacups. Lazy Susans on the larger tables held extra napkins, soy sauce, sugar and sweeteners for tea and coffee, and creamer.

He saw movement from the doorway to the kitchen. Unconsciously, his right hand moved toward the Glock.

It was a Chinese man with carefully trimmed white hair, large dark eyes. Hunched over as he walked, the man wore pressed black pants and a wine-colored shirt. Buddy estimated the man was in his early eighties. He lowered his right hand and relaxed.

The older man saw him, seemed about to tell him the restaurant was closed, and hesitated.

Buddy knew he had *cop* written all over him. So he took a couple of steps forward and badged the guy. "Detective Buddy Lock, NYPD."

The man didn't react or study the badge or the photo.

Buddy thought he was wasting his time. But now that he was here, he might as well ask. He took the medallion from his pocket, placed it in his palm, and extended his hand toward the older man. He said, "Know what this symbol is?"

The man dropped his impassive gaze from Buddy's face to Buddy's hand and the medallion. The man began to shake his head, and Buddy took back the medallion.

"Again," the man said, motioning him to show him the medallion a second time.

Buddy again held it out on his palm.

The man peered at it for a moment, then looked up at Buddy and nodded.

30

The older man showed Buddy to a table along the north wall. Buddy took the seat facing the door.

The man sat down in the other chair and faced Buddy. A waiter emerged from the kitchen with a silver-colored teapot and two cups and set them on the table. He poured steaming tea into both cups and retreated.

Buddy said, "May I ask your name?"

The man's eyes lit up, and he nearly smiled. He seemed less glum as he said, "Henry Lee."

Buddy looked around. "This your restaurant?"

Henry Lee nodded. "For forty-three years."

"A long time," Buddy said.

"Very long."

"Do you own the building?"

The man's half smile vanished. He shook his head. "I own this space where I have my restaurant. Others own the rest of the building."

Buddy nodded, not really interested in who owned which restaurants in Chinatown. He set the medallion on the table between them and said, "Would you tell me about the symbol?"

Henry Lee put his large hands together, his eyes focusing on Buddy's. He said, "This is very old, this pendant. Etched on it is a symbol not used by younger generations. They don't know about it, or, if they do, they would not wear it as jewelry."

"Why?" Buddy said.

Henry Lee pressed his lips together, knit his brow. "Some would consider it shameful, even dishonorable, to wear. You see, Detective, the writing means 'sacrifice.' But it has two meanings. The second meaning is related to Chiang Kai-shek, who fought Mao in the Chinese civil war in the late 1940s. General Chiang and his army lost the war and escaped to what today we call Taiwan. The image on this medallion is a white orchid, white with some yellow in the middle. The white orchid was the symbol of Chiang Kai-shek's elite fighting force that had the name Sacrifice. They sacrificed in great numbers but killed even greater numbers of soldiers in Mao's army. In turn, Mao swore that all members of the Sacrifice Brigade and their children would be executed."

Buddy considered this information. He wasn't sure how it applied to the case, if at all. He asked, "So the wearer of this medallion might be anti-communist, anti-Mao?"

"Maybe. But it might be a family heirloom. Perhaps the wearer of the medallion had a father or grandfather who fought with Chiang's army."

Buddy thought about revenge against family members, something he and Ben knew all too well. He asked, "Did Mao try to kill everyone who'd been in the Sacrifice Brigade and their children like he promised?"

Henry Lee nodded. After a moment he added, "But Mao has been dead a long time. I'd be surprised if China's current leadership has the same priority."

Buddy didn't understand the connection to the bodies found off Long Island, if there was one. "Do you know anything else about the symbol?"

Slowly, Henry Lee shook his head.

Buddy took the medallion off the table and pushed it into his left front trouser pocket. He was glad to have learned the meaning of the symbol on the medallion. But although Chinatown encompassed only about two square miles, its population was more than one hundred fifty thousand. He knew that without more information, determining the identity of the medallion's owner would be next to impossible.

The calm ended as the tables, the empty chairs, the restaurant itself began to shake and rumble. The metallic noise—it sounded like a military tank—grew louder and sharper. Buddy thought there was an earthquake or the building was about to collapse. He looked up at the ceiling to be sure it wasn't about to fall on him, and then down to Henry Lee, who was grinning at him.

The noise ebbed and a few moments later, disappeared.

Buddy said, "What the hell was that?"

Henry Lee said, "A construction truck on Hester Street. It's going to the building behind this one."

"Jesus. Must be one hell of a renovation."

Lee shook his head. "They're tearing it down, for a new condominium tower. These gigantic buildings are bad for Chinatown, Detective. At first, they bring new customers. But in a year or two, someone will put up a tower right here. The developers get exceptions to the zoning code. And then I'll have to close my restaurant."

Buddy thought about Henry Lee's restaurant and the new developments in Chinatown. And not just Chinatown, everywhere in the city, it seemed. He said, "Who's buying the old buildings?"

Henry Lee's eyes narrowed. "Developers."

"Any in particular?"

"Big developers. Cromwell is doing the one around the corner, behind us. With the city."

"The city?"

"Yes, Detective. Part of the city. The EDA."

"The what?"

"The Economic Development Agency. Look at the names on the construction sign around the corner. You'll see it. The EDA."

Buddy drank his tea. He didn't know much about real estate and had no interest in it, since he'd never been able to buy any. Not here in Manhattan. Not anywhere he liked in the city's other boroughs. He'd always rented until he moved in with Mei the year before. He drank more of his tea, thinking he should thank Henry Lee and get back to work. But he wanted to keep the conversation going until he'd finished. He said, "Never heard of the EDA."

Henry Lee explained, "In the case of the old buildings, the developers have to buy everybody out. They go from unit to unit, trying to get the owners to sell. It doesn't always work. People hold out. Money doesn't motivate everyone."

Buddy disagreed silently. It was his experience that money motivated everyone, with the only difference being the amount. He said, "But the longer you can hold out in the Manhattan real estate market, the richer you'll get."

Henry Lee nodded. "But if people become greedy or just refuse, and the developer isn't successful, the EDA threatens to force the holdouts from the property."

Buddy didn't follow. He said, "How do they force them out?"

"Eminent domain. You see, the EDA has the power to take people's property for a public purpose, as long as it pays just compensation. The people at the EDA can get a court order and just force people out."

Buddy thought he understood, but he asked, "What's a 'public purpose'? What's 'just compensation'?"

Henry Lee pushed aside his teacup. "Whatever the courts say they are."

Buddy thought about the courts and who paid for political campaigns. And the amount of money involved in a city where the average one-bedroom condo ran in excess of a million dollars. He said, "Are all the holdouts Chinese?"

Henry Lee shook his head. "Many who take the money right away have been here a long time. They move to a warmer climate or move in with their children. Many of the holdouts have bought more recently. They're like you."

"White?" Buddy asked.

"Yes. Or black. Or Indian. Or Middle Eastern. They bought recently and think they have the right to stay, but in the end they all leave. All kinds of people. From everywhere."

Buddy said, "How long has this been going on?"

"A long time. It started about fifteen years ago on the edges of Chinatown, over on Church Street and on the west side of Broadway. But in the last four or five years, it's come into our neighborhood."

"Nobody fights it?" Buddy asked. "The EDA never has to force people out?"

"Not that I've heard."

"I don't understand."

Henry Lee's face darkened. He studied Buddy for a moment, as if determining whether or not he could trust him. Even in the empty restaurant, Lee lowered his voice. "About five years ago, a few people refused to sell. After a while, they changed their minds and signed the papers."

Buddy asked, "Did the EDA agree to pay more?"

"No."

"So why did they sell?"

Henry Lee bent closer to Buddy. He said, "We never found out. The holdouts . . . disappeared."

31

Henry Lee took the silver teapot and poured more tea into Buddy's cup and then his own. Setting it on the wooden table, he said, "I mean, one day they were here, and the next they were gone."

"Gone where?"

"Nobody knows."

"*Dead?*"

Henry Lee shrugged. "You're the detective."

Buddy sat back in his chair. He was here to investigate bodies found in the sea off Long Island, but this was something weird. He didn't know what to think about it, but he felt the old curiosity about the break in another pattern. His chest tightened as it always did when he was close to discovering something hidden.

The restaurant door opened.

Buddy looked up. Henry Lee swiveled in his chair.

Two white men entered the restaurant and stood just inside the door. One of them, maybe five foot eight but wide as a bulldozer, had long brown hair worn in a ponytail. He stared at Buddy and at Henry Lee and took a table near the window, facing them, his expression cold. Buddy stared right back, trying to memorize Ponytail's face.

The second man was taller—maybe six foot three—with black hair combed back and shiny with pomade. His narrow face had a long nose that was broken halfway down and angled sharply to the left. His small, ratlike eyes were set deep in his skull, and they shone with menace as he stared at Buddy. Eventually he turned and sat opposite the shorter man, his back to Buddy and Henry Lee. Yet Buddy wouldn't forget Rat Eyes's face, or the outline of a handgun under his jacket.

Henry Lee pushed back his chair, stood, walked toward the kitchen, and disappeared. Buddy remained alone with the two men.

Buddy reached into his suit coat, pulled out his Glock, and held it, unseen, in his lap. He took a good look at Rat Eyes and Ponytail, and thought they were military or ex-military. With his left hand, he took another sip of tea, but it tasted as cold as the chill crawling up the back of his neck.

Now he knew he wasn't paranoid. Someone in the NYPD had heard of his case and betrayed him.

Rat Eyes turned. The men stared at him with blank expressions. Buddy looked at them and didn't blink.

He couldn't shoot them, not unless he was doing it in self-defense. They'd made no overt threat against him. Yet he was neither paranoid nor stupid.

Nor would he get into a firefight in Henry Lee's restaurant. Too much risk, and what would he gain?

In his peripheral vision to the right, he saw a waiter in black pants and shirt and a white apron emerge from the kitchen with a tray, two ice waters, and a silver teapot. The waiter spoke to the men. They held up their menus and placed their orders.

Now, Buddy thought.

Standing, he hurried back toward the kitchen.

He moved past the warming trays, the grill, the cooktops with curved woklike skillets, the dishwasher, the walk-in cooler and freezer. He came to a door on the left, and from behind it he heard faint voices—Henry Lee's among them.

Retreating, he thought. *Avoiding the problem. But surviving.*

He knew these were options he didn't have.

He kept going until he came to a wide, scuffed metal door. It had two heavy stainless-steel locks. To the right of the door was a small window, opaque with grease and grime and protected on the outside with vertical metal bars. Buddy peered through the window and saw a man standing on the other side of the door. The man was of medium height and dressed in brown work pants and a heavy jacket. He was smoking a cigarette with one hand and holding a knife with the other.

Ponytail and Rat Eyes out front with guns, Buddy thought. *Or a guy on a cigarette break with a knife.*

Not a close call.

He checked his Glock, confirming he had a round in the chamber. Then he replaced the gun in his holster, drew both locks, and shoved open the door.

32

Mei thought it was dangerous to go anywhere they might be seen. But they needed provisions and had to leave the house. Standing in the larger bedroom while Ben was in the great room, she opened her tote bag and saw the gun in its nylon case beside the box of ammunition. *No,* she thought, zipping the tote closed, the gun still inside. *Not for the grocery store.*

She drove from the house on the bluff down to Rockridge, the town in the valley below. Ben sat quietly in the passenger seat, absently staring out at the large hills and stands of evergreens. As they descended into the valley, they passed enclosures and barns for horses, everything covered by a fine layer of siltlike snow. To Mei, the landscape seemed devoid of people. When they'd arrived last night, she hadn't realized the remoteness of the house. Up there, they couldn't be seen or heard. But that meant nobody could see or hear them even if they were in distress.

Mei saw one car and then another as she drove into Rockridge. The town reminded her of Western movie sets she'd seen in California. The length of it was no more than three blocks. Storefronts faced Main Street, but behind those buildings were only parking lots and fields.

Ben pointed. "There!"

She saw Pearson's Foods, which seemed to be the only grocery store in town. When she'd parked along the curb in front of the store, they climbed out and walked inside.

Pearson's was a basic grocery store with limited produce and a lot of liquor. Mei counted two other customers in the small store, plus the cashier, a middle-aged white woman who wore a green ski cap on her head, though the store was warm.

The cashier and the two other customers, both older white men, openly watched Mei and Ben. Their faces showed interest and, perhaps, confusion.

Taking hold of a small metal cart whose wheels rattled, she ignored the stares and proceeded through the aisles, Ben at her side. He put ice cream in the cart. And tortilla chips, shredded cheese, and salsa. She also bought eggs, chicken, butter, coffee, olive oil, bread, pasta, vegetables, milk, juice, peanut butter, jelly, and more.

"You're not from here, are you?"

This was from one of the other customers, one of the older men, in a cracked voice. Three inches shorter than she, he stared up at her with yellowing eyes.

She said no and continued walking. She felt her stomach tighten. She wanted to leave her cart, leave the store and the town. But she couldn't. They needed food.

At checkout, the cashier rang up their groceries but said nothing except the amount of the bill. Ben put the groceries in five shopping bags and stood quietly, looking at his watch, responding to texts.

When Mei offered cash, the woman took it, careful not to touch Mei's fingertips. After making change, the cashier set the bills and coins on the counter, turned back toward the store, and stared into the middle distance.

Despite his limp, Ben helped carry the bags out to the Audi. After setting them in the cargo area, they looked up and down Main Street. A hardware store at one end. At the other, a sign for a bakery and café.

Mei said, "Let's get coffee."

Ben shook his head. "I don't drink coffee. And class starts in half an hour."

Mei looked at her watch. "Five minutes in the café," she told him. "And I'll buy you hot cocoa."

There were a half dozen people inside. Men and women, all white. Some openly watched Mei and Ben, the rest surreptitiously. One man of about forty and dressed in a policeman's uniform smiled at her.

After nodding to him, she turned to the girl behind the cash register, at the same time placing an arm around Ben's shoulder. She said to the girl, "I'd like a large coffee, black. And a large hot cocoa."

The girl rang them up. Mei again paid in cash, and they stepped back from the counter. She could feel the other patrons' eyes on her, and she impatiently tapped her foot.

The girl behind the counter set two large cups on the counter.

Snatching them up, Mei said to Ben, "Would you get the door?"

In the car, Ben said, "Why is everyone looking at us?"

She considered several ways to answer this question. After a moment, she said, "They're just curious."

He turned to her. "Is that all?"

Despite her suspicions, she knew that must be all. Nobody in the town could be connected to the men who'd tried to kill her and Buddy. She thought the town probably saw people like her and Ben— city people—in summer or even fall, but not in January. Residents of Rockridge had stared at them because they were obviously city people, because she was very well dressed and with a Caucasian boy who obviously wasn't her biological son. And because she was Asian.

Yet she wouldn't mention her clothes and her race to Ben. So she said, "I'm sure that's all it is. But don't worry. We'll be gone in a few days."

She hoped this was true.

In the house on the bluff, she made them omelets. Then she showered. When she emerged into the house's great room, she saw Ben sitting at the kitchen table, his laptop open and his headphones over his ears. She walked behind him and saw that he was watching one of his classes, either live or via video podcast. He had a notebook open and was writing on its lined paper.

She didn't understand how virtual classrooms could be equivalent to real classrooms, but she knew he had no choice.

Perched on the edge of the sofa cushion, she set her laptop on the coffee table and searched for job openings at galleries in Manhattan. Her body was tense. She didn't need the money, but she wanted to land something before Judge Miles could find out she'd been let go from Porter Gallery. After updating her résumé, she applied for two of them. Yet before long, the battery ran out, and the screen went dark. Getting up, she rummaged through her handbag and realized she'd forgotten the power cord. Even worse, she knew that Ben's newer laptop used a different power cord. At first her forgetfulness angered her. But then she relaxed.

It will good, she thought, *to be free of everything. For a day or two.*

When she heard Ben laughing aloud at something in his class, she felt relief. Her mood brightened. They were out of danger; he was doing his work; she'd find another job. She heard what sounded like spray against the house.

Looking up, she saw snowflakes brushing against the window.

33

Buddy drove the metal door open. It swung fast, banging on the brick wall. The man smoking the cigarette and holding the knife began to rotate toward the sound.

Buddy clamped both hands on the fist holding the knife and ran the man with the brown work pants into the wall. The man's grip loosened, and the knife clattered to the concrete.

The man brought his other hand around and tried to stub the cigarette into Buddy's left eye.

Buddy was ready. He raised his left arm and backhanded the cigarette, flipping it to the side. He put his left hand around the man's throat and squeezed.

Then he reached for his Glock, took it out, and hit the guy twice across the face with the gun stock. Hard. His anger driving explosive force.

The guy fell and lay unmoving on the concrete.

Squatting next to the man, Buddy searched the back pockets of his work pants. He found a wallet with a driver's license, two credit cards, and about a hundred dollars in cash. He took out his phone and snapped a picture of the man's driver's license. He tossed the wallet on the man and then noticed another card held by a lanyard around the man's neck.

It was an employee identification card. Turning it over, he saw the man's photograph below a name.

Cromwell Properties.

He remembered the name. Henry Lee had told him about Cromwell.

After he'd walked to the end of the alley, he peered around the corner of the building and looked up and down Hester Street. There was no sign of Ponytail and Rat Eyes, though he assumed they'd leave the restaurant via the front door. He'd try to avoid them, but he wouldn't hide.

Across the street, he saw a row of shops, restaurants, and a clothing store. Turning to his right, he watched a crew install construction fencing around an old building—the demolition job and new condominium development Henry Lee had mentioned.

After once more checking Hester Street, he walked out of the alley and around the fencing. He came to a break in the fencing and looked through it. He saw a three-story building, old and red brick, with rickety metal fire escapes painted black. Nobody would call it an architectural gem, but it wasn't a dive. Above the stone entrance to the building and the silver-colored doors, the builders had carved a word. At first he thought the word was made of Chinese characters, but then he realized it was written in an old-fashioned script. Now he could read the word. The letters spelled Nanjing.

Proceeding along the old building's front wall, he came to a new construction sign at the corner of Hester and Elizabeth. It showed the image of a shiny glass luxury-condominium tower, probably thirty stories high, called Haddon House. Below the image and the name, the sign announced that Haddon House had been designed by the architect Antoine Rousseau and would be built by Cromwell Properties, with the participation of the New York City Economic Development Agency. The addresses of Cromwell and the EDA were listed, as well as two real estate brokers helping with sales, both with ethnically English, rather than Chinese, names.

Cromwell and the EDA, Buddy thought, remembering Henry Lee's mention of them.

He took out his phone and snapped a photo of the sign. After replacing the phone in his pocket, he studied the image of the glass tower. He wasn't ignorant of basic economics. Haddon House, a project for the rich, would replace the tired Nanjing building. That sort of thing was happening all over Manhattan. Standing by the sign, he did some rough calculations. A one-bedroom unit in Haddon House—a new building with amenities—would be over $4 million. A two-bedroom would be $6 to $8 million if on an upper floor. Plus the cost of parking spaces in the underground garage. Plus association fees for the fitness center and the rooftop pool. Looking around, he saw the traditional buildings of Chinatown, many of them former warehouse buildings and tenements, and rising above them, here and there, were modern condominium towers. Reaching up into the sky around the neighborhood was evidence of hundreds of millions in profit from all the residential buildings constructed in lower Manhattan during the years Henry Lee had mentioned. And some of those modern buildings had encroached into the historic district.

Money, he thought.

He knew it had been changing the city since 1626, when the Dutch bought the island of Manhattan from Native Americans for sixty guilders, the equivalent of about fifteen hundred dollars in today's money.

And who was he to put his finger in the dike? He couldn't stop it. Nobody could, unless the laws of economics changed. But he could do one thing. He could bring justice to killers.

34

He checked all directions from the corner, but still saw no sign of Ponytail and Rat Eyes. Crossing to the north side of Hester, he began heading east. He saw small offices and shops and numerous all-residential buildings, many with signs impossible for him to read, except for the phone numbers printed across them. After going two blocks, he'd seen the same phone number three times.

He realized that he needed help.

Two women—one in her fifties, the other in her eighties—were walking toward him. They wore heavy coats and knit caps on their heads. He heard them speaking in what he assumed was Mandarin. They glanced at him and kept going.

He held up a hand. "Excuse me."

The women paused. Their eyes showed apprehension but not coldness.

He pointed to the sign and said, "Would you tell me what that sign says? Would you translate it for me?"

The women looked at the sign. The younger woman smiled at him and said, "It says there's a two-bedroom apartment for rent. And it gives the phone number to call if you're interested."

Buddy nodded. "Anything else?"

The woman looked again at the sign and then back at Buddy. She shook her head. "Nothing else except the real estate agent's name."

Buddy didn't know if this information was valuable, but he said, "What's the name?"

"Lin Wong," the woman told him.

Buddy said, "Does he work around here?"

The women chuckled and spoke to each other quickly, in Chinese. The younger woman said, "Lin Wong's offices are on Bowery, between Grand and Hester. Middle of the block. But he's everywhere."

Buddy nodded. "What do you mean, 'everywhere'?"

She shrugged. "He's a big broker in Chinatown. Many listings. All the time."

"I understand," Buddy said. "Thank you."

Both women smiled before continuing past him.

Keeping alert for an ambush by Ponytail and Rat Eyes, Buddy walked north on Bowery. Halfway down the block he found a street-level office with a large sign outside the door. Most of the words on the sign were in Mandarin, but he could read two English words: Lin Wong.

He opened the office door and walked inside. It was clean but not large. A twentysomething female receptionist sat behind a white desk. She rose when he entered and offered him tea. He shook his head and asked if he could speak with Mr. Wong.

She said, "Perhaps I can help you. Are you interested in one of our listings?"

In response, he took out his badge wallet, flipped it open, and held it up for her to see. "I'm Detective Lock with the NYPD. I'd like to speak with Mr. Wong if he has a moment."

Her smile vanished, but she nodded and walked back through a hallway to what he assumed were the offices of Lin Wong and any associate brokers who worked with him. He looked around the small reception area. On the walls were awards Mr. Wong had won, and also laminated marketing materials for apartments to lease or purchase. He hadn't been waiting more than thirty seconds when the receptionist returned, followed by an elegantly dressed Chinese man in his midsixties.

The man wore a dark-blue suit with pinstripes, a white shirt, and a solid blue tie. His thinning hair was combed back from his face, and his expression was pleasant. Buddy thought the man had the air of success about him.

The man said, "I'm Lin Wong. What can I do for you?"

Buddy said, "I'd like to ask you a few questions about real estate in Chinatown."

Lin Wong nodded. "Certainly, please come back to my office."

Buddy followed the older man into offices containing modern white furniture and iMac computers. In a conference room with a clear glass wall, Mr. Wong indicated a chair for Buddy and sat down across the table. Buddy removed his overcoat and gingerly rested on the delicate chair, fearing he'd break it and wind up on the floor. He looked over at Lin Wong and said, "I've seen your phone number on for-lease and for-sale signs around the neighborhood. You do a good business here?"

Wong shrugged modestly. "Yes, I do a pretty good business."

Buddy thought for a moment. Then he said, "You seem well connected. But I didn't see your name on the sign for the new Haddon House project. Did they ask you to list the units, try to sell them?"

Lin Wong's forehead grew lined as he shook his head. "They didn't ask, and I wouldn't have worked with those people. Haddon House and other projects like it are ruining Chinatown." Wong pointed in the direction Buddy had come. "What's wrong with the Nanjing building?" he asked, then answered his own question. "Nothing. But it makes nobody rich, and that's the problem. So they're going to destroy it, even though there are holdouts."

Buddy leaned closer. "Holdouts? How many?"

As he thought about that particular building, Lin Wong's eyes narrowed slightly. Then he said, "Three at Nanjing. One of them my friend. He ran a jewelry shop around the corner that's become an ice cream store. Everybody knew him. He was head of our neighborhood business association. My friend keeps telling me the developer is pressuring him to sell, but he and his wife won't do it. And why should they? Their place on the third floor is big. They raised their children there. And they like the neighborhood, although Chinatown is changing, becoming like everywhere else." Studying Buddy's face and clothing, Lin Wong asked, "Where do you live?"

Buddy said, "Upper East Side. My fiancée has a place there."

The man nodded, but his face showed disbelief. He flicked at his sleeve, as if a speck of dust had fallen on it.

Buddy asked, "Could you tell me where your friend and his wife are?"

Lin Wong shrugged. "I haven't seen him in a few days. Or her. But I heard they gave in, signed the papers after all." He shook his head and added, "Very strange, since he told me they'd never sell. Not now. He told me they'd sell in ten years and give their children even more money."

Buddy had two thoughts. He'd deal with the second one first. He said, "How old are the children?"

"I don't know. There are two sons and a daughter, I think. One involved in television. The others . . . I don't remember."

Buddy felt his pulse jump. He pulled out the small notebook and pen he carried with him everywhere. He said, "Would you give me the name of your friend? And his wife?"

Lin Wong considered the request. He looked away from Buddy, through the glass wall at the suite of pristine offices—his fiefdom, the generator of money for his own family.

Buddy listened to the older man's breath but didn't push him. He remained unmoving in the uncomfortable chair.

At last, Lin Wong turned to him and said, "My friend is Chen Sung. His wife is Lily."

Buddy recalled the inscription in the engagement ring worn by the Jane Doe found off Long Island. He wrote quickly and was ready with the next question. "What about the third holdout? Do you know his name?"

"No," Lin Wong said, "I don't know the name. It's a young woman from California—Los Angeles, I think. Chen told me that several years ago she inherited her apartment in the Nanjing building from her grandmother. She's rich and won't leave for any price. She'll take them all the way to the Supreme Court of the United States. But you can see the sign across the street for Haddon House. The developer must think she'll sign the papers. Maybe they're putting pressure on her just as they did on Chen and Lily."

Buddy said, "What kind of pressure?"

Lin Wong put his hands together. "I don't know. But I guess it worked."

35

Ben trusted his school friends and the text messages he received from them. Even after three weeks at Vista, he felt that they'd accepted him. Like most kids his age, they texted back and forth, before and during and after class, without paying much attention to who was who. It was their separate world, hidden from adults.

In the afternoon, he attended his social studies class remotely. He sat at the table in the great room in the house on the bluff. Staring at his computer screen, he watched and listened to his teacher. To his left was the social studies textbook, open to a page about the Transcontinental Railroad.

Now and then he glanced over his laptop screen at Mei. She was on the sofa, reading a magazine, sipping a cup of coffee.

Boring. This was a text from Alan Blackman, one of his friends. Since he'd paired his new watch with his phone and his laptop, the texts appeared on all three devices.

Yep, he replied, typing into a text box on the laptop screen, although he liked trains and wished he'd lived in the time when the frontier existed and the country was still being settled. He liked the idea of getting away, going somewhere nobody knew his name. He could take Buddy's last name. He could become Ben Lock, and nobody would connect him to his family's past.

This idea thrilled him. He was about to ask Mei if he could change his name, when a chime sounded through his headphones.

He read the new text.

Dude, where r u? She asked about u.

Ben hunched forward and typed: Vanessa?

U r right.

Ben flushed. Vanessa Knight was the prettiest girl in the fourth grade at Vista School. So that Mei didn't notice he was ignoring his class, he turned off the sound notification for texts on the devices but left on the watch's haptic tap feature. Each time he received a text, the watch tapped his wrist. He typed: Paris.

Really?

He smiled and typed: Jamaica.

BS

Africa

Nah

Ben typed: New York.

Then y not in class?

Ben typed: In the country.

Town?

Rockridge.

Ur house?

Mei's friend owns it. I get to watch Netflix.

He waited for a response. When none came, he typed: What did Vanessa say?

Still no response.

He closed the laptop and looked out the windows.

The snow had stopped, but the sky remained gray.

36

Buddy stood inside the door of the real estate office and scanned the street for Ponytail and Rat Eyes. Careful to obscure his movements from the receptionist, he pulled the Glock from his shoulder holster and put it in the right side pocket of his overcoat.

His hand gripping the stock, he pushed open the door with his left hand and walked out onto the sidewalk. He checked left and right.

Seeing nothing, he returned to the Charger he'd left on Mott Street. As he walked, it seemed at first that little had changed. The sidewalks were busier and, despite the cold, the shops had filled with customers, and all kinds of people were entering the restaurants. And yet everything was different. When he glanced above the roofs of the old buildings, he saw several condominium towers. They didn't seem like an improvement to him, they seemed menacing. He wondered if their foundations were built on the bones of murder victims.

Once inside the Charger, he fired it up, locked the doors, and put the Glock into his shoulder holster. He thought for a moment, took out his phone, and texted Ward: Injuries show Long Island couple jumped or were pushed off bridge.

Then he put the car in drive and headed north toward home. Using his right thumb, he dialed a number on his phone and switched on the speaker feature. As he listened to the line ring, he focused on Broadway, clogged as usual in the middle of the day.

The line clicked. "Mingo."

"Mario, it's Buddy. Would you run a Chen Sung and Lily Sung through the system?"

"No problem. Anything else?"

"Not now, thanks," Buddy said, ending the call. He was thinking about what Henry Lee had told him, and about what Lin Wong had said about holdouts at the Nanjing building. As Broadway became Park Avenue South, the traffic opened up. He switched on WBGO and listened to some new jazz. He didn't recognize the artist or who was playing in the trio, but they worked tightly, improvising but keeping the forward motion of the piece. He liked that about it and turned up the volume. As he made his way north on Park, passing Twenty-First Street, he glanced out his window.

He saw banks, a FedEx store, a CVS, to his left the Health & Racquet Club, to his right Saint George's Gothic façade in dusty red limestone. New Yorkers and tourists filled the sidewalks, bundled up in heavy winter coats and jackets, boots and scarves plain and outlandish. Others had their parka hoods pulled up over their heads. Some wore expensive wool or cashmere overcoats and gloves, their heads hatless and their faces pink in the gray afternoon. Ahead were the lights of the intersection at Park and Twenty-Third. In that moment, he also noticed the headlights of a large SUV speeding toward the intersection from Twenty-Third Street.

The SUV flew toward him at about forty miles per hour. It didn't halt or swerve. It kept coming, shooting into the intersection straight toward Buddy's car.

He didn't react. He didn't lean away from the headlights. He had no time to do anything except begin to turn his head to the right.

He didn't hear the smash of steel against steel.

Or feel the impact of two and a half tons crushing the Charger.

His eyes closed. He stopped breathing.

37

After dinner, Mei and Ben decided that getting out of the house was worth the risk. Not wanting to spend all day and all evening in the small house, they once again climbed into the Audi.

They drove down into Rockridge, parked on Main Street, and walked up one side of the street, crossed to the other side, and walked back down.

They tried the door of the coffee shop and bakery, but it was locked. Ben peered inside, his breath fogging the windowpane. They passed a bar that was open, then came to a theater that was showing the latest Star Wars movie.

Ben looked up at Mei. "Can we see it?"

She had no interest in Star Wars. Not usually. But tonight she decided she could use an escape. "Sure," she said, and held open the door.

Inside the theater, they walked down the sloped floor to a row halfway to the screen. The house lights were bright, and the previews hadn't begun. As they sat down, Mei glanced around the theater. About thirty or forty people were there, all watching them as if they were insects under glass.

Sliding down into her seat, she turned to Ben. Yet she saw only the back of his head, only the dark hair that was definitely too long. She made a mental note to schedule a haircut for him when they returned to the city. Her eyes traveled beyond him. In their row, not more than five seats away, sat a young couple. High school kids who were watching them. Mèi stared at them for a few seconds until they looked away. And then the lights went down.

Ben seemed to like the movie. Mei thought it might be too violent for him, but given all he'd endured the past month, it was a tame fantasy. More importantly, he enjoyed the escape, and so did she. This was the thing about children, she'd learned. You do something for them, and it ends up being good for you.

Later they drove up the bluff toward the small house. At the driveway's steepest point, she stomped on the brakes.

The Audi dug into the pavement, coming to a rapid halt, the seat belts holding Mei and Ben in place.

In the headlights ten yards in front of the car stood a coyote. The animal was the size of a medium-sized dog, with pointed ears, a narrow snout, thick body, and fur that was gray and black along its back and rust-colored farther down until becoming light gray at its belly. The coyote stared into the headlights, seemingly confident and unafraid, its breath rising wraithlike around its head.

Mei and Ben sat in silence.

She thought they should have been more like the coyote when they were observed at the movie theater. Not caring that others watched them. But this was a wild animal, a predator.

Ben lowered the passenger window. "Go away!" he shouted, motioning with his right arm. "Get out of here!"

The coyote's ears twitched. Then it turned its head and trotted off the drive and into the trees to the west.

Mei let up on the brakes and pushed on the accelerator. The car shot forward up the hill. As she steered to the patch of asphalt by the front door, she realized she was shivering.

38

Buddy lay facedown. His head hurt like hell. Something was pulling at him. Something hard. At his stomach, shoulder, chest, and side. With some difficulty, he brought air into his lungs. The air burned hot.

He opened his eyes.

He was looking up at the Charger's roof. He moved his eyes right and left. To his left the car door pushed against his shoulder, elbow, hip, and leg. Parts of the door and seat were crumpled against him like an accordion. Part of the window, too, its fragments spilling into the car like shattered ice.

He realized the thing pulling at his shoulder, side, and stomach was the seat belt. He was hanging upside down, trussed up like a deer.

Now he remembered. The SUV coming fast through the intersection toward him.

He jerked his head left, so he could look out at the upside-down pavement. He saw the SUV. Twenty feet away, its chrome grill and front bumper were bashed in. But it was upright. Its headlights were blazing at the Charger, at him.

Shit.

He knew he needed to move. He guessed the driver of the SUV was unhurt and mobile.

Shit!

Buddy shifted his body. Nothing seemed to be broken, but he was woozy. He had a vivid headache that threatened a complete mental shutdown. He thought he might pass out. But he knew he had to act now. He reached down to the Charger's roof and pushed on it to ease the weight on the seat belt. With his right hand, he pressed the seat belt release.

It was jammed.

He tried again. And again.

On the fourth try, the latch came out. He fell to the roof of the Charger, landing on his left shoulder.

Jesus. That hurt.

He pivoted and lay sideways. He pulled the Glock from his shoulder holster and scanned the pavement around the car.

To his right he saw a set of feet approaching. To his left, from the direction of the SUV, a second set of feet, these in black boots. He again looked right. He tried to make out the shoes. These were nearer. Black shoes. He aimed the Glock.

The feet grew closer.

He got ready to fire, and saw the shoes were loafers.

Not dangerous, he decided.

Swiveling left, he saw the boots were approaching too slowly, too carefully. Now the feet stopped. At some risk to himself, he pushed his head—just a little—toward the space where the car window had been.

With the SUV's headlights in his eyes, his vision was blurry, but he could see the faint outline of a man who wore dark clothes and large boots and held a gun in his right hand. The man's stance widened as he raised the gun.

Buddy was faster. He shot at the man's chest but knew the bullet had gone low.

Two rounds.

The man shouted in pain and collapsed onto the asphalt and stared at Buddy, who was lying sideways on the overturned roof of the Charger.

Now Buddy could see the man wore a black mask over his face. Buddy took a breath and gulped at air. He felt his consciousness slipping away, so he bit his tongue until he tasted blood. He raised the Glock and tried to aim.

The man he'd shot crawled and slithered hurriedly behind the SUV's left rear tire. Buddy had no shot. He saw the driver's side door open and the man climb inside. He heard the door slam.

The SUV backed up.

Shit, Buddy thought. *He's going to ram me again.*

Yet the SUV continued in reverse. Five feet. Ten. Fifteen. Threading between the stopped traffic. The SUV's headlights washed over Buddy lying in the overturned Charger before the SUV sped away, heading uptown, fast.

Buddy rested his head on the roof and blacked out.

39

Buddy woke, opened his eyes, closed them again.

A brutal pain throbbed above his left ear. He breathed deeply and again opened his eyes.

He lay in a hospital bed, the end of an IV tube taped to the back of his right hand. A blanket on the chair to the side of the bed read Bellevue Hospital.

His left wrist throbbed, though not as badly as his head. He moved his hand sideways, flexing his fingers as if he were playing octaves on the piano. The pain was bad. His movement was restricted. He wondered if he'd be able to play the piano as well as he had in the past.

Goddammit.

He shifted his weight in the bed. Nothing was broken, he determined. But the main problem was his head. Emanating from the area above his left ear was an overwhelming ache unlike anything he'd experienced.

Blinking away the faint nausea and the urge to curl into a ball, he looked around the room and through the partially open door. He saw people coming and going. The ICU was supposed to be secure, but he knew it wasn't. He doubted the access would keep out a hit man. Nobody, he realized, could protect him here. He was a sitting duck.

A nurse with a name tag that read "Juan" entered the room, gave him a quick once-over, and checked the monitors next to the bed. Juan asked, "Any dizziness or disorientation?"

"No."

"Feeling okay?"

Buddy stifled a laugh. Laughing would hurt more than coughing or even breathing. He said, "Never better."

Juan adjusted the IV drip and began to leave.

"How long?" Buddy asked. "How long do I have to stay here?"

Juan turned to face him. "You've been in a major accident, Detective Lock. You've got a concussion and a bruised rib, and you need to be under observation."

"But for how long?" Buddy pressed.

Juan raised his eyebrows. "You've been here for only two hours."

Buddy thought: *Juan doesn't know that people have tried to kill me today.* He said, "How long?"

Juan shrugged, said "Ask one of the doctors," and left the room.

Buddy hated not knowing. Hated sitting here like a turkey on a platter, ready for someone to carve up.

That image convinced him.

He wouldn't stay here waiting for his attackers. They had resources and possible connections to the NYPD. They were everywhere and they were ruthless.

He swiveled his legs around, pulled the IV out of his wrist, yanked the blood pressure and pulse monitors from his arm and right forefinger, and stood.

The monitors next to the bed emitted loud beeps and something resembling a siren.

At the same time, he put a hand on the mattress to steady himself. Dizziness and nausea swept over him.

Christ.

But instead of climbing back into bed, he went slowly over to the chair, removed the hospital gown, and began putting on his suit and overcoat. He found his wallet and the medallion in a plastic bag on a hook.

Juan was first in the room. "Detective Lock," he said loudly, "you can't leave. You aren't well."

"I'm well enough," Buddy said. "And I *am* leaving. Right now." As if for emphasis, Buddy pulled on his suit coat over the empty shoulder holster. "Juan, where's my duty weapon?"

Juan eyed the holster warily. "You need to stay here, Detective Lock."

"No."

A doctor swung into the room. She was in her early thirties, with a stocky build, blue eyes, and short brown hair.

"Detective Lock," she said, "you're in no shape to leave. You're in *danger* if you leave."

Buddy thought, *I'm in worse danger if I stay.* Keeping his voice calm, he said, "Please return my duty weapon."

She stared at him until she blinked. Shaking her head, she strode to the nurse's station, removed his Glock 19 from a locked cabinet, and handed it to him.

He took it. "Thank you." And walked along the corridor.

"Detective," she called after him. "We can't help you if you leave."

Buddy turned to her and tried to smile. "Thank you, Doctor, but I have to go."

"Detective, you don't understand. You have a severe concussion. You've been unconscious for a couple of hours."

Buddy said, "But I'm conscious now. No worries." He turned away and walked down the hallway. Once he'd turned a corner and the doctor and Juan could no longer see him, he stopped and put a hand on the wall to steady himself.

His heart pounded. He felt sweat on his face.

After a moment, he straightened and kept going.

40

In the elevator Buddy studied the other passengers. He saw members of the hospital staff in pale-blue scrubs or white lab coats. An elderly couple with gray hair and old winter coats in dark colors, the old man crying openly and the old woman with stone-cold eyes and a mouth turned down at the corners. A young Indian man and woman dressed in jeans, Nike running shoes, and Patagonia jackets. She held a baby in her arms and glanced at Buddy before looking quickly away.

Buddy hadn't looked at himself since the accident. He might be bruised or cut around the face. Yet he didn't care if he frightened this woman. Breathing deeply, he knew the elevator ride would soon end, and he'd have to walk along the hospital corridor toward the exit. His stomach tightened as the brushed stainless-steel doors opened. He didn't move.

When the hospital staff and the four civilians had filed out of the elevator, he put his right hand over his stomach, near the shoulder holster under his suit coat, and stepped into the corridor.

He looked right, then left. The fluorescent bulbs above cast everything with an unnaturally pale light. He didn't like what he saw.

Many people were walking in his direction, some slowly, some rapidly and with purpose. After the events of the last hours, he suspected all of them of murderous intent. He couldn't evaluate each of them. He wasn't up to it. The only solution was to get out of the building.

Swiveling around, he followed the corridor signs toward First Avenue. He left the old hospital and walked under the enormous glass atrium with balconies overlooking the huge space. He felt a hundred pairs of eyes on him. But he kept his head down and marched forward. Every three paces he did a three-sixty check. Eyes on him, he was sure, but no assault.

Moments later he went up the stone ramp that brought him level with First Avenue. Ten seconds more, and he was standing just inside the vestibule. He was unprotected. Standing in the open. Anyone could see him. He didn't like the feeling. With his right hand he reached under his suit coat and held the Glock. He flexed his left, ready to fight off another assault.

He knew they'd come for him again. Maybe here. Maybe at home. He thought of Mei, alone with Ben somewhere.

Jesus Christ.

He needed to get up to Seventy-Sixth Street, but he couldn't walk there. If another SUV plowed into him, he wouldn't be lucky a second time. Taking a cab wouldn't be safe, for the same reason. And in his condition, the subway would be a death trap. He considered and rejected Ward. Buddy was a cop. He should be able to handle the situation with his own resources.

He decided to trust someone he didn't completely trust. He took out his phone and dialed.

41

Mario pulled along the curb in an unmarked Ford Interceptor. From the driver's seat, he rolled down the passenger window and called, "Need a ride?"

Buddy raised a hand in greeting and hobbled to the car. He climbed in and shut the door, groaning as he did.

Mario said, "You look out of it, man."

"I am. Out of it."

"Shouldn't you stay at the hospital?"

Buddy didn't respond.

Mario exhaled. "All right." He glanced into his side mirror and merged into the northbound traffic.

As the car began to move, Buddy's dizziness worsened. Closing his eyes, he said, "Did you talk with traffic and patrol?"

"Sure did."

Buddy looked over at him. "Did they get anything on the SUV that hit me?"

Mario shook his head. "Not a thing."

"DOT didn't have a traffic cam?"

"I checked. Not at that intersection."

"Fuck."

"Yeah."

"Did you check hospitals for gunshot wounds to the feet or lower legs?"

"I did."

Buddy waited for Mingo to relay what he'd found. When his partner didn't answer, he turned to him. "Just tell me, Mingo."

"Sorry, Buddy. They reported nobody with that kind of injury."

Buddy was silent. *Who the hell are these people?* He remembered that only yesterday, Tan Jacket had disappeared after Buddy kicked him into a concrete staircase. And tonight, he'd shot someone at Park and Twenty-Third, and that person hadn't gone to a hospital.

Buddy's dizziness threatened to overcome him. He faced forward, closed his eyes, and rubbed his temples.

Mario said, "Buddy, your memory is fuzzy. I get it."

"No," Buddy said.

Mario continued, "Witnesses talked to patrol, Buddy. They said the driver of the SUV hit you and drove away. One guy said he heard gunshots or a car backfiring, he wasn't sure which." Mario reached over and laid a hand on Buddy's left shoulder. "The accident messed with your head, man. Patrol thinks there wasn't a gunfight."

"What?" Buddy sat up, shrugging off Mario's hand. He knew there was at least one witness, but the guy who'd been wearing black loafers must have been spooked.

"Don't feel bad about it," Mario continued. "I mean, you can hardly walk. No way you can remember—accurately—what happened at the crash scene."

Buddy started to reply, then caught himself. What was the point? At least he wouldn't be suspended for being involved in another shooting. He wouldn't have to deal with Force Investigations, and he could keep his service Glock.

But he'd been rammed by an SUV. He'd nearly been killed. His mood flashed black. He didn't know what had happened. But he knew that in addition to touching the proverbial third rail, he was getting closer. To something or someone he couldn't identify or touch. But that something or someone had shown lethal force that could hurt, even kill, him and Mei. Once again, he realized his enemies had clout. An unbelievable amount of it.

He opened his eyes, turned, and stared at Mario. His distrust growing by the minute, he said nothing more.

When they arrived at his building, he got out of the car and closed the door behind him.

Did he sell me out? Buddy thought. *And for what?*

42

Ward stood in the gun room of his large modern house in Greenwich. He was packing two ballistic nylon duffel bags. One with clothing, including jackets, for him, maybe for Buddy. The other with handguns, ammunition, a flashlight, face paint, holsters, a Taser, a rifle, and an Uzi. The gun room was in the basement, thirty by thirty feet, with recessed lighting, a polished concrete floor, racks of guns, and below the racks, shelves filled with everything he might need in case of an ambush.

Ms. Gallatin had gone to bed in the opposite wing of the house. The house was quiet, so the ringing of his mobile phone startled him.

"Hello?" he answered.

"Mr. Mills, this is Helmut Borer." The precise voice spoke heavily accented English.

Ward felt the twinge of anxiety, but he wouldn't express it. For a banker like Helmut Borer, he had to be cold to be respected. "Yes, Helmut?"

"I found the account."

"Where?"

"Basler Holding."

Ward said, "What's the account balance?"

"Four hundred thousand dollars."

"Were there numerous small deposits, or only one deposit?"

"A single deposit, made yesterday."

"When was the account established?"

A pause as Helmut Borer studied his information. Then: "Yesterday."

Ward thought about the money deposited into a Zurich account by a junior detective from the NYPD who made well under $100,000 a year and probably had to allocate much of that money to housing. "Helmut?" he said.

"Yes, sir?"

"Thanks for the favor."

"You're welcome."

Ward ended the call and dialed his brother. When Buddy answered, he said, "Mingo has a numbered account with four hundred grand in it."

He could hear Buddy's breathing, but Buddy didn't respond.

"Buddy?" he said.

"Yeah."

Ward stared at a Beretta M9 on the gun rack. He took hold of it with his free hand and said, "The money was a single deposit, made yesterday. Maybe a down payment for taking you out?"

"It could have been," Buddy said. "Or for the couple off Long Island. Or something else."

Ward shook his head. "Really, you think the money is for something else?"

Buddy's voice grew deeper, louder, when he responded. "No, I think it was related to this case. But I don't know how."

43

Alone in his living room, Buddy set down his phone. He checked the Glock.

It was good to have it back. Even at home he carried a spare magazine in his right trouser pocket. After a while, he held the gun at his side.

He stood by the living room windows and stared out at the city. Lights on familiar buildings on Central Park West and Central Park South: the handsome Plaza Hotel, the needle of One57, the Ritz-Carlton, the Time Warner Center's sheets of black glass, and across the park, the Dakota. At night these buildings were like child's toys—illuminated and colored shapes of different eras, the city's history brought to life.

Buddy went into the master bathroom and took two Advil. Returning to the bedroom, he retrieved the medallion from his pocket and pushed it under the mattress on his side of the bed. Then he took a hot shower, but only briefly and with the Glock on the vanity within easy reach.

The headache easing, he sat on the sofa, pulled out his cell phone, and studied the photograph he'd taken of the sign at the future site of Haddon House. Once again he read the names: Cromwell Properties and the New York City Economic Development Agency.

He pushed the home button on his phone and then the Safari icon. He searched for Cromwell Properties, clicked on the company's website, and clicked the link for leadership. There, he read about Stella Bannon, the CEO:

> Stella Bannon leads Cromwell Properties, a premier real estate developer offering the best of New York City design, development, construction, leasing, and sales. During her fourteen years with the company, Cromwell has completed eight projects in the city, five in Manhattan. *Forbes* has rated Bannon a Top 10 CEO in New York. J.D. Power has recognized Cromwell as one of America's most ethical private companies. Bannon serves on the boards of Big Brothers Big Sisters, Mount Sinai Kravis Children's Hospital, and the Whitney Museum of American Art.

Buddy thought this information told him nothing about her. Nothing of use.

So he searched for the Economic Development Agency. Its executive director was Erica Fischer. Her biography, posted on the EDA's website, gave even less relevant information.

Buddy searched Bannon's and Fischer's names.

He found news articles, mostly about new projects, a few about eminent domain controversies. *Eminent domain,* he thought, *the power of government to take property away from private citizens.* But he already knew about it, thanks to Henry Lee.

Nothing unusual. Nothing unexpected. Nothing at all.

He was grasping at air, yet he sensed movement. He just couldn't see through the fog surrounding that movement. Not yet.

He got up and sat behind Mei's Steinway. He began to play something easy, something for beginners. *Für Elise.*

He made no errors, but his headache worsened and his left wrist burned. Annoyed and more than a little worried about his ability to play, he decided to go for something difficult. He'd test himself at full volume. Something that would require strength and speed in both hands when played at the composer's recommended tempo.

The first thirty seconds of Grieg's Piano Concerto in A Minor.

The first notes had always seemed to him like icicles thrown through the air. He'd relished playing them as a young man, but tonight he was apprehensive. That he'd forget the notes. That his hands would fail him. But he hadn't become either a concert pianist or a detective with the NYPD through weakness.

He straightened on the piano bench.

Lined himself up.

Opened and closed his hands.

Visualized the opening bars, the icicles, the strength of the passage that he wanted to convey to . . . to whom?

He was alone.

Once again, he was alone in this life.

No, he thought then. *Not alone.*

I have music. And it doesn't matter if I hate it half the time.

He imagined an orchestra's timpani rising in volume. Taking two deep breaths, he raised his arms for an instant and then plunged into the opening chords. And the descending line.

He played hard, loud as he would in a concert hall. The entire room echoed the sound back to him. But he kept playing for that essential thirty seconds. His left hand hurt like hell, but it didn't fail him. Nor did his memory.

He finished the opening bars, just as an orchestra's strings would echo the theme he'd played, and stopped, breathing more easily.

He hadn't lost it. In a week, he'd be all right.

He lay on the sofa. The Advil kicked in. The apartment was silent.

He didn't trust the peace, the calm, the apparent disappearance of the menace. He knew it would come for him again. It would try over and over until it got him.

After he'd closed his eyes, he thought he was in seawater, falling from the surface of the salty spray into the depths. The cold blackness engulfed him and pulled him down. Yet he fought the current and swam upward. At the peak of a wave, he tried to see the lights of the coast, but he could see nothing. He looked up to see the stars, to attempt a primitive navigation, but the thick clouds blocked out all light.

He swam for an hour, maybe two. His limbs burned with the effort. His lungs seized up. He tried to float on his back, then his front, but the water kept dragging him down.

He reached the point where he knew he'd fail. He wouldn't reach shore. He was going to die.

Why fight any longer?

Why swim for no reason?

A few moments of life weren't worth the gargantuan effort.

He stopped moving. He sank deep into the ocean until all was darkness and he couldn't breathe. Water poured into his lungs and he was drowning. But he wasn't fighting it. He felt at peace. Then he changed his mind.

He didn't want peace. He wanted to live.

He began kicking, propelling his body upward to the surface. But it was too late. He'd sunk too far. He wouldn't survive.

He yelled in anger, in torment, in regret.

No!

He woke. He sat up on the living room sofa, gulping air, his breaths rapid and fierce.

DAY 3

44

Mei awoke to the sound of something she couldn't place. It sounded like voices—hundreds or thousands of them—in the distance. A faint vibration, almost a swishing, arced over the house. She sat up and peered through the slit of light coming between the blind and the windowsill. Yet she could see nothing in the field on that side of the house.

Her stomach tightening with anxiety, she slipped out of bed, put on a pair of jeans, and crept from the room, careful not to disturb Ben, who was asleep on the sofa.

As she entered the great room, she immediately turned to the front door. Seeing it was closed and locked, she exhaled. She walked gingerly toward the window to the right of it. There, she put a hand on the edge of the blind and pulled it to the side.

Her first impression was that the ground outside seethed with bugs. Her mouth twisted involuntarily with disgust. But then the bugs took form and moved in a dozen directions at once.

My God, she thought in horror.

Bringing her hands down, she considered what to do. Or even if there was anything she *should* do.

Almost fearful that some of them might try to get into the house, she unlocked the door and opened it. Just a crack, at first. When nothing came inside, wider.

Then she heard clearly. These—crows, dozens of them, maybe hundreds—were the sounds that had awakened her, a witches' whispering chorus. They made her feel almost ill, and they seemed touched with foreboding.

Now she felt motivated to do something, to chase off the terrible creatures.

By her feet to the side of the door, she saw her boots. Quickly, she pushed her feet into them and walked outside into the cold, closing the door behind her.

They looked up with their depthless black eyes but showed no concern. As if they belonged there, they didn't move.

Walking twenty feet out among them, she clapped her hands. "Go away!" she shouted at them. "Go away!"

Yet the crows, cloaked in sleek oily feathers, remained calm. They took no notice of her.

"Damn you!" she cried. "Leave us! Leave us!"

Two of the birds near her toddled five feet in the opposite direction before turning and pointing their beaks at her.

She clenched her fists, considered shouting again, but knew it would do no good. Yet she believed she had to make the crows leave or there would be terrible consequences.

Returning to the house, she went in and removed her boots. Quietly, she padded barefoot to the larger bedroom, where Ben was sleeping. After pulling open the closet door, she stood on tiptoe and from the top shelf took hold of a nylon case. It was heavy, but she could carry it in one hand. Kneeling down on the floor of the closet, she rummaged through her duffel bag and found the box of ammunition. In the kitchen, she unzipped the case, took out the .38 revolver, put six rounds in the cylinder, pushed the cylinder back into place, and carried the gun in both hands to the front door. After stepping into her boots, she walked outside.

The crows parted as she walked into their midst, some of them eyeing her curiously. Most ignored her, even now as she pointed the revolver skyward.

Sliding the pad of her right index finger on the trigger, she held her breath and squeezed the trigger four times.

Immediately, the birds shrieked and leaped into the air, all of them, together in a black cloud, then wheeled overhead and down, down, toward Rockridge. Their alarm echoed around her, and she shrank at the awfulness of the sight and the noise. But then everything grew quiet. Silent, even.

"Mei?"

She turned to see Ben standing in the doorway in his pajamas. His hair was tousled and nearly obscured his eyes.

"I had to," she told him. "I had to make them leave."

45

Mario called at six fifteen that morning. "You were right," he said.

Buddy sat up on the sofa, blinking at the faint light coming through the large windows, and held the phone to his right ear. He glanced around the room, remembering everything. Head throbbing, he got up and went into the kitchen.

"Buddy? You all right?"

"Yeah, Mario." He opened a cupboard, poured two Advil tablets into his palm, and swallowed them dry. He realized he needed coffee, or his brain wouldn't work today.

"The *Sungs*, Buddy. Chen and Lily." Mario spoke rapidly, excitedly. "You were right about them."

Buddy filled his Mr. Coffee with water and poured coffee into the mesh filter. He said, "What'd you find?"

"That's just it. They're *missing*. I spoke with their eldest son. He described his parents. He described his mother's engagement ring and told me it was inscribed with *for L*. Which meant 'for Lily.'"

Buddy felt relief. He may have discovered the identities of the bodies found off Long Island. But his relief was tempered with apprehension. If the Sungs' deaths had something to do with the razing of the Nanjing building to make way for the Haddon House project, then he'd opened a can of scorpions and pushed his finger inside. Forcing himself to take one step at a time, he spoke into the phone. "That's not enough for positive ID."

Mario's voice rose with excitement. "Buddy, the Sungs' oldest son went to OCME this morning for identification. He confirmed it. *They're the bodies of his parents.*"

Buddy's mind raced. "Yeah," he agreed absently.

Mario said, "The guy, though. The man. The eldest son told me he had no identifying marks except he wore some kind of medallion with the Chinese symbol for *sacrifice*. No sign of a medallion, Dr. Silva told me. But it probably fell off in the ocean. So we're good, Buddy. You solved the case."

Buddy pressed his thumb and middle finger into his temples, hoping to lessen the pulsing headache. Then he walked back to the master bedroom, reached under the mattress, and brought out the medallion. He stared at it, turned over the side with the symbol to the other side that was smooth black onyx.

"Buddy?"

"Yeah."

"Did you hear me? You solved the case."

Buddy breathed deeply. "You think this is a missing persons case?"

Mario was quiet. Then he asked, "Don't you?"

Buddy said, "How do you think the Sungs—a retired man and his wife—wound up in the Atlantic in January?"

"Must have been suicide. Right?"

"Not necessarily, Mario. We don't know." He stood over the Mr. Coffee and inhaled. He thought if he drank all the coffee, he could make it through the day. He said, "Call the Sungs' adult children. Get a meeting with them."

"When?"

"Today. Now."

46

"Now" ended up being two hours later: 8:00 a.m.

Buddy held on to the handrail serving the four steps up to the front door of the Nanjing building. The headache had faded. Maybe it was the Advil or the coffee, or both. He'd regained most of his stability.

Mario stood on the top step, checked the building directory to the left of the door, and pressed the white button next to the name Sung.

A buzzer sounded almost immediately, and Buddy followed Mario inside.

The small lobby was tired but not dilapidated. All furniture had been removed, leaving only scuffed terrazzo floors. Above them hung a dusty chandelier that might have been fifty years old. Buddy thought the building seemed abandoned, and he supposed that in a way it had been. Taped to the elevator's bronze-colored door was a slip of paper that read "Out of Order."

They climbed the terrazzo staircase to the third floor. No lights functioned in the hallway, and over the stairs, they noted only a series of weak bulbs. At each level, above their heads, an exit sign glowed cherry red. The walls were painted taupe, the carpeting was brown and marked with stains. The third unit along the right side of the hallway, marked as number 305, had a nameplate with the name Sung.

As Mario knocked on the door, he glanced at Buddy. Yet Buddy's attention had been caught by movement down the hall to his left.

The door at the end of the corridor had opened and closed.

Buddy saw a young woman walking toward him. As she drew near, he saw that she was in her early or midtwenties, with large eyes, angular features, and clear skin. Her long brown hair, which she wore under a black ski hat with a marijuana leaf sewn into it, couldn't hide her attractiveness. Nor could her puffy gray down parka, blue jeans, and expensive-looking knee-high boots.

The door to unit 305 opened. Mario held up his badge and introduced himself to a young Asian man.

Buddy took a last look at the young woman in the corridor. The light from the interior of the Sungs' living room fell on her wrist. Buddy thought he recognized a man's stainless-steel Rolex with a blue face.

He smiled at her and said, "Good morning."

She glanced at him. "Hey."

Then she was past him.

He could hear the sound of her boots echo on the staircase down to the lobby.

Mario called him inside the Sungs' home.

Buddy said, "Go on in, I'll be there in a moment."

He walked down the hall to the doorway of unit 309. Seeing no nameplate or other identification, he returned to the condo unit of Chen and Lily Sung.

Inside, he faced the three adult children of the missing couple. They were sitting on a sofa under a large window, watching him expectantly. He said, "I'm sorry for your loss. This must be a tough time for all of you. But we have a few questions."

As he spoke, he watched them closely. He was surprised to see the eyes of the Sungs' children were dry. No expression crossed their faces. They didn't cry or, for a few moments, even speak.

Then one of the young men sat forward on the sofa and said, "We were expecting this news."

47

Buddy stood in the middle of Chen and Lily Sung's living room. To his left, Mario sat in an armchair. In front of Buddy, on a large cloth sofa the color of caramel, were the three adult children of the Sungs. They'd exchanged names. Wang, the older son, on the left. June, the middle child and only daughter, between Wang and Leo, the younger son.

Wang handed Buddy a piece of heavy white paper, the kind someone would use to write a formal letter. On the paper was a typewritten note that read:

> Our dearest children,
> We love you more than words can describe. Your lives are stars that, for us, will never burn out. We do not wish to burden you with the destruction of the illness. The two of us cannot be apart.
> So we have chosen to end our time with you. We have chosen to end our lives. And we have chosen to set you free.
> Goodbye, and love always.

Under the text of the note, he saw Chinese characters.
Buddy looked up at Wang, who pointed to the characters.

"My parents' signatures," Wang explained. He then handed Buddy a second piece of paper.

Buddy read it quickly. The letterhead at the top was from a doctor at New York-Presbyterian Hospital. It was a typewritten and signed diagnosis of pancreatic cancer in Chen Sung.

Wang rejoined his sister and brother on the sofa. He looked up at Buddy and said, "They told us they were going to end their lives, but not when or how. We offered to comfort my father, to give him the best care, but he didn't want to be incapacitated. He wanted to die on his own terms. We tried to convince my mother to continue living, for her grandchildren, for us, even for the senior ballet classes she loved. But she said she couldn't live without our father."

As Wang spoke, Buddy glanced at Wang's siblings. June, a woman of about forty, was watching her older brother with rapt attention. Leo, perhaps five years younger than his sister, kept his eyes on the floor.

Buddy studied Leo. The younger man had hair to below his ears and eyeglasses with translucent frames. He wore a black turtleneck, jeans, and black leather boots. Several braided leather bracelets looped around his wrists, as well as an enormous watch of black metal. While Leo's older brother spoke, he said nothing.

The pattern, Buddy thought. It wasn't right. There was a wrong note. Played softly, but wrong just the same.

He excused himself to use the restroom and went into the back hallway. After closing and locking the bathroom door, he searched the small space but saw nothing of note. Next he tried the master bedroom. It was plainly decorated with tan walls and framed photographs of the family on vacation, mostly in California, Arizona, and Florida. There was a queen-sized bed with night tables on either side and, above the headboard, two double-hung windows with lime-green curtains. He saw a small armoire. To its left was a ballet barre, each end of the wooden pole attached to the wall with a stainless-steel bracket.

Returning to the now-silent living room, he handed his card to all three siblings. He took out his small notebook and pen and asked them for their full names, dates of birth, occupations, and contact numbers. He learned that Leo was a television director who worked frequently in London. Leo didn't meet his eye when he handed Leo a card.

He knows something, Buddy thought. *Or he suspects.*

Mario let the family know how to claim their parents' bodies. And with that, the detectives repeated that they were sorry for the family's loss and closed the door behind them.

Downstairs in the lobby, Mario pushed open the door and began walking down the steps to the sidewalk. He turned back to see if Buddy was following him and then stopped on the bottom step. Mario called back, "What is it?"

Buddy was standing on the top step. He'd turned to study the building directory just above the street door's buzzer. Two names in white lettering remained on the black background.

His headache had intensified. The names blurred. He shut his eyes, breathed deeply, and tried again.

The names took shape. The first was C. Sung, unit 305. The second? S. Richardson, unit 309. He took out his notebook and wrote down the young woman's name.

As they got in Mario's Interceptor, Buddy again thought of Leo Sung, the dead couple's youngest son. Leo's body language hadn't shown agreement with the statements of his older brother, Wang. He hadn't shown disagreement, exactly, but Buddy thought Leo had shown skepticism if not more.

He'd give Leo two hours, and then he'd call him.

Mario was speaking into his phone. "We solved the missing persons case."

This was a knife blade stuck into Buddy's chest. He turned to Mario and asked, "Who are you talking to?"

Mario held the phone to his chest. He said, "Chief Malone."

"Why are you doing that?"

Mario shrugged. "The chief told me to call with any significant developments."

Buddy gripped the seat with his left hand and the door handle with his right. He wouldn't hit his partner, not yet.

Mario ended the call and turned on the Latin pop music he liked. Buddy kept his eyes straight ahead, but he wasn't taking in the scenery of Chinatown. He said, "Mario, stop the car."

"What? Why?"

"Stop the fucking car."

Mario pulled the Interceptor along the east curb of Broadway but didn't put the car in park.

At last Buddy turned to him. He knew his face was red, and his left hand had curled into a fist. He said, "Mario, never, *ever* talk to Chief Malone or anybody else, *unless* we're on the same page. *Got it?*"

Mario let go of the steering wheel and held up his hands. "But what page are you on, Buddy? The Sungs were suicides. We have the proof. The proof, *got that?*"

Buddy ignored him, didn't respond to the lip the junior detective was giving him. He'd deal with that later if he couldn't get a different partner assigned to him in the next week. He said, "Did you hear from the lab on the prints off the credit card I gave you?"

Mario sighed. "Yes, I heard. Nothing. No matches."

Buddy considered this. So Tan Jacket had no ID, no money, and no criminal record. Something was off there; he wasn't sure what it was. Buddy returned his attention to the case and Mario's failure to be on the same page. He said, "Confirm Chen Sung's diagnosis with the doctor on the note."

"Sure thing, but it's a waste of time. The case is closed. We can move on and solve some real homicides."

"Yeah?" Buddy asked.

"Damn right. Let's do some work."

"That's what we're paid for, isn't it, Mario?"

Mario's expression tightened. "Sure, man."

Buddy said, "Ever been to Switzerland?"

"Switzerland? What the hell are you talking about?"

"Never been there?"

"Of course I've never been to Switzerland. Have you?"

Buddy remembered playing concerts at the Tonhalle-Orchester Zürich. He'd been eleven years old, traveling with his father. But that was a long time ago. He said, "Where do you bank?"

Mario turned to him and screwed up his face. "Hey, amigo, what the hell?"

"It's a simple question. Where you do bank?"

"Citi. Why?"

"No other accounts?"

"No. I've got my pension with the NYPD. Why are you asking me this shit?"

Buddy didn't answer. Instead, he said, "You have a numbered account in Zurich, don't you? At Basler Holding."

Mario reared back. "What the hell has gotten into you? Numbered account? I don't know anything about a numbered account."

Buddy kept his eyes on Mario's. He lowered his voice at the same time Mario's rose. He said, "Four hundred thousand dollars."

Mario stared at him. "I've got less than fifteen grand to my name. Wherever you're getting your info, it's bullshit."

Buddy didn't respond. He got out of the Interceptor and watched Mario steer away from the curb.

He thought Mario was telling the truth. But he'd been wrong before.

48

In the late morning, Ben heard the distant sound of a machine. He was sitting at the table in the great room, watching his math class on his computer, and at the same time completing a worksheet with a ballpoint pen.

A car, he thought as the sound increased, and he heard an engine and tires on the asphalt driveway outside the house.

He didn't move. He felt his stomach rising as if he might be sick. "Mei!" he called out. *"Mei!"*

She hurried into the great room from the hallway. Her eyes widened. "What? What is it?"

He didn't move, didn't turn toward the door. He was frozen, listening as Mei went behind him and looked through the window to the right of the door. He knew Mei had a revolver in the closet, and wondered if he should try to get it out.

He said, "Who is it?"

"The police."

"What? Why?"

"I don't know. But it's the officer we saw at the café yesterday."

Ben heard Mei open the door, but he kept his eyes on his computer screen. He thought if he didn't look at the policeman, the policeman wouldn't take him away. Because that was surely why the policeman was here. Judge Sylvia Miles must have ordered him taken away from Mei and Buddy, and she would force him to live with his aunt and uncle. Hands over the keyboard, he typed nonsense, but listened carefully.

"Good morning, ma'am. I'm Officer Lingwood."

"Hello."

"You all right?"

"Yes," Mei said quickly. "Why wouldn't we be?"

"Well, ma'am. I had a call about a disturbance up in this neck of the woods."

Ben stopped typing.

"A disturbance?" Mei asked.

"Yeah. Gunshots. A few of them. Did you fire a gun up here?"

"No, Officer. Why would I fire a gun?"

Officer Lingwood didn't immediately reply. "All right," he told her. "But if you hear anything, please let me know. And of course keep in mind that your neighbors here might be farther away than what you have in the city, but they're close by, and everybody hears everything."

Mei said, "Thank you, Officer."

He said, "You have a good day."

She closed the door. Now Ben turned toward the door. He saw her watching Officer Lingwood climb into his car. They heard the sound of the engine grow louder and then fade away.

After locking the front door, she drew close to him. Her smile surprised him, because he'd thought she was nervous, or she should have been.

He said, "I don't like it here. I want to go home."

"I don't like it here, either," she told him, standing behind him, putting an arm around his chest and hugging him.

He wriggled free, angry that they had to be in this house.

"Soon," she said. "We'll leave soon."

Ben tried to believe her, but he wasn't sure he did.

49

Staring at his phone, Buddy studied the photograph of the Haddon House sign he'd taken the previous morning. He said, "Drop me off at the EDA offices, would you? Hell's Kitchen. Forty-Sixth and Eleventh Ave." He hadn't gone to the pool to request another car but made a mental note to take the time.

Mario turned right, headed west, and lowered the volume of the music. "What's the EDA?"

"The Economic Development Agency. They're a division of the city working with Cromwell Properties on the new condo tower that will replace the building where the Sungs lived."

Mario looked over at him. "What are you doing, man? The case is closed. We need to move on."

"No, it's not that," Buddy lied. "I've got a friend who works there. I want to say hello."

"Yeah?" Mario said, looking over at Buddy. When Buddy didn't respond or return his glance, Mario said, "Sure thing."

A few minutes later, Buddy walked into the reception area of the EDA. It was on the eighth floor of a nondescript building. The tile floors were scuffed and stained, the walls white with more than a hint of yellow, the art on the walls showed color photographs of office buildings, residential towers, retail centers, and parks. He took it all in as he approached the reception desk, which was made of plastic modular furniture.

The heavy young woman behind the desk said, "May I help you?" He took out his badge wallet, opened it, and held it up. He said, "I'm Detective Lock. May I speak with the executive director?"

The woman shook her head. "I'm sorry, but Ms. Fischer is in meetings."

He nodded. "I need to talk with the person handling the Haddon House project in Chinatown."

The receptionist said, "I'm sorry, but the people working on that project are out of town."

Buddy didn't know if the receptionist was being truthful or not. But he wasn't going to settle for the runaround. He said, "I'll wait for Ms. Fischer. Please let her know I'm with NYPD Homicide."

This brought a response from the receptionist. Her eyes widened as she stood. "I'll let her know," the young woman said, and disappeared down a row of modular furniture to the right and beyond his vision.

The receptionist returned a few minutes later but said nothing to him, only sat behind her plastic desk and answered the phone and stared at her computer screen.

Buddy paced the small waiting area. He studied the photographs and read the tag below each of them that had been stuck to the wall. Printed on each tag was the name of the project and the date it had opened. He recognized Madison Square Park. The buildings meant nothing to him. Some appeared to be public housing, or what used to be called that. But the projects completed in more recent years looked to him like housing for the rich, buildings like Haddon House. Lots of granite, glass, and steel. The more recent, he noted, the more glass. He wondered about the mission of the EDA and whether it had changed over the years. He wondered how much money was involved and how much of it found its way to the EDA and its management.

Forty minutes later, a pale young woman with dishwater blond hair and a slender, formless body covered by a loose-fitting blue dress walked over to him. He was sitting on an uncomfortable wooden chair and reading the *Gazette* on his phone. Salacious stuff, mostly. Embezzlement on Wall Street. Bribes in Albany. The usual.

"Detective Lock?" asked the pale young woman.

He looked up. "Yeah?"

"Ms. Fischer is available for a brief meeting. Would you come with me?"

50

Buddy put away his phone, stood, and followed the young woman as she wove through the gray cubicles and finally reached a hallway with real walls and private offices. At the end of the hallway, the pale young woman led him into a large private office. The office's large windows looked out over the Hudson River at the bluffs of Weehawken, New Jersey. He saw houses along the river and larger houses on top of the bluffs, but he didn't have time to study the view. In the corner of this large office stood a woman about his age.

"Good morning, Detective Lock," she said in a high-pitched but strong voice. "I'm Erica Fischer, the EDA's executive director." She stepped forward and offered her hand.

"Morning," he said, noting her small hand but strong grip and the silver bracelet on her wrist. He saw that she was shorter than average height but wore very high heels to appear taller. She had a medium build with a striking face. Her hair was expensively highlighted and extended to just above her shoulders. She wore a gray skirt, a matching turtleneck sweater, and a Burberry scarf around her neck.

She let go of Buddy's hand, glanced over his shoulder, and said, "Thanks for joining us, Jack. Detective Lock, this is Jack Carlson, the associate director."

Buddy turned around. Carlson was big, with a short haircut. He looked like he spent a lot of time at the gym. He wore a nice blue sport coat with a faint check pattern but no tie. Buddy noticed immediately that he was injured. A long cut marked Carlson's forehead over his blue eyes. Additional cuts and bruises covered his hands. The cuts appeared fresh. He was using two aluminum crutches, his right foot bandaged and in an orthopedic boot.

Buddy felt himself go hot. *Coincidence?* he wondered. He didn't offer Jack Carlson his hand as he asked, "What happened?"

Carlson's handsome face tightened. "A skiing accident."

Buddy thought the injuries were consistent with a collision between an SUV and a Dodge Charger, the bandaged foot possibly the result of a bullet wound. But he had no proof. Alert to any sudden movement from Jack Carlson, he turned to Fischer and said, "Tell me about Haddon House. What was the EDA's role?"

She tilted her head as if condescending to speak to a small child. "We facilitate. Why do you ask?"

Buddy ignored the nonanswer. He said, "Who makes money from Haddon House?"

This time she answered straight. "The developer, Cromwell Properties."

"Anyone else?"

"The investors who provide the financing."

"Who are they?"

"It's NationBank. But Cromwell pays market interest rates, of course."

He said, "Who buys the units?"

Fischer's eyes widened, as if he were naive or stupid. "Anyone with money. Americans. People from abroad—Indians, Chinese, Russians, English, German, Saudi, and on and on. This is an international city, Detective."

After thinking about this, Buddy asked, "How many units in Haddon House have been sold to Russians?"

Erica Fischer smiled. "I don't know. Foreign buyers—even some American buyers—use companies to purchase real estate in New York. So we often don't know who's buying."

"What percentage of units in Haddon House," he pressed, "are under contract to companies?"

Her smile vanished as she crossed her arms over her chest. "I'm sorry, Detective, but that's confidential information."

He realized he wasn't going to get anything further, not without a warrant, and even with a warrant, it was notoriously difficult to determine condominium ownership. Switching topics, he asked, "How does the EDA deal with holdouts?"

Fischer's face became a professional mask, as did her language. "We give holdouts every opportunity to work with the city."

"What if . . . what if the holdouts refuse to work with the city?"

She said, "Then we use the power of eminent domain."

"Used it lately?"

She shook her head and walked behind her desk. On its cluttered surface, he noticed a large Louis Vuitton bag—an unusual luxury for a government employee. "Fortunately not. But the threat is always there. You see, Detective, the EDA prefers to inform rather than to make threats."

Threats, he repeated silently. He said, "Did you inform Chen Sung or Lily Sung? Or did you threaten them?"

Fischer's mask remained impassive. "I'm not familiar with those names."

Buddy thought, *I'll bet not.* He said, "Any issues at the Nanjing building?"

She smiled. "We have everything we need. Or we'll soon have. Cromwell has assured us. Haddon House will be a great project. A boon for the city."

Buddy didn't reply. His focus had shifted from her to Jack Carlson. He asked, "What did you do before you came to the EDA?"

Carlson lifted his chin. "Government work."

"What kind?"

"FBI."

Buddy nodded. *This guy is capable,* he thought. *He has friends who'll tap phones and perform deadly favors, such as shooting a police detective.*

Erica Fischer clapped her hands together once. "I have another meeting, Detective. You understand."

Buddy looked at her. She didn't offer her hand.

Jack Carlson walked him out through the hallway and the maze of cubicles. In the lobby Buddy turned to ask Carlson more about his time at the bureau, but Carlson was already returning through the cubicles to the hallway and Erica Fischer's office.

51

Downstairs in the building lobby, Buddy's phone rang. He pulled it from his suit coat and checked the screen. Recognizing the NYPD's main line, his anxiety went full throttle. He answered the call: "Lock here."

"Buddy, it's Malone. Where are you?"

"Hell's Kitchen."

"Nice work solving the missing persons case. You notified the Sung family, now you're done. So I've got a new one for you. Robbery-homicide at a bank just inside the Nineteenth Precinct—your home turf. Okay?"

Buddy said, "I'm not sure the Sung case is closed."

"Sure it is. Mario confirmed with the doctor that Chen Sung had terminal pancreatic cancer. Nobody survives that, Buddy."

Buddy's chest tightened. It always did when he thought he was being railroaded. He said, "When did Mario confirm the cancer?"

"Five minutes ago. So the case is closed. Got it?"

Buddy wondered if Malone was pushing because Buddy and Mario were needed elsewhere, or if Malone was dirty. Or maybe Mario and Malone were right, and the case was solved. It made sense, didn't it, what happened with the Sungs? Terminal cancer diagnosis. Mr. Sung wanted to die before things got ugly. His wife, a member of the generation that stood by her man, even followed him to the grave. Is that what wives of the Pharaohs had done? Yeah, it might make sense to some people.

He said, "Okay, Chief. I'll move on."

But he couldn't accept that he'd solved the case. Where Mario or another detective, even a senior one, might agree and conclude the missing persons case was solved, he saw a jarring sequence of events. For him, it was as if he'd been playing one of Bach's glasslike French Suites, and in the middle of the development section, the melody turned into Tom Petty's "American Girl." In the case of the Sungs, the pattern had broken. The musical line had fallen apart. He could see the wreckage, even if Mario and Malone couldn't. Or wouldn't.

His phone rang a second time. He saw the NYPD number again and knew it was Malone calling a second time. "Chief?" he answered.

Silence on the other end of the line. Then he heard a woman's voice, hushed but clear. "Buddy?"

Buddy felt on edge. "Who's this?"

"Rachel Grove."

The anxiety lessened. "Oh, hey. I thought you were the chief. What can I do for you?"

Rachel said, "I did the research project you wanted. About the One Police line that called the burner phone you showed me."

Buddy asked, "Who was it?"

"The call went out from the trunk line, but we couldn't trace it to a particular extension," she explained. "But we know it came from a splinter line that serves two desk phones."

Buddy pushed his phone more tightly against his right ear. "Which desk phones?"

"Chief Malone and his secretary, Alicia Bravo."

Malone, he thought silently. Had he misread the chief? And was Malone's betrayal the reason he'd ordered Buddy off the Sung case? Maybe. But what if someone else had made the call from Malone's or

Bravo's desks? Bravo was an hourly employee, required to clock out at the end of the day.

He thought about that night and standing over Tan Jacket in the darkness, taking the phone from the back pocket of the unconscious man's trousers. "Rachel," he said, "was the chief still at work at five thirty or six p.m. two nights ago?"

"No idea."

"Check the cameras in the lobby. Call me when you know when the chief left that night. Can you do that?"

"Yeah, Buddy. But that's as far as I can go."

"Understood," Buddy said, and ended the call.

As he walked out through the security checkpoint and stood in the vestibule of the building housing the EDA, his headache returned. It throbbed above his left ear. Dizzy, he touched the window facing Eleventh Avenue. He stood there for a while, the glass cooling his hand.

More help, he thought. *Rachel is good but I need more.*

He gathered his strength, planned his route north to Gracie Mansion, and stepped outside.

52

Sloan Richardson saw the bank teller notice her watch. It had been her father's favorite Rolex. A Submariner, stainless steel with a blue face and bezel. She rarely took it off. She knew it was too large for her—out of proportion to her wrist—but she didn't care. There were many conventions about proportion and what ought to be done that she ignored. Maybe the teller thought her watch had been stolen rather than a reminder of her late father's affection. Then again, many people had guessed wrong about her.

The teller counted and recounted the five hundred dollars in cash and passed the bills across the counter to her. The teller said, "Is there anything else I can do for you today?"

"Yes," she replied. "Would you jot down my balance, please?"

The teller took up a blank deposit slip and a pencil and stared at her computer screen. Her eyebrows rose, but otherwise her face remained impassive. She wrote on the deposit slip and pushed it across the counter.

Sloan Richardson read the number: $245,643.68. Still standing at the counter, she tore the deposit slip into shreds and pushed them toward the teller, saying, "Thank you."

A half hour later, she entered Baked, the sandwich and coffee shop at the corner of Church and White Streets in Tribeca, and saw him at a table at the back. He saw her and, ever polite, stood from the banquette and offered his hand.

She ignored this gesture, removed her gray knit hat, and shook out her shoulder-length brown hair. Then she sat on a white chair facing him. It wasn't that he was unattractive to her. She'd have slept with him happily if he hadn't been repulsive to her for another reason. His handsome, athletic build and dark-brown hair carefully trimmed, with a touch of gray at the temples, was the look she most liked. Maybe because he resembled her late father, dead too soon from a heart attack. He was polite, well spoken, and—he'd told her—married with children. Although she was here for a personal reason, he was here for business. Their sole previous meeting had ended in a draw. She'd agreed to meet him a second time only because he'd promised her an improved offer.

"How are you, Miss Richardson?" he asked once they'd sat down. "I took the liberty of ordering you a coffee. Would you like cream or sugar?"

She glanced at the coffee cup in front of her. Steam rose, twirling, out of the black liquid. For a second she suspected it was poisoned but then brushed away that notion as paranoid. She'd already begun to think this meeting was a mistake. *Miss Richardson,* she thought. *Does he think he's living in Downton fucking Abbey?* Folding her hands around the cup, she appreciated its warmth on the cold day. She said, "I like it straight."

He smiled. "Excellent. How've you been?"

She frowned. "I'm here for your offer, nothing else."

He nodded. "I understand." He unbuttoned his camel hair coat and sipped at his coffee.

She waited, not moving.

He said, "We're prepared to offer you four million dollars."

At the mention of money, she sensed the anger rising within her. She said, "I don't want it. You know I don't want it. Why are you offering something that won't convince me?"

He sat back in his chair. "It's a very generous offer, Miss Richardson. You should take it."

Miss Richardson, she thought again. *My God.* She narrowed her eyes. "I've told you what I want. If you give it to me, I'll sign your fucking papers and move out."

He smiled again, but this time with animosity. "It's impossible. I've told you that."

She sipped the coffee, pushed back her chair, and stood. She pointed at him and said, "I won't sign the papers. Not until I meet *her.*"

He leaned toward her. "You have to deal with me, Miss Richardson. You won't be meeting with anyone else."

"Then we don't have much to talk about." She laughed, and decided to use his first name. "Do we, *Vance?*"

His face tightened with anger and frustration, but she turned and left the table. As she left the café, she put on her hat, fished her gloves out of her jacket pocket, and walked home to Chinatown.

When she returned home to the Nanjing building, she noticed that a folded piece of letter-sized paper had been slipped under the door. She closed and locked the door and picked up the single piece of paper. After hanging her jacket in the closet by the entry, she walked into the kitchen and set the paper on the countertop. She knew what it was. It wasn't the first paper she'd found in this way.

From the refrigerator she took a bottle of half-finished chardonnay from her family's vineyard in Paso Robles, filled a wine glass, and sipped at it. Then she took the top off a cookie jar and pulled out a pack of Camel Lights. She lit one with a Bic lighter, inhaled gratefully, and blew the smoke toward the partly open window over the kitchen sink. Sipping the wine, she looked at the gray afternoon light outside and, for the first time in months, missed LA. The weather, mostly, but also her friends. And normal guys. She thought it was weird that men in Los Angeles seemed more real and dependable than men in New York. She'd met more than a few in her time here, and more than a few had wanted to date her, but she couldn't understand them. What they wanted—other than to be in bed with her—seemed cloaked in mystery. But she was familiar with mysteries, and the biggest one of her life was the reason she'd moved to her grandmother's former apartment in Chinatown.

It had taken months, but she'd solved the impossible riddle of who'd given birth to her and then given her up and left her outside a hospital. Her discovery had been by happenstance. Two weeks ago she'd been in her dentist's waiting room, paging through that morning's copy of the *Gazette*. Without thinking, paying more attention to the Fleetwood Mac song coming through the speakers in the ceiling, she'd noticed an image of a woman. The woman was smiling in a close-up. The article was about the woman, but the image was what mattered to her. The woman's eyes were pretty, like Sloan's. The woman had a perfect right eye, the lid slender and well above the brown iris, like Sloan's. But the woman's left eye was different. The lid didn't tuck up nicely but drooped, ever so slightly, obscuring, by the slightest degree, the brown iris of the eye beneath it.

Just like Sloan's left eyelid.

Still holding the newspaper, Sloan had stood and faced a mirror in the waiting room. She'd stared at herself, then held up the image of the woman in the article.

They shared the same face, except the one in the image was more than three decades older than hers.

She'd taken out her phone and called the woman who'd written the article. They'd spoken, although Sloan hadn't been sure what to do, and she hadn't revealed anything on that call.

Now she'd decided to take the next step and meet with the *Gazette*'s reporter. The reporter had assured her of maximum coverage.

Soon, she thought. *Very soon.*

Remembering the single sheet of paper on the counter, she set down the wine glass, unfolded it, and read.

When on a tiger's back, it's hard to dismount.
—*Old Chinese proverb*

She laughed aloud. "What assholes."

The cigarette lighter came in handy. She held the paper over the kitchen sink and watched as it burned brightly for a moment, and then disintegrated into gray ashes.

Going over to the window, she looked out and saw a work crew installing construction fencing. The men were below her, but as she stood under the kitchen lights, she knew they could see her.

She gave the men the finger.

They didn't react, only continued with their work.

53

The blinds were closed. In the glow of the light on the nightstand, Stella Bannon looked down at Vance McInnis, Cromwell Properties' vice president of development. At his handsome face with two days' growth of beard, small dark eyes, and short dark hair. She admired his muscular chest, and she felt him inside her, thick and firm.

He groaned and touched her breasts.

She'd waited for ten minutes, and so had he. It was time to release both of them. She quickened her pace, wrenching her hips over him, squeezing him until he came inside her.

"Yes!" she called once, loudly, but only once.

He shouted aloud, three times. Not her name nor his wife's, but some indistinguishable word.

Immediately she rotated off him and lay on her back, her slender limbs extending over the soft linens. She didn't curl up against him but lay free, not even touching him. She'd taught him to do the same. She'd taught him not to discuss what they'd done together—not their sex today or their sex any of the many preceding days over the past three years. It was a private matter, so private they never mentioned it.

She said, "Would you get me a drink?"

He caught his breath and sat up on one elbow. "I have a bottle of Dom."

"Not tonight. Do you have vodka?"

"I think so."

"Over ice, please."

As he got out of bed, his eyes caressed her naked figure. She didn't mind. She was happy with the way she looked. His lips parted, and he seemed on the verge of uttering a compliment, but she frowned. Without dressing, he left the room. His footsteps on the walnut floors were soft and soon faded from her hearing.

This wasn't her bed, but it was familiar to her. This wasn't her bedroom, but she'd approved its design before Cromwell Properties, the company she ran, had purchased the site on Little West Twelfth Street in the Meatpacking District, demolished an old warehouse, and built this tower that had become famous for its engineering and wavy exterior. This unit had two bedrooms, one of which Vance used as an office. It also featured two bathrooms, a kitchen and great room, plus a small foyer. It wasn't large, about two thousand square feet, but it was expensive. The finishes were custom. The bathrooms' surfaces were marble, the kitchen countertop white quartz, the appliances Wolf and Subzero. She knew that Vance didn't need this condo. He lived with his wife and two children in Montclair, New Jersey. But it saved him from having his wife notice hotel bills on his credit card statements, and from the risk of being recognized at various hotels around Manhattan.

As she lay uncovered on the mattress, wearing only the silver bracelet she never took off, with the sensation of him still warming her, she wondered if he'd ever taken others to this bed. And did it matter if he had?

Not to her.

Glancing around the room, she decided the architect and the general contractor had done a good job with the space. But she'd grown used to more space, to something larger. Having a huge space in Manhattan, as she did up on West Seventy-Third Street, communicated something much different than it did in the Midwest or the Southeast.

Ample space in Manhattan created not only jealousy, but awe. And she admitted to herself that she derived great satisfaction from that awe.

Vance returned to the bedroom carrying a glass filled with ice cubes and at least two inches of vodka. Sitting up, cross-legged, she took it from him and sipped.

He hadn't put on clothes or covered himself with a towel. He stood before her naked.

She didn't mind. He was handsome and had every attribute she thought a man should have, and then some. He'd gone to Yale for college and to Stanford for his MBA. He had the perpetual suntan of an avid golfer. But his pedigree hadn't made him ethical, and that was why she needed him.

He said, "Are we still at twenty percent for me, for Haddon House?"

She took another sip of the vodka before setting the glass on the night table to her left. "What about the usual fifteen percent?"

He smiled, but without warmth. "More for this project," he told her. "Because of the . . . difficulties."

She studied him for a moment. His flat stomach and the tuft of black hair around the part of him that had given her much pleasure. What was it that made her desire him so consistently and for so many years? She didn't know, and if he disappeared tomorrow, she'd find someone else. But as long as their time in this bedroom continued, she'd be generous. He hadn't been greedy about anything, ever. It was his family, not hers, that he risked by seeing her. For she had no family, not anymore. "All right," she said. "Twenty percent."

"Thank you, Stella."

"Sure."

He walked into the master bathroom, away from her view, and turned on the shower.

She reached for the glass of vodka and continued sipping the liquid that warmed her chest and stomach and helped her to relax, to take perspective and consider the deaths of others. She thought of the people who'd needed to die for the success of Cromwell Properties' projects. It was unfortunate, she'd be the first to admit, but wasn't accident and death the price for great works, great monuments? Workers had died building the pyramids at Giza, in Egypt. During construction of the Empire State Building, no? And the Eiffel Tower. Certainly, the Three Gorges Dam in China.

People shouldn't have opposed the greatness of her firm's projects, should have embraced those projects' permanence—as much as anything in the modern world could be considered permanent. Hadn't the holdouts brought misfortune upon themselves?

Yes, she thought. *On themselves.*

Work couldn't stop because a few people objected. That was the way of the world, and those who stood in its way were naive or stupid if they expected anything else.

The way of the world, she thought. She lay on her left side, facing the window and the darkness beyond the blinds, and rested the glass of vodka on the mattress.

She heard Vance turn off the shower and, a few moments later, come into the bedroom. She didn't turn to watch him put on his clothes. He didn't say anything to her, only left the bedroom, his shoes making a flat sound on the walnut floors, followed by the opening and closing of the door to the hallway outside and the elevator that would take him downstairs to the parking garage and the Lexus sedan that would return him to Cromwell Properties' offices. Her own car was waiting on the street outside, and she had the same destination. She'd work until ten or eleven, just as he would. She knew he'd then return here for a late dinner before driving out to Montclair and his family.

After climbing out of bed, she carried the empty glass to the kitchen, wiped it off with a damp paper towel, and set the glass in the dishwasher. She didn't shower. She dressed, made sure to take all her clothing and her earrings, and leave nothing. This, to avoid scandal, to show the world, if it cared, that theirs was a professional relationship. And in case she had to cut him off.

For her, self-preservation and survival were all. She'd warned Vance not explicitly but clearly—in her approach to business, by her references to a higher morality in which achievement outweighed ethics—that others might fall, others *would* fall, but she'd remain.

She'd been careful, and she was careful still. There were no connections between herself and any crimes. None that could be proven or even seen. The better part of her work wasn't the gleaming towers of steel, glass, and granite that rose into the sky, but her movements, almost imperceptible, in the shadows.

54

Buddy scanned the sidewalk in front of him and the cars on Eleventh Avenue to his left. He didn't see anyone following or waiting to attack. After the SUV had rammed him, he wouldn't chance a cab. So he walked to Eighth and descended into the subway. He went slowly, his right hand on the railing so he wouldn't lose his balance and tumble down the concrete stairs.

People jostled past him, elbowed him. He blinked, eyed everyone, but saw nobody who seemed out of place.

At the bottom of the stairs, he saw the E train about to leave. Knowing it would take him east where he could transfer, he jogged into the nearest car and sat in the back-left corner, giving himself a good view. He kept an eye on everyone who moved and everyone who didn't.

Two big guys in their twenties wearing black jeans, black jackets, and black boots held his attention. They noticed him but didn't move. He studied their faces and necks. *Too much fat,* he thought. Not like Tan Jacket. Not like the man who'd driven the SUV into his Charger. Those men had been big but strong. Leaner. Not only trained but trained recently. They moved like the athletes they were. *Military or paramilitary,* he thought again.

The train snaked deep underground, lurching to a stop every few minutes. He got off at Lexington and caught the 6 train. After a few minutes the rocking of the car grew monotonous. Buddy thought about Mei and Ben at the house in the country. He wondered if it was nice like Ward's place in Greenwich or more modest. He imagined himself arriving at a large house, taking them in his arms, listening to Ben describe their adventures, celebrating because Judge Miles had awarded custody of Ben to him and Mei. Until he caught himself.

He'd nodded off, his spine bent forward until he was nearly collapsing onto the floor. Instinctively, he reached through the folds of his overcoat and suit coat and put his right hand around the Glock. He scanned the car.

No visible threats. But also, no Mei and no custody of Ben.

The anxiety returned. He and Mei wouldn't be awarded custody of Ben. They'd lose him forever. There was nothing he could do to stop it. He made a fist with his left hand, his fingers and thumb tightening as he tried to squeeze the rising anger out of his body. Because he couldn't let it cripple him. Because Ben wouldn't return to the city until this case was handled.

Looking up, he studied the map above the windows.

Not long.

He didn't sleep again. Ten minutes later he exited at Eighty-Sixth Street and walked north two blocks and then east to the intersection with East End Avenue. There he saw the white-and-yellow guardhouse across the street.

Approaching the guardhouse from its left, he observed the closed iron gate between two thick posts of red brick. Taking his hands from his pockets, he held them easily at his sides and in plain view.

A guard walked out to meet him. The guard wore a pistol on his waistband and said, "May I help you?"

Buddy said, "I'm Detective Lock, with the NYPD. I'd like to see the mayor."

"You have an appointment?"

"No."

"I'm sorry, but the mayor's schedule is full."

Buddy said, "If the mayor's here, I don't need an appointment."

The guard hesitated, stared at him a moment. The guard's expression changed, softened.

He's recognized me, Buddy thought. *From television.*

The guard said, "Let me see your badge."

55

Buddy reached through the lapels of his overcoat and into the left breast pocket of his suit coat. He took out his badge wallet, opened it, and held it up for the guard to see.

Squinting at the ID, the guard nodded once. He said "Wait here," before returning to the guardhouse.

Buddy went over to the gate. He was going to put a hand on it but decided he didn't need to brace himself. The minute or two that he'd slept on the subway had eased his headache and vertigo, at least for a while.

Suddenly the gate swung inward, and the guard walked over to him.

The guard said, "Straight ahead. Security will meet you at the front door."

Buddy said, "Thanks, man."

But the guard had already turned away.

A few minutes later, Buddy was led by a squat female security guard into a sitting room. He knew Gracie Mansion was just that—a mansion—but this cozy wood-paneled space might have been owned by his grandmother. Wing chairs faced a sofa covered in amber fabric. A rug in blues and creams covered much of the oak floor. In the large fireplace with a gray marble mantel, a fire crackled and glowed orange and red with heat. By the fireplace stood Mayor Blenheim.

She wore black pants, a white shirt with a collar, and a finely knit black sweater. Not a strand of her light-brown-and-silver hair out of place, she seemed calm and at ease in the mansion. She gave him a warm smile. "Detective Lock, it's a pleasure."

He held up a hand. "I'm sorry for intruding, Mayor Blenheim."

"Oh, it's no trouble. None at all." She motioned toward the coffee table between the wing chairs and the sofa, where there were two silver pots. "Coffee or tea?" she asked.

He held up a hand. "Neither, thank you."

"Would you care to sit down?"

"Sure. Yeah." Buddy sat in one of the wing chairs but leaned forward, a hand on each thigh.

She relaxed into the sofa opposite him, crossing her legs and placing a hand on the armrest. "How may I help you?"

"I'm sorry for bothering you, Mayor. I thought I wouldn't have to take you up on your offer, especially not this soon. But I need help."

She tilted her head sideways. "What would you like me to do?"

He wasn't sure how to ask, how to phrase his request in the appropriate way. So he said it plainly. "Unless you put a word in for me with Chief Malone, I won't be able to do my job."

Her forehead grew lined. "Chief Malone is preventing you from doing your job?"

He said, "I'm investigating a couple—the Sungs—from Chinatown found in the water far off Long Island Sound. They were holdouts at a project that's going to replace the Nanjing building down on Hester Street. I'm trying to find out what happened to them." Buddy said nothing about the attempts on his and Mei's lives, keeping his rundown focused on the Sungs. "They got out in the Atlantic somehow," he concluded, "but it wasn't because they jumped or were pushed off a bridge close to land."

Mayor Blenheim uncrossed her legs and sat up straight. "It sounds like you're right, Detective. Why is Chief Malone resisting?"

Buddy said, "The case is 'solved.' Mr. Sung had terminal cancer. He and his wife were inseparable. They wrote a suicide note. It makes a kind of sense."

She lifted her chin and looked up at him. "But not to you?"

"No, ma'am. Not to me."

"I see."

He leaned forward. "I've got nowhere else to turn."

She watched him carefully. Silence filled the room.

He heard wood popping in the fireplace. He'd begun to sweat and wanted to take off his overcoat, but he didn't want to stand and interrupt her consideration of his request. He'd have to wait, even if he felt queasy in the hot room.

In a quiet voice, the mayor asked, "Why do you care so much?"

He turned back to her. "About the Sungs, you mean?"

"Yes, the Sungs."

He held his hands in front of him as if he were going to explain, before realizing it wasn't something he could tell anyone else. Not without offering the private details of his life. So he said, "It's the way I'm made."

She smiled. "Yes," she said, "I understand. You gave me a much better answer than some bullshit about wanting to help people or bring justice. You've been with the NYPD for too long to give me that answer."

He appreciated her thought, but then he wondered if she were cynical. He decided to push. "Why?" he asked her, "do *you* care about politics and the city?"

She didn't hesitate. "It's the way I'm made."

Their eyes met.

He said, "Thank you for your time, Mayor Blenheim."

She nodded. "No promises. But I'll make a call."

56

That night, Sloan Richardson couldn't breathe. She woke up, tried to open her mouth, tried to understand why she couldn't sit up.

A hand covered her mouth. The hand held her tightly.

Inhaling through her nose, she smelled the sweet scent of leather. A heavy weight pressed down on her chest.

What the fuck?

She kicked upward and then sideways, attempting to curl into a ball that would make restraining her more difficult, but only a moment later, she couldn't move. There were too many of them.

Several men, at least. She couldn't see well in the darkness of her bedroom. They moved around her, held her.

No, no, no!

They were going to rape her. All of them. One after the other. They had the power to pull her legs apart. She could do nothing. Nothing at all. And when they were finished with her, what then? Would they kill her?

She struggled again, tried to move, tried to kick. Now she tried to scream.

But it was no use.

She grew calm and tried to think. About what got her to a place where men invaded her home and held her on her bed half-naked.

Living in a nearly abandoned building—her mother had warned her against this very thing. She'd been stubborn, arrogant, ignorant.

Yet what she expected didn't happen. Her breasts were exposed, but none of the men had touched them. At first she didn't know why.

Then they brought her into a sitting position and put a black cloth over her head that covered her torso.

No!

A third time she struggled, but they held her tightly. She could feel the size of their hands and sense their strength. She gave up and was quiet.

They spoke in low voices about removing all her furniture and personal belongings and loading them into a truck on the street below. One man said, "Thirty minutes." This man seemed to be the leader, and she thought his accent was foreign.

A hard metal object rammed into the side of her head, and everything went blank.

57

In the night, Mei woke and sat up. The faint moonlight against the closed blinds showed the contours of the large bedroom.

She could hear Ben's rhythmic breathing from the sofa across the room. Her stomach burned, and she realized she was hungry.

Careful not to wake him, she padded out to the house's main room and switched on the lights. In the kitchen, she cut up a melon, poured a bowl of muesli, and added milk from the refrigerator. For a while she stood there, eating, not really thinking about anything, except that she'd had enough of this house, where she didn't have Buddy or any of her books or clothes. She had confidence in Buddy and knew he could solve the case. Or she hoped he could. He'd often told her about unsolved cases, cold cases that went for years and sometimes an eternity without being solved.

This is the last time, she thought. *The last time Ben and I hide.*

After going over to her laptop on the sofa, she opened the screen. When it didn't light up, she remembered she'd forgotten the right charger.

She walked over to the table and opened Ben's computer. Moving the cursor via the glide pad, she intended to close the text conversation on the screen. She wanted to read the *Gazette*'s headlines and check her email account to see if any galleries had responded to her job applications. Something caught her eye in a text Ben had sent to another cell number, presumably to one of his classmates.

Worry enveloped her. She put an arm across her chest.

In the text, Ben had given out their location. Not the exact house number or even the name of the owner, but its location near Rockridge and that it was owned by a friend of hers. Ben didn't know the name of Jessica's boyfriend, Mei realized with relief.

She leaned in closer. The text had gone to a number and the initials A. B.

No, she thought, *I'm being paranoid.* A. B. must be a classmate. And why would anyone at Ben's school care if they were a couple hours outside the city? They wouldn't. Not when many of his classmates were the children of movie stars who took them to glamorous locations all over the world. On the other hand . . .

She thought for a moment and decided she wanted to be sure.

She texted A. B. Who is this?

For several minutes she waited. The clock on the upper right of the computer screen read 2:43 a.m.

Still no response.

As she'd intended, she went into her email account, but there were no responses from galleries. Then she went to the *Gazette* website and read the headlines. A massacre in Syria. A drought in Texas. A budget showdown in Washington, DC. She skimmed all the stories, not so much interested as filling time.

She stopped reading when she heard the distinctive chime. A new text had arrived and appeared in a bubble on the right side of the screen.

The new text was a reply to her text. It read: Duh!

Mei closed the laptop. She walked into the kitchen and then returned to the computer but didn't open it. What should she do? What *could* she do? Her text might have awakened a ten-year-old boy in Manhattan, who'd typed a snarky reply. Or her text might have been received by someone who meant to pursue them.

She hugged herself and turned around. She went to the door and confirmed that both locks were set. She walked over to the kitchen window and looked out but saw only blackness, not even stars.

58

Sloan Richardson shivered in the cold. Not just shivered but shuddered. The men hadn't put clothing on her, and she was outside, where the temperature was far below freezing, maybe below zero. She also knew she was sitting in a chair—a chair that was moving.

She couldn't see anything because of the black hood over her head. She didn't how long she'd been unconscious or if it was night or day. She tried to shift her weight and move, but she couldn't. Her legs were tied to the chair or in some way restrained, a rope or cord around her upper arms. Mentally, she studied every inch of her body. Even with limited movement, she knew she hadn't been raped. This fact gave her relief. Until she realized that if they didn't want to have sex with her, they wanted something else.

Hearing the roar of a loud engine, she grew confused. She couldn't identify the kind of machine that made the sound. Not at first.

She thought it could be from a truck or a boat. She sensed that it *mattered*.

But she knew one thing for certain: this wasn't a random assault.

The chair stopped moving. She was set down on a hard surface. Her bare feet touched it, and the icy cold shot up through the bottoms of her feet.

Ahhhh!

As she raised her feet, giving them some relief, something was placed in her right hand.

Holding it, she recognized a pen.

She heard a man's voice, the same man who'd given orders to the others inside her bedroom. He said, "Miss Richardson, I'd like you to sign a document for me. A deed for unit 309 in the Nanjing building. In return, you'll receive fair market value, wired to your account within three days."

Angry despite her disorientation, she threw the pen aside. "Fuck you!" she shouted.

Something hard and heavy crashed into her right knee. The force seemed to come from a great height and blow apart her knee.

Ah! Oh, my God.

She tried to double up in pain, but she couldn't move. She heard herself crying.

Another blow fell, this time on her left knee.

She screamed. She wept loudly, tears running down her face. She closed her eyes and struggled to move her legs, to give her knees some solace, but the pain didn't lessen. She tried to get away from them, from the chair, from the men, but she couldn't move. There was no escape. After a moment she sat quietly, crying, wanting to be somewhere safe where the men couldn't get her.

"Miss Richardson?" It was the man's voice again.

And once again she noticed his unusual accent, but she still couldn't place it. She moved her covered head around, trying to turn in the direction of the voice. It seemed to be coming from her right side.

"Please, Miss Richardson, put your signature on the deed. I'd rather not hurt you again, you see."

She felt a paper slide under her hand. Its normality comforted her. The pen was threaded through her fingers again. Writing her name was something she'd done thousands of times before.

Considering her situation, she held the pen over the paper. What other option did she have?

She signed her name.

And then she was taken toward the loud engine. As it drew near, she realized the sound didn't come from a car or truck, a boat or the jet engine of an airplane.

Closer, closer, and it became more defined.

Now, when the roar grew deafening, she recognized it at last.

She grew frenzied. Struggling against the restraints, she jerked her head left and right, forward and backward. She leaned this way and that, trying but failing to tip over the chair. She screamed. She called for help.

But in the all-engulfing noise, nobody heard.

59

At two o'clock in the morning, the door to Vance McInnis's condo opened. A dark-clad figure stepped inside and closed the door.

The figure wore a black knit hat and black leather gloves and carried a nylon messenger bag.

After setting the bag on the kitchen counter, the figure unclipped the flap and removed surface cleanser with a high alcohol content, and eight microfiber cloths. Then the figure began spraying the countertop and all the door pulls, the faucet handle, the refrigerator and freezer doors and handles, and inside the refrigerator and freezer, the surfaces, bottles, and racks. Next came the dishwasher, outside, handle, inside, all glasses, utensils, plates, and bowls in the racks.

But first, using polyethylene tape, the figure removed prints from a single drinking glass in the bathroom, then set the tape inside a plastic case and put the case in the messenger bag.

The figure moved methodically, with great care and without hurry. The kitchen was the first room, then the master bedroom and the master bath.

All surfaces. Anything that had been touched or might have been touched. Because it wouldn't be long before a CSU team examined this condominium. This was nearly certain, for an order had been given.

From one of the pillows on the king-sized bed, the figure removed two strands of hair. Short hair, dark, that of the man who at times slept here.

Then the figure stripped the king-sized bed, not only the flat sheet with the damp circle in the center, but also the pillowcases, the white cotton blanket, the duvet cover, and the mattress pad. After carrying these to the small laundry room between the master bedroom and the smaller bedroom, the figure put the white linens, the duvet cover, and the mattress pad in the washing machine, added detergent and double the amount of bleach recommended, and switched on the machine.

The figure returned to the master bedroom, cleaned it thoroughly, and continued on to the master bathroom. Later, the figure applied the cleaning solution and microfiber cloths to the surfaces of the second bedroom that Vance McInnis used as an office. Then the smaller bathroom, followed by the living room and the laundry room itself. The figure took the vacuum from the closet in the laundry room and went over the carpeting in the bedroom and office. Later, after four o'clock in the morning, the figure took the mop and bucket from the laundry room, added hot water and a splash of ammonia, and cleaned all the wood floors.

Afterward, the water now only lukewarm and gray with dirt, dust, a few dead spiders, and other bugs, the figure dumped the bucket out in the laundry-room sink, set it on the floor and the mop in the bucket. The job was finished. It was nearly five in the morning.

The figure stood by the door to the hallway and the elevator, wiping down the locks on the door and the handle. After opening the door and stepping out into the corridor, the figure wiped down the exterior door handle, the lock, and the surface around it, as well as the entire surface of the door between six feet high and three feet high where someone might have touched the door to hold it open or to close it.

The figure closed the door, tucked the cleaning solution and the last microfiber cloth in the messenger bag, removed the vacuum bag and wiped down the machine, and, still wearing gloves, pressed the button for the elevator.

DAY 4

60

Chief Malone rose from behind his large desk, glaring at Buddy. He walked around the room like a wild animal, ready to kill, and slammed his office door. He faced Buddy, his forehead red with anger. "You talked to the *mayor*?" Malone shouted, his voice as big as he was. "After I gave you a fucking medal, you went over my head?"

Buddy didn't respond. When he'd woken up that morning, he'd felt his old energy return, his old confidence. Malone wasn't going to force him to back down. Not today.

Malone opened his arms wide. "After you screwed me, you've got nothing to say? *Nothing at all?*"

Buddy said, "I want to finish the job."

Malone's enormous eyes widened. Sweat formed at his temples. "Yeah, Buddy, you finish it. You can work the Sung case—their *suicide*—for another week. But"—he pointed a thick finger at Buddy—"you're doing it alone. Alone. Because I'm not going to waste Mingo's time or any other department resources. None. Got it?"

Buddy said, "I understand."

"Yeah?" Malone shook his head slowly. "I'm not sure you do. Understand. So let me lay it out for you. I expedited getting you back on the force. I let you work the suicides from *Long Island*—Jesus, I should have said no—and this is how you treat me? After I did you two big favors?"

Buddy thought about Malone's reaction, and decided it was typical. He'd expected it. Mostly. And this gave him some comfort. But he wasn't certain of Malone. It seemed pretty strange that soon after he'd told Malone about the bodies Mack Berringer had discovered off Long Island, someone had nearly killed him.

Coincidence? Maybe.

But maybe not.

Malone might be dirty, Buddy thought. *The chief might have betrayed me, sacrificed me for . . . what?*

He considered subterfuge, but it was too late for games. He'd play it straight up, at least with Malone. After this meeting, he wouldn't tell the chief a damned thing.

Buddy went to the door and opened it. Before he left, he said, "There's something there, Chief. And thank you."

Chief Malone laughed angrily. "I'll see you in seven days, when you'll have to work for real. And fuck you!"

61

Mei climbed soundlessly out of bed and looked over at Ben. His chest rose and fell under the duvet spread over him on the sofa.

She thought about the text she'd received—or Ben had received—from A. B. around two thirty that morning. Had it truly been from a ten-year-old boy? If the text had been from someone else, should they leave the house Jessica had lent her?

She didn't know where else to go. If they moved to a hotel, she'd have to use a credit card because she'd soon run out of cash. And even if she'd had enough cash, she'd have to use her ID to register at a hotel. Either way, Ben's resourceful aunt and uncle could track her and show Judge Miles that she'd violated the court order and taken Ben out of New York City—a black mark against her bid for continued custody of the boy she loved.

She could think of no solution, except to be cautious, to be prepared, to be ready to fight, if necessary.

Wearing lightweight pajama bottoms and a soft T-shirt, she took the gun in its case from the closet's top shelf, together with the box of ammunition from her duffel bag on the floor. Again, she glanced at Ben.

Still asleep.

She hurried from the room and out into the kitchen. Unzipping the case, she withdrew the revolver. As Ward had shown her a couple of weeks ago, she released the cylinder and saw that only two bullets remained. Squinting, she peered along the barrel and saw that it was clear.

Hands shaking slightly, she opened the box and inserted four bullets into the cylinder. Then she clicked the cylinder into place and looked over the room.

Where to put it?

Close, so she could get it if she needed it.

But not somewhere Ben could see.

A cupboard?

No. If I'm cornered, I won't have time to go into a cupboard.

The refrigerator. The top of the refrigerator.

She set it there, pushed it back a little, and then set the box of Triscuits and a box of granola in front of it.

I can get it there, she thought, *if I need it.*

62

Buddy stood in the lobby of One Police Plaza, but sensed that he was on melting ice. Everything was getting hotter, and he was about to fall through. He pulled out his phone and dialed.

"Hello?" It was the female voice he'd expected.

"I don't have access to your floor, so I'm downstairs," he said. "Did you check the video?"

She said, "Not on the phone. Stay where you are."

Three minutes later, Rachel Grove strode through the lobby. She wore a pair of snug black pants and a sky-blue shirt. Her heels clicked across the stone floor.

She got close to him, almost too close. She smelled like mint.

In a low voice, she said, "Malone left at six ten p.m. that night."

That must be it, he thought. *Malone called Tan Jacket. Malone has power and resources. He knew where I was and when. The chief's being dirty would explain a hell of a lot. But how does Mingo fit into the scheme?*

Yet Buddy wasn't sure it had been Malone. He knew that even if Malone had left the building at 6:10, someone else might have had access to his desk or Alicia Bravo's desk. Malone might have been in a meeting on a different floor. He didn't know how to ascertain the chief's whereabouts without broadcasting what he was doing. Being caught investigating the chief of detectives would end his career, unless he had proof Malone was dirty. And right now, he had nothing.

Rachel said, "What's this about? This phone number? This call?"

Buddy looked her in the eye and shook his head. "I don't want you involved."

She laughed lightly and smiled. "But I am involved."

"Not like I am," he told her, stepping back. "You've done enough. And Rachel?"

"Yes, Buddy?"

"Thanks. I mean it."

"You're welcome. And I mean that."

63

Fifteen minutes after Ben woke up, Mei ushered him out of the house on the bluff. They climbed into the Audi and headed down the serpentine road to Rockridge. She stomped on the accelerator. "What is it?" Ben asked, his right hand gripping the passenger door handle as the SUV shot down the hill. "Why are you going so fast?" She didn't respond but focused on the road. Yet she felt his startled gaze on her.

"Mei? What's wrong?"

"Your texts," she said. "Your school texts. With one of your friends."

He shook his head. "I don't understand. Which friend?"

"A. B.," she said. "Who is A. B.?"

"Alan Blackman. He's in my class. Why?"

Mei hesitated. Was she being irrational? Had the texts in which Ben had told A. B. approximately where they were staying been an innocent exchange? She couldn't decide how to know for sure. She didn't trust her instincts. "I'm sorry for looking at your texts," she began. "I woke up in the night and wanted to check my email on your computer, and I saw the text conversation up on your screen. I texted the person who'd asked you where we're staying for his name. He replied right away—at almost three o'clock in the morning!"

She looked over at him. His expression was one of disbelief.

He said, "Mei, it's fine. Alan's parents let him sleep with his phone. It's on his *pillow*. You woke him up and he thought you were me, being stupid."

"Don't respond to any texts, no matter who they're from," she warned. "Okay?"

He said nothing but raised his left wrist and began looking at his new watch.

She reached over and touched his chest. "Ben?" she asked. "I'm serious about this. No texting, all right?"

At last he turned to her. "All right. I won't."

"Not to anyone."

"I *know*. I won't."

He was quiet until she turned onto Main Street. Then he said, "So why are we here in town again? Wouldn't it be safer to stay at the house?"

"We're going," she told him, "to the hardware store."

He tilted his head, puzzled. "But why?"

She pulled the car along the curb in front of the hardware store, put the car in park, and switched off the engine. After taking off her seat belt, she rotated in her seat until she was facing him. She touched his arm and said, "Buddy isn't here, but if he were, wouldn't he say that we should protect ourselves? Just in case?"

Ben nodded. "Did you bring the gun? The one Ward gave you?"

"Yes, I brought the gun."

Ben looked down and studied her jacket. "Is it here, in the car?"

"No, it's at the house. But I want to do what Buddy would do. So we'll check out the hardware store and see if we can find something. Okay?"

Ben stared at her, uncertainty in his eyes.

Inside the small store, they walked through the short aisles, the shelving on either side of them reaching to twelve or fourteen feet. The selection was good for a store in a town this small.

Mei wandered, unsure of her goal. At one of the shelving end caps, she saw a display of gloves, and she looked down at the pair she held in her hand. They were shearling gloves, soft on the inside and the outside. Good for warmth and style, but not so good for gripping something. In the display, she found Wells Lamont lined work gloves in bright-yellow leather. After tucking her shearling gloves in the side pocket of her parka, she took down the work gloves, size small, and tried them on.

A little big for her, but they fit well enough.

Well enough for what? she asked herself.

Ben tried on a pair of the same gloves, same size. He looked up at her and said, "May I get some, too?"

"Yes," she told him, although his black North Face gloves were more than adequate. She walked down the store's main aisle. Lights on motion sensors would be helpful, but she and Ben had discovered on arriving that the house was equipped with at least two of these. Seeing a display of axes and hatchets, she turned away. She knew she wasn't strong enough to fight anyone with one of these, and they reminded her of terrible times in the past. God knew how Ben felt when he saw them. Realizing from his melancholy face that his thoughts were aligned with hers, she leaned over and kissed the top of his head.

To the right of the checkout, she saw, beneath a polished glass counter, a display of knives, their metal tips shiny against a spread of green baize. Hunting knives, pocketknives, carving knives for—what, eviscerating a deer? And other knives whose purpose she couldn't guess. She began to move toward the checkout, and then stopped and turned around.

I'm not strong, she thought. *But I can hide things. I can convince someone I'm not a threat, even when I am.*

She glanced at Ben, who was watching her. His eyes met hers before dropping to the shiny knives.

The older man behind the checkout counter sidled up to the other side of the case. He had gray hair, a hearing aid in his right ear, and silver-rimmed eyeglasses. He didn't smile at her, but his blue eyes were friendly. "Interested in a knife?" he asked in a rasping voice.

"Yes," Mei told him. "I'd like a pocketknife. Maybe the one here." She placed an index finger on the glass and pointed downward.

From an opening behind the counter, he reached in and touched a pocketknife with a smooth black grip. "This one, ma'am?"

She nodded.

His hands took hold of it. He straightened, closed the blade, and handed it across the counter to her.

The knife's heaviness surprised her. It was compact, and yet it must also be strong. She turned it sideways and put her left fingernail in the groove where the blade peeked out of the grip and pulled on it.

The blade emerged and clicked into place.

She turned it in the light and moved it from one hand to the other.

The man said, "Any particular use for the knife?"

"For this and that," she told him.

Ben said, "Can I see it?"

Carefully, she handed it to Ben, the blade still out.

He held it, put it in one hand, his right. His expression brightened. "I'd like this knife."

She caught herself. As in the case of the yellow leather gloves, she wasn't going to say no. *It can't hurt,* she thought, *for him to have a pocketknife. Not as long as we're living in that house.*

"Only the one?" the older man asked.

She said, "Do you have another?"

"Yes. Would you like two?"

"Yes, please." Then she turned to Ben. "You have to be careful with this knife, okay?"

"I *know.* I won't use it. I just want it."

A few minutes later they climbed into the Audi. Ben put his new gloves on his lap and then opened and closed his new pocketknife.

She put her new gloves in the pocket of the driver's door and slipped her knife down into her right boot.

For a minute or two, the knife felt cool and strange. But then it warmed, and she hardly noticed it. Yet its presence gave her confidence.

64

Buddy pressed the buzzer and waited.

"Hello?" came the voice.

"It's Detective Lock."

"Please come up. I'm on the tenth floor."

The door buzzed. He pulled it open and entered the small lobby. There was no doorman. He saw only limited furniture: four small black chairs, a wooden coffee table. The walls were white and contained abstract art. The floors were plain white stone. An understated but expensive condo building. He was in Chelsea on Twenty-First Street, near many art galleries, with the east side of the building along the High Line.

Buddy walked into the elevator and pushed the button for the tenth floor. A few moments later the door opened into a spacious foyer. Standing before him was Leo Sung. Buddy said, "Good morning, Mr. Sung. Thank you for meeting me."

"Of course. Please come in." Leo motioned him into the enormous great room.

Buddy glanced at the high ceilings. He estimated they were fourteen feet high, the same as in Mei's place. Just as in the lobby, expensive-looking contemporary art hung on the walls. One large abstract canvas. One photograph of a naked man wearing nothing but a wolf mask and stiletto heels. A third painting of a seascape with nude bathers of both genders. Gray leather furniture. Along one wall, floor-to-ceiling bookshelves, completely full. Enormous windows. Buddy knew this condo must be worth at least $10 million.

Leo pressed a button on a fancy coffee machine in the kitchen. "Coffee?" he asked.

Buddy said, "Yeah. Thanks."

He stood by one of the chairs as Leo operated the machine, a stainless-steel miracle that made a low noise before dispensing the coffee. Buddy thought the machine must be grinding the beans, but he couldn't be sure.

Buddy said, "You didn't tell me anything when I met with you and your brother and sister."

Leo's face colored. At first he didn't respond, only took two perfectly white cups and handed one to Buddy. Then Leo said, "Let's sit down."

Buddy took the chair facing the sofa, where Leo had sat. Buddy waited, allowing silence to fill the large room. He sipped his coffee. It was strong and full flavored. He liked it, but not enough to buy a machine that probably cost as much as a small car. He leaned forward and set the cup on the glass coffee table. He took his notebook and a pen out and looked up at Leo, waiting.

Leo drank his coffee, then set his cup down, too. He leaned back into the sofa and said, "I didn't tell you anything because I don't know anything."

Buddy remained silent.

Leo watched him.

Buddy said, "But you *think* something. You *suspect* something."

Leo nodded. "I'm younger than my brother and sister, and when I was a boy, my parents were tired of teaching *hanzi*, and I didn't want to learn. So on my parents' suicide note, I don't know if the signatures are theirs or not."

Buddy said, "You don't trust your brother or sister to recognize the signatures for you?"

Instead of answering, Leo said, "My father was sick, yes, but my mother told me only a month ago that she'd never leave me." Slowly, Leo shook his head. "I don't think she killed herself."

Buddy thought for a moment. He silently compared the modest condo of Leo's parents with Leo's home. He said, "How much were your parents paid for their unit?"

"Five million dollars."

Buddy made a note and asked, "To be divided equally between you and your brother and sister?"

Leo nodded.

Buddy glanced around the room, couldn't help but see the large photograph of the naked man wearing the mask. *Why put that in your living room?* he wondered. He said, "But you don't need the money."

A statement rather than question.

Leo said, "No. I have enough."

"What about your brother and sister. Do they have enough?"

Leo said, "They need the money. I've helped them in the past."

Buddy pressed, "What do they need money *for?*"

"My sister, for her children's tuition and peace of mind. She doesn't have expensive tastes. My brother, for a place to live. He's renting and can barely afford it. He's told me he's reserved a condo in Haddon House, and since he grew up on the site, I guess Wang knows and likes the location. He's a bit of an asshole."

Buddy thought Wang had made a deal. The possible murder of his parents might or might not have been part of it. He said, "Do you know who was pressuring your parents? Or your brother?"

Leo got up and went into the kitchen. Buddy watched the younger man flip through some papers on the counter. Leo picked up a business card, returned, and handed it to Buddy.

The card read: "Vance McInnis, Vice President of Development, Cromwell Properties."

65

Later that afternoon, Mei heard a noise and looked out the windows of the great room. She saw woods and snow-covered farms spread over the rolling hills below, and a single car coming up the winding drive to the house.

Immediately she went to the door and set the dead bolt. Ben watched from the sofa.

Mei said, "Someone's coming."

Ben got up and came over to her.

They stood together by the window to the right of the door.

The car was small—not an SUV. A coupe, sporty and jet-black.

Ben said, "It's a BMW, a three series. The new body style that looks like a shark."

Which doesn't belong here, Mei thought. *Not in this town at this time of year.* A chill slid into her chest.

She backed away from the window, turned, and hurried into the kitchen. One glance told her the revolver remained on top of the refrigerator.

Not yet, she thought. *Not until I'm sure we're in danger.*

Her eyes scanned the counter. There it was, right where she'd left it. Her new pocketknife.

She grabbed it. As she returned to the window and Ben, she opened the blade.

The black car made the final turn toward the house. Under the gray clouds, the car's headlights were on and shining at the door and the window beside it.

Mei squinted, trying to see the driver of the car, but the overcast sky impaired her vision, and large sunglasses obscured the driver's face.

They waited. The small house was silent.

Mei gripped the knife. There was nowhere to run and no escape. She'd fight if she had to. She'd kill to keep Ben alive. He was her son, no matter how Judge Miles ruled.

They watched the small black car slow and stop. The driver's door opened.

Out of the car stepped a tall woman with long blond hair.

"Thank God," Mei said.

"Who is it?" Ben asked.

66

Mei unlocked the door and pulled it open. "Jessica!" she called. "Thank God it's you!"

Her now-former coworker from Porter Gallery smiled but then frowned and pointed. "What's with the knife?"

Thirty minutes later, the three of them went on a hike. Jessica wanted to show them the view from the top of the bluff and at the bottom of the ravine on the other side, where there was a walking path beside a stream. Mei and Ben wanted to get out of the house. In her delight at seeing Jessica and the prospect of vigorous exercise, she wasn't thinking of danger.

Ben had put on boots as well, but he had left his pocketknife on the kitchen counter. He also wore the new yellow work gloves Mei had bought him at the hardware store.

Mei asked him, "Is your leg well enough to do this?"

"Yes."

"Are you sure? We could watch a movie instead."

His eyes had filled with light. "I'm okay. I'm going."

Mei wore her black hiking boots, her Moncler parka, and her yellow work gloves. She'd folded her new pocketknife and slid it into her right boot between the leather tongue and the lacing. It was held there, immobile and almost invisible, the black plastic grip camouflaged by the boot's black leather. Jessica looked stylish in dark-blue jeans, a puffy white parka with a hood trimmed in sable, and Vuarnet glacier glasses with leather sides to prevent peripheral glare. They set out up the hill toward the ridge above the valley.

Having taken this route before, Jessica went first, followed by Ben and then Mei.

Ben said, "What about the coyote? What if he sees us?"

Jessica turned and looked back at him. She said, "He stays away from hikers. But if he gets too close, I'll kick him all the way to Rockridge."

Ben said, "He won't bite you?"

Jessica stopped and raised one of her heavy Sorel boots. "Sure, if he wants this down his throat."

Ben smiled.

Jessica continued leading them up toward the ridge and farther and farther away from the house.

67

Buddy put on latex gloves and took out his set of lockpicks. In the unlit corridor on the third floor of the Nanjing building, he crouched down and began working the lock on S. Richardson's door. He'd had Mario check the address and unit number and learned her first name.

It was Sloan. Sloan Richardson, the young woman in her twenties he'd spoken to the day before. He recalled seeing her as he'd stood outside Chen and Lily Sung's door not forty feet from here. Her winter clothes, fashionable boots, her glossy brown hair, and clear complexion. A beautiful young woman.

He felt the last pin rise, the lock draw back. Standing, he put his pick and tension wrench into a small nylon case that he zipped shut and dropped in the right side pocket of his suit coat, and opened the door.

The rooms were dim, the curtains drawn and blocking most of the afternoon's gray light.

He entered the foyer, flicked the switch by the door, and the recessed lights in the ceiling came on.

He stood without moving.

The room beyond was barren of furniture, and the old oak floors had no rugs covering them. He walked into the other rooms: kitchen, formal dining room, two bedrooms, and a bathroom. This was a very large space in Manhattan, especially for one person.

He found nothing personal to Sloan Richardson, nothing that would tie this home to its inhabitant.

Not so much as a toothbrush. Only a single knit ski hat, dust, paper clips, a yellow broom, and a hairbrush.

No sign of violence. No sign of anything. It was like being in a vacant warehouse.

As he took out his phone and dialed, he felt as if he'd been kicked in the stomach. *Damn it,* he thought. *I'm too fucking late.*

68

Ward sat in the front passenger seat of Brick's Tesla, watching someone. Brick had a hand on the wheel, but they weren't moving.

When Ward's phone rang, he checked the screen and answered. "Buddy?"

"Yeah." His brother's voice, softer than usual.

Ward said, "You okay?"

"Not really."

"What do you mean?"

Buddy didn't answer, but Ward could hear his breathing.

After a moment, Buddy asked, "Would you call your Swiss banker and ask him if there's been another deposit in Mario's account?"

"Did something happen?"

"Later," Buddy said, ending the call.

Ward sat quietly, studying the entrance to the building into which the man had walked. He was more than a block away and hoped he hadn't missed anything. In the weak winter light, anything was possible.

After dialing the number, Ward held the phone to his ear.

"Zurich Cantonal Bank, Helmut Borer speaking."

Ward looked at his enormous watch and calculated the time in Switzerland. "Good evening, Helmut. I have a favor to ask of you."

Hearing only silence on the line, Ward continued, "I need you to check Mario Mingo's account once more."

"Mr. Mills," Helmut Borer began. "This is highly irregular. I—"

"Must I bring up the excellent service that Credit Suisse has offered me?"

More silence on the other end of the line.

Ward could picture the pale-faced banker's narrow lips pressed together in anger. He hung up, set the phone on the car's dashboard, and stared at the building entrance. He turned to Brick. "Did we miss him?"

Brick's blond hair covered part of his face, but Ward could see the former surfer's eyes were focused on the building. "No," Brick said, "he's in there."

69

Sloan Richardson's life, wiped clean.

Much too clean, Buddy thought. *And too fast.*

He believed that yesterday when he'd seen Sloan Richardson in the hallway, these rooms had held furniture, rugs, paintings or posters on the walls, dishes and utensils in the sink, food in the refrigerator, bottles of wine or beer, personal effects in the bathrooms, a computer. Someone had cleaned it out, and in a hurry.

A killer.

Or someone who could order killers to take the life of a young woman who'd done nothing except prevent others from getting their hands on millions of dollars. Sloan Richardson, he reminded himself, had been the last holdout at the Nanjing building.

The falling value of human life, Buddy thought angrily.

He returned to the living room, opened the blinds, and turned around. The space was as empty in natural light. Striding to the doorway to leave, he caught himself.

No, not yet.

He'd gone as far as most would go, but he was patient. He knew that if the medical examiner ruled Sloan Richardson's death the result of murder, a crime scene unit would be here in no time. But he doubted they'd find anything. The cleaner had been a pro.

But that didn't mean *he* wouldn't find something. He saw things others, even CSU teams, didn't.

Maybe, he thought. *Maybe.*

He turned and started going through the condo a second time, beginning in the smallest bedroom. He opened the blinds and examined the walls, the ceiling, the oak floorboards, the space between the radiator and the wall. He checked the closet, running his hands across the shelves. Finding nothing but wire hangers, a belt, and a pair of Doc Martens, he proceeded to the bathroom. He rechecked the cabinets, the mirror that swung open and doubled as a medicine cabinet. But there was nothing. He moved on to the master bedroom.

He opened the blinds, walked across every floorboard, even bending over and pressing on them where they were coming apart slightly in the dry winter air. But they held fast. He went into the closet and checked every built-in shelf. He found nothing. He looked up at the ceiling, walking back and forth across the room, but there was no water damage and no displaced or discolored plaster. It was evenly white. He checked the walls. A few minor nicks. Small holes in the center of most of the walls, evidence of picture hangers. The paintings or posters hadn't been in place long enough to show a difference in the color of the walls where they'd hung. Below the window stood the radiator.

Unlike the radiators in the other rooms, this one was covered by a wooden box enameled in white. He stood over it, arching his neck to see behind the box, but it was flush against the wall. He moved left and right, to see if there was a gap between the box and the wall at either end, but he saw no gap. Crouching down, he gripped the sides of the box and pulled. It held fast. Somehow, he knew, the iron radiator had to be connected to the building's heating system via a pipe that ran under the floor or in the wall. That pipe had to be accessible to the super or a plumber to bleed off any excess air in the pipes. He guessed the pipe would be on the left side of the box, and he sat on the floor there and studied the box. A faint line showed the border of a side panel.

Reaching out, he worked his fingertips around the panel's edges and pulled until it came free.

As he set the panel to the side and looked through the opening, he saw the dull glimmer of iron poured long ago that must be filled with more than a half century of sediment. Yet the radiator still worked. He could feel the heat emanating from the piping. And hidden to the left of the iron, flat against the oak floor, lay a white envelope.

70

With his latex gloves, Buddy picked up the envelope carefully. He examined it. The back flap was unsealed. No writing marred its crisp exterior. He turned up the back flap and peered inside.

He saw two pieces of paper. Or rather, one piece of paper, folded, and one small photograph.

He removed the photograph first. It was the color image of a baby, perhaps six months old, perhaps slightly less. The baby was fat and smiling and pretty, and wore a pink dress with ruffles down the front. She had dark eyes, light-brown hair, and chubby bare feet. A woman in a lime-green skirt or dress and also barefoot held up the child's arms so the baby could stand on an Oriental rug that was green and black. He stared at the rug, thinking he'd recently seen one like it. But then he noticed that around the woman's right wrist was a distinctive silver bracelet. Continuing to search the image, he saw that the woman's legs above the knee, and all other parts of her, were beyond the frame. The remaining details of the photograph were blurry. Buddy turned it over.

On the back, in cursive and in blue ink, were the words: *Sloan, five months.*

Buddy dropped the photograph into the envelope and took out the folded piece of paper, which was smaller than letter-sized. When he unfolded it, he recognized it immediately.

It was a birth certificate, noting the birth of a baby named Sloan Richardson on March 2, 1992. The certificate listed the father as Arthur Paul Richardson and the mother as Susan Chapman Richardson. It listed the baby's place of birth as New York City. Nothing unusual there. Except there was a blank. There wasn't anything written in the field for the name of the hospital where the baby was born. *Maybe,* Buddy thought, *the baby was born at home. Or in a cab. Did it matter?*

And yet the blank put him on alert. He studied the certificate carefully. He reviewed the birth date: March 2, 1992. He saw the date of the certificate: September 18, 1992. That seemed strange to him.

Sloan Richardson's birth certificate had been issued more than six months after her birth.

Buddy stared at the certificate. Then he looked again at the photograph, and the writing on the back of it: *Sloan, five months.*

She must have been adopted, Buddy thought. And this photograph might be the only one showing Sloan and her biological mother. Sloan had this information, and she wanted to know more.

If he had it right. If his guess was correct.

Which it might not be.

But if it were, he wondered if Sloan Richardson had been born to a New Yorker before her adoptive parents had taken her to California. Perhaps she'd grown up there, as Lin Wong had told him, and finally returned to New York as a young woman in search of her biological mother. Buddy wondered if Sloan had found her mother, had met and spoken with her. He wondered how that conversation had gone.

He considered another possibility: Sloan hadn't found her mother and at the time of her death had still hoped to find her.

He took out his phone and called Mario. When his partner answered, Buddy said, "Hey, would you check on a woman named Sloan Richardson? Early or midtwenties, lived in the Nanjing building, from somewhere in California?"

"I don't know, Buddy. Didn't Malone give orders not to help with this suicide case?"

The question annoyed Buddy, although he knew he was working alone. He said, "You got something else to do?"

"Ah, yeah, I do. *Homicides.*"

Buddy thought for a moment. Then he said, "Can you help me?"

Very slowly, Mario replied, "Chief Malone ordered me not to. He said you've got to stop working this shit. I mean, *Jesus,* Buddy. Get with the program."

Buddy paused to learn if partnership meant anything to Mario.

After a moment, Mario said, "A few more days and we'll be working together, right?"

Buddy hung up.

After using his phone to take photographs of the birth certificate and the baby picture, he replaced them in the envelope. He'd take the envelope with him and leave it with Henry Lee at the restaurant around the corner.

The safest place for it, he thought. *Until I know who I can trust.*

Standing, he considered the situation. The birth certificate. The photograph.

He assumed that Sloan Richardson's search had been cut short, had failed. Her search probably had nothing to do with the deaths of the Sungs or with her own death. But it was important to him that the young woman had wanted something badly, that she'd been trying to learn where she came from. Sloan Richardson had wanted to make a connection to her mother or father. Yet it seemed likely that she'd been murdered before she could make that connection. If her biological parents were living, they'd probably never met her as an adult and she'd remain forever lost to them. She'd reached out a hand into darkness, but no hand had taken hers.

Buddy stared at the floor, imagining a young woman approaching her mother or father, introducing herself, asking—perhaps begging—to talk with them, to hear their voices, to feel their embrace. To regain what she'd lost so long ago, in a reunion fraught with emotion, regret, and recrimination but also, just maybe, forgiveness.

But what if the meeting had taken place? What if, in some odd way, her death had resulted from that meeting?

He looked at the blank wall and listened to himself breathing. He shook his head and yearned for a drink. A deep sadness surrounded him as he left the silent rooms.

71

Buddy closed the door to Sloan Richardson's condo and returned to the stairs. He climbed up one level to the roof and walked outside. The cold hit him at once, and he buttoned his coat. He noticed the Nanjing building was lower than the new buildings. Not enough units for the land value, he understood. A taller building would yield more units, which would yield more money for the developer, Cromwell Properties. Cromwell would be his next stop.

But first he walked to the edge of the parapet wall and looked down. He saw the crew finishing the installation of construction fencing around the building. Men in hard hats and fluorescent orange vests moved rapidly. Now that the Sungs and Sloan Richardson were gone, nothing stood in the way of the Haddon House project.

The workmen noticed him. They looked up and motioned for him to get off the roof and get out of the building. While watching him, one of them took out a phone and began speaking into it.

Buddy stepped back from the parapet wall before returning to the interior of the building. After going down the staircase to the foyer, he walked out onto Hester Street.

Not having obtained a replacement car for the totaled Charger, he came to the corner and walked south on Mott Street, dropped into Henry Lee's restaurant, and handed him the envelope for safe keeping. Henry Lee nodded and carried it to his office at the back of the restaurant.

Outside again, Buddy felt his head throbbing with leftover pain from the concussion. He was glad to descend into the subway on Canal Street and begin the ride north. His plan was to go home, take an Advil, eat some lunch, and maybe sleep an hour before catching the management of Cromwell Properties at the end of the workday, when they couldn't make excuses about having meetings.

As he emerged from the subway at Seventy-Seventh Street, he walked a block south on Lexington, and then west on Seventy-Sixth toward the entrance to the Carlyle Residences. In front of him there were no cars, and on this west-to-east one-way, all traffic would be coming toward him. But his eyes roamed the sidewalk in front of him. He used his peripheral vision to check the sidewalk on the other side of the street.

Behind him he heard the screech of tires and realized that a car was headed the wrong way. Now he heard heavy footsteps rapidly gaining on him.

As he turned to face whatever was coming, something hit his head. He blacked out.

72

Forty yards behind Buddy, Ward Mills watched the white panel van's nose tilt forward as its driver stomped on the brakes. He saw the side door slide open. He began to run when he saw the two men jump out of the van, when one of the men hit Buddy's head with a baseball bat. He sprinted as Buddy crumpled and the men dragged Buddy into the van through the side door and the van sped toward Fifth Avenue.

Ward couldn't reach the white panel van in time to help his brother. But he remained calm. He'd had experience with this kind of thing before, and he was prepared.

Instead of his typical Brioni suit, today he wore black Carhartt pants, Nike field boots, a black wool zip-up sweater, and a black North Face parka. Plus black sunglasses. This was a day he'd expected harm to come to his brother, and he was right.

He spoke into his Bluetooth earpiece. "In front of Buddy's building. Where are you?"

"Right behind you!"

He turned. Instead of his silver Range Rover, he saw Brick's silver Tesla Model 3. It was maneuverable and could drive on sidewalks if necessary. Brick stopped the car.

Ward climbed in the front passenger seat. "Up ahead," he said. "White panel van turning on Fifth."

"Got it."

As the car accelerated, Ward took out his phone and dialed Ben's number.

No answer.

Ward left a message, speaking calmly, as if he were in no hurry at all. "Hey, Ben. It's Ward. When you pick this up, would you give me a call? Thanks."

Brick turned the corner and headed south on Fifth. "There it is!" he called.

Ward saw the van, which was about to turn left on East Seventy-Fourth Street.

Brick said, "Want me to get close?"

Ward shook his head. "No, they might kill him. Stay back, but don't lose them. We go where they go."

Brick said, "And then what happens? What's the plan?"

Not answering, Ward looked around to the floor of the back seat. In one of the foot wells lay a duffel bag containing several handguns, ammunition, and other high-tech objects he'd packed. He examined them for a moment. When he again faced forward, he pulled back the left sleeve of his jacket and pressed the homing beacon feature of his wristwatch. A red light on its face began blinking.

"If we get separated and I stay with Buddy, follow my beacon wherever I go, no matter the cost."

Brick looked over at him and nodded silently.

Ward said, "The plan is they die, and Buddy and I don't. But plans have gone wrong before."

73

At first Buddy was aware only of his head and how much it hurt. He blinked his eyes open. Shut them. The brightness overwhelmed him. Dizziness made everything sway. Around him he heard white noise. It was loud, as if he were standing near a high-powered fan.

What is that?

He realized that he was sitting upright but moving. His overcoat was gone. Opening his eyes a second time, he squinted in the pale light under gray clouds. He looked down and saw what they'd done to him.

Bungee cords tied him to a wooden chair with armrests. Bungee cords also tied the chair to a chrome-plated luggage trolley. The luggage trolley's horizontal bar banged against his head, and he leaned right and left and forward to avoid the bar. And to learn if the cords around his arms and legs would loosen.

But they held fast. They were so tight they hindered his circulation. His arms and legs were partly numb.

He glanced around. A man in front of him was pulling on the vertical bar at that end of the trolley. A second man, behind him, pushed against the vertical bar at the back of the trolley. They were big guys, one huge, and dressed all in black. Both with military bearing.

Rat Eyes and Ponytail, who threatened me in Henry Lee's restaurant?

He wasn't sure. Black mountaineering face masks showed only their eyes.

Buddy thought, *They're hiding their faces because they don't want me to be able to identify them. Because they aren't going to kill me.*

Yet as he took in his surroundings—the white-painted building to his left seemed empty and devoid of activity—he realized the men were more likely hiding their faces from the numerous security cameras.

His breathing became more rapid. He tasted iron, maybe blood in his mouth, maybe the tang of adrenaline.

His trepidation increased. His eyes moved faster now, darting around him. He noticed the bulges on the outside of the men's right ankles where they were carrying handguns. He also noticed the men weren't talking or communicating, perhaps because they'd done this before.

Not that he could hear them well if they'd been talking. The strange sound resembling a fan grew louder and soon became overwhelming. The men were moving him toward it. He was disoriented and couldn't place the sound. The noise assaulted him, and he blacked out briefly.

He woke a second time. Now he instantly recognized the sound.

It wasn't a fan. Not at all.

He wondered where they were taking him. But only for a moment. And then everything made sense.

How death had come to holdouts of real estate projects in Chinatown.

How two of the bodies of the most recent holdouts had disappeared, found only because of Mack Berringer's need to fish farther and farther from shore.

Sloan Richardson's almost certain end.

His entire body tensed with alarm. He wanted to run, but he couldn't move. The terror was unlike any he'd known. It was like watching a bullet in slow motion coming right for his face—and he couldn't move, couldn't avoid it. Now he was certain he had thirty minutes to live. Maybe a little more, maybe a little less. But an hour more of life? He knew that was a dream.

74

Mei enjoyed being free. She was so happy to get out of the small house on the bluff. The fresh air felt great. Her winter clothes kept her warm, and the strain on her leg muscles invigorated her. She almost wanted to run toward the ridge above them.

"Jess? Ben? Let's pick up the pace!" she called.

Jessica, leading the three of them, turned around. "I'm going as fast as I can. You in a hurry?"

Mei laughed. "Let's push ourselves."

Ben shouted, "We can run!"

Jessica held up the index finger of her right hand, and began jogging, then sprinting across the field toward the ridge that was a hundred fifty yards ahead of them and up a steep incline.

Ben kept close to her, although he was much shorter, although he limped slightly. His flexible legs pushed off and drew themselves upward for another push not much different from pistons in an engine. His boots kicked up flecks of snow. Mei watched for a moment, then took off after them.

A hundred yards and they'd stopped together, hands on their knees, catching their breath. Ben was the first to straighten and look at the ridge.

Panting heavily, he said, "Not much farther."

Jessica coughed. "But it seems as far as the moon."

Mei straightened. "We need to meet our goal."

Jessica elbowed her playfully. "What goal? You're on vacation."

"A forced vacation."

"What does it matter? Let's stop here, go back down to the house, crack open some wine. Did you buy any wine?"

"If I'd known you were coming, I'd have bought more."

"Is the vodka still in the freezer?"

Mei looked down at the house, now only a speck far below them across fields and stands of trees barren of leaves. "Still there."

Jessica smiled. "Good. We're covered."

Mei turned and saw that Ben was already climbing toward the ridge. And their route was turning into a climb. Not to the extent they'd need ropes, but it was at least a challenging hike. Jessica noticed that Ben had left them, then groaned loudly but began to follow him.

Mei remained at the back of their line. Her limbs had warmed. She felt alive, not stuck in the house, not afraid, not hiding. Her nervous energy had gone and been replaced by natural energy, even optimism. She thought her worries about the person with whom Ben had exchanged texts about their location might be misplaced or overblown. Now she didn't think Ben had given enough information for someone to discover the house's location.

Looking up at him, she saw him get closer and closer to the ridge lined with evergreens. He was stronger, and had greater endurance, than she'd expected.

As if sensing her gaze, he turned around. Cheeks red with the cold and his efforts, he smiled.

75

Buddy sat inside a dual-engine propeller plane. It had been the sound of the turboprops he'd heard, not a fan or a boat or a helicopter or a jet engine.

Still tied with bungee cords to the wooden chair on the luggage trolley, he looked around the airfield. They appeared to be in an industrial area, with the back of a warehouse or a big-box store to the north. The airstrip seemed narrow and short. He saw no maintenance crew. He peered up at the air traffic control tower above the small and seemingly abandoned airport, and saw no movement, no sign of anyone.

Where the hell am I?

He knew it didn't matter. He was on a small plane whose engines thrummed faster and faster as it began to move. To his right was a small window. To his left, the door the men had pushed him and the trolley through. They hadn't shut the door. It was open, latched to the interior of the left fuselage with a metal cable through a steel ring on the floor.

The man in the seat in front of him had removed his mountaineering mask. It was Ponytail, from Henry Lee's restaurant. Buddy wanted to grab the guy's long hair and rip it off, but he couldn't move. In front of Ponytail, in the cockpit, sat the pilot. Buddy could see only the back of the pilot's head, but the pilot had broad shoulders and light-brown hair and wore a beard and a leather bomber jacket and a headset. Buddy heard a third man moving behind him, but he hadn't seen him without his mask removed. He guessed it was Rat Eyes.

Over the engines' deafening noise, Buddy said, "I know what you did. And I've told other people what you did. It's over!"

The men ignored him.

The propellers spun faster and faster. The deafening noise cut through the small plane as it hurtled down the runway.

Buddy stared through the open door to his left. As the ground fell away and wind whipped through the cabin, Buddy feared the air pressure would suck him out.

76

Mei, Ben, and Jessica were standing on the ridge when they saw a single black Chevrolet Suburban coming up the long drive to the small house on the bluff. Its headlights had a blue tint. Mei's recent feeling of optimism vanished.

Ben said, "Who you do think it is?"

"Someone who's lost," Jessica told him. "Who else would come up to the house?"

Despite the invigorating climb, Mei instantly felt cold. She wished she'd brought her revolver, but it was behind the Triscuit box on top of the refrigerator in the house below.

She watched as the Suburban stopped in front of the house. The two front doors opened and two men climbed out. They were dressed in black and each was carrying something.

A gun.

Mei breathed in sharply, but she didn't move. She was frozen there on the ridge, unsure what to do. *Maybe*, she thought, *the men will see that we're gone, and leave.*

The men stood for a moment by the front door. They stepped back. One of the men kicked at the front door until it swung open, the interior of the house dark from where they stood on the ridge. The men walked into the house.

Jessica said loudly, "What the fuck are they doing? They just broke into the house. Did you see that?"

Mei didn't answer. She thought the scene below was like a silent film, because from the ridge they couldn't hear anything.

She, Ben, and Jessica didn't move.

Three minutes later the men emerged from the house. They looked down at the snow, then up in the direction of the ridge.

One of the men walked around to the back of the Suburban and opened the tailgate. He remained there briefly. Mei couldn't see what he was doing. But then she saw two large German shepherds jump off the rear bumper and down onto the asphalt road.

Fear grasped at her throat, and she had to remember to breathe.

The dogs made rapid circles around the man who held their leads. The other man jogged into the house and emerged a moment later. He was holding white objects.

Mei squinted and realized the objects were the pillows on which she and Ben had slept.

The men held the pillows in front of the dogs' snouts. The dogs began to bark.

Mei tried to tamp down the anxiety rising within her, to no avail. She bent over and tightened the laces of her boots, her gaze never leaving the men and the dogs below.

Call 911, she thought.

Standing, she took off her gloves and pulled her phone from her pocket. There was a signal.

The barks of the German shepherds echoed all the way up the incline to the ridge. The man holding the dogs' leads pulled first one dog and then the other close. He unlatched their leads and issued a command with a shout. He pointed to the tracks in the snow and the ridge.

The dogs caught the scent immediately. At first they trotted along the footprints Mei, Ben, and Jessica had made. Then they broke into a run, followed quickly by the men, their guns drawn.

Mei knew there wasn't time for help from the police. She put away her phone and took hold of Ben's hand. "We need to run," she told them, backing off the ridge. "They're going to kill us. We need to run. Now! *Hurry!*"

Jessica hesitated, but then followed them as they rushed in the opposite direction, down the other side of the ridge into a winding, snow-filled ravine.

77

Buddy watched through the open door to his left. He saw no land, no evidence of human habitation. He saw no islands, boats, or birds. Instead he could see only clouds and, through gaps in the clouds, the Atlantic Ocean and its whitecaps and slate-colored swells. His mind recorded what he saw but was otherwise blank, except for the pain from having the baseball bat crash into his head. Vertigo crippled him. He was frozen.

He thought about the human response to danger that evolution had provided: fight or flight. He couldn't run and hide. He certainly couldn't fly. He wasn't sure he could fight—not trussed up like an animal. But he'd watch and wait. The men hadn't made a mistake. Not yet.

The air within the plane was frigid, the noise of the engines deafening. His hands shook with cold and nerves. His breath came in short bursts. He coughed twice. His feet were growing numb. He couldn't hear much of anything. But it didn't matter.

He thought it best that men and women didn't know when or how they'd die. He wished they'd just shot him. That would have been instant blackness, forever. As the plane banked to the right, and through the open door he saw only featureless gray, he thought of Mei and Ben. The things he wished he could tell them, mostly how much he loved them. Even if he'd told them so many times, it wasn't enough. He wished that he and Mei had married and had children of their own. But she knew his feelings. He hadn't talked about them much, but he was certain she understood. In the end it seemed there wasn't more to say. There was just more to do. With them. With life. He wanted to live. This was the strongest desire he had. He also wanted to seek justice for those who hadn't been allowed to live, for Chen and Lily Sung, for Sloan Richardson.

As the plane leveled off, and he gazed down through a break in the clouds at the endless black water, he wondered if anyone would seek justice for him.

78

Jessica called forward to Mei. "Why are we running? We should stop. We should tell them there's been a mistake."

"Keep *going!*" Mei urged. She knew there was no mistake. She knew that if the dogs and men caught them, their odds of survival were low and probably zero.

Now at the floor of the ravine, they were heading west on a hiking path to the left of a frozen stream. The path was ten feet wide, the ice on the stream five.

Ben remained calm, intense, quiet. He kept his head down, sidestepping the snowdrifts over the path, the brambles, the rocks. He never slowed, even though his right leg must have burned with pain each time he pushed off. He surely felt the same urgency that she did. His life had been threatened before, and he knew to run from danger.

Jessica half shouted, "What do they want?"

Mei spoke between breaths, not turning back to her friend. *"Us. "*

"But why?"

"I don't know."

Ben continued in the lead, following the path. Mei sensed Jessica slowing her pace, and she turned to check on her friend.

Jessica was bent over, hands on her thighs. Panting, she said, "This is ridiculous. We just look guilty, running away. What if they're police or something? What if it has to do with Oliver's investment business? What if they want to question *him*?"

Instantly, Mei considered and rejected this idea. Jessica's boyfriend had nothing to do with the frightening man outside Porter Gallery. Or the conversation by text between Ben and someone posing as one of his classmates. She glanced forward at Ben, who hadn't stopped, his navy-blue coat growing rapidly smaller the farther he went. Turning to Jessica, she said, "They're after Ben and me. I don't know why. You should come with us. They'll think we told you something."

Jessica turned as Mei ran past her. "Told me what?"

Mei faced forward as she called back to her friend. "I don't know and it doesn't matter. *Come on!*"

Jessica said, "No, thanks. I'm going back to the house and calling Oliver."

Mei was tempted to stop and return to her friend, to argue with her, to demand that Jessica follow them. But she wouldn't stop. She had to protect Ben and herself. And it was true that maybe the men would ignore Jessica. But she and Ben had to push forward through the ravine, trying not to stumble on the rocks, knowing they'd lost ground and might lose more. She and Ben couldn't outrun the German shepherds, whose barks were growing louder by the minute.

"Aghh!" Ben howled, tripping, pitching forward, tumbling into the snow-covered stones.

Mei caught up with him, stopped, and bent over. She took his arm and helped him up. "You okay?"

He didn't answer, just pushed her hand away and started running, almost sprinting, continuing on the path through the ravine.

As she began to run behind him, she glanced backward. Jessica had turned and was walking east along the floor of the ravine, toward the German shepherds that were rapidly growing specks, and behind the dogs, the two men in black.

Mei kept running, following Ben. Her legs ached. Her lungs burned. She felt light-headed. But she kept on. Fear, determination, and adrenaline gave her ability and purpose.

The barks of the German shepherds grew louder.

Then she heard it.

A sound she recognized. Although she knew she wasn't mistaken, that her worst fear had been realized, she still turned and looked behind her.

Jessica was no longer walking. Mei could see only a blue-and-white mass where her friend's body lay. The white parka and blue jeans were now horizontal and motionless. Over the fallen form stood one of the men, while the dogs and the other man continued running toward Mei and Ben.

They were gaining on her, she could see it. And yet what could she do? She wouldn't stop running, because she believed standing still would mean death. They'd do to her what they'd done to Jessica. *My God!* She thought. *They killed Jess. For no reason! She wouldn't have hurt them, wouldn't hurt anyone. Why?*

Ben turned to look back at her. His eyes met hers, then searched behind her. His face grew red and he began to cry. He said, "They'll get us, Mei. They'll get us. We can't get away!"

"Keep running!" she called up to him, even though she believed he was right. They couldn't get away. They'd be caught. And killed.

A few minutes later, the dogs caught up with them.

Mei stopped and turned, ready to kick the dogs, to keep them away from Ben. Yet the dogs didn't attack, only barked loudly, their saliva spitting into the air as they circled her and Ben, who'd also stopped running. She moved closer to Ben. They stood back-to-back, the German shepherds' long snouts and enormous teeth so close she could have touched them. The dogs' barks were short, vicious, loud as machine-gun fire.

Mei reached back and put her arm around Ben's chest in an awkward embrace. She said, "I love you."

Ben looked up at her and said, "What are they going to do?" She tried to smile at him. "It doesn't matter. If we live, we'll be together. And if we die, we'll be together. But I want you to know that you're the best boy in the world. You're the best, Ben."

He began sobbing. He wiped away his tears, but those were replaced by more tears. Her vision went blurry as she cried.

Soon the two men caught up with the German shepherds. With a command from one of the men, the dogs immediately ceased barking.

Mei waited, bracing herself for the shot that would kill her.

The men were large, with blunt, impassive faces. Each held a large black handgun.

79

Buddy moved his ankles, straining against the bungee cords. They were less tight than when he'd regained consciousness on the tarmac. He slumped forward, as if passing out, and glanced down at his feet. The hooks had slid near the floor, providing more slack in the cord. *Maybe,* he thought. *Just maybe.*

The cords around his arms also were looser than they'd been. He might be able to get his wrists out of them if he had time.

He waited.

Ponytail stood, his large eyes watering in the frigid air rushing into the plane, but he didn't blink. Buddy couldn't see the man behind him, but he heard the man's voice.

The man shouted, "Time's up."

Buddy knew this was his last chance at life. They could push him out of the plane right now. They *would* push him out. He struggled with his hands.

Ponytail moved closer, grabbing the horizontal chrome bar above Buddy's head.

Buddy sensed the man behind him holding on to the vertical bar at his back. He wriggled his hands and wrists. The bungee cord's metal hook popped free.

The trolley swayed and began rolling to his left, toward the open door and the screaming engines and shrieking wind outside. He didn't think. He moved his hands. Got the right one free. His heartbeat spiked. He went for Ponytail. Hit his nose, harder than he'd ever hit anyone.

Ponytail didn't expect it, must have thought Buddy couldn't get his hands free in time. Ponytail's head knocked backward like that of a doll. Blood shot out of his smashed nose. He lost his balance and toppled over backward.

The trolley stopped. Didn't get closer to the open door, didn't move farther away.

Buddy planted his feet and threw himself onto Ponytail. He dragged the wooden chair and the trolley with him, upending them. As he landed on Ponytail's chest, he jacked his feet up and down and lost his shoes but got both feet free. He kicked the chair and the base of the trolley backward, heard them hit the man behind him, then the man crash against the side of the plane.

The plane tilted to the right and then straightened.

Buddy punched Ponytail in the nose and the side of the head. Three savage blows. Blood streamed out of both nostrils. But Ponytail was strong and even with the smashed nose, he rolled onto Buddy and punched Buddy in the face and neck.

Buddy raised his hands and tried to buck him off. Ponytail lost his balance and wavered, as if suspended above Buddy. Buddy sat up and punched him in the eyes. Ponytail swayed backward and Buddy kicked him. Three times. Fast. Buddy wanted to survive. He'd fight like an animal, scrambling, scrappy, dirty.

Suddenly, the plane banked harshly to the right, doing a one eighty, turning back in the direction of the city, before straightening. Buddy put a hand to the side of the fuselage to steady himself.

Then he rolled to the right side of the plane and kicked hard at Ponytail. Once. Twice. Kicked him toward the door. Ponytail's eyes widened with terror as he realized what was happening. He grasped Buddy's legs.

Buddy pivoted and sat up, stood up, and punched him over and over in the face. Ponytail grasped at the sides of the door and pulled himself into a sitting position. Buddy crouched low, anchored himself as best he could, and slugged Ponytail in the chest. He watched Ponytail waver and tip backward.

Ponytail's left shoulder extended beyond the doorway. The wind caught his shoulder, put him off-balance, and sucked him out the door.

Buddy didn't watch him go, didn't listen for a scream. Instead he turned to the man behind him. It was Rat Eyes. Hunched and hulking in the small plane. Now that Rat Eyes had removed his mask, Buddy could see the dark complexion, the wide face, and the eyes that resembled shiny black marbles. Those eyes were hard and filled with determination and complete confidence. The man's shoulders seemed to be five feet wide, like those of a linebacker for the Giants. Rat Eyes was climbing to his feet and pulling a gun from his ankle holster. Buddy knew he couldn't wait.

He launched himself over the wooden chair and the trolley lying on their sides. He tackled Rat Eyes. He expected the impact of a shot to the chest, but his quickness meant the man didn't have time to raise the gun very far.

Crack!

The gun discharged, the sound distinct from the violent thrum of the engines.

Buddy knew the shot had missed him, but the second one wouldn't. He socked Rat Eyes in the face, pulled away, saw the gun. Went for Rat Eyes's right forearm and hand, ratcheting them upward.

Crack!

Another shot, this one into the upper fuselage.

Buddy held Rat Eyes's right arm, the one with the gun, but the guy was huge, his arms like pythons. In close combat, Rat Eyes had the advantage. He began to hit Buddy. He knocked Buddy off his feet. Buddy scrambled up.

Shit.

With one hand he guarded his face, with the other he reached around the floor and found a wicker tray containing snacks. He picked it up and hit the linebacker in the eyes. Buddy took a step back, closer to the open door.

Rat Eyes held up the gun, aimed at Buddy.

Buddy rushed at him, forearms crossed in front of him, aiming his fists at the man's face. Instinctively, Rat Eyes raised a left forearm to block him. And didn't fire. But Rat Eyes pushed forward, bulldozing Buddy, backing him toward the open door. Bringing up his left fist, Rat Eyes punched Buddy.

Twice.

The second one like a sledgehammer.

Then Rat Eyes tossed the gun behind him and grabbed Buddy. Buddy stepped forward, enduring a punch to the head and bear-hugging the guy.

If I go, you go.

Then someone held Buddy's shoulders. A grip like a steel claw.

What the hell?

Two blows to his back, his spine.

Who?

The pilot.

Fuck.

He stood on the lip of the opening, reaching to the sides of the door to halt his progress. But they knocked his hands forward. He grasped at nothing, at air.

And they pushed him out of the plane.

No!

James Tucker

He descended into the frigid air. He couldn't breathe. He thought his heart had stopped. He was a rock thrown toward the earth at an unbelievable speed. The wind howled in his ears. He couldn't think. He was in freefall, his arms and legs outstretched in a futile attempt to slow his inevitable death.

He lived at the edge of consciousness, his heart racing wildly before slowing, before cardiac arrest.

Now on his back, he saw the plane bank right and disappear into the clouds.

80

Two hundred feet above the DHC-6 Twin Otter, Ward stood in the open doorway of another plane. A plane that had climbed faster and could fly above and behind the Otter.

After raiding the skydiving shop near the hangar, he'd taken at gunpoint a King Air jump plane that had just finished fueling on the other side of the airstrip. He'd told the pilot he was trying to save a man's life. The pilot had looked at the gun and followed Ward's instructions. They'd been airborne thirty seconds after the Otter.

As they'd followed the Otter out over the Atlantic, Ward remembered Buddy's text about the suicides off Long Island. The medical examiner had suggested they'd jumped or been pushed off a bridge.

Some fucking bridge, Ward had thought.

When he and the pilot had seen the Twin Otter's open door, they realized that the men who'd captured Buddy weren't taking him anywhere. There was no destination. Not for Buddy.

The pilot had begun to turn the plane, to return to the hangar, to get away from whatever would happen. Ward had put the gun to his head, and the pilot had straightened the King Air.

Now Ward gripped both sides of the open door to keep from falling. He watched for Buddy. He hoped the clouds would allow him to witness the moment his brother was pushed out of the Otter.

A few minutes earlier, he'd nearly jumped but caught himself. At first he'd thought the man falling from the plane was Buddy, but the man he'd seen had long dark hair.

Ward stood at the chrome-plated lip of the doorway, his legs wide apart, fighting against the pressure and the icy wind that pulled at him. He wore goggles he'd taken from the skydiving shop and tight leather gloves. The parachute harness was too tight, but that was okay. If things went right, there'd be a shitload of weight on it. He'd strapped a second harness to his left leg.

He waited, watching, squinting, straining to see. If he jumped too soon, Buddy would die. Buddy would probably die anyway. His idea was almost certain to fail, but he'd give all he could. He knew that if the situation were reversed, Buddy would do the same for him.

But he couldn't wait too long. Three seconds too long meant he'd have no chance.

He saw something.

What is it?

Movement at the edge of the plane. A man, it seemed. A familiar man.

Buddy.

The tip of a nimbus cloud passed between the two airplanes, obscuring Ward's view. He leaned forward, farther out the door. He squinted and ignored the roaring plane engines.

What was that?

The planes flew beyond the cloud, making clear his view of the Otter. But he couldn't see anyone in the doorway.

Jesus.

Did I see a fleck of black peel off the side? I think so. Or was it nothing, a dense portion of the cloud?

He thought, *Should I wait, to be sure?*

No!

His gut told him Buddy was falling. He couldn't wait. This was it. This was his one chance, Buddy's only chance.

He dived out of the plane. Headfirst, arms at his sides, jackknifing downward, away from the King Air and to his left, back to where he thought he'd seen the speck peel off the plane.

Speed, unlike any he'd known. He didn't hold out his arms and legs to slow his fall, he went faster and faster, to the edge of consciousness, to the point at which his heart began to run so fast he couldn't breathe.

He broke through the cumulus clouds and scanned the enormous space below him for a form he knew well. He saw a flock of white gulls but not Buddy.

Extending his arms upward in a stretch, he angled himself north and dangerously increased his speed.

One chance.

Come on, Buddy.

Come on!

Where the fuck are you?

81

Buddy was dropping fast, so fast he couldn't move. An impossible fatigue covered him, smothered him.

He gave up, lying still as a doll.

He tried to look up, to see the gray clouds and patches of sky during his last few seconds of life, but he couldn't help but look down.

The indigo-colored Atlantic approached fast. Now he could make out the individual swells and their relative sizes, the wind whipping up whitecaps on their crests. He saw the edge of land in the distance. The land seemed flat and white and winter brown. A few boats miles away, barely moving if they were moving at all. His eyes took in these details but he couldn't think. His eyes were an old camera with the shutter stuck open and no film inside to process the images. Nothing registered. He fell, that was all.

In his chest he felt an intense, rigid pain. He stopped breathing. He blacked out.

82

The air screamed in Ward's ears. He felt light-headed. He knew he had another ten or fifteen seconds, and he'd have to pull the rip cord or fall to his death. He screamed to stay alert. He bit his tongue until it bled. He took deep breaths. He frantically searched the airspace below him, north and south, east and west. The endless sea and the smooth rim of Long Island. Boats in the distance. He tensed. He scanned up and down and back and forth.

Nothing.

His stomach churned. He turned his head and vomited.

Then he refocused. He saw it.

A hundred yards below him and to the left, a black disk camouflaged by the dark waters of the Atlantic. But it wasn't a disk. It had a head, a torso, legs.

He went for his brother.

One chance.

83

Buddy jerked awake as he was knocked sideways.

He opened his eyes.

Breathed.

He heard screaming.

Something was on him, around him, hugging him.

No, some*one.* Someone was with him. He wasn't alone. He was dying with someone else.

He felt himself relax. He tried to ignore the screaming.

Without much curiosity, he glanced at the person with him. *A man from the plane,* he thought. But then he saw the blue eyes behind the goggles. He recognized them.

Hey, what?

He tried to focus on the voice he knew so well.

Ward yelled, "Help me! Put these straps around you! *Now!*"

Buddy reached toward the straps, tried to fit his arms through them.

And blacked out again.

84

Ward felt his brother go slack his arms.

"No, no, no. Buddy! *Buddy!*"

But his brother didn't respond.

He looked down.

Five seconds.

Five seconds to get the harness on his brother.

Not one second more.

He moved, pulling the harness around Buddy's legs. He snapped one side. The other.

Then he snapped his harness to Buddy's and yanked the rip cord.

85

Buddy came to. Water poured over him. Water so cold he shook violently.

He was in some netherworld. He lay shivering, blind and cold and wet. He lifted his head, trying to get out of the water, and breathed. Deeply.

Again. Again.

His mind began to function.

He sensed his brother near him, unclipping the parachute.

He knew that he was alive.

86

Mei hugged Ben and turned her head away from the men pointing guns at them. She inhaled and held her breath, ready for her life to be shot through and extinguished. She clung to the boy she considered her son, and he nestled against her chest. Both wept aloud.

"I love you," she told him. These were the last words she wanted to speak, the last words she wanted him to hear before they faded into time's oblivion.

Her eyes were scrunched closed, but she couldn't close her ears. She heard the men's boots crunch the snow.

One set of feet moved around her until they stood behind Ben. The other set stood behind her.

The man behind her said, "Kneel. Do it."

She had no choice. She knelt along with Ben. The knife stuck in her right boot gave her no protection. The cold of the snow passed through her pants. Immediately, she felt dampness at her knees.

Ben was shaking in her arms, as afraid as she. He, too, wanted to live. While she had less life remaining than he did, she wanted to live just as much as ever. In the past six months, it had grown sweet, with Buddy and now Ben joining her life.

A cool metal object pressed against the back of her head.

"I love you," she repeated.

Ben whispered in her ear. "Mei? Mei?"

"I'm here, sweetie. I'm here."

"They're going to—"

"*Shhh.* We'll just go to sleep."

"But Mei. Mei?"

She held him more tightly.

A cell phone rang. At first Mei thought it was Ben's phone, but a moment later she heard one of the men talking.

"Yeah. We got them. A hiking path a mile from the house. I don't see anyone else. Not here? Are you *sure?*"

Everything around them grew still. The metal moved away from the back of her head.

She waited, listening to her breath mixed with Ben's.

The screech of a hawk pierced the silence. It was overhead, unseen, now again unheard.

The men behind her didn't move.

A single gunshot filled the trough of the ravine, echoing off its steep walls.

87

Buddy rolled up and down the swells. He knew he was hypothermic. His lungs were tightening, constricting. He didn't know how much longer he had.

He watched Ward's arm rise above the water and press several buttons on the giant black watch that Buddy had once made fun of. The watch emitted a faint beeping noise that became continuous.

Through his goggles, Ward looked over at him. "Hang in there, man. Brick's on his way."

Buddy heard himself groan.

Ward worked an arm under his neck and helped support him, kept his head above the swells toppling over them. Ward said, "This is the best thing that could happen!"

Buddy wanted to shake his head, but he couldn't move his neck. He croaked, "Are you fucking kidding me?"

"Don't you see?" Ward shouted. "They think you're dead. *Dead.*"

"I'm not far off."

Ward ignored him. "Buddy, they'll stop looking for you. You're *free.* Now you can hunt instead of hide."

The argument warmed Buddy, angered him. After the fall, he felt completely defeated. He didn't want to be prodded to do anything. He wanted to get away from New York. He wanted . . . he wasn't sure what he wanted. Even lying faceup as the giant swells moved under him, he knew that he couldn't live—and Ben and Mei couldn't live—until he finished the business that had brought him to this watery grave. Yet continuing his investigation seemed difficult or impossible. He said, "I have no resources. I can't use a phone. A car. My badge."

With his free hand, Ward patted his chest. "You have *my* resources. More than what the police department has. There's no chain of command. No rules."

No rules, Buddy thought. *No shit. You get thrown out of an airplane, you get justice however you can get it.* He considered what had just happened to him and changed his mind. *Justice? No. Revenge.*

He waited, focused on his breathing. A dense cold grasped at his heart. He fought it, tried to move his arms and legs.

His eyes began to close. His legs grew so heavy he couldn't move them. He'd die here in Ward's arms. Better than alone, but he wished he were with Mei somewhere warm. In bed with her. He imagined her in his arms, sitting astride him, a smile on her full lips, her silky black hair falling around his face, her honey-colored breasts brushing his chest.

"Mei," he said aloud.

His dream continued as the water lifted and gently lowered him. His breaths became shorter and shorter. Now he felt warmth, a flame that sparked in his heart and soon spread across his body like a wildfire. Peace, at last.

But then he heard the sound of an engine. It intruded into his dream.

Ward shouted something.

Buddy blinked his eyes, tried to raise himself. He tried to speak but couldn't.

From the corner of his eye, he saw the length of a white fiberglass boat. On the side of it were red letters. They spelled *Boston Whaler.*

Hanging over the chrome railing stood Brick, Ward's driver.

Buddy tried to say something but couldn't make a sound.

He heard Ward shout, "Get him in the boat. Get him warm. Don't let him sleep. Now!"

Buddy felt strong arms pull him up out of the water and over the side. Brick pulled at his clothes. All of his clothes. For an instant he shivered in the unbearable cold, then Brick dried him and covered him with a blanket and then a down parka and a hat and mittens. Then he sat Buddy up and poured liquid from a thermos into the stainless-steel cap of the thermos and held it to Buddy's lips, pouring it down Buddy's throat.

Buddy tasted it. Coffee. But something else, too.

Whiskey.

Oh, yeah.

He drank until it was gone. He couldn't speak, but he looked up at Brick with wide eyes.

Brick seemed to understand. He refilled the thermos cap and held it to Buddy's lips.

Buddy drank eagerly. As he did, the hard cold dissipated and slowly disappeared. Genuine warmth replaced the cold. His mind began to turn like an engine starting in the winter. Slowly, fitfully, then more and more smoothly.

He watched as Ward climbed up the ladder at the stern. Ward's face was red, his lips blue. His body shook with cold. Buddy watched as he, too, stripped down, toweled off, and dressed in heavy down gear.

Wearing mittens like Buddy's, Ward turned to Brick. "Get us to your car. Fast as possible. For Christ's sake, *hurry!*"

Brick signaled to the driver, a burly older man in a navy-blue water-repellent jacket and hat who stood behind the steering column. The older man turned the wheel and pushed the throttles down, all the way. The twin two-hundred-fifty-horsepower Mercury engines thundered, powering the boat toward the shore.

Buddy held on to make sure he didn't bounce around.

Ward stared at him and then looked away, toward land.

At first Buddy thought Ward had ordered Brick to hurry for him, to get him to a hospital. But he was breathing well now. He was warm. When he considered further, he recognized the danger had started with him and had spread to everyone he knew.

Everyone I know.

Ben.

Mei.

88

Ben felt his phone vibrate in the front right pocket of his pants, and at the same time, the Apple Watch silently tapped his left wrist. He knew he couldn't look at either device. So he kept up the march as he and Mei had been ordered to do. The men had laughed when they fired the gun up into the air, when he and Mei were kneeling with the dogs circling them like devils. Laughed because they were only pretending to kill him and Mei. He hated these men, hated their dogs. He was so angry that he'd try to escape when he had a chance and when Mei could go with him.

They walked single file: first Mei, then the first man dressed in black. This man was tall with very short blond hair, a rangy giant. Strong and proud looking. Ben followed the blond man.

Behind Ben walked the second man in black. This man held the leads of the German shepherds. He was shorter than the tall man but thicker, larger, with huge arms, a shaved head, and a tattoo of a something white—a bird or a flower—on the side of his neck.

The snow crunched under Ben's boots, under the boots of the others. On either side of him rose the steep sides of the ravine, covered with patches of ice and loose stones and dotted with evergreens. The floor of the ravine was rocky and snowy, and he had to watch his step so he didn't fall. On his left lay the frozen stream, its surface like a mottled black snake. To his right was a crumpled mass. He stared until he recognized it.

Jessica.

He heard Mei crying. He watched her dash out of the line to her fallen friend. Ben stopped.

"Jessica!" Mei called, kneeling at her friend's side. "Jessica? Can you hear me?"

He saw Mei touch Jessica's face, put one hand on her shoulder and another on her hip, and roll her onto her back.

The figure so filled with life a half hour ago didn't move. Stillness enveloped Mei's friend, the blond hair tinged with scarlet. Ben studied Jessica's chest carefully, but it didn't rise or fall.

He watched as Mei turned to the men. Tears streamed down her face. "Why?" she cried. "Why did you kill her? What good did it do?"

The large man at the front of the line said, "Because she was with you."

Mei shook her head. Her eyes narrowed. "What the hell is wrong with you people?"

The phone in Ben's pocket vibrated once, briefly, indicating that someone had left him a voicemail or a text. The watch lightly tapped his wrist.

Buddy? he wondered. *Is Buddy nearby? Can he save us?*

No, he knew Buddy couldn't save them because Buddy was in the city. He and Mei would need to save themselves.

As he stared at Jessica's bloody hair, he tried not to think of what had happened to his family, what might happen to him. As he thought about escaping, he remembered what Buddy had told him the month before: *If anything happens ever again, hide. If you can't hide, run.*

Can I run? he asked himself, knowing from terrible experience that he needed to get away or he'd end up like his mother, his father, his sister, Ellen-Marie. *Not here, I can't,* he thought. *But there will be a chance. There must be a chance.*

The tall man in front pointed at Mei. "Get back in line. We're going."

Mei shook her head. "We can't leave her here."

"Get in line, or I'll bash your face."

Mei stood. "What about Jessica? What about my friend?"

The man smirked. "Coyotes will get her."

Mei's eyes showed anger mixed with fear. "Really? So why not let the coyotes get us?"

The man again pointed at Mei. "Get in line."

Mei persisted. "Why? Why not shoot us and leave us for the coyotes?"

"Coyotes?" asked the shorter man with the shaved head. "Sometimes they don't get everything."

Mei put her hands on her hips. "So we're next?"

The man with the shaved head shrugged. "We'll find out."

Mei glanced at Ben. His eyes met hers, and he again felt their bond. She tried to smile at him, but it was more of an expression of terrible pain. She rejoined the line, now behind the tall man, and they proceeded through the ravine for nearly a mile until they reached the route they'd used to come down the western side of the ridge.

The blond man in front of them walked within those footprints up the steep eastern side of the ravine. Ben dropped his head, bent his legs to lower his center of gravity, and made his way up behind Mei. She was doing the same, here and there grabbing at leafless trees to pull herself up. He looked to his left and right, but there was nowhere to run. He'd have to wait.

At the top of the ridge, they stood looking down at the small house on the bluff and, beyond the house, the town of Rockridge. From this height and distance, the town appeared to be a child's toy. But he knew the town was as real as the guns the men were holding.

Where are the people now? he wondered. *The people farther down the bluff who called the police about Mei's firing the gun? Didn't they hear the shot that killed Jessica, or the shot meant to scare us?*

Mei stopped. She said, "My leg is injured. I can't walk anymore."
The man in front of her halted his march, returned to her, stared
at her a moment. Then he brought back his right boot and kicked her
shin.

"*Aghh!*" she cried, falling over, lying in the snow, clutching her leg.
She curled up into a ball, weeping softly. "*Ohhh.*"
The man stood over her and said, "Get. In. Line." His speech was
accented, thick around the vowels and harsh at the consonants.

Ben made to rush over to her, but the man behind him grabbed his
upper arm so tightly he couldn't move.

Mei saw the man with the shaved head restrain Ben, and she
uncurled, stood with obvious effort, and hobbled forward. Her face
was wet with tears and melting snow.

The tall man in the lead turned and continued taking them down
the bluff toward the house. Mei walked with a limp. Ben kept three or
four paces behind her, trying to slow their progress, because that was
what Mei seemed to think they should do. He trusted Mei, even now.
Mei *and* Buddy, because they'd saved his life before. And because they
were the only people on earth who loved him.

When they reached the house, the tall man opened the front door.
Instead of allowing Mei to enter first, he drew his gun and walked
inside. Mei followed, then Ben. For a moment Ben realized the man
behind him wasn't there. He turned and saw the second man open the
rear door of the Suburban and command the German shepherds to
jump inside. A moment later the man closed the rear door and walked
toward the house.

Ben stared at him, but the man's expression showed no response.
No recognition, no friendliness, not even anger or disdain. The man
was like a robot or a machine.

Ben felt himself go cold, even though his running away from the
men and the dogs had made him perspire, and the march back out of
the ravine and to the house had warmed him. He realized his clothes

were damp with sweat. His right leg ached. As the man with the shaved head came up behind him as he stood in the doorway, Ben turned and entered the house.

Mei stood in the great room, facing the tall man, who was across the sofa from her. The man held his gun at his side. She said, "The boy and I are going to put on dry clothes."

The tall man looked first at the man with the shaved head, who was behind Ben. Ben couldn't see the reaction, but then the tall man nodded at Mei.

"Come on, Ben," she said, waving him toward the bedrooms.

The man behind him again grabbed his upper arm. "One at a time. You stay here. I'll go with her."

Ben saw Mei's face drain of color. He feared the man with the shaved head might kill her in the bedroom.

Mei's eyes met Ben's. Fear welled up within him. "Don't go," he blurted. "They'll hurt me. They'll hurt you!"

He saw Mei glance at the tall man in the middle of the room and at the man with the shaved head behind him. He didn't look at them but saw her turn and continue down the short hallway to the bedrooms.

Panic seized him. "Mei!" he called. *"Mei!"*

But she stepped toward the doorway.

He could hear the breathing of the man with the shaved head and then the man's footsteps as he came around Ben and followed Mei toward the bedroom.

Ben didn't move. He stood in the living room with the tall blond man. In the silence, he felt a faint tap on his wrist from the Apple Watch, now covered by his jacket sleeve.

He thought he'd received a text. But he couldn't look at the watch or the tall man would take it away.

89

Mei entered the larger bedroom, the thickset man with the shaved head close behind her.

She gathered dry clothes—dark-wash jeans and a gray Lululemon pullover with a hood—and turned to go into the bathroom. "I'm changing in private," she told the man.

"Hold it," he said, and walked into the bathroom, glanced around it, opened the drawers and the cabinets. Satisfied no weapons were hidden there, he returned to the bedroom and indicated she could go inside.

After closing and locking the bathroom door, she unlaced her hiking boots and removed the pocketknife. Carefully, so it wouldn't make a sound, she set it on the vanity. Then she changed into the jeans and pullover and put on and laced her boots. Again, she took up the pocketknife. This time she stuck it between the right boot's tongue and lacing. It held there, secure and nearly invisible.

A knock at the door.

She froze. "Yes?" she called. She could hear the low breathing of the man on the other side of the door. He was so close to her, so strong. She knew he could overpower her if he wanted . . . she tried to push away the image of him ripping off her clothes and forcing himself on her.

No, she thought. *I'll shove my fingernails into his eyes if I have to. But he's not going to touch me.*

The low breathing paused, and then the man said, "One minute, and you come out."

She stared at herself in the mirror. Doubt showed in her eyes and the lines across her forehead. But anger flashed through her as well. Anger that she and Ben were stuck with these men, that they might die, that Buddy's case had brought the men here.

Goddammit, she thought, as she unlocked the door and pulled on the handle. *What ever happened to normal life?*

She hoped that when she returned to the great room, the men would be distracted and wouldn't notice her reaching up to the top of the refrigerator, wouldn't see that she had the revolver until it was too late.

I'll shoot them, she thought, *the way they shot Jessica. It won't be murder. It won't even be a crime. Because I have no choice. It's them or us.*

Other than aiming and firing, she had no plan. She understood that if she didn't succeed, she and Ben wouldn't survive. They'd never be allowed to live, not after witnessing Jessica's murder.

Unlocking the door, she walked into the bedroom. Her body tight with nerves, her skin sensitive to any touch, no matter how light, she held her breath as she emerged into the great room.

The tall man—she thought of him as an Aryan giant—stood by the big window. He glanced at her, then at the man behind her.

She felt the blood rush through her body, warming her, making her fingers tingle as if with electricity.

I have to do it, she told herself silently. *Them or us.*

She went over to the refrigerator and opened the door. From the corner of her eye, she saw the blond man turn to glance out the window.

Rapidly, she closed the door, reached around the box of Triscuits, and took hold of the revolver. It felt heavy and too large. Her hand felt damp with perspiration. Her hand shook; the barrel shook. Yet she raised the revolver as she turned to the man by the window. She stared at him as she fired.

Bang!

An ear-splitting explosion sounded in the small room.

The Aryan giant fell to the floor.

Ben shouted.

And then the man with the shaved head was on her, tackling her, tearing the gun from her hands. He pushed himself up and off her, and she lay on the floor, turning her head to look at the giant.

Who was getting up off the floor.

She searched for blood or injury on his form but saw nothing. The Aryan giant's eyes met hers, and he smiled. Laughed.

What? she thought. *How could . . . ?* Her eyes searched behind the tall man, and she saw the large window was cracked around a small circular opening near the window's lower right side, where the bullet had passed through and out into the snow.

The squat man leaned over and smacked her across the face, making her cheek burn. He smacked her again and said, "Crazy bitch."

Heedless of the men, Ben rushed over to her, took her arm, and helped her up.

90

One minute later, Ben went across the great room, through the doorway to the hall, and into the larger bedroom. The squat man with the shaved head was behind him, his gun out, Mei's revolver in his waistband. Ben surveyed the room. He needed clothes. Then he'd check the watch.

The watch!

He went to his bag, removed a dry pair of khakis and socks, a T-shirt, a red-and-black-and-white plaid shirt, and a navy-blue wool sweater with a thick shawl collar. Without looking at the squat man, he walked toward the bathroom.

"Hold it," the man said.

Ben turned to him.

The man held out his left hand, palm up. "Your phone. Give it to me."

Ben faked a quizzical expression. "What phone?"

The man pointed at his trouser pocket, where its rectangular outline was visible.

Ben didn't think he had a choice. He pulled it out and set it on the man's hand. The man dropped it to the floor and took the gun barrel and smashed the phone into pieces.

Head down, Ben went into the bathroom, closed and locked the door. As soon as he'd taken off his damp shirt, he held up his left wrist and studied the watch screen.

It was blank. And black.

He pressed the crown on the right side of the device.

As if by magic, the time and date appeared in small gold lettering at the top. In the middle of the screen, he saw a rectangular green text box with white lettering inside it. He read: On our way.

Buddy? he thought. *Ward? Or both of them?*

His spirits rose before falling sharply. Buddy and Ward had no idea where he and Mei were staying. They had no idea of the location of the house. Because Mei had refused to tell them. And the Apple Watch needed his phone to function.

Oh, no! he thought, upset with Mei. *How can Buddy find us? How can Buddy save us?*

But then he remembered this was the new Apple Watch, with its own cellular connection. His hands warming, he typed a reply to the text: Two men got us. At the house. Hurry!

For a moment, he stared at the screen, expecting and hoping for a response. But there was none.

He put on his clean clothes—making sure the heavy wool sweater's left sleeve covered the watch—and left the others on the floor. Then he walked out of the bathroom.

As he returned to the great room, he realized he hadn't texted the location of the house. Not even the town—Rockridge. He needed to return to the bathroom and text them the name of the town and a description of the house.

He stopped, began to turn.

But the squat man with the shaved head gripped his shoulder and forced him forward.

"Stop it!" Ben called, trying to shake free of the man's enormous hand.

But the man didn't let go. And in an instant, Ben was standing in the living room, facing Mei, the left side of her face swollen and red, the tall blond man by the window.

Sadness overcame him. He went to Mei and began to cry. His shoulders and arms shook. He couldn't control himself. He didn't know what to do. And why had he thought he could escape from these big men with their guns? Or that Buddy and Ward would rescue him in time. He should stop being stupid. There was no escape. Not unless Mei had an idea she hadn't shared with him.

But . . . but . . . maybe she does.

At this thought, he swallowed. Mei wiped away his tears, her expression blank. Slowly, almost imperceptibly, she shook her head, warning him against something. Maybe against crying.

She said, "Put on your shoes."

He didn't look at the men. Instead, he went over to the entrance to the house and put on his gray New Balance shoes. When he returned to the kitchen, he saw Mei standing at the kitchen counter, making food, pouring herself a glass of water and an orange juice for him. He saw the squat man relaxing on the sofa, the black revolver in his hand. The tall man was by the large window overlooking the valley. He was slowly pacing, gun at his side.

Mei drank from her water glass. Ben stood beside her and sipped his orange juice. Its coolness soothed him, and he realized he was hungry.

He noticed Mei straighten. Her voice became stronger. She said to the men, "What do you want with us? What are you doing here?"

The tall man by the window stood still. He raised his chin and stared at her. In accented English he said, "We're waiting."

She opened her hands. "For what?"

But the man didn't answer. He only looked out the window.

91

Buddy and Ward climbed out of the *Boston Whaler* and stepped onto a private dock on the north side of Point Lookout, Long Island. Buddy had difficulty walking. His legs felt like rubber, and he nearly fell while climbing up the concrete steps onto the property owner's back-yard. Brick caught and steadied him, pulled him around the white clapboard house that appeared to be empty of people. On the other side of the house was a crumbling restaurant in red brick with a roof of asphalt shingles that needed repair. Buddy shook violently and knew he belonged in a hospital, but he steeled himself for the task at hand. Turning at the sound of an engine, he saw the driver of the *Whaler* pocketing a thick wad of bills as he maneuvered the boat into a nearby slip.

Brick led him out to the sidewalk. Brick's silver Tesla was parked at the curb. After popping the trunk with his key fob, Brick pulled out a duffel bag stuffed with clothes.

Buddy stared at the dry jeans and shirts and shoes and jackets, not sure if they were meant for him. When he noticed motion beside him, he realized Ward was stripping off his clothes. All of them. In five seconds, his brother stood naked on a jacket spread over the pavement. Then Ward took clothes out of the duffel and put them on. Buddy took a deep breath and followed suit.

Brick leaned into the trunk and pulled out hiking boots. Two pairs, one for each of them. He set them down and Buddy and Ward put them on.

Brick nodded. "Let's go."

Ward sat in the front seat; Buddy stretched across the small back seat. Brick glanced in the rearview mirror and put the car in reverse.

In dry clothes, Buddy began to feel more alert. Rather than growing calm, he became more anxious. "We need to find Mei and Ben," he said. "But I don't know how."

When Brick threw the car into drive, it burst forward with speed that surprised Buddy.

In the front passenger seat, Ward took up his phone that he'd left with Brick. As Ward held the phone in his palm, Buddy could see the green text bubble. He said, "Who sent it?"

Ward turned around and faced into the back seat. "Ben."

"What did he say?"

"They've been taken."

Dread filled Buddy. The sense he'd lose everything. His body tightened with impending panic.

The car spun around and accelerated west on the Long Island Expressway. Ward again faced the front and spoke loudly over the nearly silent motor. "When we get close to the house, we should watch for vans and SUVs. They might pass us, driving back into the city."

"The *house*?" Buddy said. "We don't know which house. We don't even know the town."

Ward shook his head. "I have their location." He held up his phone so that Buddy could see Google Maps.

Buddy squinted. "I don't understand. How could you . . ."

Ward half turned toward the back seat. "Buddy, you might not have noticed, but the Apple Watch box I gave Ben had already been opened. By me. Because I had my tech guy install a monitoring app so I could track Ben's location on my phone. He's at a house outside Rockridge."

Shit, Buddy thought. *That's fucking brilliant.* But he said nothing. He was thinking about getting to Ben in time.

In time for what?

Buddy shook his head angrily, though neither Brick nor Ward could see him. Anxiety pulsed until his entire body shook with it. He gripped the door handle and said, "The men won't keep them at the house. And they're not driving into the city. They're going to the nearest airfield."

92

Two hours later, Ben heard it. He'd been hoping for the sound of a car—Ward's Range Rover with Buddy and Ward inside. But the noise wasn't from a car.

From his perch on a stool at the kitchen bar, he looked out the big window that faced north. The tall blond man pacing by the window stopped and also stared through the glass. The sound grew louder until Ben recognized it. He searched the sky and saw a propeller plane flying low over the ridge. The house shook as the noise grew loud and the plane passed over the house. He thought it couldn't be more than a hundred feet above them.

The sound of the plane's engines faded, returned, then disappeared to his right. The plane didn't fly over the house a second time. Outside, the gray afternoon light had darkened, and he could see a few lights twinkling faintly in the distance. He turned from the window when he heard Mei give a brief cry.

The man with the shaved head had shoved his gun into her back. He said, "We go now."

Mei winced and looked past Ben to the tall man, who was by the window. In an even voice, she said, "Where are you taking us?"

Ben felt the blond man put one of his enormous hands around his neck. The man squeezed until breathing grew difficult. The man pushed him forward, across the room, past Mei and the man with the shaved head, to the door.

Squirming away from the blond man, he tried to turn around to see if Mei was following, but the man's grip was like steel. He couldn't move his head.

Then he heard Mei call to him. "I'm here, Ben. Behind you."

Her voice calmed him, though the panic had taken hold of him. Panic, because he couldn't run or hide or fight against the terrible thing happening to him. Because they were trapped. His mouth had the coppery taste of fear, but he continued walking as best he could.

As they went outside into the cold, he realized he hadn't put on his jacket. He glanced up and saw only the increasing darkness. In the sharp cold he put his arms across his chest, then dropped them, worried the men would notice his watch.

He kept waiting for the watch to tap his wrist, alerting him to a text from Buddy and Ward, but there was no tap. He knew it then: there would be no help.

The man holding his neck reached forward, opened the Suburban's left rear door, and pushed him inside. The man slid in beside him. Ben saw the door to his right open, and soon Mei was sitting beside him. She put an arm around him, leaned over and kissed him, held him tightly to her, and quietly urged him to buckle his seat belt. He did so, and then hugged her, smelling her sweat mixed with the lemon scent she wore. To him, the scent was clean and pure and comforting, even when they were headed somewhere he knew would be terrible.

The man with the shaved head walked around the Suburban, climbed into the driver's seat, and started the car. He didn't look behind him when he threw the car into reverse. Instead, he backed up quickly, and Ben heard scratching sounds behind him. And panting.

The German shepherds. He smelled them, knew the dogs were in the cargo area. Maybe in a crate, maybe loose.

There's no escape, he thought. *Not from the dogs.*

He hugged Mei more tightly. She touched the back of his head with her hand. Its warmth calmed him, but only a little.

The man with the shaved head put the car in drive. The Suburban surged forward down the long drive, away from the house, toward Rockridge and . . . *where?*

He thought maybe he should expose the watch and try to dial 911. But he knew the man beside him would tear it off his wrist before he could type the number. His only option would be to run when the door opened, when they arrived wherever they were going.

He moved his hands slowly, slowly, until they covered the buckle of his seat belt. Shifting his eyes left, he could see the tall blond man pressed against him. The man had one hand on the left rear door's armrest, and one hand on his right knee. Very close to Ben. Almost touching him.

Sliding his right thumb over the buckle, Ben pressed down on the button. It made no sound as the catch released. Keeping his hand over the buckle, he held it in place. If he allowed the belt to retract, he'd be discovered.

93

Sitting beside Ben in the back seat of the Suburban, Mei pretended to be at ease. For Ben's benefit. And to mislead the Aryan giant next to Ben and the man with the shaved head, who was driving and glancing at her in the rearview mirror. She put aside her initial failure to kill the men. Now she had to create another opportunity for escape, and for life. For her, and especially for Ben. Beneath her placid expression, she thought furiously.

They passed Rockridge and turned south on Highway 17. The Suburban accelerated rapidly.

Mei hit upon a single idea. It filled her instantly with hope, before that hope disintegrated just as quickly.

No, it won't work, she told herself. *There's no escape, not from these men with their guns and their German shepherds. Don't delude yourself, Mei. You can't win.*

But even as she tamped down her hope in the idea, its real possibility increased. Over the course of thirty seconds, it became a plan that would probably fail, yet it was their only chance.

She leaned forward and put a hand on the back of the empty front passenger seat. "You need to stop," she told the man with the shaved head. "I need to use a restroom."

The man didn't take his eyes off the road. "No."

The Suburban accelerated down a hill and began to climb up another, larger hill. To her left she noticed a dark wood.

She raised her voice. "I have to go now. Right now."

The Aryan giant to Ben's left said, "Hold it. You're a big girl. We'll be out of the car in a few minutes."

"I can't wait a few minutes. My God, we were out hiking and running, and then we hiked back. I drank a ton of water when we got to the house. I swear to God, I just need to use a restroom."

The man with the shaved head snorted. "Shut up, would you? No stops for pissing."

Mei leaned forward as if in extreme discomfort. She stayed that way for a while, hunched over, her right hand reaching down and sliding the pocketknife out from between the laces and tongue of her right boot.

The Aryan giant said, "Go in your pants, bitch. It won't matter, especially not to you."

Mei turned her face slightly to the right. Concentrating hard, she attempted to open the pocketknife with her right hand alone. Without looking at it, she tried to find the groove near the edge of the blade so she could insert her thumbnail and pull it open.

The Suburban bucked over the uneven road.

Her hand lost its place.

She began again, feeling along the edge of the blade. There it was. Small and narrow, like an invisible crease.

Her thumbnail caught in it, and she pulled. Slowly, so that the blade, extending, didn't click audibly into place.

But at last the knife was fully open, the blade sharp. She ran her index finger over it. And then at last she sat up, her right hand gripping the blade.

The Suburban's suspension jerked, and the big vehicle crested the top of the hill and began to move faster. Neither man seemed to pay her any attention.

Ben turned to her, yet she didn't return his glance.

Three times, she took deep breaths and planned the motion of her arms, her hand, the knife. She hadn't put on her seat belt as Ben had. She could move without restriction.

Her eyes focused on the bare neck of the man driving, the man with the shaved head who'd hit her in the face. His skin was mottled with the remnants of acne. It was pink and pale and, in some places, a sickly blue. But to her, it looked soft. To her, it was the target.

Now she stared out the right rear passenger window, as if in a daydream. But her hand turned the knife until she could grip it tightly, blade aimed down, her thumb over the end of the bolster.

Again she counted.

One.

Two.

Three.

She put her left hand on the raised armrest between the two front seats and half stood. Then she raised her right hand, reached to her left, and plunged the knife into the neck of the man with the shaved head.

The man screamed, put his hands on his neck.

The Suburban spun out of control, throwing her against the right rear door, knocking the knife against the window and out of her hand. Ben shouted something. The Aryan giant held the grab handle above his head to steady himself, at the same time reaching into a shoulder holster for his gun.

Mei found the knife as the Suburban spun in a circle and went up on two wheels, nearly rolling. She held it the way she had before. And she lurched across Ben and stabbed at the Aryan giant's face.

The blade caught him below his right eye. She raised it for another attack. But he punched her in the chest, causing her to fall backward onto the seat. He fumbled for his gun, found it, and took it up.

The Suburban swerved to the right and the left, then stopped abruptly, pushing her hard against the back of the front passenger seat.

The Aryan's gun banged against the left rear passenger door and fell to the rubber floor mat.

Mei opened the door, fell out, tumbled to the side, and stood. She reached into the Suburban for Ben. He was out of his seat belt and coming toward her. She took hold of his hands and pulled.

But he was held back. One of the Aryan's large hands held the hem of Ben's sweater and was yanking him back inside.

"Kick him!" Mei shouted. "Hard!"

Ben kicked at the man before dropping his feet to the floor, pushing with all his strength, and driving himself toward the open door.

His sweater stretched and then tore.

Mei saw that he was free, grabbed and nearly threw him out of the Suburban. Without waiting for him to catch his balance, she seized his right hand and tugged him into the woods, where they were instantly hidden by evergreens.

For a few yards, they ran together until she stopped him, removed her hand from his. In a low voice she said, "Go left, quietly and fast. Don't stop!"

His eyes widened with fear. "But where are *you* going?"

"We need to separate," she told him, moving her hands apart for emphasis. "We'll be harder to find."

He touched her arm. "Are you sure?"

"Yes! Now *go!*"

She watched as he headed left through the trees, running quietly and quickly, just as she'd told him to do. For a few seconds, she stood there, loving him, loving everything about him. And then she turned to the right, running fast but calling out, as loudly as she could, "Help! Help! Help!"

She knew they'd find her, but she hoped he'd escape. And live.

94

Buddy held on as Brick drove the Tesla fast. Brick aimed at the faint orange glow on the western horizon, screaming north on Highway 17. Brick swerved around other cars with increasing recklessness the farther they got from Long Island and as they ascended the hills east of Wurtsboro Ridge State Forest. Higher and higher, the Atlantic farther and farther behind them, dusk spreading across the land. Buddy's fall into the ocean part of history now. He'd been unconscious repeatedly and in shock, then his mind had begun to move and his heart to beat.

Boom-boom. Boom-boom. Boom-boom.

But his full range of emotions hadn't returned until their drive to Rockridge. It hadn't taken long, but now the intensity of his feelings washed over him as the frigid waves of the Atlantic had done, crystallizing in a way that would be difficult to control. What coursed through his veins wasn't mere anger, it was rage.

The events of the past few days, especially his fall into the ocean, had turned him into a tightly coiled spring that was about to push back. Hard. So hard he didn't care how many he took down with him. He didn't care what happened to himself. He was going to do more than touch the third rail. He was going to grab on to it and chain himself to it until he could see what it was and where it led. His hands shook with fury. He felt hot. Without looking at the Glock 19 Brick had handed him, he ejected the magazine, confirmed it was loaded, and reinserted it. His eyes weren't on the gun or on Brick and Ward in the front seats. No, he was searching outside the car.

For an SUV that didn't look right. A panel van. A truck that didn't belong.

They were approaching the small town of Rockridge, ninety minutes northwest of Manhattan. He saw farms, pastureland, modest houses, hardware stores, and farm implement dealers. Gas stations and a McDonald's, their lights beacons in the dusk.

"How far?" he asked, not taking his eyes from the oncoming traffic.

Ward said, "Fifteen minutes."

Shit, Buddy thought. *They passed us. They're behind us. We've got to turn around!*

But he said nothing. Despite his anxiety and fury, he wasn't sure how much time had elapsed. He continued to stare out the windows, right and left, at the oncoming cars to his left and at any parking lots, for Mei's Audi or for anything suspicious. He hadn't noticed anything. In his peripheral vision, he could see Ward's left hand holding an iPhone with Google Maps on the screen. Ward was giving Brick directions to the airfield closest to the house on the bluff over Rockridge. This was Sha-Wan-Ga Valley Airport, several miles southeast of the house. Buddy knew that if Brick's Tesla reached the airfield after Mei and Ben had been forced onto a plane, he would have lost the two people he most cared about.

Ward said to Brick, "In three miles, take a right on Burlingham. There's an airfield a mile or two to the northeast." Ward held up the phone he was using to track Ben's watch. "They're between us and the airfield."

Buddy worked to keep his breathing even. He was shaking with adrenaline, but he could only look out the windows. They were getting close to failure or success, and there was nothing in between. But at the speed Brick was driving, everything would happen in the next few minutes.

Ward's voice rose as he said, "Two miles to Burlingham, and they're three miles from us."

Buddy tightened his right hand around the Glock. He kept his vision outside the car.

He watched as a Suburban drove toward them in the oncoming lane. He strained to see the driver, the color, and year of the SUV. In the rapidly fading light, it was difficult to see it well. He opened his mouth to say, *Hold on!*

But at the moment the Suburban passed them, he saw that it was at least ten years old, with a middle-aged woman behind the wheel. Letting out his breath, he leaned back in the seat and transferred his gaze to the right side of the car. He saw snow-covered fields and wires stretched between telephone poles that ran along the side of the road, seemingly to infinity. To the north lay a forest of evergreens, tall and dense and dark in the fading light.

Two minutes later, they passed Burlingham.

Ward stared at his phone and said, "They're not moving."

Buddy's stomach churned. He felt both the car rise as it climbed a steep hill and then a bump that briefly shook the Tesla. At the crest of the hill, he looked forward. He'd expected to see a broad vista on the right and only the forest on the left, but instead he saw the red taillights of a black Suburban on the shoulder of the west side of Highway 17. The right rear door was open. The left front door was open.

The Tesla was doing close to ninety and would soon pass the Suburban.

He put a hand on Brick's shoulder.

He shouted, "Slow down!"

95

As the Tesla slowed, Buddy glanced right at gray rolling fields. He saw no movement, no sign of Mei or Ben or anyone else.

Brick swerved across the southbound lane and pulled slowly up behind the Suburban. Buddy waited until the car was nearly at a stop and opened the door.

Barking. Frenzied barking. He heard it clearly as he stepped from the car. It took him a moment to figure it out. But then he crouched down, Glock drawn, and jogged toward the Suburban.

Dogs in the back, he told himself.

He checked the SUV's interior, but it was empty. When he turned, he saw Ward and Brick behind him. Ward held his Beretta M9. Brick held the Tesla's key fob.

Buddy said to Brick, "You need a gun."

Brick shook his head, his sun-bleached hair swaying in the dusk. "No way, man. Not me."

Buddy looked at Ward and held out his hand.

Ward reached into his jacket, pulled out a second M9, and set it on Buddy's palm.

Buddy offered the gun to Brick. "Take it."

Brick took a step back. "Hey, man. I'm a pacifist."

Buddy narrowed his eyes and stepped forward rapidly, shoving the gun at Ward's driver. "*Take the gun.* You're not in fucking Malibu."

Brick looked down at the Beretta as if it were poison. Reluctantly, he took the weapon. He said, "How do I use this?"

"Point and shoot," Ward told him.

Buddy said, "Here's the plan." He pointed at Brick. "You go in straight. Ward goes left and I go right. Don't shoot before you confirm it's not one of us or Mei or Ben. Got it?"

The other men nodded.

They turned toward the densely growing evergreens that reached almost to the edge of the road. Buddy led, peeling off to the right, followed by Brick heading straight in, and by Ward, angling left.

"Buddy!" Brick called in a hoarse whisper.

Buddy stopped, looked left. "Yeah?"

"We won't be able to see shit."

"Use your head, Brick. Use your ears. And stay calm."

He didn't wait for Brick's response. Instead, he crouched down and in the last wisp of twilight walked into the dark evergreen forest.

96

Buddy could hear his breathing in the quiet of the wood. Few cars passed behind him on Highway 17. The night was still.

Then Buddy heard Ben's scream.

An invisible hand grabbed his heart. Took hold. Squeezed until he began to sweat.

He pushed forward, using his left forearm to bat away the low, brittle tree branches. The trees were so close together that in the darkness, his visibility was no more than twenty feet.

Boom!

The sound of a gunshot echoed through the woods. Terribly loud and final. Yet from which direction, Buddy couldn't tell.

Buddy felt the earth fall away from him. *Ben! Mei!*

Now he heard Mei, her voice faint, maybe straight ahead, maybe to the right. He knew she had the same fear he had: Ben was dead.

She called out: "Ben! Where are you? Ben!"

If the boy made a response, Buddy didn't hear it.

If Ben was gone, he could try to save Mei. He *had* to save Mei.

Resisting the urge to run headlong through the woods, he crouched into combat position and proceeded toward his one o'clock. Rapidly. There were at least two killers with him in the woods. He kept his breathing even, his eyes alert to shapes that didn't belong.

Stopping, he turned and swept his eyes behind himself and to the sides.

Clear!

Forward again. Faster, careful to avoid branches that might crack if he stepped on them.

Movement. He saw it. At two o'clock.

He squinted in the charcoal-colored light. *Not Mei,* he thought.

Buddy followed, closing the gap. He could see the man more clearly now. Not tall but wide, with a shaved head.

Yet he saw no sign of Mei. Not her dark hair or her slender frame. He didn't know if she might be creeping to where she believed Ben's scream had come from, or if she were lying, immobile, on the fine layer of powdery snow, hoping to be invisible.

Buddy continued, getting closer and closer to the man with the shaved head. Drawing nearer, he saw the man touch his left hand to his neck. The man groaned audibly.

Injured.

Buddy thought proudly of Mei and what she must have done to the man.

Still, Buddy couldn't see Mei. He was forty yards from the man with the shaved head, who suddenly jogged forward and then abruptly stopped. The man seemed to be staring at something or someone hidden.

97

Ward could see Ben. The boy was trying to run—hobbling on his good leg—through the woods just inside the tree line, along the fields to Ward's left. The echo of the gunshot had deceived everyone, but not Ward.

Thirty yards into the wood, he'd seen a tall blond man raise a gun and shoot at Ben.

But the shot had missed.

Now Ward sprinted, going deeper into the wood but moving northeast, slightly away from the line Ben and the man following him were making as they strove northwest, so that the man was to the left of Ben. They were two points of a triangle, with Ward the third point.

Ward gained on them, pushing branches away from his face as he ran.

He saw the man again raise his gun.

Ward stopped and knelt down. He aimed the Beretta and pressed the trigger.

98

Buddy sprinted, faster than he ever had. He raised his gun, but even as he neared the man, he knew that at that speed, racing through the woods, with his arms in constant motion, he'd miss the guy and might hit Mei.

He lowered his gun but kept going.

Closer.

Closer.

99

Mei heard a second gunshot from a direction she couldn't determine. Falling to the ground, she curled up and lay still. Her left cheek rested on the snow. Its cold soothed her. Her heart slowed just a little. Above her towered evergreens whose tops rose so far she couldn't see them. And these trees hid her, for a moment at least, from the man with the shaved head and his gun. In the stillness, she thought of Ben.

Is he alive?

She didn't know. She couldn't see anything out here in the cold woods.

She heard footsteps in the snow. A soft, dangerous sound.

Listening carefully, she heard a man trying to catch his breath. He was near, so close she could hear the wrinkling of his jacket as he moved his arms.

Slowly, she turned and looked behind her. He stood ten yards from her, and she realized why he'd stopped running.

He sees me.

Although his features were obscure in the moonlight, she could tell he was facing her. She could see the dim outline of his shaved head and of the gun in his hand.

She knew it now: she was going to die.

In an instant she made a resolution. *I'm not going to lie here and wait to be shot. Like an animal. Maybe my death will give Ben some advantage, and he'll escape. I'm going to lose, but I'm also going to fight.*

She sprang up, with her feet at shoulder width. Defenseless, she found her voice. "Why are you chasing me?" she shouted at the man with the shaved head. "What do you want from me?"

He didn't answer, didn't move.

Clenching her fists in front of herself, she rushed toward him and saw him raise his gun.

100

Buddy stood behind and to the right of the man with the shaved head. He couldn't see Mei directly. His vision blurred, his eyes watering from being struck by branches. He saw two men, and then his vision cleared, revealing a single man whose right arm was extending out.

Mei screamed furiously.

He didn't hesitate or think. He had no time for either. He aimed and pressed the trigger.

He fired two rounds, both at center mass.

The man fell forward as if he'd been shoved from behind, collapsing on the snow-covered ground as the piercing sound of the gunshots echoed through the woods and quickly faded.

Buddy ran toward the man in the snow. As his ears cleared, he heard Mei shouting. He could see her now. She'd jumped on the man and was hitting him, hitting him in the face as he lay motionless. She struck him over and over. But the man didn't resist.

"He's dead," Buddy told her, putting his arms around her as gently as he could and pulling her away.

For a moment she fought him, pushing toward the man, punching at air. But then she slowed her movements and stood quietly. She turned to him, embraced him, kissed him once, briefly, on the mouth, and then pushed him away.

"You," she said loudly, her eyes wild. "You're here."

"I'm here. So is Ward. And Brick."

Her brow winkled with worry. "What about Ben? Is he—"

"I don't know," he told her.

For a moment, she stared at him before returning through the woods toward the Suburban. He followed her, relieved she was alive. Yet he felt a lead weight in his stomach as he thought about the gunshots he'd heard moments ago in the near distance, and the boy who'd run away by himself.

101

Buddy wound his way out of the woods, moving toward the headlights of the Suburban. Although Mei had jogged ahead of him, he kept close to her. With the Glock at his side, he remained alert. He didn't know what had happened to the large man or to Ben.

And then he was clear of the woods. In the thick dusk on the west shoulder of the remote highway was the Suburban and behind it, Brick's Tesla. From the back of the SUV came the barks of dogs. Hysterical, angry, perhaps afraid. The Suburban's doors had been closed, and behind it stood four figures.

Her breath visible in the cold, Mei stood with Ben but apart from Ward and Brick. Brick walked past Buddy to the Tesla, climbed into the small car, switched on its driving lights, and remained in the front seat. Mei's arms crossed over the boy's chest. Ben's face bore scratches, undoubtedly from running through the trees. His hair was wet with sweat. But when he saw Buddy, he grinned.

"Buddy!" he said, breaking free of Mei's arms and rushing toward him. Ben stumbled over a crack in the asphalt, caught himself, and lurched into Buddy's arms.

Buddy had crouched down and now held the boy, taking in his warmth and his boyish scent. He hugged Ben tightly, holding him and not letting go. He didn't want to let go—ever. Ben's chest pressed in and out against him, and Buddy savored the sensation of Ben's warm breath against his neck. "Thank God you're okay," Buddy said.

Ben squeezed harder. "I knew you'd find us. I knew we wouldn't die."

Buddy didn't remind him how close he'd come to losing them, how they'd nearly died.

Ben pulled away and looked him in the eye. "They killed Jessica," Ben said. "They shot her."

"What?"

"They shot her."

"Who's Jessica?"

"From Porter Gallery." Mei spoke clearly, her voice low, resigned, melancholy. "My friend. Jess came up to the house to see us, to make sure we were okay. And they killed her at the bottom of a ravine when we tried to escape."

Jesus.

Buddy stood up slowly. A cold tremor passed through him. "I'm sorry. I'm so goddamned sorry."

Mei stepped forward and put an arm around Ben. She said, "I'm sorry, too." For a moment she watched him, her eyes meeting his.

He saw they were strangely blank, as if a wall had formed behind them.

She continued, "But that isn't enough, Buddy. I'm leaving. With Ben."

Good, he thought, as a car passed them on the highway, a rush of air waving over them and then subsiding into silence. *They need to disappear for a while until I solve this case.* He said, "Where are you going?"

Her expression was cold. "Somewhere," she replied. "I don't know where, and I wouldn't tell you if I did."

Now he understood. She was hinting at more than taking Ben to a safe place. No, he realized, she was doing more than hinting.

The solid ground beneath his feet cracked, and he was toppling over the edge of a bottomless crevasse. Something tore within him. He thought it might be his heart.

He tucked the gun into his waistband at the small of his back and held out his hands, palms upward. "We can do this," he urged. "We can make this work."

Slowly, she shook her head. And then she pulled off her engagement ring and offered it to him.

Buddy stared at the ring and lowered his hands to his sides. "Please, Mei. Please don't do this. I love you more than anything."

Ben began to cry. "Mei, we can't leave Buddy. We can't leave him. What will we do? What will *he* do?"

Yet Mei stepped forward and dropped the ring in Buddy's coat pocket. Standing on her toes, she leaned forward, kissed his cheek, and backed away.

He caught her lemon scent, he feared for the last time. He said, "Would you reconsider?"

"No. Not tonight. Not tomorrow. Not this month or next. Maybe never."

His mind spun, searching for a way to prevent what was happening, to halt time, to change the consequences of all that had happened over the past few days. He could think of only one way to stop her from leaving. "If we don't stay together," he argued, "we'll lose Ben. The court won't give us custody."

Raising her chin defiantly, she said, "Better for him to live with his aunt and uncle than to stay with us and die. No, Buddy, I can't jeopardize his life and his future because of your job. And *don't* use him as a bargaining chip to talk about us."

Buddy knew he was guilty of doing just that, but fear and anger squashed any remorse he might have felt. His voice rose. "It's not a bargaining chip, it's reality."

She put a hand on Ben's shoulder. "We're leaving. Now." She pulled Ben toward the Suburban's front passenger door and helped him climb inside. She buckled him in. The barking of the German shepherds grew fiercer, sharper. After closing the door, she walked around the Suburban. "I'll quit!" Buddy called after her, more loudly than he'd intended. This was a decision he'd just made. He'd never considered leaving the force. He was a police detective, and his work defined and motivated him. His work gave his life purpose. Quitting meant not knowing what to do. Quitting meant having no money, and having no money meant having to return to the concert stage. He wasn't sure he could do that. Yet he had to make a choice.

Mei put a hand on the driver's door, stopped, then turned to face him and Ward.

When she hesitated, Buddy spoke rapidly. "I'll quit my job. I'll go back to the piano and learn to perform again. Maybe make another album. We can have a normal life, a safe life."

Her face showed no sign of agreement or disagreement. Thinking for a moment, she breathed deeply, once, twice. Then she sighed. "I don't believe you. You are who you are, Buddy. You can't change. You're a detective, a hunter of criminals. I love you, and I love how you work so hard for other people, including Ben and me. But"—she shook her head—"I can't be part of it anymore. Part of *you*. I want to have children and a career. I want to live to be old. And I don't think those things are possible with you. I mean, *Jesus Christ*, Buddy—those men killed Jessica, then you and Ward killed them. And now that they're dead, what will happen?"

He was silent. He knew this wasn't the time to tell her he'd been thrown out of an airplane, and the same had nearly happened to her and Ben.

"*What?*" she demanded.

He couldn't move. Every part of him felt paralyzed. At last he said, "I don't know."

Her eyes narrowed. "But I do. I know that *others* will come for us. They'll keep coming. Until we're dead. So the only way Ben and I can survive is if we leave you. I'm sorry, Buddy, but this is over. You can stay in our—in my—home for another week, then you need to be gone. Goodbye."

My home, he thought. *Hers, not ours. Not anymore.*

She pulled open the driver's door, climbed into the Suburban, and started the ignition.

Buddy wanted to grab hold of the rear bumper, to keep the nearly three-ton vehicle in place. But he knew he couldn't stop it, couldn't stop Mei from the consequences of her decision, couldn't stop her from tearing them apart.

So he didn't move. He stood motionless in his misery, frustration, and anger. And in his helplessness.

Mei drove the Suburban forward and made a half circle on the highway. As the SUV's headlights shone south, he held up a hand to block the blinding light.

The Suburban headed west, passing him and Ward, and he lowered his hand. He had a clear view as the Suburban climbed the hill. A moment later, at the hill's crest, the red taillights grew smaller, flickered, and disappeared.

102

At midnight Buddy stood alone in Mei's living room. Brick and Ward had dropped him off and left. Nobody else knew he was here. He'd gone from the hotel, through the door and the narrow hallway to the Carlyle Residences, sneaking past Schmidt, the doorman, as Schmidt had helped an older couple out of their taxi. He was alone in what had been his home but now was another place he had to leave.

Despite the view and beautiful room, he felt an increasing pressure, like one of those sleeves a nurse uses to check your blood pressure, tightening around his entire body. He couldn't loosen its grip. He couldn't be with Mei because he hadn't solved the case. And even if he solved the case, she and Ben wouldn't return. Because his pursuers had destroyed his family.

Obliterated his family.

But it was worse than that. He'd lost the *only* two people he truly loved. Now he was completely alone, with the fleeting exception of a half brother who lived in a different world than he did.

Just great, he thought. *Just fucking great.*

He couldn't call the police. They'd investigate him, as he was AWOL when he should have been working.

But when he returned to the kitchen, he realized the NYPD had contacted him. Mario had left a message on his home line.

"Where are you, Buddy? Did something happen? Hey, I checked out Sloan Richardson. She's early twenties, from Beverly Hills. Dead daddy was a movie studio exec, moved into Grandma's condo in the Nanjing building about a year ago. Grandma died about fourteen months ago. Did you need more on Sloan? Let me know. The chief's on us, Buddy. I'm telling him you're working with me, but I can't cover for you much longer. Adios."

Buddy considered the source of this information. If Mario had known he was dead—or had played any part in making him dead— Mario wouldn't bother doing Buddy favors. Plus, the information made sense to him. Girl from sunny LA moved to Manhattan. Didn't want to be forced out of her inherited condo that had sentimental value. But was that all there was to it? Or had her stubborn refusal to leave and take the money Cromwell had surely offered been a move in a chess match he couldn't see?

He didn't know.

Buddy wouldn't return Mario's call. Mario might mention it in passing to the wrong person. If anyone learned he was alive, he'd be an easy-to-find target. Especially easy if his enemies were cops or people who had influence with the NYPD.

The solution? He didn't know of one.

The phone in the kitchen rang. He turned quickly, went over to it, and paused. He was supposed to be dead, and dead men didn't answer the phone.

Can it be Mei? he thought. *Did she realize she made a mistake?*

He picked up the phone and listened but didn't answer.

At first he didn't know who was on the line. He heard only crying. "Ben?" he said. "Is that you?"

A moment of quiet and then, "Yes."

Buddy tried to make his voice calm and casual. "Hi, Ben. How're you doing?"

"Buddy?"

"Yeah?"

"Will you come get me?"

Buddy wasn't sure how to respond. He said, "What's wrong?"

"I want . . . I want to be with you."

These words raised Buddy's spirits, but they also hurt him. He said, "Is something wrong with Mei?"

"I want to be with *you*," Ben repeated. "With you *and* Mei."

Anguish coursed through him. He wanted the same thing, but he didn't know how to tell Ben that it was impossible. At least for now. Yet he hadn't given up. Despite all evidence to the contrary, he began to think he could regain Mei's hand, that he'd marry her, that the three of them would again form a family. "I'll find a way for us to be together," he promised. "For the rest of our lives. Things will work out. They *will*, Ben. I'll resign from the force and find something else to do. All right?"

Ben was quiet. Then he said, "Can you do it now?"

Buddy breathed deeply, trying to control his frustration. "No, not now. I have to find out why you and Mei were taken by those men. After that, we'll see what happens."

Ben's voice rose, "But you promised! You promised we'd be together!"

Before Buddy could respond, he heard Mei's voice in the background and then Ben quickly whispered bye and hung up.

Cut off, that's how Buddy thought of it. Cut off from Mei and Ben. He became angry at Mei but realized that she'd done what she needed to do. She was protecting Ben, even at the cost of separating Ben from him.

He was trapped. He was stuck in his life and there wasn't an exit. He slammed his open left hand on the kitchen countertop.

"Fuck!" he said aloud.

He left the kitchen and walked into the living room. Pacing by the windows, he thought about his options and decided there was only one. To be with his new family, he'd give up everything else. Even the NYPD, for twenty years his reason for existence, for sanity, for pride. *Solve the case. Quit the force. To make a living, return to his first love and first curse.*

He went over to Mei's baby grand, sat on the bench, and played the same pieces he'd played two nights before. *Für Elise.* The first thirty seconds of Grieg's concerto.

This time, his playing was improved. His left wrist hurt—hell, his entire body hurt after being beaten and thrown from an airplane—but he had reason to hope. If he laid off his wrist for a couple of weeks, he'd recover. Maybe he'd record something again and make a little money. Or maybe he'd play in a jazz club, but not the concert stage. Definitely not that.

Lifting his hands from the keyboard, he sat silently at the piano. The black lacquer showed his faint reflection. He could see his face's outline but not his eyes.

He knew he was getting stronger. He remembered that Ward had called him a hunter. Mei had said something similar. He thought they were right. He thought about his prey.

One dirty cop, he thought. *Or more than one.*

What else did he know?

His investigation needled Erica Fischer and Jack Carlson of the EDA. It threatened Cromwell Properties, the big real estate developer.

He'd begin there. He'd be relentless. He'd put down whomever he had to. He'd show no mercy.

But to succeed, he couldn't be himself. He couldn't be Buddy Lock with the NYPD or even Buddy Lock, failed concert pianist and private citizen. He'd have to become nobody. A nobody who worked mostly at night.

He'd become a ghost. A ghost with a gun and the freedom to use it.

DAY 5

103

Ward entered the office of Stella Bannon, CEO of Cromwell Properties. "Thank you," he said hurriedly. "Thank you for seeing me."

"Of course, Ward," Stella Bannon replied, standing from behind her modern desk, a glass top set on four legs of black steel. "We ought to see each other outside the trustees' meetings."

Stella Bannon was of medium height, fanatically thin, with black hair pulled straight back from her face and clipped behind her head with a tortoiseshell barrette. She wore a tailored dress so devoid of ornament and so plain that he knew it was expensive, likely Dior. From her ears hung simple silver hoops that matched the bracelet on her right wrist.

They met in the center of the large office and shook hands. She motioned him to one of the four armchairs covered in bright orange leather, and they sat down.

He kept his face expressionless as he said, "I'm sorry, Stella, but my brother, Detective Lock, couldn't make it. I'm not sure where he is, but he's undoubtedly working."

As she nodded once, he thought he noticed the beginning of a smile, quickly suppressed. He, in turn, suppressed his anger and suspicion.

He said, "I know a little about music but nothing about real estate development. It's Greek to me, Stella. But could you tell me about the

Haddon House project? I might buy a place in the city because I'm tired of my usual suite at the Four Seasons." He crossed his legs, revealing gray socks patterned with miniature images of the *Mona Lisa*.

Stella Bannon described the amenities of Haddon House, but noted that most units were already under purchase contract. Ward widened his eyes at the description of the planned fitness facility. Stella talked about the brilliant design by Antoine Rousseau, the famous Parisian architect.

When she paused, Ward nodded and said, "But my brother has told me you have a problem with some occupants of the present building on the site, the Nanjing building. Holdouts. They're refusing to sell you their units, aren't they?"

Stella Bannon showed no frustration with the question or the situation to which he'd referred. "Your brother is mistaken," she replied. "There are no holdouts at the Haddon House site. Zero holdouts, Ward. And even if there were, the EDA could use eminent domain to remove them."

Remove them, Ward thought. *That's one way of putting it.*

Ward gave her a confused expression, shaking his head as if the whole business was beyond him. He said, in a low voice, "What about Chen Sung and Lily Sung? What about Sloan Richardson?"

Stella Bannon's face went blank. She shook her head and said, "I don't recognize those names."

Ward's voice rose in volume. "Strange, but those are three people who were discovered over the past week. Off the coast of Long Island. The last three holdouts of the Nanjing building you're demolishing to make way for Haddon House."

Stella Bannon stared at him but didn't respond.

Ward said, "My brother told me that one of the Sungs' children gave him a business card from Vance McInnis, your vice president of development. May I talk with him?"

Stella Bannon regarded him silently as she considered this request. Ward watched her carefully, but she betrayed nothing. He imagined that she was thinking of how to show she had nothing to hide. But perhaps she was thinking of something else entirely.

A moment later she stood and pressed a button on her desk phone. She said, "Would you have Mr. McInnis come to my office, please?"

Ward watched her as she proceeded to type on her computer keyboard while standing. She didn't speak to him or look at him. He stared at her as she pretended he wasn't there.

The door to Stella Bannon's office opened, and Vance McInnis entered. Ward saw that he was tall and lean and well built around the chest. He had a Mediterranean complexion, dark hair, and small dark eyes set deeply within his face. He was dressed in an expensive but off-the-rack blue check sport coat and wool trousers, no tie.

Stella Bannon straightened from her keyboard and addressed McInnis. "Ward Mills"—she tilted her head at Ward—"wants to know about any holdouts from the Nanjing building. What's the status there?"

McInnis shrugged and turned to Ward. He had a low, clear voice. "They signed the papers—the three of them. We paid their money. I don't know or care where they went. They caused enough trouble."

Ward stood and faced McInnis, who was about one inch taller than he was. Ward said, "I thought they were holdouts."

McInnis nodded. "They were. Until I received packages via messenger. The packages contained their signed agreements to sell, along with deeds to their units."

Ward said, "How . . . convenient and lucky for Cromwell Properties. Do you have the envelopes?"

Vance McInnis's eyes narrowed to slits as he crossed his arms. "No."

Stella Bannon said, "You see, Mr. Mills, we can't help you—or your brother, if he's . . . wherever he may be."

Ward gave a wan smile and shook his head. "My brother is probably on his honeymoon. Where else would he be?"

Stella Bannon smiled back at him and said, "Indeed."

Ward began walking toward the door, then stopped and turned around to face Stella Bannon and Vance McInnis. He said, "Would you tell me about your corporate and personal aircraft?"

Stella Bannon looked annoyed. "What?"

Ward raised his chin. "You heard me."

Stella Bannon looked over at Vance McInnis. His expression had gone blank.

Vance McInnis said, "How is that information relevant to Haddon House?"

"Your planes, helicopters, whatever, will be registered with the FAA," Ward told them. "So I can find out. Save me the trouble, would you?"

Vance McInnis pointed to the door. "Time's up, Mr. Mills. Time's up."

Stella Bannon went past Ward and opened the door. She said, "I have another meeting. Goodbye, Ward."

104

A half hour later, Ward walked into the lobby of the Carlyle Residences. Dressed in his customary Brioni suit, this one a medium gray, and handmade shoes, he greeted Schmidt, the doorman, and held up an access card for Mei's condo.

Ward said, "I'm going up to Buddy and Mei's place to take care of a few things while they're away."

"Sure thing." Schmidt nodded. "I haven't seen them in a couple days. Where'd they go?"

Ward smiled. "Skiing, up in Vermont."

"Oh, yeah? That's good. Let me know if I can help."

Ward was carrying a large Dunkin' Donuts coffee and a heavy black nylon duffel over his shoulder. The contents of the duffel clanked as he walked. He said, "Thanks, man." He held up the coffee cup. "Now Buddy's got me hooked on this stuff."

Schmidt laughed. Ward touched his good shoulder and walked into the elevator. When the elevator door closed, he thought, *It's working. If Buddy's doorman believes he's gone away, who could disagree?*

But then he realized the consequences of the dead men in the woods along Highway 17. When those men didn't report in to whoever had hired them, someone would wonder what had happened.

105

Buddy had to play dead. He'd returned late last night from Rockridge and remained all day in the apartment. He couldn't let anyone see or hear him or, if possible, think about him.

In the kitchen, Ward handed Buddy the coffee and set down the large duffel bag. Buddy noticed that Ward had dressed to the nines.

Weird choice, he thought, *for surveillance.*

But he wouldn't be critical of his brother, not today, maybe not ever.

Buddy removed the plastic lid and took a couple of large mouthfuls of the coffee. After an Advil half an hour ago and now the coffee, he was feeling ready to continue the hunt. He took a step forward and watched as Ward unzipped the duffel bag and pulled open the sides.

He could see clothes Ward had brought him—for the new Buddy, not the now-deceased police detective. This Buddy had independent wealth. Ward took out a pair of Tommy Bahama khakis and dark-blue cotton pants, some expensive button-down shirts and a dark-blue fleece, a black Patagonia parka with a hood, gloves, a black baseball-type cap with the Under Armour symbol stitched above the bill, and expensive-looking Persol sunglasses. Under the clothes were black shoes that appeared to be lace-up dress shoes but were more like sneakers. When Ward removed these from the bag, Buddy saw an arsenal.

Buddy bent down. In the bag he counted one rifle, five handguns, an ankle holster, two shoulder holsters, plus an IWB holster. Carefully, Ward removed each piece and placed it on the granite countertop. With the equipment removed, Buddy again looked at the duffel and saw two sets of body armor, four boxes of ammunition, two knives, and two sets of lockpicks. As Ward lifted these from the bag, his eyes met Buddy's.

Ward said, "Leave the investigation in the city to me. You should move up to my place in Greenwich. I'll be your eyes and ears. You can tell me what to do. I'll follow your instructions to the letter. You won't have to leave my house."

Buddy felt anger, but only for a second. He knew his brother was trying to protect him. "No," he said calmly. "I need to do it myself. I need to see and hear. I need to think right there in the moment. With the clothes you brought me, I'll become someone else."

Ward eyed him warily, seemingly trying to decide whether to argue. Then he said, "Don't shave, all right?"

Buddy nodded.

"And dye your hair."

"No."

Ward's mouth twisted with frustration, then he said, "Okay. Wear these clothes I've brought you. Think of how Buddy looked and acted, then do something different. Not hugely different, but different enough to throw people off." Ward pulled from his coat pocket a burner phone and several hundred dollars in cash and handed them to Buddy. He said, "Dead men don't use credit cards or ATMs."

Buddy hesitated—he already owed his brother, not money, but more than he could repay—then took the phone and the money.

In the master bedroom, he tried on the clothes Ward had brought him, with Ward standing by the window, relating his meeting that morning with Stella Bannon and Vance McInnis. He put on the dark-blue fleece over his T-shirt and slipped his set of lockpicks in the generously cut left front pocket of the dark-blue pants. Finally, he added an

IWB holster at the small of his back for his Glock 19. And an ankle holster weighted with a Glock 26. Plus several spare magazines for the 19, pushed into the left side pocket of the Patagonia jacket.

Ward said, "McInnis is a hardcore athlete. He's in great shape. Must go to the gym. Maybe he runs or rides a bike, but he lifts weights, there's no doubt."

Buddy thought about the man who'd thrown him from the plane. He turned to face Ward and asked, "What's he look like?"

Ward told him.

"Small eyes?" Buddy asked. "Like a rodent's?"

"Maybe smaller than normal."

A coincidence? Buddy wondered.

Ward continued relating the meeting, and how Stella Bannon and Vance McInnis had refused to provide him with information about their corporate and personal aircraft. "Yes," Ward said, "they clammed up. McInnis stands there like an elementary school teacher and tells me, 'Time's up, Mr. Mills. Time's up.'"

Buddy's skin felt like static electricity was brushing it, making it almost crackle. He said, "'Time's up?' That's what McInnis told you?"

"Yeah. He's a prick."

"No," Buddy said. "That's not the point."

"What do you mean?"

Buddy raised a fist. "The guy who pushed me out of the plane? He looked like Vance McInnis. And before he threw me out, do you know what he said?"

Ward didn't answer.

Buddy said, "The asshole said, 'Time's up.'"

"Shit," Ward said.

Buddy nodded. "Yeah. Shit. It's the same fucking guy. So it's got to be Cromwell Properties that's crooked here. Cromwell Properties that's killing people to push its projects forward and make hundreds of millions of dollars."

Ward nodded. "I'm with you, Buddy. But that's *if* McInnis is your guy. 'Time's up' is a common expression. You can't build your case on it."

Yet Buddy's mind was spinning forward. He thought about confronting McInnis, arresting him. He wanted to kill McInnis, but he'd settle for sending him to prison for life. But that wouldn't work. Not right now. He had no evidence that Cromwell Properties had done anything illegal, let alone commit multiple murders. And even if he saw McInnis and confirmed that McInnis had thrown him from the plane, he had no proof that had happened. He had no proof of anything, not yet.

Turning from his brother, he slowed his breathing and tried to focus. *Hard evidence,* he thought. *Irrefutable evidence.* He thought silently for another moment, then he put on the black Patagonia jacket with the magazines in the left pocket, the baseball cap, and the sunglasses that Ward had brought him.

"Let's go," he said. "Their time's up."

106

To avoid Schmidt, he led Ward into the laundry room and down the interior fire stairs. As they descended from the twenty-fifth floor, he grew apprehensive about the way the afternoon and evening might play out. He was about to break the law. Several laws. If he were caught, the repercussions could be prison or death, depending on who caught him. But he reasoned the law was a thing that protected the innocent, and in this case the only people he'd hurt by breaking the law were killers. His conscience cleared. Or cleared enough.

For a moment they waited on the other side of the door from the lobby, until they were certain that despite the cold, Schmidt was standing outside under the sidewalk canopy. Then they hurried across the lobby and along the narrow hallway that led to the lobby of the adjacent Carlyle Hotel.

Out on Madison Avenue, Buddy looked right and left. Seeing nothing suspicious, he turned to Ward and said, "We're going after Cromwell. But first, we need to clear away the dirty cop or cops. You take Chief Malone. I'll take Mingo. Depending on what we find, we might focus on Stella Bannon."

Ward nodded. He lifted his phone and called Buddy. Buddy felt the burner phone in his pocket vibrate and heard it ring.

Ward ended the call and said, "You have my number."

"Yeah." Buddy nodded. "But remember, you're watching the chief but you're not doing anything to him, okay? He might be clean."

"And if he's not?"

Buddy said, "If he's dirty, call me."

Ward nodded, walked to the curb, and held out a hand for a cab.

Buddy walked south, alone. He wouldn't take a taxi because he wasn't in a hurry, not for what he needed to do. And he liked the walk, no matter how cold it was. It would give him time to think, time to plan.

As he went, he glanced in the window of a restaurant and caught his reflection. He almost didn't recognize himself. The hat and the sunglasses helped to hide his features. Nobody paid him attention, and that made him feel dangerous.

The familiar weight of Ward's unregistered Glock 19 at the small of his back helped the feeling. He'd forgone body armor. He didn't think he'd need it for surveillance. Because surveillance, he'd told himself and Ward, was all they were going to do tonight.

107

A few minutes after five o'clock that evening, Ward followed Chief Malone out of One Police Plaza. Malone didn't get into an unmarked and drive home, but instead walked out of the massive brick building and descended the steps into the subway at Brooklyn Bridge–City Hall station on Centre Street.

Malone didn't spot Ward, but how could he? He'd never met Ward, and Ward was dressed like any of the dozens of other businessmen waiting on the platform, although Ward was better dressed than most of them.

Better than all of them, Ward thought to himself.

Malone, NYPD's chief of detectives, wore a nondescript suit and a gray wool coat that stretched over his bulky stomach. His bare, domed head shone in the dull lights of the subway car as he sat near the front and took out a copy of that morning's *Gazette.* Ward sat on the other side of the car, toward the back. The train lumbered through the depths and stopped again and again and again. Eventually, at the Newkirk Plaza stop in Brooklyn, Malone got up, folded the newspaper, and tucked it under his left arm. When the doors opened, he walked out of the train, Ward five paces behind.

Above ground, Ward dropped back to forty feet behind Malone. From the other side of Foster Avenue, Ward saw the chief of detectives enter a liquor store. Ward waited in the cold, watching the door, not quite trusting his vision. It was beyond dusk now, everything dark except under the streetlamps or lights from stores and restaurants along the sidewalks. The other pedestrians ignored him as he paced back and forth outside a clock repair shop, closed for the day.

Five minutes later, Malone emerged from the liquor store carrying a bottle in a tan paper bag. He walked south on Foster another two blocks, turned left on Rugby Road, and a hundred yards farther, walked up the steps of the third-row house on the left.

Ward watched the door close. After waiting a moment, from his pocket he pulled a black knit ski mask. He put the mask on his head, but he didn't pull the forward part of it over his face. Moving quickly, he approached Malone's doorway and withdrew the set of lockpicks from his overcoat pocket. At Malone's doorway, he pulled the mask over his face.

He knew people might see him, approach him, or alert the police. Speed was everything. Yet he'd practiced for years, and he was calm and fast. Four seconds, and the lock drew back with a nearly silent click.

He opened the door and stepped inside the row house. Moving quickly, he slipped the picks in his jacket pocket and pulled out a Beretta M9.

As he proceeded along the left wall of the center hallway, he heard voices from the television news. Then he heard the kitchen floor creak and knew that Malone had heard him.

No good options, he thought.

He didn't know the layout of the house. He was flying blind.

He pressed up against the wall by the doorway from the kitchen to the hall. Not breathing, he watched the door open and studied the scuffed oak floor for a shadow. Straight through the doorway he could see a family room, a television set at its far end. To the right of the doorway, he could see the side of a white refrigerator.

Except for the noise of the television, the house was silent. He heard no traffic outside. The kitchen floor didn't creak a second time. For a second he suspected the noise he'd heard earlier was the house shifting. Or perhaps Malone had put his feet up on a living room coffee table beyond Ward's field of vision.

But then a shadow moved from behind the refrigerator into the doorway, followed a second later by a six-inch kitchen knife held by Chief Malone's enormous fist.

Ward crossed to the other side of the hallway. He encircled Malone's forearm with his left arm and pulled Malone into the hallway, knocking him off-balance with a kick to the shin, and hitting him in the chest with the Beretta.

Malone was a bureaucrat and hadn't been in the field for years. He went down quickly, still holding the knife. Ward stomped on Malone's wrist.

"Aghh!" Malone shrieked.

Ward reached down and took away the knife, threw it back into the kitchen, and pointed the M9 at Malone's chest. He tilted his head, as if studying Malone's fear and thus eliciting more fear.

This seemed to work. Malone raised his hands. Bubbles of sweat appeared on his domed forehead. "Take anything you want," Malone blustered. "Anything. But leave me alone. I don't know who you are, and I don't care!"

Ward ignored the suggestion. He knew Buddy would be furious to learn about the break-in and his holding Malone at gunpoint in the chief's own house. But he knew the danger of a traitor on the force. He knew all too well. So he leaned closer to Malone and said, "Tell me about Haddon House."

Lines appeared across Malone's expansive forehead. "What?"

"You heard me."

"Yeah, I heard you. But what's Haddon House?"

"The project?"

"Project? What project? I think you've got the wrong guy."

Ward was starting to think he did, too, but he'd make sure. "When did you last meet or speak with Stella Bannon?"

Malone laid his head on the floor, closed his eyes. "Shoot me if you have to, but I've never heard of Stella Bannon. Is she the victim of a crime? Did we arrest her?"

Not yet, Ward thought.

He raised the gun, turned it sideways, and hit Chief Malone on the side of the head.

Malone's head slammed against the baseboard and then was still. His eyelids dropped like curtains.

Ward watched to be sure Malone's chest continued to rise and fall. Convinced the chief of detectives would live without permanent injury, he raised the mask and left the row house. Outside on the street, he called the number for Buddy's burner phone.

Buddy answered, "Yeah?"

"Malone's not involved."

"You're sure?"

"Yes."

"How do you know?"

Ward wasn't going tell his brother anything further. He ignored the question and said, "Where are you?"

"At an airfield."

Ward stopped walking and clenched the phone. "Buddy!" he shouted into the phone. "Are you all right?"

108

Buddy recognized the airfield. He'd been here yesterday, and this time he could see the signs: Republic Airport. And knew where it was: Farmingdale, on Long Island. But this time, he wasn't tied to a chair and a luggage trolley. Today, he was hunting.

In order to follow his partner, Mario Mingo, he'd positioned himself behind the stairs going up to the Park East Synagogue on East Sixty-Seventh, outside the Nineteenth Precinct, a red brick building with stone detailing around the windows. This was Buddy's home base. Where he had his cubicle. Where he'd spent years of his life.

Just before five o'clock, Mario had run out of the building, jumped into his Ford Interceptor, and headed north.

Luck had been with Buddy. An available yellow cab, a Toyota Prius, was dropping off an older woman on the precinct steps. Buddy raised a hand and hurried across the street, hoping his disguise was effective against anyone from the building who might glance out one of the windows as he crossed the street.

"Follow the Ford Interceptor," he said, slamming the front door.

The driver, who Buddy thought was West African, looked over at him. "Hey, man . . ." the driver began.

Buddy handed over some of the twenties Ward had given him and pointed forward at the rapidly disappearing Ford. "Come on!" he said, his voice rising. "Let's go!"

The driver put the car in drive and pulled into traffic. He said, "But the guy driving the Ford is a cop."

"So am I," Buddy said. "Fucking step on it."

Now, as they approached the airstrip, he put up a hand and said, "Hold back, okay? *Hold back.*"

The cab driver slowed the car, and Buddy couldn't complain. The guy had kept up with Mario despite breaking speed limits the entire way out of the city—north to the RFK Bridge and then Interstate 278 down to the Grand Central Parkway.

Most airfields, even those as small as this one, were surrounded by extensive flat ground. Visibility extended hundreds or even thousands of yards. To the west of the runway was the dun brown wall of a big-box store. To the east from the cab, Buddy could see flashing police lights and spotlights arrayed around a small plane a quarter mile away—a plane that seemed awfully familiar.

At an eighth of a mile, he could make out the plane. It was the white dual-propeller plane in which he'd flown yesterday.

Jesus, he thought. *Could Mario have figured it out?*

"Stop the car," he told the driver.

"Sure."

As the car rolled silently to a stop, Buddy saw the plane illuminated by the eerie white glare of the sodium vapor lights used by CSU. And CSU was there in force. Two teams, each with several detectives. He watched Mario drive the Ford close to the scene and get out.

Mario approached plane, one of the detectives speaking with him, gesticulating toward the open door. Mario nodded as he peered in through the doorway, talking further with the detective standing to his right. Then he returned to his car, stood beside it while typing on his phone, then got in the car and headed away from the airfield and toward the taxi and Buddy.

"Turn around," Buddy said, hunching over so Mario couldn't see him when he passed them. "Follow the Ford."

The driver put the car in drive and turned the wheel. Buddy heard the sound of the Ford pass them.

What's Mario doing?

Buddy's driver stepped on the accelerator, and the Toyota surged forward. Buddy sat up and saw the Ford speeding away.

They followed Mario's car.

West on Interstate 495.

Through the Queens Midtown Tunnel and back into Manhattan.

Across the island on Thirty-Seventh Street.

Down Ninth Avenue, arriving eventually at Little West Twelfth Street on the Lower West Side.

It took over an hour and twenty minutes.

Mario pulled up to a newer building in the Meatpacking District. He made no effort to find a parking spot for the Ford, just double-parked by the building's front door. Four uniforms were waiting for him.

Mario got out of the car and approached the uniforms at the door. All five drew their guns, and Mario led them into the building.

Buddy handed over most of his money to the taxi driver. Then he walked into a coffee shop across the street from the building. He stood by the window, not bothering to order anything. Five minutes later Mario and the uniforms came through the building door, leading out a man in handcuffs.

Buddy watched carefully. At first he thought it was Rat Eyes, who'd thrown him from the plane. Same Mediterranean complexion, same dark hair, same level of fitness.

But the man in handcuffs was taller, softer, handsome as a movie star. And he was more than confused, he was stunned. He looked up at the sky as if waiting for deliverance from God. But there was no deliverance, not as Mario pushed him into the back of a black-and-white and slammed the door.

Buddy watched from the coffee shop as Mario climbed into the Ford, pulled into traffic heading south, then turned left, the black-and-white with the perp and the second black-and-white following. Buddy knew they were headed east to One Police Plaza. That's where you booked a high-profile guy like . . . like who?

Vance McInnis, Buddy thought. *Ward's description of the guy to a tee. But what did Mario find on McInnis? What did I miss?*

As he stood behind the window and watched the cars pull away, he wondered if it had been Mario who'd missed something. Or been misled.

He took out his phone and called Ward. When his brother picked up, he said, "Meet me in the Meatpacking District. Little West Twelfth Street. I'm at Grind It Coffee."

Buddy remained by the window without moving. His breath fogged the window as he waited. And waited. He expected a CSU team to arrive and examine Vance McInnis's condominium. Yet nobody showed up. Maybe they were busy with the plane at Republic Airport.

He wasn't sure what had happened, but he knew an opportunity when he saw one.

109

Buddy worked the pick and tension wrench in the lock. He crouched low and wore latex gloves. Ward stood to his right, blocking an immediate view of Buddy from the elevator and the empty corridor. Four seconds, and they entered Vance McInnis's condominium. They stood in the foyer, listening, making sure Mario hadn't left a uniform inside the place to maintain the integrity of the potential crime scene.

"Hello?" Buddy called.

There was no response.

Buddy turned to his brother, amazed that Ward wore a beautiful suit and overcoat for this kind of work. He shook his head silently.

Ward noticed. "What?"

Buddy didn't answer. Instead he asked, "How were you sure Malone wasn't involved?"

"He convinced me."

"You *talked* to him? I told you not to—"

"I made an executive decision," Ward interrupted.

Buddy felt his face go hot. He held up a hand. "I told you to follow him and nothing more. What the hell did you do?"

Ward shrugged, looked away.

"Tell me, goddammit."

Ward faced him. His lightly tanned face showed no sign of embarrassment. Ward was confident about everything he did. Buddy wondered how that felt.

Ward said, "I roughed him up."

Buddy couldn't believe it. "Where?"

"His house."

"You broke into his *house*?"

"Had to."

"And he told you he knew nothing about Haddon House or Cromwell Properties?"

"Yeah."

"You put pressure him?"

"Certainly. The pressure of a Beretta."

Buddy knew his face showed shock. "Sometimes I don't get you."

Ward was silent.

Buddy wanted to slug his brother, but at the same time he was relieved—relieved that Malone was clean and someone he could trust.

Buddy reached into his jacket and handed Ward a pair of latex gloves. He said, "Put these on. We'll go room by room. But fast. CSU won't be long."

He led Ward on a search of the condominium. Bedrooms, baths, living room, kitchen, small laundry room, everywhere.

As Buddy searched, he found no evidence of anyone, not even Vance McInnis. No photos of family. Nothing but a bottle of vodka in the freezer, some white wine in the refrigerator, and red wine in a small rack on the marble countertops. Plates, dishes, bathrooms—all of it clean. *Or cleaned,* Buddy thought.

He stood in the master bedroom, with the gray area rug and the king-sized black lacquered bed frame. The mattress had been stripped of linens, even the mattress pad. A few books partly filled one shelf.

349

On the wall opposite the bed hung a flat-screen television but no DVD player, no movies.

Listening to his breath in the quiet, he thought more about the condo. Then he walked into the kitchen and began opening the cabinets. He saw very few pots and pans, a few bowls, plates, drinking glasses, and cheap flatware.

Ward followed and pulled out the plastic garbage can and peeked inside. When Buddy glanced over, Ward said, "Dirty napkins and take-out containers, used chopsticks. A pizza box."

Buddy said, "Guys with everything eat the same shit as everyone else." And then he checked the cupboards for weapons, ammunition, anything to indicate McInnis knew how to threaten or get violent.

But there was nothing.

He went into the room next to the kitchen, which turned out to be a laundry room. Opening the washing machine door, he saw the barrel of the machine was filled with white sheets and a white mattress pad. He sniffed, smelled the stench of bleach. Far too much bleach.

Someone beat us here, he thought. *Did that person set up McInnis?*

He returned to the kitchen, studied the faucet handle, the stainless-steel refrigerator door. Then he hurried into the bathrooms. Checked the faucet handles, the handle of the toilet seats, the toilet seat itself. He stood and looked at the gleaming space before going back into the master bedroom. Leaning over, he put his eyes at the level of the nightstands. He heard movement behind him, straightened, and turned around.

Ward was staring at him. "Did you find something?"

Buddy laughed angrily. He said, "It's too clean. I see no prints on anything. The guy's here eating greasy pizza, and everything is spotless. No, this place has been cleaned professionally, and I don't mean by a cleaning lady. The person who did this job was careful and in no hurry. The paper towels or cloth towels or rags or whatever were used are gone."

Ward said, "Maybe Vance McInnis knew they were coming for him and wiped it down."

Buddy didn't respond. He left the master bedroom and walked along the hallway into the living room. There, he switched on the television to the local NBC station.

Perfectly done, he thought.

110

He saw live coverage of the arrest of Vance McInnis. Stock photos of the Cromwell Properties vice president of development; images of McInnis, his wife, and two children at a neighborhood barbecue. Video of McInnis teeing off at a Pebble Beach charity event. Buddy turned up the volume and listened.

The newscaster, Leonard Baldwin, a man in a dark suit and a dark tie, announced to the world that the NYPD had charged Vance McInnis with first-degree murder in the death of Sloan Richardson, having thrown her out of a two-engine propeller plane—the image to the right of the announcer's shoulder changed to a distance shot of the plane Buddy knew only too well, at rest under the glare of CSU's lights. The newscaster stated that the murder had been two nights ago, according to air traffic control records, between midnight and 1:00 a.m.

Buddy felt confusion and anger. He noticed Ward was standing beside him, but he didn't speak. He listened as the newscaster passed the narrative over to Gabriela Stone, a reporter at the airfield. He grew distracted, not by the news story but by what hadn't been included.

The Sungs, he thought. *Not a word about Chen and Lily Sung.*

Gabriela Stone lifted her chin and said, "Sources inside the NYPD have revealed that the airplane contains fingerprints of both Sloan Richardson and Vance McInnis. Yesterday morning, Sloan Richardson was reported missing by a friend. A highly placed source with the Federal Aviation Administration has told me exclusively that footage from an exterior security camera may show McInnis, hiding himself under a knit cap and black clothing, dragging Sloan Richardson onboard the aircraft two nights ago. The strange thing, Leonard, is that the plane's regular pilots have airtight alibis. So it's unclear who piloted the plane on its fateful voyage. Maybe McInnis himself, as he had a pilot's license and was rated on this aircraft. This is in conflict with McInnis's story that he was with Ms. Stella Bannon, the CEO of Cromwell Properties, at the time he was to have killed Sloan Richardson. The NYPD has yet to confirm. But I've learned from a confidential source that Miss Richardson was the lone holdout preventing a new condominium project in Chinatown by Cromwell Properties."

Buddy saw the video cut to a different reporter, in a live feed, standing with Stella Bannon outside the offices of Cromwell Properties. Enormous tinted windows and slabs of granite behind her, Bannon stood before a dozen handheld microphones and phones.

Buddy leaned forward and turned up the volume.

Stella Bannon looked confidently at the cameras, her eyes steady despite the bright lights, her shoulder-length raven-colored hair pulled back from her face. She said, "Two nights ago, and last night, I was at home, alone, working. I didn't see Vance McInnis after I left the office on either night. I'm shocked and saddened by the charges against my associate, and I hope that he takes responsibility for his actions. I must state for the record that I knew him to be hardworking and ethical. I'm as surprised as anyone by these charges against him regarding the young woman, Sloan Richardson, and her murder."

Stella Bannon then turned from the microphones, ignored the shouted questions, and walked calmly yet briskly into the building housing the Cromwell Properties offices. Her hair shimmered in the lights and then was lost behind the tinted glass of the large doors.

Buddy switched off the television. He stood next to Ward in the silent room and stared at the black screen. He thought the scene was out of a movie. There was the young, attractive female victim. The rich guy who kills her in a terrible way. The evidence in a private plane. A motive viewers could understand: McInnis killed Sloan Richardson so construction on Haddon House could begin, leading to his continued success and millions of dollars. A crime, a motive, the bad guy caught. *Perfectly done,* he thought again.

Buddy hated perfection because it was found only in movies.

Instead of the movie he was meant to see, he saw an investigation that was too easy and that had progressed too fast. It was a movie, limited by a show time of no more than one hundred twenty minutes. He tried to ignore the newscast they'd watched, for he had questions the reporters hadn't thought to ask.

How did Mario Mingo find out about Sloan Richardson's murder?

He was too young, too green, too out of the loop to make that discovery by himself. He must have been fed information about Sloan Richardson, just as someone had fed the Swiss bank account established in Mario's name. Fed by someone with endless money—someone like Stella Bannon of Cromwell Properties. By someone who'd known Sloan Richardson was dead and could connect Sloan to the location of that particular plane.

He also knew why. Since he'd been thrown out of an airplane, his killers needed a new fall guy for Sloan Richardson. Soon, they'd probably add his own death to McInnis's crimes. As a cop killer, McInnis wouldn't last long in prison. McInnis would be silenced, forever unable to give interviews or write a book claiming his innocence.

Buddy turned to Ward and said, "Let's go."

They went through the condo, switching off the lights. At the door to the hallway and the elevator, Ward looked through the peephole.

"Clear," he said, and began opening the door.

Buddy raised his hand and pushed hard against the door until it closed. "Hang on."

Ward turned to him. "What is it?"

Buddy said, "McInnis's dinner."

"Cheap delivery pizza. So what?"

Buddy walked back through the dark rooms to the kitchen. He switched on the overhead light and pulled out the plastic garbage can. It was empty except for the crushed box and a few napkins stained yellow with grease and red with tomato sauce. He lifted out the box and looked at it.

Ward said, "You hungry?"

Buddy ignored him, turned the box on end, and saw the printed label stuck to one of the sides of the box. The label read: "Mediterranean, extra olives. McInnis. Apt. 804, 56 Little West 12th 02/02/15 12:51 a.m."

He rotated the box so Ward could read the label. He said, "This was two nights ago, at the time McInnis was supposedly throwing Sloan Richardson out of one of Cromwell Properties' planes."

Ward looked at him, eyes wide. "But McInnis was home, eating Mediterranean pizza with extra olives."

Buddy nodded. "Take a photo of the box and label, would you?"

Ward took out his phone and snapped a dozen photos, and then Buddy returned the pizza box to the trash.

Buddy said, "Maybe CSU will find the label and establish the alibi, but maybe not. This case was closed before it was opened."

At the door, they stood for a moment. Ward checked the peephole a second time.

"Clear," he said, and opened the door.

Buddy went first, his hand near the Glock. He pressed the button for the elevator and waited. When both of them were inside the elevator and the door had closed, he said, "The police and the media will be all over McInnis. But McInnis is a frame job."

Ward looked at him. "So who's at the top of our list?"

111

Buddy and Ward crossed Little West Twelfth Street and climbed into Ward's idling silver Range Rover. It was 8:00 p.m. and they were hungry, but Ward's car was stocked with food. Brick had picked up sandwiches and coffee at Petrossian. Buddy reached for the coffee and thought about Ward's question.

"At the top of our list?" he repeated, and then drank deeply of the coffee. The caffeine went right to his heart. The hot black liquid gave him energy and sharpened his mind. He sat forward and turned to Ward, who sat next to him in the spacious back seat. "People with money," he said. "People with power. Think about Haddon House. Who gains if the project moves forward?"

Ward said, "Cromwell Properties. Stella Bannon."

Buddy looked out at the street and saw that snow had begun to fall. It came down almost sideways between the residential buildings, turning golden as it passed under the streetlamps. Fast, and a lot of it. He thought the snow would cover the city's dirt and make the hard buildings softer, prettier. It would disguise the ugly parts of the city and make the attractive parts even better.

If only I'd solved this case. If only Mei and Ben hadn't . . .

He pushed away these thoughts. He couldn't allow himself to consider all he'd lost, because those losses would cripple him. They'd interfere with his work on this, the last case he'd handle for the NYPD. And to solve this one, he'd need total focus.

The cold had gotten him down, but it wasn't cold in the Range Rover. In the cabin, the seat cushion and back were heated. He ate part of a turkey sandwich, washed it down with coffee, and said, "That's part of it. Cromwell makes millions on the project. If they run into trouble, the EDA threatens eminent domain. The EDA is a nonprofit, so it would be Erica Fischer, the executive director, or someone on her staff—maybe Jack Carlson—who get payoffs from Cromwell. If the holdouts fail to make a deal, they disappear. Remember, the Nanjing building is one of many projects. Add up the profit from all the projects over, say, the past fifteen years, and you have a shitload of money. So what we're missing is who makes the holdouts like the Sungs and Sloan Richardson disappear? And why do they do it? Are they paid in cash or in some other form?"

Ward said, "Other than Cromwell—and Erica Fischer, if she's paid off—I'm not sure who else benefits, other than people who buy condos."

Buddy set down the turkey sandwich on the wrapper and wiped his mouth with a paper napkin. He sat, immobile, for half a minute. His pulse spiked, and suddenly he became so hot that the warm interior of the Range Rover stifled him. He reached to the back of the center console and turned off the seat heater.

It's obvious, he thought. *So obvious I didn't even . . .*

He looked at Ward. "*That's* who benefits. The people buying the condos."

Ward shook his head. "I'm not following. That could be anyone—anyone rich enough to afford a place in Haddon House."

Buddy leaned closer and said, *"No, it couldn't."*

112

"No, Ward," he said. "Not in this case. Not in the cases of the other projects where the holdouts have died. These aren't your usual buyers."

Ward opened his hands. "I'm lost. This is capitalism, the free market. People with money can buy as many condo units as they can afford."

Buddy smiled, remembering what Erica Fischer had told him. *This is an international city, Detective.*

In response to Buddy's silence, Ward said, "Who, then?"

Buddy said, "You've read the articles. People use shell companies to buy properties in New York. You can't figure out the real buyer. Maybe it's a prince from Saudi Arabia. Maybe a billionaire from China. The buyers could be any of these."

Ward said, "Or none of them. They don't have to kill for condos."

But they do, Buddy thought. *They kill for condos and money and maybe for something else.* He said, "Cromwell Properties set up and sacrificed Vance McInnis. Cromwell has to be involved."

Ward sipped from his bottle of Perrier. "They're either involved, or they know what's happening and don't object. Maybe they're making too much money to rock the boat. Maybe they've been threatened."

Buddy thought there must be a connection to the NYPD. This connection would be the string that led to the truth. Facing Ward, he said,

"Here's my working theory. Maybe it's more than a theory. Cromwell builds condo towers. If Cromwell has trouble getting people in the existing buildings to leave, or if those people want too much money to go, others—maybe Erica Fischer and Jack Carlson—threaten eminent domain. But if the holdouts still don't sell, someone makes them disappear. Probably someone in the NYPD or someone who coordinates with the NYPD. It's not Mingo. He's a junior detective and this would have to go higher. After tonight, we know it's not Malone. So we don't have the name of the person or persons at the NYPD. But the force is part of it, part of . . ." Buddy let his voice trail off.

Ward wiped his mouth with a napkin. "Part of what?"

Buddy thought about each person who'd died for a reason related to the building site for Haddon House: Chen Sung, Lily Sung, Sloan Richardson. He could explain the Sungs' deaths because they were holdouts. So was Sloan Richardson. But had there been more to Sloan's death?

Had she been killed because she refused to sell her condo in the Nanjing building? Or because she'd threatened to make public her mother's identity?

His mind raced. *Who is her birth mother?* he wondered silently. *And why did her birth mother give her up for adoption?*

He thought perhaps Sloan Richardson had been on the cusp of discovering a secret that might damage someone. Maybe her biological mother. Or biological father, whoever he was.

He finished his sandwich, crumpled the wrapping paper, and drank the last of his coffee. The more he thought about these possibilities, the more he doubted they were true. He tried to remember that theory, the one about Occam's razor. The idea that the simplest explanation is the one most likely to be true. In this case, he believed the simplest explanation was that Cromwell Properties had murdered the holdouts to keep the Haddon House project on schedule and under budget. Maybe buyers of the condo units were involved. Maybe not. The success of the scheme didn't rely on anyone else in power. But it did rely on at least one dirty cop. As did the framing of Vance McInnis.

His mind went around and around for another minute. Finally, he hit the side of the door with his knuckles. "Fuck!" he said aloud.

Ward regarded him warily. "You figured it out?"

"Just the opposite."

Yet he was beginning to see large sections of the puzzle, as if from a distance. It was like climbing over a hill and looking down into a natural amphitheater, the sound of the music rising up into the night sky. But the music was only sound. He could almost hear the melody, but not quite. Not yet. But now he knew the key in which the music was played. He recognized some of the instruments. He was close to hearing the theme around which everything had been structured.

Stella Bannon, he thought, *and Erica Fischer. You need each other to make money. To threaten the holdouts with eminent domain. To pressure the holdouts to sell for a reasonable price. Failing resolution, to make the holdouts disappear.*

Zipping up his jacket, he said, "Take me up to Forty-Ninth and Eighth. I'll watch Bannon. You take Erica Fischer."

Thirty minutes later, when Brick pulled along the curb on the other side of Eighth Avenue from the offices of Cromwell Properties, Buddy opened the door of the Range Rover and climbed out. Looking upward, he saw snow falling thickly across the city, in great waves of white, whose cold pricked his eyes. He knew that by tomorrow morning the city would be white and almost pure. But tonight it would be slippery and lethal.

113

Buddy stepped inside Coffee Club, the high-end coffee bar across from Cromwell Properties. He ordered a large black coffee and found a place by the window. He sat in a hard wooden chair and unzipped his jacket, but he didn't take it off, because he needed to keep the Glock in his IWB holster hidden from the other customers and the staff. He watched the front door of the Cromwell Properties offices, the very place where Stella Bannon had given her press conference making a human sacrifice of Vance McInnis.

He checked his burner phone. The clock read 8:34.

She's already gone, he thought. *Or she's at a meeting. Or maybe, after the news conference, she left the office and took the evening off. She might have had regrets, after having sentenced Vance McInnis to death.*

But he sipped his coffee and didn't get up. *No,* he told himself, *she's there.* Doing damage control. Interviews by phone or with a TV camera brought into her office.

So he waited, watching the door to Cromwell's offices. He drank his coffee. He ordered a refill. After a while, he took out his burner phone and called Ward. When his brother answered, he said, "Status?"

Ward's voice was calm. "Erica Fischer took a cab from her office to the Ritz-Carlton, Battery Park."

Buddy thought about the southernmost tip of Manhattan, the view of the Statue of Liberty, the expensive condo and apartment buildings, the Ritz-Carlton Hotel and residences. He pictured Fischer's highlighted blond hair and generous curves. "Is she meeting someone?" he asked.

"She *lives* there. Not in the hotel, but the residences."

Buddy thought he might have missed something, something big. He said, "Fischer works at a nonprofit, and she lives at the Ritz-Carlton?"

"Sure does."

Buddy recalled that she wore no wedding ring. He said, "Does she have family money?"

Ward said, "Her parents were schoolteachers. Want me to stay with her?"

Buddy considered Erica Fischer and what guilty people did to close deals. "Yeah," he said. "Give her another hour."

Hearing the sound of an engine, Buddy turned and saw a black Mercedes S-Class sedan pull along the curb in front of the Cromwell Properties building. It sat there like a sumptuous coffin, idling silently. Nobody got in, and nobody got out.

He said "Talk later," and ended the call. Despite it being night, he put on his sunglasses, got up, threw away his coffee cup, and went outside.

One glance told him the sleek Mercedes was waiting for Stella Bannon. He hurried to the intersection to the north, crossed the street, and walked back south toward the doors to the Cromwell Properties building. He stood off to the side in the darkness, zipping up his jacket to hide more of his face. He didn't think he could be seen by anyone coming out the building doors. And besides, he'd never met Stella Bannon in person. She might have seen him on television related to the Death Clock Murders or the case involving Ben's family, but he hoped that he remained a stranger to her, especially given his new look. He looked left for a cab but saw none.

The snow was falling harder now, and a moderate wind pushed the mass of white almost horizontal. He narrowed his eyes to keep the snow out as he looked over the Mercedes.

If Stella Bannon were to climb into it, he'd have a hard time following. He had no Uber app on the burner phone. Even if he did, he couldn't use Uber, because if anyone were monitoring his accounts, the charge would show he was alive. He thought for a moment, then changed position.

He walked closer to the Cromwell building doors, passed them, and stood as if looking into a window of one of the ground floor offices. He decided that nobody would buy this ruse because an opaque screen covered the window. So he held up the burner phone and pretended to type out a text. He stood there, unmoving, for several minutes, his bare hands stiffening from the cold. And then, from the corner of his eye, he saw the doors to the Cromwell Properties building open.

Stella Bannon walked out onto the snowy sidewalk. Wearing a black cashmere overcoat with a thick belt and a hood hanging off the back, she was accompanied by a well-dressed couple in their fifties. Both the man and the woman were taller than Stella Bannon and shared refined features, but next to her they seemed weak. She remained imperious and regal as she stood facing them, in black high heels, her silky black hair setting off her fair complexion. After she'd described the Haddon House project, she promised the couple there would be no delays. Yet only the third-floor unit they'd been discussing remained unsold. All units on the higher floors were under contract.

The man said, "Ms. Bannon, we're ready to commit, but we'd like to be sure of the view facing west."

Stella Bannon pointed at the Mercedes. "Here's my car. Why don't we take a look, and you can commit now if the view meets with your requirements?"

The couple glanced at each other and nodded.

Stella Bannon moved toward the car, and the driver—an older Caucasian man who was gaunt with white hair—emerged from the driver's seat and opened the rear doors. As they climbed in, she told him, "We're going to the Nanjing building, please."

When the older man had returned to the driver's seat, he maneuvered the sleek sedan away from the curb and into the sparse traffic heading uptown on the one-way.

Buddy didn't watch the car. He was already jogging south, trying to find a cab.

114

"Stop here," Buddy told the cab driver.

They had just turned from Elizabeth onto Hester Street and were headed west. He'd been lucky and found a cab one minute after beginning his search outside the Cromwell Properties building. Now he handed the fare through the Plexiglas divider to the front seat and climbed out of the cab. Thirty yards farther on the left, he saw Stella Bannon's black Mercedes idling by the front steps of the Nanjing building.

But it couldn't wait there. One lane of traffic had been fenced off for demolition, so there was no lane in which to park. After suffering the horns of cars behind it, the driver of the Mercedes accelerated, merged into traffic, passed through the intersection with Mott Street, and continued up to Mulberry Street, where it turned right and disappeared.

Buddy jogged forward. The Nanjing building's exterior lights shone down over the steps up to the front door. Pale white lights filled the lobby with a ghostly luminescence. From the sidewalk, he couldn't see Stella Bannon or her potential buyers. He knew that if he got into the lobby, and Bannon and her clients came down the interior staircase, he'd have nowhere to go but out the front door. And the driver of the Mercedes would soon return, probably in a minute or two.

Not enough time.

Reversing course, he jogged through a break in the traffic to the other side of Hester. He stood in front of a dark shop window in his hat and sunglasses and waited.

Very soon, the black Mercedes passed by and approached the steps to the Nanjing building. The large luxury car slowed but once again, due to traffic, couldn't stop. Instead, it kept going, passing the empty steps.

Buddy dashed back across the street, was nearly hit by a car, rushed up the steps, stood at the door, and tried the handle.

It was unlocked.

He pushed it open and entered the lobby. He stood there in the silence, listening, hearing nothing.

Once again, he noticed the sign on the elevator: "Out of Order."

The adjacent staircase was poorly lit.

He knew the Mercedes would soon return, and he'd be spotted. *Either retreat now, or press on.*

He removed his sunglasses, tucked them in the side pocket of his jacket, and began climbing the stairs.

115

A woman in her home office heard the chime of her phone. She was sitting at her desk. Still dressed in her work clothes, she was sipping a glass of sauvignon blanc.

She set down her pen, slid the phone closer, and peered through her reading glasses at the green text window. It read: They want to meet. Come now. Nanjing building. Chinatown.

That was all. Immediately, she pushed back her chair and stood. Through a crack in the curtains, she could see the heavily falling snow and an expanse of dark water. She didn't want to go out, not tonight, not in a storm.

But she would. They needed to meet. And the text had been from the person she trusted most.

116

Ward checked his watch and said, "See anything?"

Ward thought that in the snow, the verdigris-colored Statue of Liberty in the harbor looked grand and resolute. As he swung his gaze right to the large Ritz-Carlton Hotel and residence building, with the profile of a thick-maned lion attached to the side of the glass and granite, he thought that structure, too, appeared grand and immovable. But perhaps a little quiet. A few people had emerged, and several more had gone into the hotel. Yet there had been no sign of Erica Fischer.

"Yeah, man. I do." Brick pointed at the entrance.

Startled, Ward looked and saw Erica Fischer walking down the steps toward a waiting shiny black Cadillac Escalade. The lights allowed him to confirm her identity and to see that she wore a long black coat and a dark hat over her blond hair. The driver held open the right rear door, and she ducked into the SUV. The driver jogged around the back of the car and jumped into the driver's seat. A second later, the Escalade jerked forward, maneuvered east on Battery Place, and accelerated rapidly.

Brick put the Range Rover in gear and turned to Ward.

Ward said, "Don't lose her."

In response, Brick pulled the car forward, increasing speed so quickly the Rover fishtailed before he regained control, and they shot forward.

Where's she going in such a hurry? Ward thought. *In a snowstorm?*

To their right, the river was black as the sky. To their left, the buildings of the Battery Park neighborhood, residential towers made of stone, steel, and glass, their higher floors with views of Governor's Island and, in the distance, Staten Island.

The Escalade swerved north onto the FDR. Brick followed, and they found only sparse traffic on the expressway lining the eastern edge of Manhattan. They sped up as they got closer to Chinatown.

The heavy snow made the going slower than usual, even if it was after nine o'clock and well after rush hour. Brick, an excellent driver, struggled to keep the Rover in the paths through the snow made by the cars ahead of them. Ward ignored Brick's struggles, instead staring intently at the Escalade's red taillights.

As the large vehicle approached the Brooklyn Bridge, it slowed.

Ward squinted as the large black SUV seemed to hover in mid-decision. He sat forward, hands on his knees. He stared as the Escalade slipped off the FDR and soon turned west toward Chinatown. They passed a Toyota Camry and accelerated wildly, nearly spinning out of control before regaining traction.

Brick stomped on the accelerator, and the Rover sped forward, pushing Ward back into his seat. Ward grabbed the door handle and slid forward on the seat.

He said, "Close the gap, Brick. Close it."

"Roger."

Ward broke his stare with the Escalade, switched on the reading lamp over his head, and pulled out the Beretta M9. He checked the magazine and the slide. As he put the M9 in the shoulder holster under his Brioni suit, he swallowed and noticed the metallic taste in his mouth. It wasn't blood that caused this taste, but foreboding. Buddy was in Chinatown by himself, and God knew what awaited him there.

117

Buddy stood at the top of the stairs on the first level of the Nanjing building, listening. Because he couldn't see more than twenty feet in front of him. Other than in the lobby and above the internal staircase, the lights in the building had been shut off. He gazed out into darkness, even the red exit signs having been disconnected.

Making up for his blindness, he listened.

He heard no sounds from the floors above. No sign of occupancy. He kept his jacket zipped. Any water in the radiators had gone cold and still or been drained away. He'd have expected this silence if the building were vacant, but he knew it wasn't. He'd seen Stella Bannon's Mercedes idling at the curb after she and the potential buyers had gone inside. He hadn't seen anyone else enter the building, but there might also be others who'd arrived earlier. Squatters. Homeless who'd somehow gotten inside to avoid the fierce winter storm.

Others, he thought, and pulled the Glock from his waist holster.

There were no sounds from the street outside. He thought that nearly all vehicles must be off the roads, avoiding the storm. He heard no whispers of car tires, no truck engines, no beeping of plows. It was like being sealed in a tomb.

Yet the quiet didn't lead to relaxation and calm but to anticipation, anxiety, and adrenaline. He moved the Glock to his left hand and wiped his perspiring right hand on the thighs of his pants. Then he transferred the gun back to his dominant hand. His heartbeat sped up as he climbed the stairs.

Aware only of the sounds of his own breathing and the press of his rubber-soled shoes on the terrazzo staircase, he reached the landing. For ten seconds he halted. Hearing nothing, he began climbing up to the second floor.

Above him, a single bulb covered in translucent plastic cast a feeble glow over the steps. He went slowly, making sure not to slip, not to make a noise. When he reached the second floor, he stopped, held his breath, and listened.

But he heard nothing.

Standing at the perimeter of the stairs, he looked upward, aimed the Glock, and curled around the wall like a snake as he climbed to the third floor. Nearing the top few steps, he heard voices.

Taking one step, then another, he could peer down the corridor, his eyes just above the level of the third-floor carpeting. The corridor was empty, but now he had a better read on the location of the voices. They were beyond unit 305, the Sungs' former home. Leaning forward, straining to hear, he realized the discussion must be emanating from unit 309, two doors down from the Sungs' condo, where Sloan Richardson had lived.

He considered waiting but realized he might become trapped between Stella Bannon and her driver on the street outside when she and her clients came down the staircase. Being trapped was something prey did. And this time, he was hunting—hunting outside the law. He ran up the last few steps and along the dark hallway to unit 305.

The door was open, and as he ran he could see the doors to all the units were propped open with black rubber doorstops. He could make out the spaces as faint light came in through the windows overlooking Mott Street. He rushed into 305 and scanned the interior. All traces of the older couple had been removed. The living room was barren of furniture, paintings, rugs, and plants. Cromwell Properties—or perhaps it had been the Sungs' eldest son—hadn't wasted any time in removing all evidence of the older couples' lives. Their former home would be demolished in the next few days, and little of their time on earth would endure except their children. The building was worse than a graveyard because there were no remains. Its emptiness echoed Buddy's feeling of abandonment. He began to doubt himself.

Do I have it wrong? he thought. *Is Vance McInnis, the VP of Cromwell, truly guilty? Or was the EDA involved, and I failed to understand how?*

He recalled that Jack Carlson, the EDA's associate director, had claimed a ski injury, but might have been driving the SUV that had crashed into him.

Ignore it, he told himself. *Stick with what you know. What got you into this mess in the first place: the Sungs, the Nanjing building, real estate development in Chinatown.*

Now he heard Stella Bannon and her potential clients returning along the corridor toward the Sungs' door. She was praising Antoine Rousseau, the architect for Haddon House, and the future project's timeless but modern design, the floor-to-ceiling windows in every room, the roof deck, and the fitness center. As the voices grew closer, Buddy backed into the hallway that led to the bedrooms of unit 305.

Stella Bannon and her clients paused by the door. They talked about the neighborhood and how it was changing for the better, according to all of them, while retaining its original vibe. The man walked into the Sungs' condo. His footsteps made the oak floors creak softly under his weight.

Buddy backed into the master bathroom, putting more distance between himself and the other man. He listened carefully, ready to react and avoid the man if possible.

Buddy heard the man stroll around the living room, proceed to the windows, stand there a moment, and then retrace his steps to the doorway and the exterior corridor. As Buddy listened to their voices and retreating footsteps, he emerged from the master bathroom and hallway and reentered the living room. He walked slowly, mindful of where he placed his feet on the tired oak floorboards, staying close to the walls to keep the boards' creaking to a minimum. Bobbing his head into the corridor, he watched Stella Bannon and her clients disappear down the staircase, the voices growing faint and soon inaudible.

He moved rapidly across the hallway to another vacant condo, walked to the living room window, and looked down.

He saw the building door open. For a brief moment nobody left. But then he watched as Stella Bannon and the rich couple grasped the metal railing and walked down the snow-covered steps. The older man driving the Mercedes pulled alongside the construction fencing and hurried out of the car, his shoes kicking up the white powdery snow that covered everything. He held open the rear passenger door. The rich couple climbed into the back. Stella Bannon remained by the building steps, waved once as the older man returned to the driver's seat, and the car drove off.

What's Stella Bannon doing? he wondered, but only briefly. Then he was certain. She was meeting someone.

He let the air out of his lungs and looked around. He saw that like unit 305, this one was vacant of everything. He could see the room clearly, but only because the layer of white on the street and sidewalks outside reflected the streetlights' illumination up into the room, giving it an ashen hue. In the calm and silence, he tried to make sense of the broken pattern. In contrast to his thoughts a minute ago, he considered the possibility that Stella Bannon was innocent. Unlikely as it seemed, she might be no more than the unwitting beneficiary of someone else's crimes—maybe those of Vance McInnis.

Voices, he thought. *Outside.*

Returning to the living room window, he gazed down. He could make out one woman in a black overcoat, a hood pulled up over her head. The color of her hair was impossible to discern. He thought it must be Stella Bannon, but he couldn't be sure. Opposite this woman was another woman in a similar black coat and a dark-colored hat. This second woman had her hair tucked into the hat.

Unable to see her face, he cocked his head and stared through the glass.

118

Buddy wiped away the fogged-up window and stared down at the steps below. A moment ago, a third woman had joined the first two, appearing from across the street. This woman had a long black coat and hood that obscured her face. Now all three stood outside the Nanjing building, on the top step above the sidewalk, their backs to him. They were standing as one, gesturing, talking.

Anger surged within him, yet he didn't move from the window, didn't go down the stairs to confront them. Something held him back. Something told him to remain where he was, out of sight. Because he sensed the show wasn't over. Not by a long shot.

All three women continued to face Hester Street. He could see only their hats or hoods. They'd become interchangeable. He saw the women extend their right arms and shake hands with each other, exposing for a moment the pale skin of their wrists to the faint light of the streetlamps. He saw it then. The flicker of silver bracelets on the wrists of two of the women.

The flash of metal jogged his memory; he wasn't sure why.

Two women descended the steps together, turned right on the sidewalk, and walked east along Hester. His eyes followed them until they'd disappeared from his vision.

When he again looked down at the steps below him, the third woman was gone.

He hustled along the third-floor corridor to the top of the stairs. From there, he heard a distinct sound, a metallic clap that could only be the lobby door closing.

He stopped moving, remained completely still, held his breath.

Then he heard footsteps—more than one set of them—climbing the stairs toward him. Low voices, men's voices, rose up through the stairwell.

Tightening his grip on the Glock, he walked backward along the corridor and farther into the darkness.

119

Across Hester Street, in a darkened doorway of a closed shop, a shadow watched the door to the Nanjing building. The dark figure wore a heavy down parka with the hood pulled up over its head and brought low over the forehead. A scarf obscured the face, except for two dark eyes. Black gloves covered the hands. The shadow didn't move. It wasn't going anywhere, despite the snowstorm. The shadow's eyes were trained on the stainless-steel door and had seen much during the past hour.

Several people had arrived and left since the shadow had been watching.

Two women the shadow knew had met with a third woman on the steps outside the Nanjing building and left minutes later. The third woman had gone inside the building.

And then, several minutes ago, two large men had entered the building. Even from the alley, the shadow had seen that these men were armed. They'd made no attempt to hide the handguns at their sides. The shadow had expected these men to meet with the third woman. This was, after all, the plan, the purpose.

One minute ago, the shadow had turned and seen a handsome, expensively dressed man with brushed-back sandy-colored hair who might have been going to a business meeting, but who instead entered the lobby of the Nanjing building, drew a large handgun, and began climbing the building staircase.

The shadow waited a moment, then followed.

120

Buddy sprinted down the hall and returned to unit 305. He waited inside the door. As the men's voices neared, he retreated to the master bedroom. The men entered unit 305 and stood in the empty living room, on the other side of the wall and maybe ten feet from him.

In low voices, they used a language Buddy didn't recognize. *Not Chinese,* he thought. *Not Spanish or French or German.* He listened further and compared it to phrases he'd heard in movies. He tensed when he placed it.

Russian.

This formed another note he could hear clearly for the first time, a note that fit within the pattern he'd been trying to see, that completed another section of the musical line. He'd read that Manhattan real estate was a giant washing machine for money. Foreigners with cash bought real estate. They got the money out of countries like China and Russia and parked it here, where it was safe. The money had been stolen from the people and governments of those countries. Or the money had come from the drug trade. Or the girls trade. Or from corruption in government or business. Or all of the above. Wasn't this the reason so many of the high-end condos in the city were vacant? Those condominiums and town houses weren't homes, they were washing machines.

Buddy thought about the need to make dirty money appear clean. He thought the logic held.

These buildings paved the way for money laundering on a massive scale in the strongest real estate market in the world. People who got in the way of that gusher of money had to be silenced, removed, and "disappeared." Billions of dollars depended on the washing machine, and what were the lives of a few people—the Sungs, Sloan Richardson, Mei, and Ben—standing in the way?

He heard a new set of footsteps on the oak floor of the living room. These steps were lighter, faster, and purposeful, yet not hurried. There was a shuffling sound as the men in the living room moved across the floor. And then Buddy heard a woman's voice, higher pitched but practically inaudible. He couldn't place it, not then.

He took out his phone, muted it, and turned on the audio record function.

A man's voice: "Detective Lock is gone."

After a pause during which Buddy heard the near whisper of the woman's voice, a second man said, "Unless he can fly, he's gone."

The woman's voice. Buddy held his breath and didn't move, but he couldn't discern any words.

The first man said, "His fiancée, and the boy."

Buddy leaned forward, something inside of him tightening with anxiety. He held his phone closer to the hallway entrance.

The second man's voice: "We'll find her and the boy, and everything will be tied off."

Tied off, Buddy thought. He realized that if he died tonight, Mei and Ben would be killed. He had no illusions about their ability to survive.

His phone vibrated once, the noise loud in the empty room. He tried to muffle the device, thrusting it into his jacket pocket.

Shit!

As the phone grew still, he pulled it from his jacket and checked the screen. The text from Ward read: In the Nanjing building. Where are you?

Before he could type out a response, he realized the voices in the adjacent room had gone silent. The woman, and the men with her, had heard the vibration of his phone.

121

The shadow took shape in the lobby of the Nanjing building. The gloves were removed and placed in the parka's side pockets. The parka was unzipped by several inches, enough to allow the figure's hand to reach inside to a shoulder holster and withdraw an NYPD-issued Sig Sauer P226 DAO.

The gun had no safety. It was ready to fire.

The figure held the gun with both hands and proceeded slowly, silently, up the stairs.

122

Buddy thought furiously. He had the Glock 19. The Russians in the living room almost certainly had superior firepower. And there were at least two of them.

Somewhere in the building, Ward waited. His brother could be downstairs in the lobby. Or on the staircase. Or on the first or second floors. His brother might even be on the third floor, not thirty feet from him. Buddy decided it didn't matter. Ward wasn't with him in the master bedroom of unit 305, and Buddy knew he couldn't fight two or more Russians at once.

Why aren't they storming the bedroom? he wondered.

And then it came to him: They didn't know who he was, but they thought he might be armed. They believed if they came through the door, he could kill them all. But this hesitancy wouldn't last. The Russians wouldn't wait forever. If they chose to attack the master bedroom, he'd die. He probably couldn't shoot both of them before they could shoot him. He'd lose, he'd die, and from what he'd learned from the conversation, Mei and Ben would die.

Shit.

Shit, shit, shit!

He'd have to find a way out, if he could. Scanning through the room lit only by the streetlights' reflection on the snow outside, he saw the wall-mounted ballet barre. If he tore the barre and brackets off the wall, he'd have something to work with. But what the hell was a ballet barre against a hurricane of bullets?

He studied the room further. There wasn't anything else in it except for the radiator over two windows.

Windows.

Quietly, he moved toward them. They were double-hung, a single latch securing each. He chose the window to the right, swiveled the metal lock until it was free, and slowly, achingly slowly, began to raise the lower part of the window.

123

Sheltering in unit 303, Ward didn't look at the shadow across the corridor in the doorway to unit 302. He gave no sign he'd seen it. Standing against the wall inside unit 303, he began to count how many people might be in the building, how many guns.

Too many, he thought. *Too many to keep the peace.*

It would, he knew, be war.

124

The shadow stood inside the doorway to unit 302, listening carefully, hearing nothing.

Stomach in knots, teeth clenched.

Carefully, slowly, the shadow let air from its lungs. Loosened, but only for a moment, the faintest pressure on the trigger of the Sig Sauer held with both hands. The shadow straightened before returning to combat position. Kept a low center of gravity. A steady base for firing or attacking.

Absent danger to an innocent bystander, protocol required nonlethal force. Required continued stalemate until backup arrived.

But the shadow knew two facts. Nobody was innocent. And having backup in the Nanjing building would lead only to questions.

Take players off the board, the shadow thought. *Reduce the danger from two to one. Not protocol, except in a war zone. And this is war. This is survival.*

The shadow raised the Sig Sauer and aimed at the doorway of unit 303, at the visible sliver of shoulder of the man with the sandy hair.

The shadow slowed its heartbeat.

Counted one, two, three.

Pulled the trigger.

125

Ward felt searing pain before he heard the shot. It doubled in intensity, and tripled. His right arm went limp with pain.

Fuck, that hurts!

He threw himself backward, away from the door and farther into unit 303. Midair, he grabbed the Beretta with his left hand from his right and aimed it at the door opening.

Aghh! He landed clumsily, half standing, and fell onto his shoulders. He lay there, unmoving, not blinking, his eyes on the doorway, the Beretta steady.

He waited.

The shadow from the doorway across the hall wasn't pursuing him. Gritting his teeth, he got up and returned to the doorway. This time, he made sure to keep his shoulder and every other part of him out of sight of the doorway to unit 303.

He was trapped, but so was everyone else in the Nanjing building. *Buddy,* he thought. *What's the plan here? What's the fucking plan?*

126

Buddy heard the gunshot. He knew it wasn't from inside the Sungs' condo. Instinctively, he took advantage of the deafening blast, lifting the window as far as it would go, and put one leg outside so he was straddling the sill.

Ward! he thought then.

If someone . . .

No!

He couldn't stop, couldn't think about it. He had to survive.

Without taking his eyes from the point where the hallway opened into the bedroom, he moved his right foot down, trying to find the horizontal section of the exterior metal fire escape. He felt only cold air.

He shifted rightward, moving his torso farther outside. There it was. Solid metal. Carefully, he placed more weight on the fire escape. It held, and it didn't creak.

Rapidly now, he worked his way fully onto the fire escape so that he was standing outside, three floors above the alley between the Nanjing building and the one housing Henry Lee's restaurant. He felt the cool snow land on his head, dampening his hair. Without hesitation, he put his back to the building wall and moved left, forcing himself to go slowly, gradually increasing the weight on his right foot with each step, confirming the metal wouldn't shift or squeak.

But the escape remained stable and made no sound. Along the escape's exterior edge was a narrow snow-covered railing supported every few feet by spindles.

Like being on a balance beam three floors up, he thought, his throat tightening with anxiety.

He neared the first of the two living room windows. Crouching down, he leaned against the wall for stability, turned his head, and tried to peer into the living room.

He saw the window's reflection of the outdoors. The ambient amber-colored light of the city that formed a phosphorescent dome overhead.

Lighter outside than in, he thought.

It was difficult for him to see inside, but maybe not impossible.

He considered the situation. The optics. His own safety.

In order to have visibility, he'd have to stand on the escape directly in front of the window. By doing so, he'd block some of the light streaming into the living room. He'd also be able to see the portion of the interior near the window, and anyone in that portion of the living room. If the Russians were far from the window, he'd be a perfect target, highlighted for them by the light behind him.

Breathing deeply of the ice-cold air, he took his left hand and wiped the melting snow off his face. He thought about the living room on the other side of the glass.

If I were in that room, where would I stand?

They're there, he thought. *On the other side of the wall from me. Just two or three feet away. But invisible, at least from here.*

He breathed and looked down over the alley. Soft powder covered the unforgiving concrete. He didn't like heights and didn't trust the fire escape.

How old is this thing? he asked himself. *Fifty years? A hundred?*

Turning toward the building, he saw the pale red brick, cracked and spalling in some places, rough everywhere. And the exterior windowsill, painted black and almost shiny even in the dull light. He stared at the area of the fire escape where he'd plant his feet and become a target as he fired.

Department rules required that he call for backup. But he was dead, and dead people didn't call anyone. Even if the NYPD arrived, what then? He'd be reprimanded and again put on administrative leave. Ward would be arrested and sent to prison. Everyone else would escape. Meaning Mei and Ben would be killed.

I'm dead, he thought. *And dead people don't follow rules.*

To save Mei and Ben. To punish. Those were his goals—the goals of a hunter.

No mercy.

Visualizing his motion, he began to slow his breathing. He tamped down the rising adrenaline, the almost electrical current surging through his body. He swallowed twice.

Then he took one large step to the right, crouching slightly.

His heartbeat spiked. Boom-boom! Boom-boom! Boom-boom!

In the dimness of the living room, he could make out only a single figure, a woman with a fair complexion. In that instant, he didn't recognize her. His eyes scanned what he could see of the room, tried to find the Russians. Were they closer to the hallway, or . . .

The glass window shattered to the right of his face.

He stumbled backward, the fire escape's metal railing catching him just above the knees. For less than a second, he balanced precariously on the railing, but his momentum drove him away from the building.

Beginning to fall into the alley, he let go of the Glock. He reached forward, grasping for some kind of handhold on the escape.

127

Buddy hung on to the tread of the fire escape. The metal's cold stung his fingers. At the same time, his warm hands melted the snow on the metal's surface, making it slippery.

His primary weapon had fallen into the snow in the alley. But instead of looking down, he looked up toward the living room window.

The escape blocked his view, meaning the Russians in the living room above couldn't see him. Yet he knew they'd open one of the windows, step out onto the escape, and shoot him. Or they might step on his hands until he dropped. The fall would take him down three stories to paralysis or death.

Time, he thought. *Ten seconds. No more.*

Now he did look down, not to the sidewalk below but to the fire escape's connection between the third and second floors. It was just to his right. He could slide his hands sideways and reach the stairway. But the horizontal part of the escape had an opening for the stairs. He'd gain a solid foothold, but he'd have no cover.

He hesitated, thinking of the Glock 26 in his right ankle holster. Could he reach it? Could he hang on to the wet metal fire escape with one hand?

He heard it then. Someone raising the living room window. At least one Russian would soon be standing on the fire escape.

Letting go with his right hand, Buddy hung there, ready to put that hand back on the escape if his left began to slip.

But his left hand held.

He bent his right knee, bringing the ankle close, and with his right hand reached for the holster. Then his left hand began to slip.

Fuck!

He straightened, grabbed the metal escape with his right hand. Put most of his weight on that hand, in order to ease the weight on his left.

The escape shook with a footstep, with the weight of someone above him. Buddy couldn't see the person and didn't know if the Russian could see his fingers curled around the outer edge of the escape.

Now!

He bent his right knee, let go of the escape with his right hand, and reached for the Glock. Putting his hand around the gunstock, he pulled and raised the weapon.

His left hand held the railing firmly, for now.

Turning to his right, he could see a gun barrel extending into the hole where the stairs came down. He wasn't going to shoot at something as small as a gun or at the fragment of the Russian's arm. He had time for one shot, and he wanted center mass.

Yet he couldn't lift himself up by one arm in order to take a shot. *Impossible,* he thought.

He began pushing off the brick wall with his feet, and swinging his legs outward, not too much, but enough to give himself momentum.

One.

Two.

Three.

He pushed hard off the wall and swung his body up so he had a line of sight above the escape. To his right, a large man dressed in black was leaning toward the opening created by the stairs.

Buddy fired two rounds at the man's chest.

The man collapsed and fell headfirst down the stairs. His gun flew from his hands and he dropped like a stone.

Buddy watched as the man lay unmoving on the escape below. Then he shoved the Glock into the waistband at the small of his back, put his right hand on the escape, and moved sideways to the right, toward the stairway.

The second Russian won't try the same move, he thought. *He won't be that stupid. Or that smart.*

Buddy reached the stairs, relieved to be standing. After opening and closing his left hand in order to warm it, he pulled the Glock and held it with both hands.

His prey waited in the living room upstairs, undoubtedly with a gun or two. But standing on the fire escape without cover remained dangerous. He couldn't climb up to the escape along the building's third floor, but he had to do that very thing.

He thought quickly, pulled out the burner phone from his jacket pocket, and dialed Ward, hoping his brother was alive and could answer.

128

Ward's phone vibrated, audible in the silent room.

Buddy? he wondered, chest tightening.

He tried to think of how to answer it.

Set the Beretta on the floor?

No.

Yet he had just one functioning hand. He backed into the condo, around the corner of the living room, and along the short hallway to the single bedroom. He kept going until he reached the far wall. Then he set the Beretta on the windowsill and pulled out his phone.

"Buddy?" he asked.

"Yeah."

"You okay?"

Instead of answering, Buddy said, "I need a distraction for the Russian in this condo's living room."

Ward watched the hallway, waiting to react if he heard or saw evidence of the shadow's entrance into *this* condo. He said, "What kind of distraction? And for how long?"

A pause. Ward heard . . . wind? Was Buddy outside?

Buddy said, "Five seconds."

Ward thought about distractions. He said, "I can't leave this condo. Someone's in the corridor, someone who's a fucking great shot."

Buddy said, "Start now."

"Start *what?*"

"Count to thirty. Starting now."

"And then what, Buddy? What do you want me to do?"

"Don't use all your ammo, but shoot the shit out of the corridor."

Ward thought about this. Then he said, "I'll start the count now. All right?"

Silence, because Buddy had ended the call.

Ward shoved the phone in his pocket and made his way out of the bedroom, through the hallway, and toward the small foyer and doorway. He counted to twenty, then began firing into the empty unit directly across the corridor.

Again and again, chewing through the rounds, more than one per second.

The M9's blasts perforated the silence of the building, shaking it, making the air around him smell like a Roman candle.

129

Buddy heard Ward's first shot. Moving rapidly, he climbed up the fire escape stairs, staying low but otherwise leaving cover. Two steps at a time, he reached the third-level platform, then kept going until he was near the living room windows. Through the right window, he saw nothing. He stepped to his left, to the window with the bullet hole. The lower portion of that window was open where the first Russian had climbed out onto the fire escape.

He saw the second Russian. It was Rat Eyes, and his body faced the window and the fire escape where Buddy stood. But Rat Eyes's head was turned to the right, toward the building's interior corridor and the volley of shots from Ward's M9.

Once again Buddy saw the woman's pale, elegant face. She pointed at him. She opened her mouth to speak.

Buddy ignored her and raised his gun to fire through the glass. He aimed not at Rat Eyes's center mass but at the side of his head. Because it was personal. Because he wasn't in a forgiving mood.

He fired.

Rat Eyes's skull jerked sideways, at a weird angle and toward the corridor. Buddy saw an explosion of bone and blood, and the clump of the big man falling to the floor, already a corpse.

Then Buddy stepped through the lower part of the open window and entered the living room.

"Don't fucking move," he told the woman there, even as she shrank against the wall.

130

Hands gripping the Sig Sauer, the shadow in unit 302 didn't move. Couldn't move, or the man with sandy hair across the corridor would shoot. Had to wait, although waiting proved difficult and painful. The shadow's chest burned with worry for the woman in unit 305. If a bullet pierced that beautiful warm skin, the shadow would have no future.

"Clear!"

The shadow tensed at the sudden call of Detective Lock's voice. *Detective Lock, alive?* the shadow thought. *How is it possible?* The Russians were dead, the shadow now understood. Just as Lock's vulgar instruction had meant the woman was alive.

But the shadow understood this woman would be destroyed. Personally, financially. Her wealth and reputation, her power and dignity, gone, the remainder of her life spent in prison. Where she'd be murdered, probably.

Silently, the shadow cried out: *No, it can't be! I can't let it happen. Not when we've come so far.*

Frustration and anger charged through the shadow's arteries. Fear, too, but more than fear, *confidence*. What had the woman told the shadow? *History remembers those with power, not how they got their power, but how they took it like ripe fruit from a tree and wouldn't let go.* But the shadow's tightening chest betrayed more than these emotions. There was passion, shared only in a large, ornate bedroom. That was the foundation underlying all the others, all the years of service, all the compromises made, and the crimes committed. It was this love that led the shadow to determine another way. Another path forward. A final risk to retain all they'd worked for and all the woman had become.

131

Buddy was staring at her. She was calm, holding up her hands.

Buddy knew that nobody would come into unit 305 via the corridor. Ward would shoot anyone who tried.

He got up and approached her. As he raised his left hand, she shied away to the side. He put his hand on her left shoulder, turned her around, and shoved her forward, so her face and chest were against the wall, though her hair remained straight and untangled. In three seconds he patted her down.

Ward called out: "Across the corridor from you. Ten o'clock."

"10-4."

Buddy walked over to the doorway to the corridor. But he didn't bob his head into the space. He knew Ward was just inside the doorway to his left. He knew that across the corridor and two doorways to the left, a third person waited. Once again, he realized, nobody could move without being shot and killed. Not unless they wanted to die. Unless . . .

He had an idea, but one that was illegal and so far outside his police training that he was ashamed to think of it. And yet it might work. He decided to find out.

He turned back and waved her toward him.

132

The shadow looked along the short gun barrel at the doorway to unit 303, where the man with the sandy hair was hiding. But there was new movement in the doorway to unit 305.

She was there: always elegant, even now self-possessed. The woman emerged from the doorway. Her hands were at her sides. Her brown eyes were narrowed with fear, yet she was steady on her feet.

One step, and another, along the corridor and toward the doorway where the shadow waited. Their eyes met, but the shadow broke that meaningful connection to look behind the woman.

133

Buddy waited until the woman was between him and the shadow in the doorway of unit 302. Then he launched himself across the corridor and through the open door of the condo there.

The shot seemed louder than a bomb in the empty building, but it went above his head and wide to the left.

He stood, reentered the corridor, and slid with his back against the wall. Without pause, he moved toward the door to unit 302. He'd seen her go into that condo. He sensed but didn't look at Ward, standing in the doorway across the hall from him. He knew that if the shadow in the doorway to his right tried to shoot him, Ward would take it out.

Buddy stepped closer to the doorway, the Glock trained on the opening.

134

The shadow heard Buddy's back skim along the corridor wall, the sound of clothing against plaster moving closer and closer. It was a brushing noise, and it grew louder.

Years of training, the shadow realized, and this was the final event. Or the beginning. One or the other.

The shadow thought briefly and decided the situation had changed. Before Detective Lock had crossed to this side of the corridor, waiting had been smart. Now it created more risk.

Go!

The shadow crouched into combat position, stepped into the hallway, and began to squeeze the trigger to fire at Lock.

135

Buddy saw the movement in the doorway to his right. He fired.

Once. Twice. And again.

He heard Ward firing from the doorway across the hall, the sound of both weapons explosive and shocking. He watched the figure in front of him fall and never get off a round.

136

Buddy hurried forward, kicked the Sig Sauer away from the smallish hands, and bobbed his head into unit 302. He saw nothing, yet in the dimness he couldn't see well. Slowly, he stepped into the foyer and listened.

A keening noise, like a badly injured animal, came from the corner of the living room. He waited a moment to be sure no bullets would be fired at him. Then he moved forward.

She sat on the oak floor, her legs straight out, her back leaning against the wall. Through the window above her head, Buddy saw snowflakes resembling ashes.

As she looked up at him, he could see her tears.

She said, "Why?"

Buddy ignored her. He returned to the hallway.

Ward was pulling a black scarf and black knit hat off the figure on the floor. Ward said, "Who is it?"

Buddy stepped closer and leaned in. "I can't see."

Ward took out his iPhone and turned on the flashlight feature, shining the LED light at the body.

As Buddy recognized the face, he felt stunned. As if the earth had fallen away beneath him.

He'd been set up from the beginning, he knew now. As soon as he'd taken the call from Mack Berringer and lobbied Chief Malone to work the case, he'd been undermined at every turn. From that moment, he'd been in mortal danger.

Now he understood how his whereabouts—and those of Mei and Ben—had been discovered. How, as his investigation had brought him closer and closer to the truth, the menace had increased and ever more severe attempts were made on his life to silence him, to make him disappear. How Vance McInnis, the vice president of Cromwell Properties, had been so easily set up, with the crime scene laid out perfectly.

All of it managed by this person, who knew police procedure and everyone with power in the NYPD.

He felt anger and sadness at the depth of the betrayal—the betrayal of trust, of mission, of oath. Disgust in his voice, he said, "Turn off the light. I don't need to see Rachel Grove anymore."

Ward shut off the light, put away his phone, and asked, "Who is she?"

Buddy straightened and looked away. "Force Investigation Division, NYPD."

"What?"

"Used to be called Internal Affairs."

"The cops of the cops?"

Buddy said, "Supposed to be. But this one was a traitor."

At the sound of the name, the elegant woman emerged from unit 302. Buddy raised his gun, but she held nothing in her open hands.

Seeing Rachel Grove's body on the floor, she knelt down and embraced it, worked her hands under the shoulders, lifted it toward her in a pietà. Rachel's head lolled heavily at the end of a neck rubbery in death, her curly brown hair spiraling into the air, her eyes half open.

In agony, the living woman cried without decorum. "My sweet darling. No, no, no. No, darling. Come back to me. Come back to me. *Come back!* Oh, no. No, my love. My love. My . . ."

Buddy watched. Through the snowstorm outside, he heard the distant peal of sirens.

Suddenly, she glared up at him. "You'll pay for this, Detective."

He made no expression, though very slowly, he shook his head. "I think you'll be the one paying."

"You *killed* her, Detective. She was a police detective, in *FID*! *You'll burn for this!*"

Buddy ignored her and looked over at Ward, who was holding up his phone, recording audio and video of the entire scene.

"Do you have any idea who I am? Any idea of the sacrifices Rachel made?"

Buddy couldn't help it. He felt a burning heat roll through his body. He knew his face was flushed and he was about to lose control of himself, but he also knew this was the moment to jab her. She remained confident, despite her precarious legal position. He said, "Yeah, I know the sacrifices Rachel made. But they were the sacrifices of other people, not herself. How many people? How many had to die for your shitty condo projects and your money and power?"

She gently set the body on the carpeted floor and stood. She assumed her imperious bearing—in heels she was about his height—raised her chin, and looked down her nose at him. "*Nobody*, Detective. Nobody *had* to die. Not if they didn't choose it."

Buddy stared at her. "Choose it?" he repeated. "Chen and Lily Sung, from across the hall. Did they choose to die?"

She didn't respond. She noticed that Ward was holding up a phone and she was being filmed.

"And what about Sloan Richardson?" Buddy asked. "Wasn't she a special case?"

The woman in front of him pulled up her left sleeve and checked her watch. "It's time for me to leave."

Buddy pressed, "Why did you order Sloan Richardson to be killed?"

The woman's eyes flickered angrily. "I don't know any Sloan Richardson."

Buddy angled his head. "Sloan lived down the hall, in unit 309."

She shrugged.

"She was raised in California but born here in New York."

"Detective, many people are born in New York. They move to California because they want more space or more sunshine. Or for whatever reason. It's a free country. Now if you'll excuse me."

Buddy blocked her path. "No, I will not excuse you. Because I found out about Sloan Richardson. I couldn't put it together until tonight. But yesterday, I found something under the radiator cover in her bedroom. Do you know what it was?"

The woman gave no response.

Buddy said, "I found her birth certificate."

Her porcelain complexion grew flushed, but she was silent.

137

"It was interesting," Buddy continued. "It didn't list her mother or father. Not her *biological* mother or father. Apparently she was a foundling, left at five months old on the sidewalk outside Mount Sinai Hospital in the early morning hours of August 3, 1992. But you wouldn't know anything about it, would you, Mayor?"

Mayor Blenheim straightened. "Of course not," she said, though her voice grew strained and hoarse.

Buddy said, "Sloan Richardson had tracked you down, hadn't she?"

"Detective, I don't know what you're talking about."

"Chen and Lily Sung were just one problem you solved by murder, weren't they? The Russian money laundering brought you some campaign dollars, but that wasn't the main reason you needed to demolish the Nanjing building, was it?"

Mayor Blenheim's face showed frustration and annoyance, perhaps feigned, but her face also showed something else—something Buddy recognized. He'd seen it before in the rich and powerful. It was the thing they hated more than anything else.

Fear.

Fear they'd been found out and would lose all they'd gained. That they'd lose everything.

Right now, he was the person threatening to take it away.

He said, "All of this—all the people killed, the pursuit of my fian-cée and the boy we're trying to adopt, the death of your own daughter, Sloan Richardson—you did for money. For help winning elections."

Mayor Blenheim said, "Detective, I've supported your work, but I think you need professional help."

Buddy heard the sirens outside. They were close. He had no more than a minute. He said, "The power of other people is based on their competence at their jobs, their connections, their money. But your power is based on voters' support. That's all you've got. So if the public learned you'd once had a five-month-old daughter that you abandoned outside a hospital . . . a daughter you'd ignored your entire life. A daughter you had not when you were sixteen but when you were in your midthirties and about to run for city council. That public knowledge would have destroyed your career. So when Sloan learned your identity, when she refused to vacate her apartment in the Nanjing building— because you wouldn't recognize her or even meet with her—you made her disappear. Your discovery that she lived in the Nanjing building gave you the chance to kill two birds with one stone. She couldn't hold over in the building, because she was dead. And because she was dead, she couldn't end your career." Buddy pointed at the mayor and said, "Do you have anything to say about your decisions?"

Mayor Blenheim seemed shaken. But she said, "Nonsense."

Buddy said, "We'll do a DNA test on you and on Sloan Richardson's body. The truth will come out."

Mayor Blenheim glared at him.

"Your own *daughter*," Buddy said. "Murdered in the name of your career."

Mayor Blenheim pointed at him. "You have no idea, Detective. You'll never achieve what I have, and you don't know the cost of that achievement. But everything I've done has been in the service of this city, the greatest city on earth."

"No," Buddy said, shaking his head, "it's been for you. And the costs have been borne by your daughter and many other residents of Chinatown and the surrounding area you've had killed over the past fifteen years. In return"—Buddy pointed at her—"you got campaign contributions and fame and power, and the holdouts got death. Russians supported you financially and in God knows what other ways, and as mayor you did nothing to stop their use of Cromwell's condo projects to launder money. You and Stella Bannon and Erica Fischer—all of you made a devil's bargain. Now all of you are going to pay. I'll make damned sure of it."

The mayor crossed her arms over her chest. "That's crazy, Detective. And you can't prove any of it."

"You sure about that?"

She looked down her nose at him. "Of course."

Buddy said, "You're wrong."

The mayor raised an eyebrow.

"Yeah, Mayor. I've seen the photo. I *have* the photo," he told her, although in fact Henry Lee had the photo in its white envelope. He said, "Do you remember the photo, Mayor?"

She didn't react.

"No?" he said. "Then let me tell you about it. I found it with Sloan Richardson's birth certificate. It's the image of Sloan as a young girl. She's standing on an Oriental rug. For a few days I thought it was the rug that was familiar to me, that I'd seen it before, and recently. But it wasn't until three minutes ago, when you were bent over Rachel Grove, that I remembered the thing in the photo that was familiar."

Buddy paused to see if the mayor would say anything, but she remained silent. He said, "I've learned a lot about jewelry over the past week. It can mean commitment or the end of commitment, such as an engagement ring. It can mean a symbol of war, like the one Chen Sung wore when a fisherman found his body off Long Island. It can also be a status symbol or a gift from one's adoptive father, like the stainless-steel

Rolex that Sloan Richardson wore when I saw her in this very building. But jewelry can also be a way of remembering the dead. Or the missing. When I was a kid in middle school, one of my teachers wore a silver bracelet with the name of an American soldier and the date he went missing in Vietnam. I've always remembered that bracelet because the missing soldier wasn't a relation or even a friend to my former teacher. At the time, I thought it was strange to wear a bracelet every day to remember someone you'd never met. But other people wear those silver bracelets for people they *do* know. For friends and family members who've died or are missing."

The mayor shrugged. "What of it?"

Buddy stared at her and said, "Didn't your husband go missing in Iraq, after Desert Storm?"

She didn't respond, but she glanced down at her right wrist. As she'd bent over Rachel Grove, her right jacket sleeve had been pulled back. Even in the dim corridor light, the silver bracelet flashed.

Buddy said, "The NYPD lab will blow up Sloan's photo and increase the resolution of the bracelet. I'm confident we'll find the name of your missing husband stamped into the silver."

Slowly, almost imperceptibly, her face lost its marble perfection. The firm set of her mouth softened. Her eyes dropped down to the floor, to Rachel Grove, and a single tear descended her cheek. For a long while she was silent. Then she said, almost in a whisper, "I made a mistake. I shouldn't have . . . I shouldn't have treated Sloan that way. I shouldn't have let her go, shouldn't have abandoned her. It was a difficult time for me. With work and the first election coming the next year. And she wasn't . . . she wasn't the result of anything, really, just a warm day in San Francisco with a man whose name I never learned. But I shouldn't have listened to Rachel. I shouldn't have let her . . . let her arrange to have Sloan taken up in the plane and . . ." The mayor shook her head and sobbed once, only once, loudly, and then continued, "But what I've done, what I've accomplished, those must count for something. Weren't my mistakes a small price to pay for making this city great?" She raised her head and stared directly at Buddy. "I stand by what I've done. In my shoes, wouldn't you?"

Buddy looked at her and didn't turn away. In her eyes he saw the pain recede, to be replaced only by endless darkness. He said nothing.

And then the mayor's composure fully returned. She pushed back her shoulders, glanced once more at Rachel Grove by her feet, and said, "It's late. Goodbye, Detective." Then she turned toward the stairway at the end of the corridor and began to walk away from Buddy and Ward.

Buddy stepped forward, grabbed one of her arms, and held her tightly. He took her other arm as well and pushed her up against the tan plaster wall. He put her hands behind her back and held her. "You have the right to remain silent," he began.

He had no cuffs, but the sirens outside became terribly loud, then stopped. He heard the sound of the lobby door opening below and many footsteps coming up the stairs.

138

Buddy walked west along Canal Street in Chinatown, his head bent into the rising wind from the west. Snow reached the ankles of his boots and made the sidewalk slippery, yet he kept going, zipping up the jacket Ward had given him. When he looked up, the flakes stung his eyes, but in a pleasant way. All around him the city was coated with white like confectioners' sugar. Few cars passed by, and in one of those rare moments that came only a few days each year, the city was quiet and exceptionally beautiful. In these moments, the snow covered up the imperfections, the dirt and broken sidewalks and potholes, the buildings with roofs that needed repair or replacement. To him, the city looked like one of those photographs from the eighteen hundreds, all black and white and somehow easier to understand. And that was why he was outside rather than underground in the subway.

At a café, he stopped and ordered a large black coffee. After taking it with him outside into the cold wind, he held up his burner phone and dialed Ben's number.

After eight rings, the line went to voicemail.

Sadness hit him. He couldn't talk with Ben. Yet he left a message. "Ben," he said. "It's Buddy. I want you to know that you and Mei can come back home. The city is safe."

Then he ended the call.

He walked north up Lafayette until it turned into Fourth Avenue and then Park Avenue. Kicking up snow as he went, he walked at a rapid pace through the bitter cold, his chest warming with the effort. He walked for a couple of hours, all the way to the Carlyle Residences on East Seventy-Sixth Street, and then he stopped.

In the darkness he watched his breath rising in the frigid air until it faded and disappeared. He stood by the familiar canopy and stared through the plate-glass window to the lobby that for months had been his. But now he remembered it was his no longer. He had no home or fiancée, no hoped-for son. And no job. Because the next morning, he was going to tender his resignation to Chief Malone. He was leaving the NYPD.

His chest hurt with the anguish of these losses. He was damaged and melancholy and shocked by the extent to which everything and everyone he cared about had been stripped from him. Yet he also felt something new. Something unexpected and surprising.

Hope.

Even freedom.

He could change his life. Nobody could stop him. And he would.

He'd chart a path to win back Mei. To become Ben's father. He'd earn a living as a pianist. Somehow. And if not, he'd figure something else out. He wouldn't give up, because giving up wasn't in his nature. But as he thought more about it, he realized his hope was tinged with uncertainty. Not fear of failure but of his ability to live without the job, without the badge. He'd known for years that he needed it more than it needed him. He'd built his life around it until the job had become part of him. By resigning he'd be cutting off something as important to him as his left arm. Maybe more important. And yet the sacrifice would be worth it.

As he turned and wandered almost aimlessly in the direction of Central Park, he wondered if he truly could give up police work. He'd have to think about it. When he was done thinking, he'd act. He turned again and looked back down Seventy-Sixth Street toward his former home and above it, the canyons formed by the buildings and above them, the sky brushed amber by millions of burning lights.

ACKNOWLEDGMENTS

The author wishes to thank Will Roberts, a literary agent with a deep understanding of how stories are made; Jessica Tribble, for her support of this book and her suggestions to improve it; Peggy Hageman, for her careful readings; and the rest of the team at Thomas & Mercer. Most of all, thank you to my wife, Megan, for your partnership in our life together.

ABOUT THE AUTHOR

Photo © 2017 Jonathan Conklin

James Tucker is the author of the acclaimed Buddy Lock Thrillers *Next of Kin* (Book 1) and *The Holdouts* (Book 2). He holds a law degree from the University of Minnesota Law School and has worked as an attorney at an international law firm. Currently he manages real estate strategy at a Fortune 50 company, where his work includes frequent travel throughout the United States. Fascinated by crimes of those in power, he draws on these cases for his novels. One of four fiction writers awarded a position at a past Mentor Series at the Loft Literary Center in Minneapolis, Tucker has attended the Community of Writers at Squaw Valley and the Tin House Writers' Workshop in Portland, where he was mentored by author Walter Kirn. He lives near Minneapolis with his wife, the painter Megan Rye, and their family. *Visit him at www.jamestuckeronline.com, or follow him on Twitter @JamesTuckerRTR.*